"Another addition to Frost's delightfully entertaining Southern Witch series . . . 100 percent entertaining and satisfying . . . The romance really steams up and love takes hold. Sassy, sexy, and seriously fun."   —*RT Book Reviews*

"A brisk pace coupled with colorful characters and light humor makes this an enjoyable romp. Tammy's inept use of magic, a cool ocelot familiar, and quick thinking under pressure carry her through astounding family revelations."
                                                —*Monsters and Critics*

"Plenty of action . . . Pick up this series, you won't be disappointed . . . If you are a fan of Sookie Stackhouse then [the] Southern Witch series will fit right in with your reading."
                                                —*Once Upon a Twilight*

"*Halfway Hexed* is a laugh-out-loud magical ride that I didn't want to stop. There's humor, romance, and action all rolled into a fun, entertaining read with great characters and an intriguing plot. I was hooked from the beginning and can't wait for the next installment!"   —*TwoLips Reviews*

BARELY BEWITCHED

"Frost's latest Southern Witch novel has all the fun, fast, entertaining action readers have come to expect from her . . . Populated with fairies, goblins, vampires, wizards, rampant plants, and a few nasty-tempered humans thrown in for good measure, there's no end to the things that can and do go hilariously wrong."
                                                —*Monsters and Critics*

continued . . .

"What an amazing author! Kimberly Frost's Southern Witch series is fated for great things. *Barely Bewitched* was full of romance [and] magical havoc, and goes from one wild scenario to another. I was definitely hooked all throughout the book and couldn't put it down . . . I am definitely going to read Kimberly Frost's next novel!"
                                                    —*Romance Junkies*

"The author is on a roll with Tammy Jo. Book two has as much action as the first, if not more. Ms. Frost's sharp wit and interesting characters propel the story to a satisfying end."   —*A Romance Review*

"Kimberly Frost's Southern Witch series is destined for great things. Full of action, suspense, romance, and humor, this story had me hooked from the first page until the last."   —*Huntress Reviews*

"*Barely Bewitched* is filled with humor, sass, and sizzle! Every page is a new adventure in a world of hilarious antics and smoking chemistry. I love this series and I am really looking forward to the next Tammy Jo fiasco . . . I mean, story!"
                                      —*The Romance Readers Connection*

"The amusing story line is fast-paced . . . Fans will enjoy the escapades of Tammy Jo in this jocular urban fantasy."
                                              —*Genre Go Round Reviews*

"Kimberly Frost can tell a tale like no other . . . A can't-miss read."   —*Fang-tastic Books*

WOULD-BE WITCH

"Delivers a delicious buffet of supernatural creatures, served up Texas-style—hot, spicy, and with a bite!"
          —Kerrelyn Sparks, *New York Times* bestselling author of
                                                    Wild About You

"*Would-Be Witch* is an utter delight. Wickedly entertaining, with a surprise on every page. Keeps you guessing until the end. Kimberly Frost is a talent to watch."
              —Annette Blair, *New York Times* bestselling author of
                                                Tulle Death Do Us Part

"Kimberly Frost makes a delightful debut with *Would-Be Witch*. It's witty, sexy, and wildly imaginative. Great fun to read. A terrific new series from a wonderful new author."

—Nancy Pickard, Agatha Award–winning author of
The Scent of Rain and Lightning

"More magically delicious than Lucky Charms—Kimberly Frost's *Would-Be Witch* is bewitchingly fantastic!"

—Dakota Cassidy, national bestselling author of
the Accidentally Paranormal novels

"A big, heaping helping of Southern-fried magical fun! If you like a lot of laughter with your paranormal fiction, you'll love Frost's series."

—Alyssa Day, *New York Times* bestselling author of *The Cursed*

"Hilarious start to the new Southern Witch series that will keep you laughing long into the night! . . . Ms. Frost is an author to watch for in the future." —*Fresh Fiction*

"A wickedly funny romp . . . The story trips along at a perfect pace, keeping the reader guessing at the outcome, dropping clues here and there that might or might not pan out in the end. I highly recommend this debut and look forward with relish to the next installment in the Southern Witch series." —*Romance Junkies*

"What a debut! This quirky Southern Witch tale of a magically uncoordinated witch with an appreciation of chocolate is likely to win over readers by the first page. Just when I think I need a break from the fantasy genre I read an author who reminds me why I fell in love with [it] in the first place." —*A Romance Review*

"One heck of a debut from Kimberly Frost . . . This is definitely an excellent read, and for a debut, it's nothing less than fantastic . . . I sure don't want to miss what further misadventures Tammy Jo becomes involved in." —*ParaNormal Romance Reviews*

"Delightful, witty, and full of sass, this new series promises mega action, comedy, and romance. With this first Southern Witch novel, Kimberly Frost has made a fan of me. *Not* to be missed!"

—*Huntress Reviews*

Berkley titles by Kimberly Frost

Southern Witch Series

WOULD-BE WITCH
BARELY BEWITCHED
HALFWAY HEXED

Novels of the Etherlin

ALL THAT BLEEDS
ALL THAT FALLS

HALFWAY HEXED

KIMBERLY FROST

B
BERKLEY SENSATION, NEW YORK

THE BERKLEY PUBLISHING GROUP
Published by the Penguin Group
Penguin Group (USA) LLC
375 Hudson Street, New York, New York 10014

USA • Canada • UK • Ireland • Australia • New Zealand • India • South Africa • China

penguin.com

A Penguin Random House Company

HALFWAY HEXED

A Berkley Sensation Book / published by arrangement with the author

Copyright © 2011 by Kimberly Chambers.
Excerpt from *Slightly Spellbound* by Kimberly Frost copyright © 2014 by Kimberly Chambers.
Penguin supports copyright. Copyright fuels creativity, encourages diverse voices,
promotes free speech, and creates a vibrant culture. Thank you for buying an authorized
edition of this book and for complying with copyright laws by not reproducing, scanning,
or distributing any part of it in any form without permission. You are supporting writers
and allowing Penguin to continue to publish books for every reader.

Berkley Sensation Books are published by The Berkley Publishing Group.
BERKLEY SENSATION® is a registered trademark of Penguin Group (USA) LLC.
The "B" design is a trademark of Penguin Group (USA) LLC.

For information, address: The Berkley Publishing Group,
a division of Penguin Group (USA) LLC,
375 Hudson Street, New York, New York 10014.

ISBN: 978-0-425-26757-8

PUBLISHING HISTORY
Berkley trade paperback edition / February 2011
Berkley Sensation mass-market edition / March 2014

PRINTED IN THE UNITED STATES OF AMERICA

10 9 8 7 6 5 4 3 2 1

Cover art by Tony Mauro.
Cover design by Rita Frangie.
Interior text design by Kelly Lipovich.

This is a work of fiction. Names, characters, places, and incidents either are the product
of the author's imagination or are used fictitiously, and any resemblance to actual persons,
living or dead, business establishments, events, or locales is entirely coincidental.

The publisher does not have any control over and does not assume any responsibility for
author or third-party websites or their content.

If you purchased this book without a cover, you should be aware that this book is
stolen property. It was reported as "unsold and destroyed" to the publisher, and neither
the author nor the publisher has received any payment for this "stripped book."

For my mom, Audrey.

ACKNOWLEDGMENTS

I would like to thank the librarians, reviewers, and booksellers who recommended the Southern Witch series to their readers and customers, especially Karla and Jan from KBB, Anne from Murder by the Book, and Laura from Barnes & Noble on Holcombe. I'd also like to thank the book and readers' groups who invited me to their events. I had a great time visiting with all of you.

Special thanks to my amazing family and friends, my critique partners David and Bonnie, my agent Elizabeth, and the team at Berkley, especially Leis and Caitlin.

And, of course, many thanks to my readers/fans. I write for you.

1

THE REASON I don't normally bother to plan my schedule is that something unexpected always seems to come up and throw it off. That Friday when I got kidnapped was a prime example.

It was only four days after I'd almost been incinerated and drowned, but I was hopeful that I could balance my new life as a witch with my old life as a pastry chef. I'd accepted a commission—my first ever—from an accountant who donates her time to the Texas Friends of Fish and Fowl. As a celebration of their third anniversary, they were holding a regional fund-raiser in Duvall, and the centerpiece was to be a chocolate sculpture designed by yours truly. They wanted it to involve birds and fish, which was a bit of a challenge to my creativity because although fish are tasty—as anything but dessert—I just don't see them as art.

I was hard at work on a woodland scene with fish popping out of a brook when the bells chimed, announcing that someone had opened the front door to Cookie's Bakery. I glanced at the clock. It was twelve twenty, so Cookie hadn't returned from her lunch break yet. In the bargain we'd struck, Cookie would let me use the bakery, if I covered her lunch hour and one Saturday.

I wiped my hands on a rag and walked out to the glass counter to find my mailman, George. Technically he's not mine. He belongs to the town, but he's delivered the mail to our house since I was five, and his route always seems to be expanding. Truth be told, George would like to be the only mailman in town. He considers postal work a calling.

"Hey, George. Are you in the mood for a cinnamon roll or a caramel pecan one?" I asked with a smile.

His bushy silver eyebrows rose. If a hedgehog ever mated with a hobbit, George could've had a twin. "I'm not on a break, Tammy Jo. I'm here on official postal business."

I smiled a little wider. "Okay, then. I'll take the bakery mail," I said, holding out my hand.

"No need," he said, rounding the counter to set the mail into Cookie's straw mail basket. That was George. Mail delivery with military precision.

"All right, have a good day on your route," I said, moving toward the back.

"Just a moment, young lady."

"Yes?" I said, turning to face him again.

"We've got to discuss the situation at your house."

I frowned, thinking about our family home, which had sustained fire damage and was under repair. I was staying at my ex-husband Zach Sutton's house while he was out of town. I'd had my mail forwarded there. "Well, the situation at my house is being handled. Between TJ's construction crew and Stucky's brother-in-law, Chuy Vargas, who's the best carpenter in a hundred miles, they'll put it to rights. Chuy did the built-in bookshelves at Bryn Lyons's house, and I can tell you firsthand, he does the most beautiful work you've ever seen."

"That may be the case, but that still doesn't address the situation *I'm* talking about."

"I had my mail forwarded, George. Filled out all the paperwork two days ago, and the mail already came yesterday. You guys are a top-notch operation."

George rattled off Zach's address with a frown.

"Right, that's where I'm staying."

"It's not on my route."

My jaw dropped a little. "Right, but I'm not moving off your route permanently. It's just until my house is fixed."

"Shoreside is on my route. Highest tax bracket in Duvall, and I'm on that route *by request*. I believe you could stay there if you wanted to."

"I can't move in with Bryn Lyons just so you can deliver my mail!"

"You've got a package all the way from London, England. Airmail. Express with insurance attached. You going to trust something of that nature to the likes of Jeffrey Fritz?"

"I've got a package from England?" I asked, half amused that George couldn't stand for a high-priority package to be delivered by his rival. "I haven't ordered anything. And I don't know anyone there."

"International mail," George said with a solemn nod.

"Sounds important. Do you happen to have it on your truck?"

"In my bag," George said in a grave whisper, as if the package contained state secrets that spies in foreign countries had lost their lives to bring us.

"Well, that sure is convenient. Do I need to sign for it?"

"No. I've got my computer. I'll take care of everything," he said. He took out the small package and scanned its label, then handed it over. "Zach Sutton's mailbox isn't large enough to hold that."

"George, how did you know I'd be here today? I didn't arrange with Miss Cookie to use the bakery until last night. I can't imagine who even knew I'd be here."

"You're part of my route," George said crisply.

I laughed and couldn't help wondering whether George might have one of the town ghosts as some sort of spirit guide. No one was better informed than the Duvall ghost network.

With his sworn duty fulfilled, George marched out of the bakery, head held high.

I took a pair of scissors and carefully opened the box. There was a double layer of bubble plastic, which I unfolded to find a disc-shaped object, heavily wrapped in white foam packing sheets, making it about three inches in diameter. I raised it. Concealed underneath was a folded piece of thick stationery. I lifted the corner to read the note.

Never let it be taken from you. Keep it secret. Keep it safe.

A chill ran down my spine. I turned the paper over. No signature. Nothing written on it besides the three sentences in fancy black script.

I flipped up the box flap to look at the label. No return address. I set the note down carefully and returned to the mystery object. I pulled off the tape and slowly unrolled it. Peeling away layer after layer, I finally uncovered a beautiful antique cameo brooch. It was about two inches tall. The carved white image of a young woman's profile stood out from the pinkish-red background. There were flowers tucked into her upswept hair, and she had delicate features, angelic and pretty. The oval rim of the brooch was laced in gold and dotted with the tiniest pearls I'd ever seen. So many precious details. It made me feel like factory-manufactured jewelry ought to be outlawed.

Could Momma or Aunt Melanie have sent it? If so, why hadn't they written a longer message? And why would they be in England? Or, if it wasn't from them, who else in the world would have sent it to me?

I reached down to touch it, and a jolt of electricity shot up my arm. My brain seemed to rattle in my skull for a moment and then my vision blurred, the bakery receding.

I staggered, blindly catching myself on the counter just as she appeared. A woman with thick chestnut hair and high cheekbones. Her disheveled clothes, a blouse and skirt, flared out as she ran. I heard her panting breath, the clicking of her heels, and I smelled damp, rain-soaked streets. The haunted look in her wide eyes made my heart contract, and her fear consumed me. I reached out to her, to rescue her, but she went past me and disappeared.

I stood, staring at the spot where she'd been, but there was only black. Trying to catch my breath, I sank shakily to the floor.

Who is she?

The darkness faded, and the bakery reappeared around me. The smell of melted chocolate and baking bread. The ticking of the wall clock that was shaped like a country apron. I shook myself. I was safe at home in Duvall. The girl had been part of a premonition—my first ever. Were they always like that? Yikes. I hoped not.

And who or what had been chasing her? She'd been terrified, running as if her life depended on it. I'd felt what she was feeling. I wasn't sure if that was normal with psychic visions or not, but it didn't really matter. Only one thing was important; I had to find out who she was so I could save her from whoever or whatever was chasing her.

2

I SHOOK THE brooch gently, trying to get the vision to play again, but nothing happened. Turns out, magical brooches aren't as reliable as DVD players. I was just getting up and dusting myself off when Cookie returned from her lunch. She's as tough as gristle but has a good heart. At work she wears crisp white shirts with cotton pants under one of her twenty different aprons, and today was no exception. She looked me over with a questioning expression as she grabbed the top apron from the hook and slipped it over her head.

"Good lunch?" I asked, closing the box's lid on the brooch.

She nodded. "What have you got there?"

"Nothing much. I'm going to step out, but I'll be back for my meeting with the Fish-and-Fowl ladies," I said, grabbing my tote from the back and hurrying outside. I glanced up at the overcast sky. It looked and smelled like rain. Just like in my vision. Except there was something that made me think that the woman in the premonition wasn't going to be chased through the streets of Duvall. Although, if she did come to town, it would be a lot easier for me to help her. But what if she didn't? What then?

I paused for a moment. Why did I feel so strongly that I

had to help her? She was a stranger. Presumably wherever she was, she had family, friends, and a local police force. Her problems didn't have to become my problems . . . but I couldn't shake the feeling of a bone-deep connection to her. Could she be a distant relative? Some second cousin that I'd never met or heard of?

I drove to Zach's house and tucked the box under his bed. I could've left it in the car, but I didn't think that was a good idea since I was headed to Bryn Lyons's mansion for advice. When the note said to keep the brooch secret, I assumed it meant keeping it hidden from Bryn, because he and I were the only magical people in town at the moment.

I pressed the security button at Bryn's gate and waited.

A voice that I didn't recognize said, "Can I help you?"

"Sure can. Can you open the gate for me? I'm Tammy Jo. Mr. Lyons probably has me on the list as Tamara, even though no one but him calls me that," I said, slightly disgruntled at the fact that I'd lost the battle with Bryn over my first name. "My last name is Trask," I added.

The gate swung open, but I didn't drive in immediately. Instead, I pressed the button again. "Hello?"

"Yes, ma'am?"

"You're new, huh? Are you Steve's cousin?" Steve was night security at Bryn's, and I remembered that Bryn had planned to interview his cousin for the day post.

"Right. I'm Pete."

"Nice to meet you, Pete. Steve's a good guy. Maybe he told you that we're kind of friends?"

"He mentioned you. He said that letting you sneak into the house was how the last daytime security officer got fired."

That was what Steve had told him? *All* he'd told him? What about the fact that I'd saved Bryn's life. Twice! Once from poison. The second time from a flame-throwing warlock. Steve should've practically considered me his assistant when it came to safeguarding Bryn and his property. Unless you counted the cars I'd wrecked, which I didn't think anyone should, considering what we'd been up against. I couldn't believe Steve had told his cousin about my brief stint as a persona non grata at Casa Lyons. I frowned.

"Well, me being off the list and sneaking in—those were unusual circumstances."

"Let's hope," Pete said.

I huffed and drove through. I parked on the circular drive near the mansion's front door and rang the bell.

Mr. Jenson, Bryn's elderly butler, opened it and greeted me warmly.

"Is he here?"

"In the dining room. He's just sitting down to lunch. Have you eaten, Miss Tamara?"

"Breakfast a few hours ago."

"Very good. You'll dine here then. We have a special guest chef for the day."

"He had you bring in a guest chef?" I smiled and shook my head. "Being rich isn't the worst thing in the world, is it, Mr. Jenson?"

"It has never appeared to be," he said with a conspiratorial smile. I followed him down the hall, and he opened the door to the dining room.

If anybody could've resisted thinking *wow*, it sure wasn't me.

There were antique mirrors on one wall and two crystal chandeliers overhead. The wall opposite the mirrors was all windows, showing off the landscaped grounds. The enormous dining room table could've comfortably seated fourteen.

Bryn sat at the head of the table closest to the door. He was take-your-breath-away good-looking, but I mostly pretended not to notice. Bryn looked up when Mr. Jenson announced me, and then stood, matching the room's formality. Mr. Jenson pulled out a chair for me.

"She's agreed to stay for lunch," Mr. Jenson said before slipping out.

"That explains the memo I got about hell freezing over," Bryn said dryly. He'd invited me over for dinner every day since our near-death Halloween night. But I hadn't been to his house since then, because I'd been working a lot . . . and because I'd been avoiding him. We'd gotten pretty close, which made me nervous. Bryn, of course, never got nervous about anything, even when he had good reason to.

"I've been crazy busy, but here I am now, and it's real good to see you." I gave him my sweetest smile.

He appraised me with a look that said he wasn't going to be taken in by a pretty smile. "I'm glad to see you, but dropping by for lunch isn't the same as accepting a dinner invitation, and we both know it."

I glanced at the oriental place setting and the white potbellied teapot. "I don't see what the difference is," I fibbed. "Mr. Jenson said there's a guest chef here today, and this dining room's as fancy as any restaurant. So, what's for lunch?"

"Sushi," he said. "My favorite."

"Makes sense that that'd be your favorite," I said.

He drew his brows together. "Why?" he asked.

"Your selkie genes."

After a moment's contemplation, he burst out laughing. A few days earlier we'd figured out that we're each part magical creature.

Bryn continued smiling. "I guess that's one possible reason for my preference, but let's not spread that theory around."

I glanced at the empty chairs, then to the room's corners. "I thought the video surveillance of the downstairs didn't include sound."

"It doesn't, but now's an excellent time for us to practice concealing our secrets."

Thinking of the brooch, I agreed, though we clearly had different secrets in mind. "Why?" I asked.

"Several members of the Conclave are en route to Duvall."

The blood drained from my face, and I braced my hands on the table. The Conclave was supposed to be the World Association of Magic's version of the CIA and FBI, but the only Conclave guys I'd met had been more into lawbreaking than law enforcement. Plus, the people on the way were sure to be angry and suspicious because of the recent deaths of their colleagues.

"When will they be here?"

"Tomorrow, according to my sources."

"Well, what should we do? Leave town? Move into a cave or a jungle hut? Somewhere without telephones or ley lines?"

Bryn and I had broken WAM's laws. We weren't supposed to associate with each other or to share magic, and all they would have to do to find out Bryn and I had spent time together last week was to ask Bryn's neighbors. Then the Conclave could lock us up. Or worse.

Bryn reached into his suit coat and slid out a piece of paper. He set it in front of me.

I opened it. It was a fax dated the day after the WAM wizards had come to town. It said that Bryn had won the appeal against the injunction that prevented us from seeing each other. I was shocked. All the sneaking around I'd done was for nothing?

"Why didn't you show me this last week when it came!" I bit off the rest of what I was planning to say when the door opened. Mr. Jenson came in with lunch and a place setting for me. I glared at Bryn, who was as calm as ever. I clenched my fists in my lap until Mr. Jenson left. "Well?" I demanded.

Bryn poured me tea and said, "You're going to tell them that I did tell you about this back then. That's why we've been seeing each other, because as far as we know, it's perfectly legal for us to do that."

I cocked my head. On the one hand, it was a nice simple solution to our problem. On the other hand, I couldn't understand why he hadn't told me about the ruling earlier. I glanced at the signature on the bottom. John Barrett. The president of WAM. A guy that hated Bryn for interfering in his politics and for stopping him from getting too much power. Barrett had sent wizards to get evidence against Bryn—and to kill him. Why would Barrett have sent the letter to clear Bryn of wrongdoing? Had someone made him do it?

"Did he have to sign this because you won the appeal?"

Bryn smudged some ginger on a California roll and shook his head.

"So then why did he send it?"

"He didn't. It's going to be proven a forgery."

My jaw dropped.

"But we're going to lie convincingly about it, or we'll end up in jail."

"Can't we just say that the wizards they sent were homicidal maniacs and that we did what we had to do to survive?"

"We'll say that, too, but it wouldn't be enough. There are proper channels—"

"But I don't know the proper channels!" Could the wizard government really be so rigid that they wouldn't take into account extenuating circumstances? People had been trying to kill us! The town had been under siege! There'd been no time for magical red tape. I wanted to explode with fury and couldn't understand how Bryn could sit there so calmly.

"Right, but I do know the protocols, and they'll say I should've used them, whether I suspected internal corruption or not. They'll claim there are safeguards to ensure that any communications reach headquarters intact. So if there was a problem here last week, I should've reported it and asked for assistance, rather than breaking laws to handle it myself. I wasn't supposed to be interfering in what happened to you."

"Right. You should've just let me get killed or whatever."

"The documents that have been filed so far don't reflect that you were in danger. The ones I sent apparently haven't made it to the WAM offices in London."

My eyebrows shot up. *Intercepted? Stolen? Destroyed?*

"How do you know?" I asked.

Bryn didn't answer, which was probably for the best. I didn't need the names of the people who spied for him.

"Look, it's your choice," he said. "This is dangerous business. If you tell the truth and agree to do whatever Barrett says, they'll probably let you off with a warning."

"But you couldn't get off with a warning, and I'm the reason they're coming. My using magic is what started all this."

"You didn't know what you were getting into. Now that you do, I'll understand if—"

I held out a hand. There was no way I would let Bryn go

down alone for helping me. Not if I could prevent it. "You showed me the letter last week."

The corner of his mouth curved up. "You should bind yourself to me, Tamara. If you're going to take risks with me, you might as well reap the rewards." He ran his fingertip over my left ring finger. Warmth and magic danced up my arm and seeped into the deepest parts of my body.

I shivered, trapped for a moment in his dark blue gaze. *I can't.* "That would be crazy. We barely know each other."

"We know each other in the way that counts most."

I blushed, drawing my hand away from his. Not that I really wanted to pull back. What I really wanted was for him to keep my hand and to take the rest of me along with it. Except I wasn't supposed to let him have any part of me. I tightened my muscles and looked away from his face. "What else do I need to say about the last couple weeks?"

"There are two things that you have to remember and never waver about. First, that you saw the letter saying I'd won the appeal. Second, that the curse from the wizards caused the pixie-dust spill. You can't let it slip about your fae ancestry."

"I won't."

He had another bite of sushi while studying me. "Do you know how lawyers help witnesses prepare to give testimony?"

I shook my head.

"They practice with them. After lunch, why don't we spend a few hours getting you ready for their interrogation? I'll play a Conclave member and ask you questions. You can try to evade the traps I set for you."

"I have to go back to the bakery for a little while, but I can practice until then, and I'll come back afterward if you think I need to."

"Good. Let's plan on that."

"Let's see first how the afternoon goes. I'll be back tonight *if* I need to practice, not just because you want me to come over."

"Oh, right. Thanks for setting me straight." The sarcastic

edge to his voice caused a stab of guilt to shoot through me. He'd done a lot for me, and we both knew it. I should've been sweeter to him, or at least more gracious. And honestly, I wanted to be. That was the trouble. I couldn't trust myself around him, so I was doing my best to keep us apart.

"I wasn't—it's not that I don't want to see you, but you know things are complicated," I said.

"Because you allow them to be. And, since we're setting the record straight, if I wanted to use coercion or trickery to get you here, I would've already done it." I saw the calculation in his eyes and wondered what things he'd contemplated doing to draw me to him. Not for the first time, I felt a little out of my league.

"Well, I appreciate your restraint," I said with an exaggerated drawl. "I know it must be tough not to use coercion and trickery. Probably goes against all your lawyerly tendencies."

"Tamara." The one word was a warning.

I smiled at him, and he rolled his eyes, but the hint of a smile curved the corners of his lips. The man had a lot of patience.

"With Barrett's entourage on its way, the other thing that I should do is reinforce the protective wards on the property. Unfortunately, I'm still tapped out after the Valley of Death spell. The easiest way to amass power would be for me to do a spell that includes you," he said.

"And then you'll hold on to the magic we generate? Mine and yours?" I asked, thinking that I wanted to cast a spell on the brooch to find the woman from the vision.

"Is that a problem?"

I didn't answer.

"Why would that be a problem, Tamara? You're not planning on casting any spells, are you?"

"Well," I said, trying to decide how much to tell him. I needed his advice on what kind of spell to try, so I'd have to tell him something. "There's a premonition that I want to learn more about."

"What premonition?"

I folded my hands on the table. "My great-great-grandma

Lenore had a lot of visions, and she was an expert at interpreting them."

"So?"

"She was Edie's twin sister." Bryn frowned at the mention of Edie's name. He and the family ghost didn't get along. "And the reason my family doesn't want me to have anything to do with you is that your last name is on a list. Lenore's List of Nine. Getting involved with you is strictly forbidden."

"She made the list based on a dark vision she had?"

"Yes."

"Did the Lyons premonition pertain to you and me specifically? Or to your family and my family in general?"

"I don't know. That's what I need to find out." It sounded like the truth because it was the truth. The thing I didn't say was that I had no idea where to begin to get a glimpse at one of double-great-grandma's premonitions. So I needed to start with something that I hoped would be easier—like the brooch. "I remember Momma said that premonitions are natural windows into the future. Some witches just get them, like Lenore did. But other witches without the gift of sight can unlock glimpses of the future through divination."

Bryn nodded.

"You said you use a kind of tarot card reading, right? That's how you knew to give Mercutio to me?"

"Yes, cartomancy, but that won't show any visions."

"I know, but what would?"

"There are a lot of approaches, depending on your magic. Lampadomancy, radiesthesia, capnomancy—"

"Hey, I didn't go to wizard summer camp, remember? And Momma and Aunt Mel sure didn't use all the formal names for stuff when they talked about magic."

"Maybe it's time you did learn the terms. An informal education works for some things, but when there's a vast amount of information, getting it in a haphazard way just makes it harder to understand and remember. I've offered to teach you anything you want, if you'll—"

"No. No strings that tie us together. Especially not before we know what that prophecy says."

"It's a catch-22. You want my help to find out whether you can accept my help."

I huffed in frustration. "You were willing to share power. You break the rules well enough when it suits you."

Bryn smiled. "I can take power from you and use it because I'm allowed to use magic. I'm trained. Unlike you. It's not legal—or wise, for that matter—for me to give you information or spells that you go off to use unsupervised. You, better than anyone, know how spells can go wrong."

Okay, he had a small point there. I'd only come into my magical power in the past two weeks, and, since then, when I tried to use it . . . mostly disaster. Though sometimes, when I really needed magic to work, it did. And the brooch made me feel compelled to try more spells.

"Look, I'm curious about your ancestor's list, too," he said. "But if the premonition's almost a hundred years old, I think it can wait until after we've dealt with the Conclave investigation," Bryn said. "Also, it may have already happened and then we won't be able to see it anyway."

"What do you mean?"

"Well, the gift of sight is always foresight. Once something happens, the energy that created the vision is expended, and the actual events become part of memory. The memories belong to the people who were part of the event. Memories aren't accessible through divination."

"Well, if whatever's supposed to happen already has happened, then I don't care about it. It might have been your dad stealing my family's locket. If so, there's nothing wrong with me being friends with you now that that's over."

"No matter what your great-great-grandmother saw all those years ago, it wouldn't make sense to let it come between us. Magical synergy is incredibly rare, but we have it. There are witches who would kill for it, you know. It's not something to be squandered. Think about what we've already done and the possibilities of what we could do—"

"Stop! Don't tempt me. I'm already tempted enough just looking—never mind. Listen, this synergy stuff, it's not going to go away, is it?"

He shook his head.

"So if there's an emergency, I will share power with you. But I won't do it just for fun or as a precaution, because I don't want to be low on power either. I might have to cast a spell in a hurry when you're not around."

"To cast a spell that will probably go wrong, since yours often do. I can use the power to protect both of us." When I didn't respond, Bryn frowned. "You're not being reasonable."

I tipped my head slightly so that some of my red hair shielded me from him. "Is being reasonable what I'm known for?" I asked.

Bryn narrowed his eyes. "I don't always agree with your logic, Tamara, but I can usually follow it." He continued scrutinizing me. "What aren't you telling me?"

"I've told you all I can," I said. I took a bite of sushi. It was the freshest I'd ever tasted. "Wow, this is good. That guest chef's worth whatever you're paying him," I said to change the subject. "Why don't you start asking me Conclave questions now? We don't have that much time before I have to leave."

Anger flashed in his beautiful blue eyes, but he didn't say more about sharing power. Instead, he launched into the practice interrogation. Over the next couple hours, he trapped me dozens of times in contradictions. He did it so smoothly that it was a little scary. It was also extremely annoying since I'm pretty sure he enjoyed tangling me in knots.

3

MY HEAD ACHED by the time I got back to the bakery. If I ever give up being a pastry chef, don't put me down for becoming a politician or a criminal or anything that requires me to be questioned by a smug and annoyingly handsome lawyer with an axe to grind.

I mixed food coloring with melted white chocolate to make green chocolate paint for my hummingbird. When I finished adding decorative details, I rested the bird on a sheet of wax paper and checked my tree bark. There were a few pieces that were still a bit loose, so I used some melted semisweet as glue to secure them.

Cookie called out from the front that she was leaving for the day and reminded me to lock up after my meeting. *As if I'd forget*, I thought with a roll of my eyes. I glanced at the clock and wondered if Mercutio, my feline supersidekick, was awake yet. As an ocelot, Merc's basically nocturnal, so he's only up during the day on a need-to-fight basis. When I'd left in the morning, he'd been asleep in a tree in Zach's yard. Since it was quarter to five, Mercutio was probably awake and hunting by now. I hoped he didn't leave Zach's. I didn't want a lot of neighbors seeing him. Jenna Reitgarten had had it in for

Merc ever since he helped me burgle her house—which I should add we'd had a really good, life-and-death reason for doing. Not that I could explain that to Jenna. Not that I wanted to explain. The less I ran into her, the better.

I moved quickly around the display table, wiping away excess chocolate. I arranged the sculpture so that it was perfectly centered, then admired the brook. I'd dusted sugar crystals on the white chocolate, so the faux-white water sparkled. It looked magical, and I hadn't even used magic. I couldn't help but smile. I was sure they were going to love it. I took off my soiled apron and tucked it away before I washed my hands. I was just finishing when I heard the bells.

Here we go.

I poked my head out. "Come on back," I said to the first woman through the door. She was tall and built farm-girl solid with close-cropped auburn hair. I recognized her face from around town and wondered if she was Sue, the accountant, who'd called to hire me. I eyed the sculpture once more. The base was three feet in diameter, and one of the tree trunks was almost two feet tall with a pair of sparrows on one branch and a blue jay on another. I'd handcrafted each piece of chocolate bark, each stone, each flower, and each patch of moss and grass. It was a masterpiece.

As the ladies filed in, I smiled and stood up straighter. Then I spotted the pair bringing up the rear. Lucy Reitgarten, who still had a henna stain on her forehead from when I'd had to save her from a passionflower-potion poisoning, stalked in with her sister-in-law Jenna. They each wore a polo shirt and khaki pants. They also wore matching scowls. I exhaled heavily, my moment of triumph melting like semi-sweet chips in a double boiler.

"Hi, there," the leader of the group said. "I'm Sue Carfax. This is Mindy, and I think you know Lucy and Jenna."

I nodded to the group, looking them over. Jenna was blond, and if she wrote a cookbook it would be called *The Anorexic's Guide to Not Eating.* Her sister-in-law Lucy had high cheekbones, thick eyebrows, and dark brown hair peppered with gray. Mindy was a dumpling with legs, and her cherubic face should've been cute except for the small, unfriendly eyes. She must've been a Fish-and-Fowl member from one of the neighboring towns because I didn't recognize her.

"This is quite a work of art," Sue said with false cheer.

I took a few steps back so they could circle the sculpture. The silence dragged on for several moments, then they began murmuring to each other. Behind my back, I clenched my fists. If they made up some excuse to not pay me or were overly critical, I wasn't sure I was going to be able to keep from shouting at them. My run-in with Jenna two weeks ago over the price of a cake I'd made had already cost me my job.

"Well, it's really lovely," Sue said. A little of the tension in my shoulders eased. "That's a great catfish," she said, pointing.

"Thank you," I said with a careful smile.

"Did you go to one of the creeks around here for inspiration?"

"Nope. Zach's got copies of *Field and Stream* at the house. And I used the Internet." I went to my tote and took out my file of clippings and pictures. They passed them around.

"So, what's your plan for this hummingbird?" Sue asked, tapping the edge of the wax paper.

"I'm going to tack a piece of clear fishing line into its back and suspend it from this branch," I said, indicating the lowest one. "The beak will point down into this blossom."

"Makes sense," Mindy said. "But we were wondering . . ."

"Yes?" I asked, nodding encouragement.

"Is there another way you could make the bird airborne? Not for the public to see, but for us—right now."

I cocked my head. "What did you have in mind?" Clear fishing line would be pretty much invisible. I supposed a thin wire could be used, but I didn't think it would be as good.

"We were thinking you could do a trick," Lucy said.

"A trick?" I echoed.

Four pairs of eyes stared at me, and I felt my face warm.

"A magic trick," Mindy said.

Uh-oh.

"Or maybe you'd call it a spell." Jenna's voice rang out clear and sharp. An accusation.

They know! No, they can't. They suspect. Don't panic, I thought, panicking. "It's a chocolate bird," I said slowly and carefully. "It doesn't fly."

"Couldn't it levitate? If you helped it?"

"No, it couldn't! I'm a pastry chef, not a magician." My heart thumped in my chest.

"We want you to try," Jenna said, taking a step toward me. Lucy moved, too. I stood my ground, refusing to let them back me into a corner.

"I'm not trying anything. You hired me to do a chocolate sculpture. That's it."

"Look," Lucy said. "Jenna saw you practicing with a magic wand. And I remember you chanting when you threw that mixture on us—"

"My brother works at Glenfiddle, and he said you shouted some weird poem before splashing the poison on him," Mindy said. "Then he passed out. What was in that Tupperware?"

"Was it blood-based?" Sue asked.

"Blood?" I asked, wrinkling my nose. Why would they guess there'd been blood in it? Had they done research? I needed to throw them off-track. But how?

"Witch's herbs?" Lucy asked.

This is not good. My mind reeled. *I saved lives. I shouldn't end up in trouble for it after the fact.* More evidence—as if I needed any—that life isn't fair. *What would Bryn tell me to do?* "Look I really can't talk about that night."

"Are you in league with the devil?" Sue demanded.

I gasped. "Of course not!" That was going too far. God and I are on good terms.

"Satan, be gone!" Sue said, taking a menacing step forward. I pushed her away.

Lucy thrust a small gold cross at me and shouted, "That it may not hear the voice of enchanters casting cunning spells!"

"Oh God, my lord, smash their teeth—" Mindy said.

"Smash their—all right, that's enough. Get out!" I said, pointing to the door.

"Get her!" Jenna ordered. Then they knocked me down and piled on top of me.

"The fallen shall not rise," Sue said.

"I didn't fall. I was pushed!" I snapped. We were a mass of scratching fingernails, kicking legs, and tangled hair. I didn't want to hurt any of them, so I didn't actually hit anyone with a closed fist. In retrospect, that was a mistake. I should've treated them like any killer werewolf or vicious faery that I'd fought the past two weeks. But hindsight is twenty-twenty and foresight is more like twenty-two-hundred.

With my wrists, ankles, and lips duct-taped, all I could do was glare at them when they picked me up and carried me to the back door.

I shouted against the tape. It came out sounding something like, "Mm-errrr-mum-hu-mmurma." Predictably they ignored my garbled protests. I squirmed and struggled until they dropped me, making me bang my butt and left elbow on the tile floor. Scowling and snarling, they picked me back up.

"Stop moving! You're only hurting yourself," Lucy snapped.

"That chocolate sculpture is really great, by the way. It's going to make a wonderful focal point for the fund-raiser," Sue said.

What the fudge? They were still expecting to use my work? Not if I had anything to say about it. Unfortunately, at the moment I really didn't, but I shouted against the tape anyway.

"If you cooperate, maybe you'll be free in time for the fund-raiser. Wouldn't that be nice?" Mindy said, sweet as a Stepford wife.

I flailed until they dropped me again. My left butt cheek was going to be one big bruise tomorrow.

Jenna leaned over and grabbed my arm, squeezing hard. "That's enough," she hissed.

I glared at her.

"You brought this on yourself, you know," she said as they lifted me again. "We're taking you into custody on behalf of DeeDAW."

Who? "Uutt?"

"Defending Duvall Against Witchcraft. DeeDAW," Jenna

said triumphantly as they dropped me into a car trunk. "Now be quiet in there." With that, the lid whumped shut and plunged me into darkness.

My very first chocolatier's commission, and the clients turned into witch-hunting kidnappers! Apparently, my plan to keep my regular life as a pastry chef separate from my new life as a witch wasn't going to work out as well as I'd hoped.

4

I ROLLED AROUND the trunk, curling into a ball, trying to get my duct-taped hands around my butt and legs so I'd have them in front of my body. It was like a Cirque du Soleil contortionist audition gone wrong.

Sweating and cursing behind the duct tape over my mouth, I wasn't in the best mood for company when a greenish orb of light signaled the arrival of Edie, former flapper, former witch, and full-fledged family ghost.

"Surely not," she said dryly and eyed me with those almond-shaped peridot eyes.

I wriggled like a fish on a hook, some strands of hair plastered to the side of my face, as I tongued the tape over my mouth. If Edie was planning on mocking me, I had to get the tape off so I could get in a retort or two. I continued trying to wrestle my arms to the front of my body.

"What do you want?" I garbled against the tape. I knew it was unintelligible, but it made me feel better anyway.

"Kidnapped by the PTA brigade? Several of whom are dressed in bad shoes and worse lipstick," Edie said, clucking her tongue. "No part of the face should ever be painted yellow-orange," she said with a phantom shudder. I did agree that Sue's lipstick had been kind of pumpkinish. "Someone at the department store really should've intervened."

I stopped to pant as I finally got my bottom wedged between my forearms.

"And them getting the best of a McKenna." She shook her head, her waved black hair gleaming in the metaphysical light. "Now that you've come into your powers, we really have to get you properly trained."

I dragged my straining arms around my legs, twisting painfully to get my wrists past my ankles. I groaned, jerking my arms forward.

"Well done," Edie said with a smile. "That can't have been easy for someone with your flexibility . . . or lack of it."

I rolled my eyes and yanked the tape off my mouth. "I'm the normal amount of flexible for a human being who still has a skeleton." I gnawed at the duct tape around my wrists. "I need to carry a knife," I mumbled, making faces at the unpleasant taste of the adhesive.

"And perhaps a spell or two," Edie said mildly. "In my day, I'd have brought them to their knees. I must try to remember that Depth of Despair spell, so I can teach it to you."

"Why the hell does duct tape have to be so sticky?" I complained.

"As interesting as your Houdini routine is, I did have a specific reason for visiting."

I rubbed my arms together furiously, loosening the tape bit by bit. "What's up?" I asked before chewing again on the tape.

"I saw Melanie."

I froze. My momma and her twin sister had been incommunicado for months. "Where is she? Are they okay?"

Edie waved an elegant hand toward mine to encourage me to continue trying to escape. "I suppose that depends on how you define *okay*. She's healthy, but she's neglected her powers terribly."

"What about Momma?"

"I'd like to let Melanie explain everything. Before she can come home though, she's rather in need of my help."

"Then go help her! What are you doing here? Wait. Just

tell me. Did she find Momma? Does she know if she's okay?"

Edie gave an exasperated sigh. "All right. I'll tell you. Marlee found what she was looking for."

"Her lost love?" I asked excitedly.

"So she calls him. Though how any witch worth her salt could fall in love with a member of the fae is beyond comprehension."

I smiled. "Well, the fae are awfully pretty in some cases," I said, thinking about Bryn and his one-quarter selkie genes.

"In any event," Edie said tightly. "Marlee's in Faery, and she can't come home if she hopes to keep him. So she's stuck there . . . by royal decree."

I gasped. "How long does she have to stay?"

"I don't know. Time passes so differently there. Melanie had no idea they'd been gone so long. To her it felt like a couple of weeks."

"Huh." I got my right hand free of the tape. "Is Momma happy though? Did Aunt Mel say?"

"Yes, apparently she's pleased with her descent into—"

"Well, I'd like to meet him. My dad."

"Absolutely not! They must never know about you. The fae are extremely possessive. Narcissistic. Petty. Nasty."

"Hey, I'm half. Remember?"

"You're a witch," Edie said firmly, making me think that it wasn't only the fae who were possessive. "Did you know that in the Never, no other magic exists? So Melanie depleted all hers when she went in after Marlee. Now she's risking life and limb doing a series of power spells just to get back to normal. And that's why she needs me. I can do the sort of research that she can't. Ghost gossip. No one knows history better."

"Okay, go help her."

"It's not that simple. I need to stay with her. You'll have to mail the locket."

"Mail the locket! To where? What if it gets lost?" Edie's soul had been attached to an antique family heirloom since she'd died, and the locket had to stay in the possession of someone in the family for her to come out of it safely.

"It's either mail the locket or take it to London yourself."

London, I thought with a thrill. Wouldn't I love to go there? Absolutely. Too bad I had to face the Conclave with Bryn.

"I can't go right now."

"Then you'll have to send it. You'll have to bind the locket with a spell. I won't come out until it's lifted. When you mail it, you'll need to insure it, of course. Take every precaution."

"I will, but why didn't Aunt Mel call me? I want to talk to her."

"Everything shorts out. She's not staying in a place that's magically grounded, so doing the power spells leaves phone and computer services out of order a great deal of the time."

"Oh, right. Well, where do I mail it to?"

"It'll be in her letter. She's sending you several packages. I told her about your powers. She's very excited. Her letters will arrive separately to protect us from discovery, in case the packages should be opened before they get to you."

"The brooch? My gosh, I almost forgot. Who's the girl in the vision attached to the brooch? Am I supposed to help her?"

Edie cocked her head. "I don't know about a brooch, but then my conversation with Melanie was really focused on other things."

"Could you ask her to call and let me know? Or to write I guess. In the meantime, it can't hurt for me to try to see a little more of the premonition attached to the brooch. What's the best spell for divination?"

"I never did that type of spell. Lenore saw more than enough for both of us. I know flame-gazing is supposed to work well for some witches."

"And you're sure you don't remember anything about why the Lyons family is on the List of Nine?"

"I've told you a dozen times, I can't remember. Lenore had hundreds of premonitions. The only ones I paid attention to were the ones that had to do with me."

I pulled my right ankle loose of the tape and shook it triumphantly. "Free!" I whispered fiercely.

"Yes, rather nicely done, but there is still the small matter of you being trapped in a trunk."

"Not really," I said, lifting the glow-in-the-dark piece of plastic that showed a person leaping from a trunk. "There's a get-unkidnapped cord."

"My stars. The gangsters must be so annoyed with the car manufacturers."

I pulled the tab and the trunk released, afternoon light pouring in. I laughed. "At the next stop sign, we're out of here. DeeDAW be damned."

"Who?"

The car slowed and out I hopped. I kept my body low, pleased that they were chatting and hadn't even noticed the trunk open. I darted into some bushes. Chuckling and giddy, I watched them drive away.

Edie appeared for a moment. "I'm fading, biscuit, so I'll have to see you later." She pressed a phantom kiss to my cheek. "Don't forget to get tons of insurance when you mail the locket! I don't want to end up somewhere besides London. Like Hell. Or Liverpool."

5

IT TOOK ME almost an hour to walk back to the bakery. As I'd suspected, DeeDAW hadn't locked the front door. Very inconsiderate kidnappers! Luckily, everything seemed to be in order. I quickly cleaned up the mess I'd created while working. I needed to head back to Bryn's to fill him in and do some more Conclave prep work.

The front door chime made me stiffen. If the felonious prayer group was back, they were going to be sorry. This time, by Hershey, there would be bloody noses. I cracked my knuckles and straightened my spine before I walked to the front.

The stranger stood just inside the door. His hooked nose and the jagged scar along his right cheek made him seem sinister, but looks, of course, are one thing we don't have control over, so I wasn't going to jump to any conclusions about his personality.

He looked to be in his midforties. His dark brown hair was clipped short, his tailored black trousers and charcoal overcoat proclaiming him wealthy and powerful in the human kind of way.

"Hello," I said with a smile. "Welcome to Duvall, Texas. And to Cookie's Bakery. What can I get for you?"

He pointed behind me. I couldn't imagine what he saw in the back room that he wanted. I'd cleared the table except for the sculpture. I turned to be sure that there wasn't a stack of brownies or something that I'd forgotten.

It was only a pinprick at first. Then pain blossomed into a stabbing sensation. I jerked my head to look at my backside. A stainless steel dart was sticking out of the seat of my pants.

"But? What?" I mumbled as wooziness washed over me.

I looked at him through my lashes. He wasn't watching me. He was locking the front door and putting the Closed sign in place.

Considerish—considerate Tammy-napper, I thought blearily as I crumpled to the floor.

THERE WAS A rushing sound in my ears, and my head felt three times its normal size when I woke. The head congestion might have had something to do with the tranquilizer dart the stranger shot me with or it might have had something to do with the fact that I was hanging upside down.

Are you freaking kidding me!

I raised my head to look up at my bound ankles. They were shackled together, the chain between the cuffs looped over a thick metal hook stabbed into the ceiling. "I am not a side of beef!" I muttered to myself.

Where was the guy? Was he from WAM? But no, pretty sure if he was, he would've introduced himself before he shot me. The WAM guys I'd met were all about following rules and protocols—right up until the time they tried to kill you.

My head pounded and my stomach muscles bunched as I continued to hold myself in a half-crunched position in order to look around. It was a cellar workroom. A nearby bench had tools scattered on it. All of a sudden, I thought of those serial killers who built lairs to keep their victims captive in, and my heart hammered a major protest.

The walls and floor were solid concrete. If I screamed would anyone even hear me? I pictured a nice family of four

living upstairs, not even knowing the psycho dad had yours
truly hanging from a hook downstairs.

Nope. No possible way am I staying here!

I looked at my cuffed wrists and frowned. I could still feel
the sticky duct tape residue from earlier. Too bad I couldn't
gnaw through metal.

I tipped my chin forward, looking up the line of my body.
Yep, more circus performer acrobatics were going to be
necessary. But if Scarface thought I wasn't up to it, he was
sadly mistaken. Or at least that's what I told myself to get
in a positive frame of mind.

I bent my elbows and brought my forearms against my chest.
If I'd been my ex-husband, Zach, I'd already have been standing. Zach could do like two hundred hanging-upside-down
sit-ups. That's why Zach was in a training program for human
champion superathletes. Me, on the other hand, I had maybe
one or two dangling-from-a-hook sit-ups in me—at most.

Get ready. Get set. Go!

I jerked upward at the waist, getting to ninety degrees.

Gravity pushed down on me like twenty tons. I fought
hard, thrusting my hands out to grab my pant legs. I held on
tight, panting with exertion, bending my chest toward my
knees. The muscles in the backs of my legs screamed a protest. About not being flexible, Edie had a little bit of a point.

I bent my knees and clenched all my muscles. Almost
there! With grasping pulls, I walked my hands up. God bless
American denim for being stronger than gravity. My fingers
got to the hook. *Ha!*

I gripped it with sweaty hands and pushed my feet up.
With some jerking, bending, and arching, the chain popped
over the hook's curve, leaving only my slippery hands holding the entire weight of my body—which didn't work out
all that well.

I crash-landed on the floor with a thud and a weary groan.
Being an action hero . . . I can't say I really understand the
appeal.

I stretched out my aching muscles and let my breathing

return to normal for a few seconds. Then I heard quick footsteps on stairs.

Damn it! I am not going back on that hook!

I scrambled up, my eyes darting around the room. No keys to free myself, but standing in front of a fireplace, there was a set of pokers.

I tried to run to them, but my stride-length was only a few inches with the shackles on, so I tripped and landed with another bitter thud. Adrenaline poured through my veins.

Hurry up!

I pressed up and crawled, swinging both my legs forward as one.

He's almost here!

I grabbed a poker. There wasn't time to get behind the door. I moved quickly from the fireplace and lay down on my belly, concealing the poker under me. The door banged open.

I ordered my muscles to relax, playing possum. I was under the hook so I hoped it would look like I'd knocked myself out during the fall.

Okay, you jerk. Come roll me over. I dare you.

I tried to keep my breathing slow and steady.

I felt his hands. One on my left shoulder, the other on my left hip.

That's it. And over we go.

Crack!

I'd given the swing my all, and his look of shock wasn't even complete before he crumpled into a heap. "Mark Mc-Gwire, eat your heart out," I mumbled. I shoved Scarface off and got on my knees. I dug through his pockets.

There's a God, and contrary to what DeeDAW has to say, He loves me, I thought as I held the keys aloft and dropped onto my sore butt. I unhooked my ankles, but froze momentarily when Scarface moved. I lurched forward and grabbed his hair. I lifted his head and then banged it on the floor. I winced. "If you're not a serial killer, I'm sure sorry about that. But you did start this."

Getting the key in the lock of the cuffs seemed to take

forever. Isn't that just the way when you need to hurry and escape?! I finally managed it, eyeing Scarface.

He stirred.

"Stay unconscious, darn you!" I snapped, worrying that if I ran outside, he might chase and catch me. I wasn't going to be *that girl*. The one in the scary movies who only gets away for a couple minutes. I glanced at the cuffs, my eyes narrowing.

Now you're talking.

I grabbed him and hauled him onto his stomach. I closed the shackles around his ankles and pulled them toward his butt. I fed the handcuffs' chain underneath the chain that connected the leg shackles, so the two chains made a cross. Then, with some effort, I dragged his hands down and cuffed them one-by-one. He was on his belly with no way to get his hands more than a few inches from his feet.

Sweat dripped from my temples and my muscles ached, but I was pleased with myself. Now, I'd just call the police. Actually, since he hadn't serial killed me, this was still only a kidnapping, which fell under the FBI's jurisdiction. But I didn't know their phone number. Whatever it was, it was nowhere near as famous as "nine-one-one."

I jogged upstairs. The house was a butcher's dream. Cowhide border paper, and deer and elk heads protruded from the walls. Would I have been his first human trophy? I shuddered.

"Where the Sam Houston do kidnappers hide their phones?" I searched for about five minutes, but when I finally found one tucked under a stack of magazines, it turned out not to have a dial tone.

"Darn you, Scarface!" I snapped, stamping my foot, but then I calmed myself. He wasn't going anywhere. Sooner or later, I'd find a phone. Or a sheriff's deputy.

I marched out of the house, keeping a close eye in case he had any accomplices. I didn't see anyone. Behind the house, I found a black pickup truck with no license plates. Nothing says criminal quite like a lack of license plates. Well, except for hanging unsuspecting pastry chefs from hooks.

There were keys in the ignition.

"Now we're talking."

I hopped in the driver's seat and started it up. As I drove away, I was careful to take note of the address and the road signs I passed. Had to be sure that I could give the police good directions.

Scarface picked the wrong chocolatier to mess with.

6

IT TURNED OUT I'd been about twenty miles from Duvall. Once I got back into town, I went straight to the police station. Inside, I found Smitty, my least favorite deputy, on duty. He looked me up and down.

"Hear from Zach?" he asked.

"Yep. He's doing great."

"Where's he at?"

"I guess if he wanted you to know, he'd call you up and tell you," I said in a deceptively sweet voice that wasn't deceptive at all.

Smitty glared at me.

I ignored that and sat in the chair across from his desk. "I'd like to make a police report." He didn't move. I repeated what I'd said. He sighed heavily, got out his notebook, and dropped into his chair.

"What?" he asked.

"I was kidnapped."

He raised an eyebrow. "Come again?"

"Kidnapped. I was working at Cookie's Bakery—"

"Cookie fired you."

"I was working at Cookie's," I repeated firmly, "and I was

taken forcibly from there by four women. They knocked me down, duct-taped my wrists, ankles, and mouth, then put me in the trunk of a car. Their names are Sue Carfax, Lucy and Jenna Reitgarten, and Mindy whose last name I didn't catch."

"Get the hell out of here," Smitty said incredulously.

"I'm totally serious," I said.

With some hesitation, he jotted notes.

"I managed to get myself out of the duct tape and escape the trunk. I returned to the bakery, and a man I don't know from Adam came in and shot me with a tranquilizer dart."

His eyebrows shot up.

"I woke up hanging from the ceiling in his basement. There was no sign of any of the four women, and I don't really think he was working with them. He seemed way more professional. Plus, his house was pretty far out of town. Gimme your pad. I'll write down the address."

Smitty stared at me.

I reached across and yanked the pad from his fingers. I wrote down the address and directions to Scarface's place.

"You should go now. I left him chained up in the basement for you to arrest. You can scoop the FBI," I said with an encouraging nod, pushing the pad back across the desk at him.

"Let me get this straight. You were kidnapped. *Twice.* In one day." He shook his head. "Just how dumb do I look to you?"

I was sure tempted to answer that, but I managed to stop myself. "I'm a hundred percent serious. The guy's truck is parked outside. He took the plates off. If that doesn't smack of 'seasoned criminal,' I don't know what does. I'm willing— and fired up—to press charges." I glanced at the clock overhead. "Why don't you go get him, and I'll come back tonight to sign my statement?" I slapped a key on the desk. "This is for the shackles."

Smitty narrowed his eyes at me. "You're putting me on, right?"

"No, I'm not. You better go get him. By the way, he's gonna tell you I hit him with a fireplace poker. I'm not going to lie to you. I did. I was a kidnap victim, and I deemed it necessary force. Pretty sure a judge is going to agree with me on that."

I sucked in a breath and let it out. "There's more to my statement, but I'll tell it to you later. Can you drop me off at the bakery? I need to get my car since I assume you want the truck for evidence."

Smitty wrote some more things in his notebook, then flipped the cover closed.

"This better not be bullshit," he said, walking me outside.

I pointed to the truck. "Exhibit A."

"Uh-huh," he said skeptically. "I'll drop you off, and I'll take a couple of the boys to this address. We better find a kidnapper chained up in the basement, or, so help me, I'll haul you in for making a false report."

I rolled my eyes. We rode in silence to the bakery.

I realized that I didn't have my keys, so I had to call Miss Cookie. She wasn't very pleased, but she let me inside to get my tote bag. I didn't tell her about the kidnappings. I decided that since I was already late getting back to Bryn's, information would be given out on a need-to-know basis, and Miss Cookie didn't need to know.

I went home and picked up Mercutio, who looked like he'd just woken up. I envied him his quiet day since most of my body ached at the moment.

On the drive over to Bryn's, I said, "Wait until you hear what happened to me."

He looked at me as he licked a paw.

"I'll tell you and Bryn at the same time. It'll be easier that way." I ran a hand through my hair. "After the day I've had, I deserve to have *something* be easy."

BRYN WASN'T AT all skeptical about my story and neither was Mercutio. Bryn said I should stay the night at his house until the police had picked up the kidnapper. I didn't agree to that, nor was I inclined to agree to what he suggested next. He was going out and wanted me to join him.

Since I was lying on my back, sucking down aspirin and whiskey-spiked tea provided by Mr. Jenson, I protested.

"I've been all over town neutralizing residual magic, but there's one place I forgot about," Bryn said.

"Where?"

"Tom Brick's."

I grimaced. "I don't even want to go to Baskin Robbins, let alone to a murder victim's house."

Tom Brick had been a wizard from Austin with ties to Duvall and the tor. A couple weeks earlier, he'd refused to help the WAM wizards, so Incendio, the fire warlock, had killed him. Mercutio had seen the whole thing. A few days later, Mercutio and I had had a standoff at that house with Incendio, and Bryn and I had nearly died trying to escape.

"Did we cast any spells there?" Bryn asked. "You know my memory's fuzzy from that time."

"You definitely didn't. You spent most of that visit in a coma. I don't think I did either. But you know me, sometimes I throw magic around without even realizing it."

Bryn nodded, walking over to the couch. "It'll be one of the primary locations for the Conclave's investigation. I want to be sure there are no traces of your magic there, Tamara, and I'm not sure I remember how to get to Brick's."

I rubbed my eyes, but mumbled, "Okay, but if I'm leaving the house, I want a gun. I'm tired, and I'm not fixing to get kidnapped anymore today."

Bryn chuckled and leaned down. He brushed his lips over mine, making them tingle with his magic.

"Hey. We're not supposed to kiss," I said.

"I don't remember that being the promise you made to Sutton."

I cocked my eyebrow up.

"All you promised was that you'd wait to choose between us until he came back."

Just like a lawyer to instantly find the flaws in a normal person's plan. "Well, yes, but things should be fair," I said.

"You were with him for years. If anyone needs to make up for lost time, it's me," he said with a wicked smile. He stole another kiss before I could protest.

When he moved away, I sat up dizzily. My voice was slightly breathless as I said, "I want a gun. I need it to protect myself."

He only grinned wider.

WE WENT OUT the back door, and I gaped at the black sports car parked there. It was low to the ground and compact, the kind where about half of it is engine.

"What's this?"

"My new car."

The week before we'd had to park Bryn's Mercedes on the bottom of the Amanos River. I'd also dented his limo up pretty good.

The passenger door of the new car opened vertically, like an alien spaceship.

"They put the doors on wrong," I said.

"Yeah, I'll have to let them know about that."

There were only two seats, so Mercutio had to sit on my lap. "Mind your claws, Merc. These seats probably cost more than our house."

Once we got off Bryn's property and onto the open road, he pressed his foot down, and the car roared forward with so much force that I was pinned to my seat.

"Well, it's sure a nice little car. Who'd you buy it from? NASA?"

He chuckled. "After last week, I decided I wanted a car that could outpace anything that wasn't powered by jet fuel."

"Is the undercarriage equipped with inflatable inner tubes in case of a water landing? 'Cause that would've come in handy."

Bryn laughed softly. "I'll check the owner's manual."

I gave him directions, and several miles outside Duvall, we reached the dusty road to Tom Brick's. The road was lined by wildflowers and unmown grass. Bryn got out and opened the property's gate. I smelled soot.

The car's tires crunched over the gravel as we rolled slowly to the side of the brick house. The scent of charred wood grew stronger as we parked. Mercutio banged a paw against the passenger window, looking out.

"I smell it," I said. Climbing out, I set Merc on the passenger seat. "You don't have to come if you don't want to. I know how much bad stuff you've seen here. First the murder. Then the body when it was dinner for the bugs." I wrinkled my nose, feeling slightly sick at the memory.

Merc cocked his head thoughtfully, then hopped down.

"Is he all right?" Bryn asked, coming around the car.

"He's fine. Like always. Me, I could've lived one or two lifetimes without coming back here and remembering the state of that body."

Bryn gave my arm a squeeze. "You can wait here, if you want."

"If I can wait here, why the heck did I have to come?" I grumbled, suddenly realizing that I could've drawn Bryn a map to the place. Bryn had known most of the route already. I wondered if claiming he needed me to navigate had just been an excuse to keep me with him.

I followed him through the field. The cool breeze carried the smell of the river, which helped. When we came to the clearing, I stared at the empty space. There wasn't a single piece of wood left upright. It appeared that Incendio had completely burned the barn down, leaving behind only a black rectangle of ash.

"Nothing left," I said.

Bryn held out a hand, frowning. "You're more right about that than you know."

"How's that?"

"You're sure that Incendio used magic to burn this place down?"

"Positive. I saw him start the fire."

"With this kind of destruction, there should be plenty of residual magic." Bryn went down on one knee and picked up a handful of soot. "There's barely any here. Definitely not enough to use to identify it as Incendio's."

"So he covered it up?"

"No," Bryn said. "Grounding magic so completely, that's complex spell-casting."

"Jordan?" I asked, referring to the wizard who'd been traveling with Incendio.

"Not in a million years."

"So who then?"

Bryn blew out a slow breath and shook his head. "I don't know the exact witch or wizard who cast the spell, but I certainly know who sent him."

I cocked my head. "Uh-oh."

"Yeah. The Conclave's already here."

7

IT WAS A sobering drive back to Bryn's. He was convinced that the Conclave had snuck into town to tamper with the scenes of the magical crimes. I wanted to look on the bright side, so I tried to figure out what that was.

"At least they were just covering their tracks, not trying to frame us."

"Covering their tracks does make the things we did harder to defend," he pointed out.

"Oh." I definitely wasn't happy to think that the Conclave was cheating on the investigation, but then again, we had the false fax, so we weren't exactly being honest either. Since I didn't think Bryn would appreciate me pointing that out, I said, "Darn spies. Just like them to be sneaky."

Bryn's gate swung open, and he pulled onto the drive.

"The house where the man with the scar took you, think back, was there anything around to suggest he was a wizard?"

"You think Scarface was sent ahead? Just like Incendio and Jordan were in Texas before they showed up in Duvall?" I asked with a sinking feeling. Of course, Bryn was right. It was way too much of a coincidence that a serial killer or some regular criminal had grabbed me right before the wizard assassins came to town. "I didn't see anything that made me think he was magical." I bit my lip. "I sent the police to get him. They don't have any way to protect themselves against magic."

As soon as Bryn stopped the car, I jumped out and ran to my car. "I have to check on them and to sign my statement. I'm going to the police station," I called to Bryn.

"I'll come with you," he offered.

"It's better if you don't."

He gave me a questioning look.

"To those deputies, I'm still Zach's girl. They don't take kindly to me hooking up with you. Even if we are just friends."

"All the more reason for me to come with you," Bryn said, but I waved him off.

I drove over and left Mercutio in the car when I went in. I was glad to see that the place was mellow, not showing any signs that they'd had to battle a wizard into custody. Had they already gone to get him? If not, should I go along? Or even take Bryn with us? That would go over like liver and licorice, but it was better than letting the deputies get hurt.

"Well, well," Smitty said, coming out with a paper in his hand and licking powdered sugar from the corner of his mouth. He adjusted the gun belt around his belly.

"Hey," I said, picking up a pen. "So you went already? What did he say when you arrested him? He tell you his name?" I asked. *And his hopefully nonwizard occupation.*

"There was no one in that house, and there was no sign that it had been used as a kidnapper's lair."

My brows shot up. So the guy had gotten away? Did that make him a wizard? Had he used a spell to unlock those cuffs? Momma had that talent. When I was little she used to play games with me. I'd tie her up and she'd get herself loose. The Houdini game, she called it. I didn't know how common it was to have that skill, but it sure would come in handy if someone was a spy.

"And that truck you left here was reported stolen a week ago from two counties over. For all I know, you stole it yourself," Smitty continued.

My gaze snapped back to him, and I scowled. Of all the things to say! I'd never stolen anything in my life. Well, except for taking my family's jewelry back from Jenna, which she didn't have a right to in the first place. Besides, I'd sent her money anonymously to pay for it only a couple days after I burgled her, so could it really be considered stealing? Technically, kind of. But morally, I didn't think so.

"Now as to the other part of your story," Smitty said, leaning forward. "Lucy, Sue, Mindy, and Jenna all say they were at a prayer meetin' when you claim they were kidnapping you. Reverend Fuller says he saw them at the church."

"Maybe they were at church before they came to the bakery or maybe they went there after. It's only a five-minute drive."

"Well, I've got the word of a reverend and four solid citizens against your cock-and-bull story, so here's what I think of your statement," he said, tearing the statement in half and then in half again. "You want to get Zach's attention, you better call him up. 'Cause if you ever waste our time again with false claims, we're throwing you in a cell. I got the sheriff's permission and he says the magistrate will back us up."

I glared at him. "I didn't make this stuff up. I've got better things to do with my time than to lie about getting kidnapped. And for your information, I don't have to make up stories to get Zach's attention. He calls me all the time. Now then," I said, grabbing the scraps of paper from the round trash bin. I slid the tape dispenser toward me and taped the pieces together. I signed across the bottom. "This here is my statement, and I want it filed."

"Not a chance," he said, yanking it from me and ripping it into about sixty-four pieces.

"Isn't that against the law? If a citizen wants to make a report, you've got to take it down and file it."

He folded his arms across his chest. "Why don't you get your new boyfriend to sue me?"

I thumped my fist on his desk, but held back the string of curses that threatened to spill out. "As a general rule, I'm not vindictive, but I do believe I'm gonna make it a priority to see that you lose your badge." With that, I got up and stalked out of the police station with plenty of dignity, but not an ounce of law enforcement support.

I WAS SO tired when I got to Zach's house, I fell facedown into Zach's bed fully clothed with unflossed teeth. I was dead asleep in seconds, so I wasn't very happy when Mercutio used his claws to pull my hair and wake me up.

"What time is it?" I mumbled, trying to focus my eyes on the clock. "Merc, it's four a.m. I count that as still night. Remember how I sleep at night?"

Then I heard a noise just beyond the bedroom door. I rolled quietly off the bed and reached under it to where I'd set the gun. I clicked off the safety and crept to the door. I'd left the living room light on for Merc, so there was a stretched triangle of light on the bedroom floor. I moved until I was standing just behind it.

I peeked around the door and saw two women dressed from head to toe in burglar-black outfits, including ski masks, rifling through Zach's drawers.

"Jenna—"

"Don't use my name," Jenna whispered fiercely.

I frowned and flicked the safety back on, then tucked the gun into the back of my jeans. I tiptoed to the bedroom closet and got Zach's spare handcuffs. Then I stepped out of the room, flicking on the hall light.

"Hey, y'all," I said.

They both jumped and then yanked out crosses and held them out toward me.

"Get back," Lucy snapped, and they both started quoting scripture.

Merc and I rushed them, him nipping and distracting them, while I handcuffed them to each other through a cupboard handle.

"Okay," I said, catching my breath. "Now, I'll just call the police and we'll see who's making up stories about kidnapping plots."

Mercutio yowled and bounded to the front door, waiting for me to open it.

"What, Merc? Is somebody else out there?" Had their accomplices Sue and Mindy come along? If so, I'd better tie them up or run them off. I didn't want them sneaking in and conking me over the head.

I hurried to the front door, rubbing my eyes. Why did they have to break in during the middle of the night? I padded outside, instantly anxious when I heard the crunch of leaves. I dropped to a crouch and waited.

The noise had come from behind a row of hedges. My breath came and went in shallow sips. I crept along, trying to find an opening in the hedge that I could look through. Then I heard another crunch and looked up just in time to see Scarface behind the row of bushes. His right arm started to rise.

No!

I drew my gun and whipped it up even faster than he got his pointed at me.

"Don't move," I snapped, but he did. He turned and bolted.

I stood and chased his footfalls, not able to see him clearly enough to be sure that if I shot him that I'd only wound him. A car's interior light clicked on when he opened the door, and I ran faster, but couldn't reach him before he peeled away.

"Coward!" I shouted in frustration. I walked back to Zach's, nearly jumping out of my skin when Merc padded up.

"Lost him," I said. "That was Scarface, who kidnapped me today. Looks like he's not giving up."

I marched into the house to confront the Reitgartens about whether they were connected to Scarface, but the kitchen was empty and the cupboard door was missing. They'd yanked it off the hinges. Darn them!

Plus, when they'd escaped, they'd left the back door wide

open for any Tom, Earl, or Scarface to waltz right in. I smacked my hand down on the countertop in annoyance, then walked over and slammed the door shut and locked it.

"Well, Merc, we can't stay here. First off, I don't want Zach's stuff getting messed with or his house getting damaged like mine was," I said, stalking into the bedroom. "And secondly, if people are after us, what better place to stay than someplace with a big gate and twenty-four-hour security?" I asked, retrieving the package with the brooch from under the bed and then taking my pink-and-black-checked roller suitcase out of the closet.

Merc purred, obviously agreeing with my plan to stay in the one place that, for so many reasons, I wasn't supposed to stay.

8

I DIDN'T WANT to wake up everyone at Bryn's house before dawn on a Saturday, so I decided to run an errand to my house first. The front was still boarded up while the reconstruction was going on, so I used a key to let myself through the gate that led to the yard, then went through the sliding door. The house was unswept and smelled like sawdust, but I could see the progress. The Sheetrock in the front room had been completely replaced.

I went upstairs to a locked trunk and took out my antique spellbook. Merc sat next to me on the rug while I read about the various things that could be used to stir up visions: looking glasses, tea leaves, horse apple seeds, flames, and smoke. I ran a hand through my hair and wondered which divination spells our family's witches had used most successfully. When Momma and Aunt Mel left, they'd taken the family spellbooks with them.

The thought of getting my hands on those books excited me. I hadn't been free to read them when I was very young. Later, it'd made me too sad to read about magic when I'd thought I would never have any. When Aunt Mel came back with the books, it would be my first chance to study them as a witch. Assuming I could get my powers under control.

Bryn and I had discovered the reason why my powers had been dormant was that my fae magic worked against my witch magic and vice versa. But my magical synergy with Bryn caused a disruption in the way the two magics neutralized each other. Now all we had to do was to come up with some brilliant plan to get them not to cancel each other out so much.

"Should I try a spell here?" I asked Mercutio. "It's only divination . . . a passive kind of spell. Nothing that'll send magic spiraling out into the neighborhood to affect other people. At least, I don't think it could."

Mercutio put his paw on the book, tapping it.

I smiled. "Come on then."

Downstairs, I found a jar of tart apples in honey that I'd canned myself. I opened them and ate several, the sweet and tart fruit sliding down my throat.

"Yum."

Merc licked my fingertips, but I don't think he likes honey as much as I do. Well, probably hardly anyone does.

I collected two pairs of candles, a box of matches, and the brooch. I took off my socks and shoes and went into the yard. I positioned the tallest candle at true north and then set the other three at east, west, and south. Mercutio sat next to me in the center of the candles, and I propped the brooch up against the north candle. I lit the wicks and then dug my toes and the fingertips of my left hand into the dirt.

I stared at the dancing flames. My gaze fixed itself, unblinking, until I seemed to get sucked into the light. I saw my childhood self near the Corsic Creek Bridge with Zach. We were small. Only eight. It was our first kiss.

And then a swirl of things. On my bike. On a tire swing. Bryn walking down the corridor of the fancy hotel in Dallas where I'd first talked to him. A smile curved my lips. I'd been in awe of him back then, had never dreamed we'd become friends. Never dreamed of a lot of things.

Then I saw myself in a pale gold dress that I'd never

worn, my hair upswept. My mouth went dry as I watched myself walk down an aisle, a creamy bouquet of flowers in my clasped hands. Someone waited. Waited for me to come and marry him? Who? My heart pounded and I felt slightly sick. I was afraid of seeing my own future.

I stretched a trembling fingertip to the brooch and stared at the flame. The scene changed and the beautiful dark-haired woman was there. This time she faced me. She flung her hand, as though casting a spell. A rush of fragmented images, running, falling, cobbles. Blood! The flame shot unnaturally high, and I jerked, falling out of the vision trance as I knocked over the candle with my foot. Merc yowled. He smacked out the flame of the fallen candle as I tried to catch my breath.

"It was all mixed up. I couldn't tell what was happening."

I rubbed my arms and glanced at the house on the property behind ours where the local judge and his family lived. They'd spied on me before, and their lights were on now. I was pretty sure the lights hadn't been on before I'd started the spell.

"We need to go," I said.

With a still-pounding heart, I blew out the other candles and collected everything. Inside, I dropped the candles and matches on the kitchen counter and put the brooch carefully into its box. I wiped the dirt from my feet quickly with a damp paper towel and washed my hands.

"Okay," I said, grabbing the brooch box and the spellbook. "We'll go to Bryn's. We'll be safe there, and maybe I can sneak a few books from his library that'll give me more control over looking into the brooch."

ON THE DRIVE to Bryn's, I saw George's mail van. I slowed down and waved to him out my window.

"Morning," he said.

"George, I need to stop my mail. I'm not going to stay at Zach Sutton's house after all. Can you hold my mail and then I'll pick it up from you?"

"Where will you be staying?"

"I'm not entirely sure yet. I'm in a bit of spot. Would it be okay for me to get it directly from you?"

"I always keep to my schedule." He glanced at the clock on his dash. "I start my route by five a.m. on Saturdays, so people's mail is waiting for them when they wake up. Otherwise, they go out and don't open it until Saturday afternoon or night or—Sunday morning," he said, pursing his lips as though Congress ought to really have passed a law to prevent mail-opening delays.

"Well, that sure is sweet of you to make sure people get their mail early."

"But it's not five yet, so I could give you your mail. Your new mail from England."

"From London?" I asked excitedly. "I'll pull over." I wheeled the car into a driveway and threw it into park.

I met George next to the van. He took out a heavy-bond envelope and handed it to me.

"George, you're one in a million," I said, giving him a quick hug.

"Just doing my duty." He swung the van door closed, checked to be sure it was secure, then went back to the driver's seat. With a brief hand out the window in a make-shift wave, he drove away.

I got in my car, setting the envelope on the dashboard. "A letter from Aunt Mel, Merc," I exclaimed as I drove to Bryn's. "Hopefully she'll explain who the woman from the brooch vision is. Did you see the way she thrust her hand in the vision? A witch, I'd say."

At Bryn's gate, I pressed the security buzzer. After a bit of hesitation, Steve's familiar voice filled the air.

"It's Tammy Jo. Let me in?"

"Sure. I'll meet you at the front door," he said.

The gate opened, and I drove up the fancy paved stone circle drive and parked. I got my suitcase out, but left the brooch locked inside the trunk. Somehow I didn't think it would be good to bring it into Bryn's, where security cameras recorded everything that went on except for in the bedrooms.

"A suitcase?" Steve asked, running a hand over his brush cut.

"Yeah, think he'll mind?"

"No, but we'd better ask him."

"Well, I'll put it here until he wakes up," I said, rolling it to the corner of the foyer.

"He's up."

"Already?"

"He's on the back lawn."

"The back . . ." I glanced at Mercutio. "Where's his dog, Angus?" Bryn's Rottweiler and Merc got along like—well, like cats and dogs.

"Gone. Lennox came by yesterday and took him."

"Oh, Bryn's dad is back. Isn't that—" *Too bad.* "Nice."

"Yeah, I can tell you're thrilled," he said with a grin. "Look, I've got to go back to the monitors. You'll wait here until he comes in?"

"Sure, I've got an important letter to read," I said, sitting on the settee.

Steve went back down the hall, and I opened the envelope. The letter was on thick stationery with filigree cutouts along the top. Super delicate. Ivory paper with black ink. Also inside the envelope, there were two thick strands of black satin ribbon.

Dear darling,

I'm so sorry we haven't called! So much time passed without our realizing it. Things are very different in the N.

"The N? The Never? Slang for faeryland, I think," I said to Merc, who was licking his paws.

We're both doing well. Marlee found the one she was looking for. Not everyone is happy about that, but he is.

Unfortunately, his kind are very possessive, and if he and Marlee want to be together, they have to prove their devotion. The one who lords over everyone—we'll call her the Queen Bee—insists that Marlee stay there.

I want her to come home, but she's determined to stay with him—at least for now.

Meanwhile, I did manage to get out of there. Thankfully! I have a few things to do in the UK before I can come home. I've sent some packages. Look for them and keep them safe.

Edie tells me that you've been having some adventures. She says you've entered into a new phase in your life and that you're doing brilliantly, especially considering that there's no one from the family to help you. (Please don't turn to anyone that you shouldn't for advice. You know better!) I promise I'll be home as soon as I can. Or you could come here. I would love for you to! I miss you. If not, if you can spare Edie, would you send me the locket? I really need her to be at her strongest and having the locket close would be best. Bind the locket with the special satin ribbons to cushion its journey. I've said a prayer for it to get here safely. If you want to say a little prayer as well, the kind that binds, that would be good, too.

Send it to me at the Savoy hotel in London.

That's all for now. We love you! Stay out of trouble!

Aunt Mel

I reread the letter, so happy to have proof that she was okay. She hadn't mentioned the brooch, but there was the "keep them safe" line about the stuff she was sending. Maybe I was just supposed to hold on to the brooch for Aunt Mel, and she'd take care of it when she got back to America. But what if she didn't get back in time? I really needed more information about what she wanted me to do.

At least she'd sent the satin ribbons that she'd cast a spell on. Her binding to keep Edie in the locket would probably work, even if my spell was useless. I smiled at her use of the word *prayer* instead of *spell*. Smart and careful. Who knew if the mail would fall into the wrong hands. DeeDAW hands. Boy was Aunt Mel going to be mad when she heard about them.

"Well, that's it for now," I said to Merc, putting the letter and ribbons in the envelope and slipping it into the pocket of my suitcase. "Momma's shacked up with a faery. Aunt Mel's trying to rebuild her magic. Edie's going airmail to England. And we're staying here to face the Conclave." I blew a strand of hair out of my eyes. "You think I should have let her or Edie know about the Conclave or Scarface or DeeDAW?"

Merc purred.

"But if most of her power was depleted from visiting Faeryland, she wouldn't be able to help much, right? So she'd rush home before she was ready, only to end up in danger along with me. I think it would be better to let her come home when she's ready, when she's built up her power again. I think Bryn and I can handle things here. Look at all that we've done over the past couple weeks. Although, he did lose a lot of his power during that Death spell a few days ago." I sighed. "Maybe I should ask him what he thinks about telling Aunt Mel."

I strode to the kitchen and out the back door. It was near dawn, and most of the outdoor floodlights had gone off. I walked diagonally toward the water, figuring I'd bump into Bryn somewhere along the way.

A pulse of white light blinded me. I tossed an arm over my eyes and Merc yowled.

"What the heck was that?"

9

I LOWERED MY arm carefully. In the distance, I could see tiny needles of bright light coming from the sky. I followed the lines of illumination down with my eyes and hurried toward them.

Bryn was standing shirtless on the lawn with his arms outstretched to the sides, his head tipped back so his face was turned up to the sky. The beams of light pierced his forearms. As I drew closer, I could hear that he was murmuring in a foreign language.

I paused, not wanting to disturb whatever spell he was casting. I heard Merc's breathing get faster, then he made a high-pitched sound and darted away.

What? I looked over my shoulder, trying to see where he'd gone, then I felt sharp pain in my shoulders. I whipped my head back and saw that two beams of light had bent from Bryn's arms and were striking me. I dropped to my knees, but the slicing beams followed.

"Ow!" I yelled. "What are you doing?"

He went on with his incantation. I leapt to my feet and raced toward him, the searing pain becoming unbearable.

He stopped speaking and the lights disappeared, but not

soon enough for me to stop. Momentum made me crash into him. We landed hard. Him on his back. Me sprawled half on top of him, half on the dewy grass.

I checked my shoulders, surprised that blood wasn't coursing down them from gaping wounds. On my shirt, there were a couple dots of blood, about a centimeter in diameter, but nothing more. I jerked the fabric down to expose my left shoulder. It was too dark to see, but it looked like there was only a tiny puncture.

"Good morning, Tamara," Bryn said mildly.

I slugged his left ribs. "What was that?" His power crawled over my skin like scorpion stings. It wasn't the way his magic usually felt. I rubbed my arms, trying to make the sensation go away.

Bryn turned his head to look at me, and his eyes were wrong, too. They were usually bright blue-violet, as if light were being refracted off them like the facets of a jewel. But now his eyes were blue-gray, like storm clouds, and opalescent. Still beautiful, but unfamiliar and kind of disturbing.

"What have you done?" I whispered, unable to keep the disapproval out of my voice. I sat up and scooted back. The stings dampened, and I continued rubbing my arms. He didn't answer.

I glanced at the horizon as the sun rose. The golden orange light framed him as he stood, but didn't gild him. It was as though the sunlight folded around him, leaving several inches of darkness as a barrier.

"Bryn?"

"You weren't willing to be part of the normal power spells I could've cast." He shrugged and then turned toward the house.

"What do you mean?" I said, jumping up. I followed him, leaving several feet between us.

"This was not the optimal time to draw power from the heavens, but it had to be done."

"You used black magic?"

He didn't answer.

"You shouldn't have done that!"

He turned his head slowly and cocked an eyebrow. "I appreciate you sharing your vast wisdom and experience with me."

I could feel that he wasn't himself, but his sarcasm still made me flinch. "I may not have a lot of experience, but I can certainly feel how wrong this is. Magic that pricks and stings? Bad idea!"

"There wasn't a better choice. If I hadn't done it, when they arrived I'd be like an unarmed soldier behind enemy lines."

"I wish you'd have explained more."

"I wish you trusted me." He strode to the kitchen's back door and went inside.

"Black magic, for the love of Hershey. I can't leave him alone for one minute," I murmured.

When I got inside, Bryn was rinsing his arms under cold water. There were dozens of tiny puncture wounds in the middle of his forearms, and the skin was raised and red around them, like burns.

"Are those constellations?" I asked.

"Yes."

"You pricked your skin? Made a tattoo for the stars to send down their light?"

He nodded.

"Did it hurt?"

"Not as much as drawing power with bright magic does. Black magic is less painful. That's why a lot of people turn to it when they need to draw more than they should."

"But it feels wrong, doesn't it? After it's inside you?"

"It feels different," he said, turning off the water.

"It feels wrong," I repeated firmly.

He moved so that he stood in front of me, his hands on the counter on either side of me. The magic didn't sting as much as it had at first. It was more like fingernails trailing along my skin, hard enough to leave a mark.

"Well, let's hope that I'm never on the brink of death again and forced to sacrifice all the magic that feels right to you," he said.

Bryn had gotten poisoned saving my life. "I'm sorry about that," I said.

"I'm not. It was worth it."

Even under the influence of black magic, his charm was as seductive as ever.

I slipped my arms around his neck and hugged him. The magic wrapped around us, thick and heavy. It was hard to breathe at first, but then I got used to the feeling. I had some vague idea that I could fix things without really knowing how. It was instinctive, like everything between Bryn and me.

"Tamara—" His voice was low and smooth. "Be careful."

I ignored the warning. Instead, I pressed my lips to his collarbone and drew the darkness, like smoke into my lungs. It was damp and cold and made me cough.

He snaked a hand up to my hair and drew my head back. Then he kissed me, and it consumed us, pushing the natural world away. I tried to draw the magic out of him, but he didn't let me. Not even a sliver.

A terrible pain in my leg finally made me jerk back. I looked down at the bloody scratch where Mercutio's claw had torn my jeans.

"Merc!" I snapped.

Bryn glanced down and spoke to Mercutio in Gaelic.

"What did you say?" I asked, taking a damp washcloth to clean the scratch.

"That's between him and me."

Merc licked my leg and rubbed his head against my arm. I petted him. "I don't think Merc cares for black magic."

"I think you're right."

The wall phone rang, and Bryn strolled over to it. He stared at me as he answered it.

"What's up?" He listened for a few moments and then said, "Sure, let her through."

"Jenna Reitgarten?" I asked.

"No."

Bryn retrieved a white button-down shirt from the seat of a chair. He slipped it on and began buttoning as I followed him to the foyer. He glanced at my suitcase.

"You pick now to move in?"

"People are trying to kidnap me."

"Can't really blame them for that," he said with a sexy smirk. "I've had the same temptation myself."

"Very funny."

His blue-gray eyes darkened, making me realize that he wasn't totally kidding.

I gasped. "You wouldn't!"

"No, I wouldn't." He studied me intently. "I don't like waiting for you to turn up. But you are always worth the wait."

I blushed, having to bite my tongue to keep from kissing him with it. "Um, that's enough flirting."

"You're right. No point starting something when someone's going to interrupt us. I'll put your suitcase upstairs in my room. We can finish this conversation later."

He reached for the handle, but I scowled at him and grabbed it, rolling it out of his reach. "I'll stay in the downstairs guest room!"

"Better to sleep under the stars," he countered. "With me."

Magic and lust and all kinds of other dangerous energy undulated from his body to mine, curling around me like smoke, warming me to the core. For several long moments, I stared at him, trapped by what I wanted to do, but knew I shouldn't.

I sucked in a cool breath. "Cut that out. That's not fair." I shuddered, pulling back from the brink of launching myself into his arms. I narrowed my eyes. "You see," I said, snapping my fingers. "You see what happens when you get buzzed on black magic?"

"Yes, I see," he said, still smiling.

I rushed to the downstairs bedroom that I'd slept in a couple times before when I'd been too wounded, poisoned, or exhausted to make it home. Boy, Bryn and I had a strange relationship.

I heard the doorbell and threw my suitcase into the room and shut the door. Then I hurried back down the hall, stopping at the end, in a spot where I wouldn't be easily seen.

Bryn opened the door, and there was a young woman in a tailored navy blue suit standing on the threshold. Caramel-colored hair and peaches-and-cream skin. She had the kind of fresh, pretty face you'd see in a soap ad, but the clothes were all business. I waited for her to introduce herself, but instead Bryn spoke.

"Hello, Gwen. You know, I didn't think you could possibly be as beautiful as I remembered, but it turns out you are."

I froze, a horrible knot of jealousy twisting inside me.

She smiled a lovely supermodel smile at him. "Hello, Bryn," she said in a perfect British accent. She studied his face for a moment and then touched her thumb to his lid just under his left eye. She clucked her tongue. "That color's different. What wicked things have you been up to?"

I wanted to scratch her eyes out.

He ignored her question, asking instead, "What are you doing here?"

"I'm here for the investigation."

His eyes widened for a moment in surprise. "You're here to investigate me," he said and frowned. "You're part of Barrett's entourage?"

"I'm training under the Winterhawk. I'm here as a Conclave junior operative."

"Congratulations." The chill in his voice made her blush, and I shifted uncomfortably.

"For heaven's sake, you mustn't take this personally," she said.

"Since you're here officially, I should introduce you," he said, calmly turning toward me. He waved, and I stepped out from around the corner.

Gwen's perfectly arched brows rose, and her hand fell away from his face. "Well, it seems it's my turn to be surprised. The notorious Miss Trask, I presume. She ought not to be here, Bryn. Badly done," she said, but she held out her hand to me.

A part of me wanted to sock her, but good manners left me no choice but to shake her perfectly manicured hand.

"You've got quite a good grip," she said.

"If you pushed power into her palm and are surprised that she didn't pull back or flinch, it's because she didn't feel it," Bryn said. He was right. Bryn's was the only magic I ever felt. I was tempted to tell her all about our magical synergy, but I managed to hold my tongue.

"Didn't feel it," Gwen echoed. "We had heard there was an impairment. I wasn't sure how accurate the account was." She gave me an appraising look. "The hair's every bit as red as reported. So unlucky, that."

I fumed.

"Depends on where one's from. Red hair isn't considered the thing in England, but in Ireland there's nothing luckier."

I heard the trace of his Irish accent when he spoke, and I guessed she did, too, because she pursed her lips into a tight white line. The corners of my mouth turned up in a small smile.

"Well, if she's such a lucky charm, you won't need any advice from me." She turned on her heel and with crisp steps and military posture walked to a silver Jaguar that was parked in the drive.

Bryn sighed and watched her drive to the gate before he closed the door.

I folded my arms across my chest. "She's an ex-girlfriend?"

He nodded.

"And now part of the Conclave," I said.

"She's only the second woman ever inducted."

"So she's a powerful witch?"

He nodded.

"More powerful than you?"

"No."

"Does she know that?"

"Yes, why do you ask?"

"Because didn't you say that John Barrett's petitioned to have your wizard class raised above four? So they can prosecute you differently for any rules you break?"

He tipped his head back and stared at the ceiling. "Christ," he mumbled.

"Yeah," I said softly. "When you've got secrets, the only thing more dangerous than a whole mess of tequila shots is pillow talk."

10

I TOOK THE locket from around my neck with trembling fingers. I'd been its guardian for months, and I didn't want to part with it—with Edie.

Normally, Momma and Aunt Mel shared the locket, but when Momma left to find her lost love, she'd left it with Aunt Mel. And when Aunt Mel had gone to look for Momma, she'd left the locket with me. I wondered if ghosts couldn't pass into the faery realm. Was that why they'd had to leave Edie behind? Whatever the reason, I'd liked having her to myself. Edie had irresistible charisma. Even when she made cutting remarks or made life difficult, I'd never wanted her to stop coming to see me.

I bent my head and kissed the locket. "Be safe, and come home soon," I whispered. I tied the ribbons carefully, then closed my hands around it. "Edie, the ties will keep you inside the locket. The ties will keep you at home in the locket." I let my lids drift down and repeated the incantation over and over.

When I opened my eyes, my cupped hands were resting on my lap with the locket warm and safe within them. I felt calm. She would get to Melanie okay.

Feeling reassured, I went to the post office and mailed her to London. When I got home, I followed the smell of coffee and found Bryn sitting at the kitchen table, drinking freshly brewed French Roast. I poured myself a cup.

"Are you hungry?" I asked, taking out a frying pan and stainless steel bowl.

Bryn nodded.

"So who's the Winterhawk?" I asked, setting flour, eggs, and milk on the granite countertop.

"You know your way around my kitchen," he said with a smile.

"Well, I did make all those desserts for the party you didn't have last week." I cracked eggs into the bowl. "Winterhawk?"

"Mrs. Thornton," Bryn said. "Her personal life and background are murky. The rumor is that she was an assassin in the sixties and seventies, but the Conclave blocked her entry into their ranks for years. In 1980, she uncovered a plot. A powerful Croatian vampire coven planned to kill Rutherford—he was president of the World Association of Magic then."

I got out a small saucepan.

"She led a day raid and slaughtered the vampires, but even after she saved his life, Rutherford didn't recommend Mrs. Thornton for promotion into the Conclave. It was Barrett who supported her induction. She's semiretired now, but whenever he travels to potentially dangerous political meetings, she goes with him, overseeing security." Bryn smiled. "And he brought her to Duvall with him. We should be flattered."

"That's just what I always wanted growing up—to make WAM's Highest Threat to National Security List," I said and snagged a bottle of Grand Marnier from the bar.

Bryn ran a hand through his glossy black hair. "Don't worry. The worst that can happen is they'll lock us up for a couple decades."

"Is that all?" I swallowed hard, trying to keep my mind

on food, which I always find so much more appetizing than jail.

I made crepes with strawberries and a cream liqueur sauce for breakfast. Probably it was too early in the day for a hundred-proof dessert, but who knew what was going to happen to us. I planned to treat every meal like it might be our last.

"Delicious," Bryn said when he'd swallowed the last berry. "You're a culinary genius."

"Thanks, candylegger," I said, making him laugh. Edie had called him that once. It had been a backhanded compliment, some twenties slang about him being too charming to trust. Turned out she was right since he'd done a spell that blocked her from seeing me.

"How is the family ghost? Still dripping venom from her phantom fangs?" he asked.

I clucked my tongue. "She doesn't have fangs."

"That you know about," he said, getting up and putting his dish in the sink.

"She's going on a trip."

"Good for her. Tell her she should include a tour of the world's cemeteries. Bangkok to Belfast. Shouldn't take her less than a hundred and twenty years if she takes her time."

I smiled. "You're terrible."

"Am I?" He leaned close and stole a kiss. While I caught my breath afterward, he emptied the pocket of his black bathrobe onto the table, looking for something. When he pulled out a small silver flask, he didn't set it down. Instead he uncapped it and held it out to me.

"I made you something."

"What is it?" I asked.

"I don't know how bad the interrogation will get. This is a precaution in case they try to drug us. A serum that protects against mind-altering potions. It'll last about twelve hours."

I drank some. It tasted like onions mixed with dishwashing soap. I made a face and forced it down. So much for only consuming scrumptious stuff during the Conclave's visit. I gagged a little, while he drank the rest of the liquid in the flask and glanced at the clock. Then he picked up a pill from the table. It was about half the size of an M&M.

"This stone has a custom spell on it—one I call a resolution spell."

I tilted my head, giving him a questioning look, then I looked closely at what he'd given me. It wasn't a pill. It was a pebble, stained with gritty reddish-brown paint.

"Swallow it," he said.

I wanted to ask what was on it, but was afraid I might not want to know. So I poured some more milk into my glass, then placed the stone on the back of my tongue and washed it down.

"What was it?"

"It's from a collection of porous rocks that can absorb power and potions. I put a drop of my blood on that one."

I grimaced. "Yuck," I said, taking another swallow of milk. "No offense, but whenever I've thought that you're pretty darn appetizing, I never meant it literally."

He smiled. "Not planning to become a vampire anytime soon, huh?"

"Ugh, no." I ran my fingers over my lips. "So what was the blood rock for?"

"I don't think they'll resort to physical torture, but they'll try other things. So long as I don't break, you'll be able to draw strength of will from me."

"Will that weaken you?"

He shook his head.

"What about you? Where will you get help from if you need it?"

"Experience."

"Not from me? I can be pretty tough, you know. I don't mind you pricking my finger." I held my hand out. "To make a Tammy Jo blood rock for you to eat."

He brushed his lips over my knuckles, sending the kiss all the way up my arm. "I'm not sure yet what kind of help

I'll need, if any, but it won't be that kind. I'm stubborn to a fault."

He glanced again at the clock. Almost ten. "I'll be back down after I take a shower." He paused in the doorway. "If you want to help me with that, I wouldn't say no." His dark lashes framed blue-gray eyes that seduced the light and stole my breath.

I shook my head and pointed a finger at the door. He winked at me and was gone.

I exhaled slowly. When it came to willpower, defying the Conclave wasn't really the worst of my troubles. I wondered if Bryn had a little stone that I could swallow to resist the temptation of him. I went to the sink and washed our dishes, thinking I really needed to find a safer place to stay.

The sound of music coming from behind me made me turn off the water. I recognized it. "Where the Streets Have No Name" by U2. I walked to the table and found Bryn's pearly white iPhone. It was one of the things he'd taken out of his robe pocket.

There was a text message from an unknown caller.

Mirror in closet. One minute.

"What?" I asked, but, of course, the phone didn't answer. "Whatever happened to using a phone to talk?" I exclaimed.

Carrying the cell, I jogged up the stairs and knocked on Bryn's bedroom door. When he didn't answer I went in. The door to the master bathroom was closed, and I could hear the water running. Summon him out of the shower? That would sure put us in an interesting position, and just when I'd been planning to stay out of trouble.

"Bryn?" a voice said.

I spun toward his walk-in closet and crept into it. At the back of the closet, the small door that led to the secret study was open. Sitting on the desk was an old mirror with a gilt frame. And inside the mirror, there was a man.

He had thinning sandy brown hair, wire-rimmed glasses,

and a cheerful round face. When he saw me, he tilted his head slightly and smiled.

"Hi," I said, leaning forward.

"And hello to you. Has he been kidnapped, incarcerated, or knocked unconscious?" The man's accent made me feel like making strudel.

"No, not kidnapped or anything." I glanced around to be sure we weren't under siege. "He's just in the shower. Should we expect that to happen?"

"These days are uncertain." A soft breath, and then, "This is so good—to finally meet you. I am Andre Knobel. I will be the best man at your wedding."

"My what?" I gasped.

"Unless you agree to marry me instead. Then I will be the groom, and he can be the best man. He will not like this, but he has suffered worse disappointments. I know this because I am his oldest friend."

"He—he's never mentioned you. Or suffering disappointments. Or marriage. Definitely not marriage." I did know the name Andre. Someone named Andre worked at WAM headquarters and had gotten information for Bryn last week.

"No, he would not have done. Not yet. I have a message for him. You will tell him?"

My eyes darted around the room. I was still half distracted by the earlier part of the conversation.

"Tamara, you will convey a message, yes?"

"Yes."

"Good. Tell him someone tried to hack into the network, so I've shut it down. Backup in effect as of twelve-oh-one London. Repeat, please." He looked over his shoulder, quick like someone might sneak up behind him.

I repeated the information, then asked, "Is everything okay?"

"Tell him, too, that someone broke into my flat. They took all the computers and electronics, my audio bootlegs—the bastards—and the Egypt journal."

"A break-in. My gosh! I'm sure he'll be out of the shower any minute. I'll go—"

"No, I must go. I am actually on the run. Just a precaution."

"On the run!"

"I will come again. And so nice to talk to you," he said. Then he was gone.

I stared at my reflection in the mirror, wide-eyed and slack-jawed with shock. Plus, my hair was kind of messy. I smoothed it down absently as I padded out of the closet. Warm orange sunshine streamed in through the prism skylight, flooding the large room with light. I rapped on the bathroom door.

He didn't respond, but he'd turned off the water. I tapped again.

When the door opened, steam billowed out. I looked up at the ceiling to avoid looking at Bryn.

"Hi, sorry to interrupt. Um, there was a—Andre in the mirror."

"An Andre in the mirror," he said, amused. From the edge of my vision, I saw the movement when he wrapped a towel around his hips. He ran a hand through his slick hair and walked to the closet.

"He's gone," I said.

"When will he be back? Ten minutes?"

"No, I don't think so." I relayed the messages, and Bryn frowned.

"How did he look?"

"Friendly. Cute."

"I meant, did he look disheveled? Or hurt?"

"No, he looked fine. He said going on the run was just a precaution."

Bryn nodded. "If he didn't ask for help, then he's okay."

"He said he's your oldest friend." I waited for confirmation.

"He's my best friend," Bryn said, taking clothes from the hangers.

"I didn't know you had a best friend. He knew about me though. Didn't even have to tell him my name."

When he walked out of the closet, I stayed behind, staring absently at the rows of designer suits.

"Bryn?"

"Yeah?"

"Well?"

"Well what? I didn't hear you ask a question."

"What have you been telling him? About me, I mean."

There was a pause and then he appeared in the doorway. He was tying a cobalt blue silk tie around his neck. "Why? What did he say?"

"He seemed to think we were in a relationship. A serious relationship."

"Hmm."

"Why would he think that?" I asked.

"Why do you care what he thinks?" Bryn countered.

"I—I don't know. That's not the point."

Bryn walked past me to the closet within the closet and opened the drawer of the desk. He took out something wrapped in dark purple velvet and walked out to the bedroom.

"Come here," he said.

I moved to stand next to him as he unwrapped the velvet to reveal a stack of cards that were about twice the size of regular playing cards. The back of the cards had shimmering constellations.

He began flipping them over in pairs. The pictures were beautiful, inlaid with gold and silver. When he came to the picture of a red-haired witch, he paused a moment before flipping the second card. When he did there was a pair of hands, a man and woman's, and they were laced together with a white ribbon.

"Since the night of your friend Georgia's party, these two cards come up together. Every time."

"What's that picture supposed to mean?" I demanded, feeling like there wasn't much air in my lungs. I knew, without knowing how, that those intertwined hands meant commitment. *For life or longer*, the words seemed to echo in my head.

"It means that your great-great-grandmother's premonition is irrelevant." He shuffled the cards, then flipped them again in pairs. The red-haired witch. The hands with the ribbons.

I felt such a mix of emotions. I wanted it to be true, but I also dreaded it being true. If I was with Bryn, for real, for good, it would change my life. Momma and Aunt Mel were dead-set against the Lyons family. Would I lose them? What about Zach? What about his family? What about my childhood friends? Even though Bryn lived in Duvall, he wasn't a part of the world I'd grown up in. He hadn't gone to school in town or rooted for the high school football team. He'd been all over the world. His best friend had never even visited Duvall, for pete's sake. Probably Andre had never even been to Texas. I stiffened my spine.

"We're in charge of our own destiny. Just 'cause a deck of cards says something, doesn't make it so," I said.

"You're right. It isn't just the cards that make it so."

I took a step back, feeling unsteady. I hated when he sounded so confident. It was almost impossible to believe he could be wrong.

"You know," I said defiantly, "you could've told your friend to appear in the mirror and tell me something that would make me ask you questions. You could've put a spell on those cards, so the red witch and the commitment card came up together."

His eyes went as blue-black as his hair, and his expression matched them. "I *could* do a lot of things, but I don't want anything that badly. Not now. Not for a long time."

There was something raw in the emotions just below the surface. Something painful that I instinctively wanted to soothe, which was ironic since my insulting him was what had made it rise up in the first place.

"What did you want so badly?" I whispered.

He rewrapped the cards in the velvet. "Don't ask me personal questions, Tamara. I don't trust you with the answers."

I winced, my heart aching. I really had hurt him. "I'm sorry, but you do stuff—like blocking Edie—because you think it's for the best or will work out in the end."

"I apologized for that."

"I know, but you can be tricky and secretive. How can I help but be suspicious? Plus, you're so smart and so smooth. Sometimes I forget that you're human, too."

He nodded, but his face was a cool mask. "When it comes to cartomancy, I'm pretty skilled with this deck, but I'm not infallible. The pairing of those two cards may not be as significant as I'd first thought. Maybe it meant that we'd be bound together in dealing with the trouble of the past couple weeks. Maybe when the Conclave's gone and everything's back to normal here, the cards will separate again."

The words stung me. They shouldn't have, since I was the one who always resisted Bryn and me getting closer.

He strode into the closet and put the cards back in the drawer, then closed it and closed the panel that hid the small room.

Bryn's phone, which was still in my hand, rang. This time the ringtone was different. "Sunday Bloody Sunday." And a dark picture appeared of a clock tower looming over a river.

He took the phone and answered it. He listened for a moment, and then said, "Okay." When he hung up the phone, he said, "The president of the World Association of Magic and members of the Conclave will be here in ten minutes."

"What?" I gasped, my gaze sliding back to the closet.

"Tamara, forget everything else. Remember the practice sessions. You have to be focused and on your guard. These people are dangerous."

I nodded and rubbed my hands together nervously, my heart thudding a tattoo on the inside of my chest.

"Are you ready?" he asked.

"Since when does it matter if I'm ready?"

11

JOHN BARRETT WAS not what I expected. He looked like a trimmer, more stylish version of Santa Claus. He had white hair and a well-kept white moustache and beard. He wore a maroon sweater under his dark blue sport coat and stood in Bryn's foyer, looking around approvingly.

"Well, this was the right choice," he said to me with a twinkle in his eye. "We're staying at a place called the Duvall Motor Inn. Each room has a theme. Mine, I regret to say, is catfish. The bedside lamp, the border paper, and the bedspread are completely covered with them." His smile was jovial.

"The Yellow Rose Bed and Breakfast would've provided better accommodations. It's unfortunate that it burned down," Bryn said in a voice that was cool and hard.

My eyebrows rose, but Mr. Barrett didn't turn a hair. He stepped farther into the house. "Now, am I correct in assuming that you are Tamara Josephine Trask?" he asked, holding out his hand.

I nodded and let him take mine. He didn't shake it. He held it in his right hand and patted it with his left.

"I want to talk with you first." He moved me to his side

and away from Bryn. "And here is the brilliant young attorney who steadfastly refuses to come and work for the Association. I daresay you could better be our conscience from London than from across the Atlantic."

"Really? I thought I'd managed pretty well from here."

Barrett laughed, a short shotgun blast of hearty mirth. "So you have. Should I offer my hand now or would you refuse to shake it? Perhaps we'd better wait until our business is concluded. Now, let me see. You know Gwen, of course."

I glanced at Gwen and the sleek silver-haired woman who had come in behind her.

"Do you know Margaret Thornton?" Barrett asked.

"Only by her impressive reputation," Bryn said, and to the Winterhawk, he did extend his hand. "My father doesn't have any interest in politics or state security, but he speaks highly of you."

She had light green eyes, made more striking by dark gray liner and very black lashes. She wore a navy trench coat over charcoal trousers and tall black boots. She looked like a former Bond girl who'd turned spy herself.

"You're in a bit of trouble, my lad. Let's see if we can't get you out of it," she said crisply. Then she turned her gaze onto me. She glanced up and down. I was wearing a simple black turtleneck with black jeans and brown cowboy boots. Probably I should've worn slacks and high heels, but I hadn't known what to expect, and jeans and boots work better for me when I end up in a scuffle or running for my life.

"And here we have the child who started it all," Mrs. Thornton said. "Well, you do know how to make an entrance onto the world stage, I'll give you that, but, given the lack of magical talent, perhaps you should have tried your hand at acting and left the witchcraft to real witches." From over her shoulder, Gwen smiled.

"Actually, I'm a pastry chef."

"Indeed? And the slight bulge in the back of your sweater, is that a cake-decorating device? You have it on your person in case a cake happens to wander by in need of icing?"

I blushed. She'd spotted the gun. "No, ma'am."

"So you have a third occupation then? Pastry chef. Poorly trained upstart witch. And armed bodyguard for Mr. Lyons?"

"Well, now and again he does need rescuing," I said.

John Barrett, Gwen, and Bryn all laughed.

The Winterhawk didn't smile, and her green gaze never left mine. "Not terribly often I should think."

"No, ma'am. Not often."

"Are you good with a gun?"

"I mostly hit what I aim at, but I suppose that's true of a lot of people who know how to handle a gun."

"Not necessarily. Gwen, what do we know of Miss Trask's skill with weapons?"

"She's highly skilled. Excellent accuracy even during times of extreme stress."

So they'd been checking up on me? Who'd told them I was good? My friends and neighbors? Guys from the werewolf pack? Couldn't have been the faeries. They don't normally fraternize with witches, excepting Momma, of course.

The last thing I wanted to talk about was how I was a natural with weapons because that might lead to how I'd probably inherited my ability from my faery knight father, which was something I was not going to tell.

"Well, I'm a Texan. Guns are kind of a hobby here," I said. "Anybody want coffee or tea?"

"We had a very early breakfast, so tea and biscuits would be welcome," Mr. Barrett said.

"Jenson's not here," Bryn said.

"I can manage," I said quickly, anxious to escape for a few minutes.

"Let's not stand on ceremony," Mr. Barrett said. "I'll help you. It'll give us a chance for an informal chat. Gwen, get set up in the dining room." Seeing Bryn's dark expression, Barrett added, "If that's agreeable to you. As I've said, our rooms—such as they are—won't accommodate a formal interview. The alternative would be for you and Miss Trask to return with Margaret and myself to London while Gwen finishes up the investigation here."

"The dining room's fine," Bryn said.

I turned toward the kitchen and felt metal slide against my lower back. I turned sharply. Mrs. Thornton had my gun and was tucking it into her pocket. Annoyingly quick for an old lady!

Barrett smiled. "Now, Maggie, I don't think the young lady was going to assassinate me."

"Definitely not before I served the tea anyway," I said tartly. "That wouldn't be good manners."

Barrett laughed heartily and followed me to the kitchen.

I motioned for him to take a chair, and I put on a kettle of water. I took out two silver platters. One of them had a swirled leaf pattern etched in it, but the other had stars and planets. I smiled, wondering where they'd found the second pattern. Bryn and his celestial magic.

Barrett asked casual questions about my childhood in Duvall and about my friends and my divorce. I acted like I wasn't paying too much attention as I answered, but, of course, I was.

I made cucumber sandwiches and arranged cranberry scones, gingersnaps, lemon curd, strawberries and orange wedges, assorted cheeses and smoked salmon, and cracked pepper crackers on the tray.

I scooped some tea leaves into the platinum-rimmed teapot and poured hot water over them.

"There's something rather important we need to talk about. Before I begin, I want to assure you that you won't have to make any decisions today."

A chill coursed down my spine. He was going to ask me to betray Bryn, and, if I didn't, there would be some terrible consequence. I leaned back against the counter to brace myself.

"I know that your mother doesn't get along with your grandmother, but have you considered that there are two sides to every story?"

I stared at him. My grandmother? What was he talking about? My granny had died when I was young.

"Your grandmother would very much like to get to know you, and if you chose to come to England, to live with her for a time, you could get the very best training available, beginning your instruction with her. An unparalleled opportunity. She was one of the most celebrated teachers at the Paisley School, you know."

I realized too late that I was gaping at him in shock. I tried to compose myself, but he'd already seen.

"Did they tell you she was dead?" he asked.

I couldn't answer. Was he lying? Or was this another enormous secret that Momma, Aunt Mel, and Edie had kept from me?

How could they?

Barrett sighed. "I'd intended to say so much more, but I suppose—" He shook his head. "That's enough for now."

I sank into the chair, staring at him, bewildered and overwhelmed. Did I have living family that I'd never met? Why had Momma and Aunt Mel lied?

"What did she do to them?"

"Sorry?" he asked, putting the teapot and cups and saucers onto the second tray.

"Why didn't they want me to know her? What did she do to them?"

"They had a falling-out. I don't know the details. Only that she regrets the estrangement."

"Uh-huh." There was a large lump in my throat. I couldn't imagine what in the world could've happened to make them claim their own momma was dead. It must have been something very bad.

"There is one other thing to consider."

"What?"

"Young Lyons."

I stiffened. Did John Barrett really think he could bribe me with information?

"He's got tremendous potential, but he's keeping very dangerous company. It'll be the death of him, this underground movement." Barrett shook his head.

I kept my face perfectly still. No way was I going to let him trick me into admitting anything.

"Most of them are misfits and troublemakers. Not a great

loss to the craft, but Lyons and Knobel are the greatest minds of their generation. No one wants to see a pair of wizards who have been awarded the Granville Prize destroyed. You spoke earlier of rescuing him. I'd like to help you do that."

You could've knocked me over with a soufflé.

"I don't know what you're talking about," I said woodenly.

"I don't expect you to confirm or deny his involvement in the Wizard's Underground. Or to advise him to leave it. I'm sure no one has that much influence over him. That's the trouble with geniuses. It's hard to dissuade them from their own judgment. But he does seem very taken with you, and if you came to London, perhaps he would, too. Think about it. That would be good for you both."

At first, I was speechless. It was like he'd sat down and said, "We'd like to make you an astronaut so you can fly a rocket ship to Pluto. It'll be good for the space program."

"Everything's ready. We should take it to the dining room," I said and picked up the platter with the tea, making sure the cream and sugar bowls were there with the cups and saucers.

"One last thing," he said, lifting the food platter. "During the interrogations, things will be done that won't be pleasant. Try not to hold it against us."

12

WHEN I ENTERED the dining room, I was still reeling from Barrett's last remark—and from everything that he'd said. I really wanted to talk to Bryn alone, which also gave me a jolt because normally when I need to talk something over, I always turn to Zach or my best friend, Georgia Sue.

Bryn sat at the head of the table, signing some document. I poured him some tea and set the cup next to him while Barrett and Gwen helped themselves to tea and food.

"President Barrett, you'll want to see this," Gwen said, passing a sheet of paper to him. The fake fax.

He looked it over, silently, for a long time. Finally, he said, "It's a forgery, of course, but a very convincing one. I suppose we can guess who sent it. I got a message this morning that Andre didn't come in to work yesterday. I hope his illness isn't anything serious."

Bryn never looked up from the document in front of him. He initialed some sections and put an X through others. When he finished the last page, he slid it to Gwen.

"Should we get started? I've got a six o'clock dinner to attend," Bryn said.

"You can't be serious," Gwen said.

"If I'd been given more notice of this, I could've canceled, but I wasn't. I'm supposed to give a speech, so failing to appear isn't an option."

"That won't be a problem. If we're not through with everything today, we'll continue tomorrow, and Miss Trask can join us for dinner tonight," Barrett said.

"She's coming with me. She did an elaborate chocolate sculpture for the event and will be needed to supervise its assembly."

The DeeDAW dinner! Bryn wanted me to go? For the love of Hershey, they'd probably try to toss a bag over my head and drag me out. Well, maybe not in front of witnesses, and I definitely didn't want to get stuck with the wizards, so I just nodded and poured another teaspoon of sugar into my teacup. I probably deserved a lot of credit for not letting my surprise show, but after the kitchen conversation, I guess not much would shock me for at least a week.

"Do you want me to start with a statement?" Bryn asked.

"No, I have a copy of your statement. I've read it thoroughly," Barrett said. "In the interest of time—fortunate since you have a dinner engagement—we're going to help you to be exact in your account of the events as we question you."

Bryn didn't say anything, but my heart thumped faster. What did Barrett mean by "exact in your account"? Truthful? They were going to use a truth serum? I hoped that counted as being drugged and that Bryn's onion-and-dishwashing-soap potion would work.

"We have some new technology. It's actually based on research that Andre Knobel did with the Corps of Wizard Engineers. Though, as usual, his paper was on theoretical magic, and I don't think he foresaw this particular application," Barrett said.

From out of her briefcase, Gwen lifted a black leather box. It was about seven inches in diameter and a couple inches deep with a fancy crest embossed on it in gold. She opened the case and turned it around. Inside there was a kind of necklace. The pendant was a flat metal square with a pentacle engraved on it and hooked to its sides were fabric-covered straps. When I leaned closer, I realized that there were tiny needles protruding from one side of the straps.

"Which side faces the skin?" I demanded.

"The pentacle faces out."

I glared at them. "Then the answer is no."

Barrett smiled. "The needles are extremely fine. They're the diameter of acupuncture needles. He'll barely feel them."

"Tamara—" Bryn said in a tone that sounded like he was going to try to calm me down and go along with them sticking needles into his neck.

"No," I said, jerking my head to look at Bryn. "Needles? And something wrapped around your throat? Some new thing they're experimenting with? No! No way! What if it tightens? What if it chokes you?"

"*Our* magic doesn't malfunction," Gwen said.

I snatched the case and flung it. The Winterhawk's hand shot out and she said, "Suspend."

I dove across the table after the box, determined to disrupt everything long enough for us to escape.

Gwen flung out her hand. "Repel!" she said, but the magic wasn't strong enough to knock me back. It only made me slide from the table to the ground next to Mrs. Thornton's chair. I dipped my hand into the pocket of Mrs. Thornton's trench coat and jumped up with the gun. I swiveled and pointed it at John Barrett's head.

The case dropped from the air where Mrs. Thornton's magic had been holding it up, and the box landed on the floor. Mrs. Thornton's hand jerked toward me and so did Bryn's.

"Enclose!" Bryn shouted as Mrs. Thornton said, "Fall."

Bryn's magic closed around me a moment before her energy rocked the barrier. I stumbled, barely keeping my balance. Mrs. Thornton rose to her feet and raised both hands.

With his hand still outstretched, Bryn strode around the table to me, coming to stand just behind me.

His left hand slid through the magical force field and rested on my shoulder. "Lower the gun," he whispered.

I kept my right arm up, my finger over the trigger. "If they promise not to try to make you put that thing on." My voice was steady even though my pulse drummed frantically in my head.

I felt Bryn's magic pulse as he stepped forward. He brought his mouth to my left ear, and his voice was so soft that I knew only I could hear him. "You can help me, but not this way. Lower the gun."

My instincts screamed a protest, but I let my arm fall so the gun was pointed at the floor.

"We need a moment," Bryn announced to the room as he closed his left hand around mine.

"Yes, it seems you do," Barrett said. "Go ahead."

Bryn tugged my hand, and we backed out of the room. He pulled the door closed and then dropped the shield around us. He grabbed my arm and hurried to the kitchen.

"I need a favor," he said.

"We have to get out of here!"

"Did you hear what I said? I need a favor."

"I heard, but—"

"I'm going to cast a spell. Then I want you to leave. Go somewhere and stay out of sight. Don't talk to anyone under any circumstances."

I opened my mouth, but he covered it with his hand.

"There isn't time to discuss it. You either trust me or you don't."

My breath was quick and uneven, but I nodded.

"Don't talk. Just wait." He closed his eyes and didn't move. "Night and flame part ways in haste. She in truth, his words false-laced." Then he kissed me and honey-soaked peppery magic flowed down my throat.

He let me go, and I swallowed hard. He grabbed my tote from next to the kitchen table and shoved the straps onto my left shoulder, then yanked the door open. "Don't come back here today. Come to the fund-raiser. If I'm not there, leave Duvall."

"I'm not leaving. Where would I even go?"

He pushed me out the door. "Go to Zach. He'll protect you."

I couldn't believe he'd suggest I go to Zach. They made

no secret of disliking and being jealous of each other. For the Conclave to worry Bryn enough to send me away to Zach—such a bad sign.

I felt his spell's magic coiling around me, squeezing my chest tight. *Now what?*

"I don't think I should leave you alone with them!" I said fiercely, feeling a little breathless.

He glanced over his shoulder to see if anyone was coming. "Why not, Tamara?"

"Because they're obviously maniacs!"

"Why is what happens to me important to you?"

"Because I love you—" I slapped a hand over my mouth. Why had I said that? Was it true? I'd felt compelled to. What the Sam Houston?

He smiled at me. "Go on now. And don't talk to anyone." Then he closed the door.

"I love Zach, too. Just because I love you a little bit doesn't mean we can be together," I told the door. I slapped a hand against my forehead and turned around, tucking the gun into the back of my jeans under the turtleneck.

"I can't believe he zapped me with a truth spell," I muttered. I didn't see how forcing me to tell the truth was going to make him able to lie through that needle lie detector, but we did have our magical synergy, so maybe he could divide the truth between us unevenly.

Should I really leave him with them? I didn't want to. There were three of them and only one of him. But he was Bryn. Maybe he did know what he was doing.

If I was getting off Bryn's property, I should do it before the wizard brigade came looking for me. I looked around quickly. Merc was somewhere on the grounds, and I wanted him.

I jogged along the back lawn, looking up into the trees. When I found him, I called in a hissed whisper. "Mercutio!" Then louder, "Merc!"

He opened his eyes lazily. "It's after noon, and I have to get out of here. Come on down if you want to come with me."

He yawned and came headfirst down the trunk in that gravity-defying way of his.

I started talking as we raced across the lawn and didn't stop until we were halfway down the street in my car. Merc licked his paws thoughtfully. I exhaled hard, then worked to suck in another breath. Turns out truth spells feel kind of like an asthma attack.

"Where should we go? There might be workmen at my house. There might be kidnappers at Zach's." I bit my lip. "I love Georgia Sue, but you can trust her with a secret like you can trust me not to eat a chocolate chip cookie. So if I'm under an I've-gotta-tell-the-truth hex, I better not go there. Tom Brick's? It's isolated and deserted. But what if the Conclave takes Bryn there for a 'scene of the crime' interview?"

Mercutio set a paw on my leg and looked out my window. I glanced over. We were passing Macon Hill, the magical tor.

I swung the wheel. "Good thinking. Hardly anyone uses the chapel on the tor. We can hide the car behind it."

I looked in the rearview mirror several times as I sped up the road to the top of the tor. I parked my car on the grass. No other cars around.

I rolled down my window to get some fresh air and launched into telling Merc how worried I was about Bryn. I wanted to think of a way to get the police to go to his house and break up the Conclave's interrogation, but I couldn't call and make a false report on account of having to tell the truth. And, if I told the truth, they either wouldn't believe it or that would start another whole mess.

Then I started talking about the state of my life in general. Kind of chaotic and confusing was my assessment. When Merc stopped making any noise, I glanced over and found him asleep. Sometimes having a sidekick who's nocturnal works out. Sometimes not so much.

Feeling restless, I looked out the window at the grass swaying in the breeze.

I shouldn't be sitting around wasting time.

Plus, I needed a distraction from worrying about Bryn. The tor was a place of concentrated magical power, which might help me to see more of the brooch vision.

I didn't have any candles or matches or bowls of water, but I could always come back with those things if this attempt didn't work. Also, it seemed to me that those things were mostly used to help the mind drift. If I could get relaxed and let my mind roam, I might be able to achieve the same effect.

I rubbed the top of Mercutio's head for luck and then got out. I pulled off my boots and set them on the driver's side floorboard. I tugged off my socks and set them on the seat. The ground was cold under my feet and I shivered.

I retrieved the brooch from the trunk, waiting for a moment to see if the vision would just come, but it didn't. I closed the trunk and went around to the stone bench in front of the chapel and dug my toes into the dirt there to let the Earth's magic flow into me.

I held the brooch lightly in my hands and stared at the rippling grass. For a long time, nothing happened.

"Powerful Earth, show her to me." I whispered the request over and over until I was barely aware that I was saying anything at all.

She rose suddenly, partly transparent at first, then the slope of the hill faded and she came sharply into view. She was running with her back to me, getting farther away. I rushed after her.

The sound of her feet on the cobbles. A narrow street with gas streetlamps. An alleyway. Heart banging. Breath short. Something hit us, and we fell.

A cold lance of pain in my side made me scream. Blood spilling. Dry lips.

How could you?

I held my side and my hand cramped, fingers tingling with pain. She was on her side near me, starting to turn and then she was gone for the blink of an eye before she appeared again, standing over me.

"Help me. Please help me," she said, voice soft as the wind.

Mercutio leapt over me, yowling in fury. He passed through the apparition, and she vanished. My hand felt like it was dipped in ice water. Gasping in pain, I pried the fingers of my right hand open with my left. I let the brooch fall onto the grass and my mouth hung open, trying to get enough air. Mercutio hissed and knocked the brooch away from me with an angry paw. He clawed the dirt and stamped it down into the earth as if to bury it. The terrible pain in my side faded to a dull ache, and I blinked away the tears that had formed in my eyes.

"Oh, Merc." I ran a hand over my sweat-dampened forehead and looked at the chapel that I'd left behind when I raced headlong down the grassy embankment after her. I sucked in air and blew it out. "I don't think I can save that girl."

I let my head fall back onto the grass, staring up at the clear afternoon sky.

"I think she's already dead."

13

MERCUTIO DIDN'T WANT me to take the brooch. He was really vocal on that account, but I picked it up anyway. I used the lower edge of my shirt to keep from touching it with my bare fingers.

"I sure don't understand, Merc. If she's a ghost, why didn't she appear as a ghost and talk to me from the start like Edie would've? And if it's a vision, then why am I so sure that she was talking directly to me when she asked for help?"

I sighed. "Maybe it was a vision and then the girl astral-projected to me?" I put the dirt-covered brooch into its box and closed the trunk. I put my hands on the car and leaned over it, shaking my head. "I don't know. I felt that pain. It was *really* bad. Somebody stabbed her, I think. I felt it cut something deep inside me and then all the blood was gushing out." I shuddered.

I turned my head to look at Mercutio, who was eyeing the area suspiciously. "I'm not sure that Aunt Mel sent that thing. Why would she? Where would she even have gotten it if she's been in Faery?" I rubbed my damp hands on my jeans and straightened up.

"Maybe the Conclave sent it to me as some kind of a test." I licked my lips. "But I feel like I'm connected to that woman. Like she's someone in our family line. Maybe my grandma in London sent it to me." The breeze blew across my skin and I shivered, chilly and exhausted. "I feel terrible. Let's sit for a minute."

We got in the car, and I closed and locked the doors. I started it up so I could turn on the heat, then I put my seat back, trying to get my muscles to relax.

"I know I'm not supposed to tell anybody, but I think I might have to talk to Bryn about this brooch." That thought gave my heart a slight pang. "I sure hope he's okay."

I WOKE UP when Merc's paw bumped my arm, and I jumped when I realized someone was standing next to the car. The sun in my eyes had me half blind, but as my vision started to adjust I realized with relief that it was Bryn. I lowered the window.

"Hey there," I said with a smile.

"What are you doing here? I thought you were at my son's house?"

I jerked forward, blinking. It wasn't Bryn. It was his dad, Lennox. "I was there. I pulled a gun on John Barrett, and Bryn kicked me out for my own safety."

"You managed to pull a gun on the president of the World Association of Magic?" Lennox asked with a smile. "What was his security detail doing? Admiring your pastries?"

"They were distracted. Listen, I don't know if Bryn's okay. They were going to use some magical collar on him that was covered in needles! *Needles!* They thought they could make him tell the truth with it. I didn't want him to go along with them."

"He agreed to put it on?"

"I think so. He cast a spell on us. I think he thought he could outsmart the device."

"Then he probably will."

"You don't know. Why aren't you there helping him? You're his dad."

"Why isn't your father here helping you?"

"Because he's not a wizard. He's not even human—" I slapped a hand over my mouth, muffling my words.

"No?" he asked, cocking his head.

The pressure in my chest was building. I clutched the steering wheel hard enough to make my knuckles go white. "He doesn't live here," I said, forcing out a breath. "Plus, I don't think he cares about what happens to me." I winced. The truth was hard. I rubbed the space between my collarbones that ached from trying to keep all of the truth from spilling free. "Can you go away? Bryn told me to be by myself."

"Why?"

I hesitated, trying to find the right words, the pressure building again. "I think he thought I would get myself into trouble if I talked to people today."

"And that would make today special how?"

"Can you go away?" I gasped.

"I can," he said in a tone that implied he wouldn't.

I needed to stop talking. If I could get him talking that would help. "You know some things about my family, don't you?"

"A bit."

"Do you know anything about my grandmother?"

"I know she lived in Houston."

"Yeah, my granny Justine, but she's dead for sure. I saw her in the casket with my very own eyes. She looked like they'd stolen her from a wax museum, but I'm sure they didn't. Well, pretty sure." I slapped a hand over my mouth again. What an awful thing to say!

Lennox smiled in an expression that was just like Bryn's.

"He looks like you. Bryn does," I said.

"Yes. Except for the eyes and the hands."

"What's the Granville Prize?"

Lennox looked surprised for a moment. "Are you—Did he mention it?"

"Nope. John Barrett did."

"Ah." Lennox leaned against the car and looked at the setting sun. "The Granville Prize is the highest award someone from our world can receive. It's rather like a human Nobel Peace Prize or a Pulitzer."

"How do you get it?"

"There are different ways. In his case it was for writing a spell that changed the way wizards think about celestial magic. He didn't do it alone, but that didn't make it any less remarkable."

I smiled. I could hear the pride in Lennox's voice. Usually Lennox acted like the end of the world was next Tuesday, and the rest of us were too dumb to know it. No need for him to be civil. No need for him to care about much.

"He wrote it with his friend Andre?"

Lennox looked at me closely then. "Taking the Bryn Lyons 101 course, are you? Is that because you need him to sort out your magic?"

"Nope. He just interests me."

"He interests most people," he said dismissively.

I waited.

"Andre's a genius in his own way. Mathematics and science are his forte. Especially physics. When Bryn met him at school, Andre was an outcast, an oafish boy with no discernable social skills. The only things he and Bryn had in common were celestial magic and a fascination with theoretical magic—spells that should work but cannot be proven to work because no wizard has enough power to cast them.

"Bryn wanted Andre to be allowed into an exclusive club at their prep school, but the other members refused. That club was a ticket to unlimited success, but Bryn left it because they wouldn't admit Andre. It seemed a terrible decision at the time, but Bryn could see what others could not. Andre understood the universe on a fundamental level, but one he could not communicate or apply. Bryn saw its potential, and Bryn has an unparalleled gift for spell-writing that he inherited.

"The two became such close friends that Andre insisted

on going to Dublin for the summers to study alongside Bryn. And late one July, they wrote a spell that left the master spell-writers speechless. It later won the Granville and other awards." He looked at me then. "When they wrote it, they were fourteen years old."

"Wow."

"Yes, wow," Lennox said dryly. "At that point, in terms of magic, Bryn could have done anything with his life. But a year later he got expelled, and everything changed."

"Expelled? Why?"

Lennox looked back at the horizon. "Because he needed something that no one could give him, and he was determined to get it, no matter what it cost. Sometimes even when he knows a thing has the potential to destroy all he's worked for, he cannot let it go." Lennox shook his head and looked at me. "Which is why I wish you'd leave him alone."

"Me? You think I'm bad for him?"

"I know you are. See what he's gotten himself into because he couldn't resist helping you?"

"You got him into this, too. You stole the locket."

"Yes, I did, but I never expected him to get involved with you or you with him. You'd barely even met, and your family had some sacred rule against it. Your mother and aunt certainly said as much."

"But they didn't explain? You don't know why?"

"No, I don't know why. Nor do I care."

As he walked away, I added, "Well, I do. A lot."

THE INSTANT THAT Bryn lifted the spell, I felt the change. It was like my chest had been duct-taped for hours and someone had just cut the tape off. I twisted and stretched and breathed in huge breaths, feeling much better.

"Well, now I know how a mummy feels. Getting wrapped up in constrictive bandages, I really can't recommend it," I said to Mercutio as I started the car.

I couldn't go to the banquet at City Hall in jeans and a turtleneck, so I had to stop by my house. TJ and his crew had put a new door on my house, but I didn't have the key so I went in the back way again. Merc didn't come in. He went over the fence with a pounce, and I suspected he was going off to hunt for his dinner, which made me feel like a bad friend for not having fed him sooner.

"Merc can take care of himself. Better than you can most of the time," I mumbled, closing and locking the sliding glass door. The house was stuffy and a little dusty, so I opened the kitchen window above the sink, figuring it was too small for Scarface to climb through and that I'd be able to hear Merc yowling if he wanted to come in.

After I took a shower, I went to Momma's big closet where all three of us kept our party dresses. I leaned inside so I could see them well enough to pick one, then a flash of light behind me nearly made me jump out of my skin. I was only wearing a pink tank top and panties, which left me feeling underdressed for a fight. My eyes darted to the closet floor, and I grabbed a blue stiletto heel that had to be Aunt Mel's. I jumped up and turned with the heel facing my would-be attacker.

I was shocked to find Craig Cuskin, my fifteen-year-old neighbor, snapping a picture with a little digital camera.

"What the Sam Houston do you think you're doing?"

"Taking pictures of you."

"Give me that camera," I said, transferring the shoe to my left hand so I could hold out my right one.

"Can't do that," he said, tucking it into the pocket of his khakis.

"Have you lost your mind? You know my ex-husband's a sheriff's deputy and won't take kindly to you breaking and entering and taking pictures of me in my undies. Plus, you're the judge's son. You ought to know better than to break the law."

He smiled, revealing clear plastic braces. "First off, everyone knows Zach Sutton left town 'cause you started running around on him. And second, the back door was open."

"That is not why he left town! And the back door was

locked." How in the world had he fit through the window? He was almost as tall as me, but I guessed he was kind of a string bean.

"Your word against mine," he said. "I don't think you wanna ask the police to make that choice right now. I've heard you're not too popular around the station."

"Even if the door was open, you can't just two-step in."

"I called out. I guess you didn't hear me over the running water."

I rolled my eyes. "Tell you what. Let me put on some clothes and then we'll take a walk over to talk to your momma about this."

"I don't think you should do that. You see, some ladies have been to talk to my dad about you. They think you're practicing witchcraft."

My eyes widened.

"He didn't believe them, but he'd probably have to rethink it if he saw the footage I picked up on my video camera that I rigged to the top of your fence."

"You've been spying on me?" I said.

"Yes, ma'am," he said with a smug grin. "First it was just to get you watering the yard in a tank top and shorts. Me and my friends, we take pictures around town and trade 'em. I lucked out living behind you; shots of you in a swimsuit are worth ten of any other girl. Then you came out that one night naked." He let out a low whistle. "I don't know what you were saying, but it was hot! The video's kind of grainy, but the guys didn't complain, even when I made them pay to download it."

I socked him. His head jerked, and he buckled, landing hard on his knees. When he looked up, I slapped his face hard enough to leave a bright red handprint, then I snaked my hand into his pocket and pulled that camera out before he even had a chance to recover.

I deleted the pictures on the card and then slammed the camera lens down on the dresser, smashing it to pieces.

He looked up at me, startled, his face pale except for the red swelling under his eye and the handprint on his cheek.

"In this life, Craig, we've all got our choices to make. If you act like a man, I'll treat you like one. If you act like a bad man, I'll treat you like one. You get me?"

His cheeks flushed. "Did you kill Earl Stanton? Some people think you did, but I said there was no way. Thought you were too sweet."

"Stand up."

He got to his feet and looked me straight in the eye.

"Earl Stanton caught me in the woods and tried to rape me. I hit him in the head with a rock. Hit him hard enough to crack even the thickest skull." I paused to let my words sink in, then added, "He didn't die from that, but he could've."

"Sounds like he deserved it."

"He did."

"But look, these were just pictures. I wouldn't have touched you, unless you wanted me to."

Unless I'd wanted him to, I thought wryly. Like I'd take a tumble in the grass with a fifteen-year-old? The things boys get in their heads. "Well, I'm sure glad to hear it. Go on home now."

He was halfway out the door, when he turned back. "I'm sorry. The pictures—it was just us fooling around."

"No, it wasn't. Go do what you can to make things right by getting those videos erased. Then come tell me again that you're sorry, and I'll forgive you."

He nodded and left.

I rubbed the back of my neck and shook my head, grimacing. So now, on top of everything else, I was an occult porn star.

14

I CLIMBED OUT of my Focus with an amethyst-colored crystal pin in my upswept hair and an automatic handgun duct-taped to my calf. I wore a royal purple floor-length taffeta gown with very high heels that had a black lace over-lay, which made them look more than a little like lingerie. Except for my underwear and the strip of duct tape, not a thing that I wore belonged to me.

The black-and-white banner hanging over the doors to City Hall announced the night's benefit. I fell in step with the Shoreside crowd who made their way inside.

The lobby sported an eclectic mix of decorations, and guests moved from table to table admiring what people had done to celebrate the occasion. The high school art class's framed collage of photo clippings of Texas wildlife had dabs of fall colors that the students had painted on. Really pretty. I wondered if any of them would want to consider cake decorating as a weekend job.

Hanging from rods and spilling over a table was a beauti-ful quilt from Duvall's First Sewing Circle. Next there was a table from the Duvall Hunting Club with all kinds of stuffed wildlife. That seemed kind of crazy to me. It was like the hunters were saying, "You protect the animals, so we can kill them later." But since I'm not a vegetarian, I guess I've got no room to judge.

I spotted Jenna Reitgarten in a black-and-white striped dress. Her hair and head moved as a single unit. When it came to hair spray, someone at the drugstore needed to cut her off.

I ducked behind the very robust Mrs. Schnitzer so that Jenna might not see me. That put me in a position to see my chocolate sculpture. DeeDAW had had the good sense to use clear fishing line to suspend the bird just like I'd planned. People were circling the sculpture and pointing and smiling. I got a warm feeling in the pit of my stomach. They liked my work.

I kept watching the people until I locked eyes with Mindy.

Uh-oh.

I hurried to the ballroom doors where Smitty was standing guard. Well, technically it wasn't a ballroom, more of an all-purpose meeting room, but the council had it decorated real fancy for formal events.

"Hi."

"Ticket," Smitty said flatly, holding out his hand.

"I don't have one."

"Can't get in without one." He pointed to a pair of ladies who had a short line of people in front of them. "It was seventy-five dollars per person if you got them in advance. A hundred bucks at the door."

"She's with me," Bryn said with a voice that was slightly hoarse.

I looked over my shoulder and gaped at how good-looking he was. Dressed in a tuxedo, he plain took my breath away. Luckily Hollywood wasn't there to see or they might've tried to drag him off to California.

"Your voice?" I asked.

"Sore throat. The change in weather, no doubt." Bryn's eyes stayed on Smitty's face as Bryn handed him the pair of tickets. He all but dared Smitty to challenge him.

"If you're sick, you could have stayed home," Smitty said, then looked at me. "And you *should* have stayed home."

Bryn ignored him and guided me inside. Sue Carfax waved at Bryn, but her bright smile slipped when she recognized me.

"How did it go? Did the spell work?" I whispered.

The corner of his mouth curved up in a devilish smile. So it had worked. Hurray for us. We were sneakier than the superspies.

"But what about you? How are you?"

"Better now that I've seen you in that dress. You look amazing."

I smiled. "Thank you. Does it hurt your throat to talk? How are you going to make a speech?"

Bryn didn't get a chance to answer because Sue walked up.

"Bryn, it's wonderful to see you. When you asked at the last minute for an extra ticket, we wondered whether it was for Tammy Jo here or if it might be for your friend from England. Gwendolyn. She's so lovely."

Yes, so lovely and so *magical*! She was probably ten times the witch I was.

"This kind of event isn't really to Gwen's taste. She prefers the city, doesn't really appreciate the incomparable beauty that can be found in small towns."

"My goodness, your voice."

"Yes, let's see if I can smooth it out. Is the bar open?"

She pursed her lips, but pointed with a nod.

Bryn led me away. "Whiskey. Double," he told the bartender. "What would you like, Tamara?"

"Me? Nothing. Well, maybe juice. Half pineapple–half orange."

Bryn slipped a twenty-dollar bill into the tip glass and took his drink. He swallowed slowly, grimacing.

"Come here," I said, pulling him by the arm to where a curtain hung down. We stepped behind it, and I plucked his tie open.

"How am I going to get that straight again without a mirror?" he said mildly.

I unbuttoned the top button and cursed like a sailor at the sight of his neck. The bruising was two fingers' width and a violent blue-violet. It circled as far as my eyes could see, and brought my blood to a furious boil.

"I'm going to sock each one of them in the nose. I'm going to make them sorry. You see if I don't." When I looked up, he was smiling. "You're not going to tell me not to?" I asked.

"No."

"Good."

"Wouldn't do any good. You don't listen to me when you're angry." He finished the drink and ran his thumb over my cheek.

"Would it make your throat feel better to kiss me?"

"Undoubtedly."

"I meant could you do a spell to split the pain in half and give me part of it?" I whispered. He'd done a spell once to take away part of my pain from an arrow wound. Now seemed the perfect time to pay him back. Before Bryn got a chance to cast a spell or to answer, Jenna and Lucy Reitgarten yanked the curtain back, making me yelp in surprise.

"Here you are," Jenna said, grabbing my arm in a tight grip. "We need your help adjusting the lights on the chocolate sculpture."

Bryn's arm came around my waist, lightning fast. "Ladies, so nice to see you."

Jenna and Lucy tugged on my arms, but Bryn's grip tightened.

"Miss Trask's not working tonight, and we need some privacy to finish our conversation," he said.

"Bryn, honey, you need to get your tie back in order," Jenna said. "People are sitting down for dinner. Plus those folks you invited are at your table all by themselves."

Folks he'd invited?

I craned my neck and frowned. John Barrett and Mrs. Thornton were sitting at the front table, shaking hands with the mayor and his wife as they sat down.

"Oh boy," I said.

"We'll be right out," Bryn said, tugging the curtain so that they had to step behind it.

"Tammy Jo, we're going to catch you later on," Jenna said.

I frowned at her choice of words. "Barrett and the Winterhawk here? What do we do?" I whispered fiercely.

"Nothing for the moment," Bryn said, fixing his collar. "Unless you'd like to commence with the nose-socking."

I laughed. "I would like to. You have no idea how much."

"I'd probably find it really entertaining, but it's not in our best interest. Let's try to get through the night quietly. No scenes. I want them to see how unflappable we are."

"How unflappable you are. I'm very flappable actually."

My smile faded as we approached the table. I frowned and sat between Bryn and the mayor. We managed small talk, until the speeches started.

Bryn was really charming when he talked about the environment. He explained how he'd had solar panels installed on part of his house and shared the story of when he'd decided to invest in windmill energy production. He had half the people ready to sign up for new solar roofs and the other half for electric cars. Everything was going really well, until the men with assault rifles showed up.

15

MY BACK WAS to the doors, so I didn't see them come in. The gunfire sounded a little like hail as the four gunmen in brown hoods and brown camouflage fired into the ceiling, shattering several lights and raining glass down on the tables.

People dove from their seats to get cover.

"Tammy Jo Trask!" one of them yelled.

My heart cramped. They'd come for me? Destroying the event? Why?

Heads turned to look at me, and I blushed.

"She's there," Jenna said, pointing.

You rotten—

Bryn jerked me out of my seat and flung the table over, sending all the dishes crashing to the floor. He shoved me behind the table and then walked to meet the two men who were advancing.

"What's this about?" he asked.

"She's responsible for everything that's been going on. We've seen the video that proves it, and we're taking her."

Oh no!

Four of them, and me with just a handgun. I didn't like my

chances of escaping, but I couldn't let other people get hurt while trying to keep the gunmen from getting me. I stood.

"Get out of my way," one of the men said, pointing his gun at the middle of Bryn's chest.

"Nobody needs to get hurt," I said. "There's been some misunderstanding, but I'm willing to come talk to you."

Still seated calmly in her seat, Mrs. Thornton asked in a low voice, "Are you armed, my dear?"

"Yes," I whispered through my teeth, which were clenched into a big fake smile.

"Then proceed with your plan."

What plan? I walked forward, and two of them converged on me, grabbing my arms.

"I'm okay," I said to Bryn, whose eyes had gone blue-black. I could see his fingers twitching, anxious to hit them with a spell.

"They wouldn't hurt me in front of so many *witnesses*. We're just going to talk," I said.

Bryn remained still, but I could feel his power rolling over my back, energy that pricked my skin in its dark intent.

When the gunmen got me to the doors that opened to the lobby, I looked over my shoulder. The other two gunmen faced the people in the room as they backed out.

Bryn rushed toward one of them. He looked like he was just going to grab the gun, but I saw the gunman's arm jerk up from the force of Bryn's power striking it. Then a speaker exploded into blue and white flames.

I made like dead weight, and my arms jerked from the hands of the ones holding me. One of them was startled, but the other swung the nose of his gun toward me. I rolled away, hearing the eardrum-popping sound of bullets hitting tile.

It took two yanks to get my gun free of the duct tape. My heart slammed against my ribs, and I only had a second to decide what to do.

I shot the firing gunman in the leg and he fell back, his gun discharging overhead. I snapped my arm around to point my gun at the second guy's head. His eyes narrowed.

"Don't!" I snapped.

He didn't listen. I shot him in both arms before he could get his gun up all the way. As my second bullet hit, he pulled the trigger reflexively. I felt a rush of air and a sharp sting in my leg.

Jumping to my feet, I grabbed his gun away from him, then I swiveled and saw the guy I'd shot in the leg crawling to his gun. I rushed forward, my long skirt making me slip on the tile. I landed right on the first wounded guy. He grabbed my throat, so I clocked him in the temple with the butt of my gun. His eyes rolled up, then his head flopped back.

I sat just long enough to fling my heels off, then was up again. There would be at least one more guy besides the four I'd seen because Smitty wasn't accounted for. Smitty was either a casualty or he was on their side.

I crossed behind the big stairwell, which kept me out of sight. I circled toward the front, staying behind the kids' art table, so I wouldn't be seen.

Smitty wasn't on their side. He was sweating and trying not to show how scared he was. The gunman had one arm across Smitty's throat, and a gun pointed awkwardly at his body.

I sized it up. He had Smitty pretty well positioned as a human shield. Only the guy's head was cocked to the side and available as a target.

My stomach churned. If I shot the guy there, it would kill him. Sweat popped out on my forehead and between my shoulder blades, saliva pooling in my mouth. I swallowed, trying not to gag. I didn't want to kill a person in cold blood. But, no matter how much of a jerk Smitty had been lately, I wasn't going to let him get killed either.

I raised my gun, but heard a pop and they crumpled to the ground. Smitty jerked free, got his gun out and shot the guy twice in the chest even though the guy hadn't moved since someone had shot him in the head.

Smitty yanked his radio up and barked into it. "Shots fired at City Hall. Deputy needs assistance."

I spotted Bryn and the Winterhawk moving across the lobby. They were both armed, and I wondered which of them had killed the guy. They split up and did a sweep. She came to my side of the lobby.

"Well done," she said in her clipped accent. She moved past me, eyes roving, taking everything in.

I stood shakily and winced at the pain in my calf. I looked behind me at my bloody footprints and bit my lip. Smitty dragged the groaning guy I'd shot in the arms to the guy I'd shot in the leg and cuffed them together. He yanked off their hoods, and I studied their faces. They didn't look familiar. Who were they? From another town? If so, who had blabbed to them about what had been going on in Duvall? They said they had proof I was at fault for the town's recent trouble. I thought of the video that Craig Cuskin had let people copy. Had someone e-mailed the one of me doing backyard spells?

Smitty went into the dining room and got the other guns, then came to the lobby and piled them on the center table next to my sculpture, which had been hit by stray bullets and was broken into pieces. Why that should've made me more upset, I can't explain, but it did. I unhooked the red velvet rope so I could sit on the bottom stair. As I lifted the hem of my dress, I heard a noise. I grabbed my gun and swung it around, barely stopping myself before I shot that idiot Sue Carfax and her idiot friend Mindy.

"For the love of Hershey, don't sneak up on people right after they've been in a shootout," I snapped. My hand shook as I set my gun next to me again.

"This'll cool you off," Mindy said, her eyes narrow and malicious.

I didn't see the bucket until the last second. They each had two hands on it as they flung the contents. A torrent of water splashed me.

"That's holy water," Mindy said triumphantly as rivulets of water ran down my face and Aunt Melanie's expensive dress.

"Is it indeed?"

I jerked my head to find Mrs. Thornton standing on the opposite side of the stairs from Sue and Mindy. Her icy green eyes looked them over.

"There's a lot more going on here than a foreigner could understand," Sue said softly.

"Sometimes outsiders see a great deal."

Maybe it was her tone. Maybe it was her eyes. Maybe it was the sleek little gun in her well-manicured hand, but something about Mrs. Thornton made Sue and Mindy slink back into the shadows. I didn't blame them a bit. She was impressive and scary.

She put her gun back into her silver handbag just before Sheriff Hobbs and two deputies rushed in with guns drawn. One of them stopped at the table piled with assault rifles, but the other went past us into the dining room.

"How badly are you wounded?" Mrs. Thornton asked as Bryn hurried up from behind her. He dropped to a knee in front of me.

"Where are you shot?" he demanded.

I extended my left foot. He caught my ankle, setting it on his knee.

I raised the hem. As bullet wounds go, it wasn't too bad. As scrapes go, it was a whopper. The skin was gone, the flesh open with clotted blood along it and fresh blood trickling down.

Bryn felt along the bone. "Does that feel like it's broken?"

"Not broken," I said, pushing back wet strands of hair. I examined my skirt and found the hole, poking my fingertip through the fabric. "Do you know how many outfits I've ruined the past two weeks? Another week of this, I'll be walking around naked." I spotted the glint in Bryn's eyes and could almost hear him thinking: the silver lining.

"Don't you dare flirt. I'm wounded here."

"I was only going to say that I'll buy you a new dress."

"Sure you were."

Smitty came out of the dining room. I pulled my leg back and set it on the step as he walked up to me.

"We're going to need statements from everyone, but

seein' as you're wounded, an ambulance is coming. I'll ride with you to the clinic and take your statement there."

"Okay."

He paused for a moment. "They were gonna have to kill me. No other way," Smitty said.

I stared at him, knowing he was right.

"Saw you 'round that corner. Had the bastard's head in your sights. Saw your eyes, too. You would've taken the shot."

I nodded.

"Zach'll be proud of you when he hears."

Luckily the paramedics' arrival saved me from having to talk about Zach with Smitty in front of Bryn.

"I'm okay, fellas," I said, standing up with a little limp.

"Hang on," the guys said, grabbing my arms. They lifted me and set me on the stretcher.

Bryn came around the far side of it. "I'll make a statement, then I'll pick you up at the clinic."

"I'll drive her," Smitty said, squaring his shoulders. "Either here or back to Zach's place. Wherever she wants to go."

Bryn sized Smitty up, and I did not like the look of Bryn's eyes. There was still some dark magic swirling around behind them.

"Um—" I began.

"No matter who's driving, it's always up to her where she goes," Bryn said. He gave my arm a brief squeeze as the medics rolled me away.

It took a little maneuvering to get through the lobby and out to the cement ramp. John Barrett and Mrs. Thornton were standing on the steps, and Gwen was with them. Barrett's face didn't have any of that friendly charm that I'd seen at Bryn's. His face was world-leader, willing-to-torture-someone-with-a-needle-choker hard. As we passed them, I heard him say to them, "Is that so? Well, if it's the Bible they want, someone should give it to them."

I stiffened, and one of the medics pulled the blanket up to cover me to the chin. Unfortunately, it wasn't just the icy cold of wearing a holy water–soaked dress in the November Duvall wind that had me shivering.

Somehow when he said someone should give them a Bible, I didn't think he meant he'd be popping a couple of Gideons in the mail. I clamped my jaw shut and grimaced.

This here falls under the category of things that are not Tammy Jo's problem, I told myself.

If the Conclave's superpowerful witches and wizards were going to do something nasty to retaliate against DeeDAW, I didn't have to get in the middle of it.

But the Conclave came to town because of you.

But DeeDAW's guys had assault rifles, for pete's sake!

You don't know that DeeDAW called those guys.

I believe I do. I believe I know it in my gut, I thought stubbornly.

Well, maybe it doesn't have to be your problem . . . tonight.

16

I GAVE SMITTY my statement while Dr. Suri cleaned my leg. He froze the wound with a painkiller and stitched up the skin with what looked a lot like blue fishing line.

"This is a deep wound. I'm afraid you are going to have a scar," Dr. Suri said.

"I'm not worried. I'm a real good healer," I said, then thought about the fact that there was barely a mark on me where Bryn had pulled an arrow out of my chest only a few days earlier. I'd always healed scratches quickly as a kid. I actually didn't have a single scar from growing up, but I'd never really been hurt back then either. Recently though, I'd been seriously wounded. I should've still been healing. My recovery had been abnormally fast, hadn't it? Half-faery fast? If so, that could be a real advantage, all things considered.

Smitty was really nice on the drive back to City Hall. He asked me a lot of questions about who I thought the gunmen were, but I couldn't say very much on that subject because I didn't have any real facts myself. I did say that I thought the gunmen showing up might be related to Jenna and her friends trying to kidnap me.

He frowned and said, "I'm going to take a closer look at

their alibis that day. I'll question 'em separately and make sure the stories match up."

"Sounds good," I said. I didn't tell him about them forming DeeDAW, since then I'd have to explain why they thought I was a witch in the first place.

After we ran out of case stuff to talk about, he started reminiscing about the old days in high school. He brought Zach up about a hundred times. Smitty's a lot of things. Subtle isn't one of them.

"I can drive myself home," I repeated.

"Where are you going to stay?"

"People are after me, Smitty. Bryn's got big iron gates and an armed security guy."

"I'm armed, and Heather decorated that guest room up. No one's even used it yet. It's got its own bathroom that she filled with some spa soap that cost twelve dollars a bar."

I whistled. "Twelve dollars a bar? That must be some good soap!"

"So she says," he muttered skeptically.

He waited for me to say more, but I didn't take him up on his offer. To his credit, he didn't get mad, and I decided I'd be happy to almost save his life anytime he needed me to.

I climbed out of the car, feeling the stitches tug as they worked to hold my skin together. The throb let me know the medicine Dr. Suri used to deaden my leg was wearing off. I waved at Smitty and waited until I got in my car to call Bryn. He said he was just finishing up at the station and I told him I felt well enough to drive, so I'd meet him back at his house.

When I parked in the driveway, Merc stood by the front door, waiting for me.

"Hey there," I said. "The party wasn't so hot. Ended up in a gunfight."

He purred.

"Yeah, I got shot. Nothing too bad obviously. I sure don't know what I'm going to do about DeeDAW or the Conclave. I'd like to stay away from both and concentrate on the brooch."

Merc cocked his head, and I walked around to the car's

trunk. "When Bryn gets home I'm going to show it to him. Maybe he can help me figure out whether she's alive." I opened the trunk, and my jaw dropped. It was empty. I bent closer.

"Are you kidding me? You have got to be kidding me!"

Neither my spellbook nor my brooch was there. I hurried to the side of the car and peeked in the windows. Nothing on the seats. I went back to the trunk and checked once more before exclaiming, "For cryin' out loud, Merc!" I slammed the trunk shut. "We've been robbed."

I examined the lock. It didn't look like it'd been tampered with. Could a regular person pick the lock without leaving a mark? Or had someone used magic to open it? I barked out these questions to Mercutio, who only looked at me thoughtfully.

"C'mon," I said, going into the house. I was still sitting on the settee in the foyer when Bryn opened the door.

"I got an interesting message while waiting to give my statement. A call from a WAM solicitor who wanted to congratulate me," he said as he closed the door. He shook his head with a grim smile. "I won the appeal. Days ago. I knew there was a reason that Barrett didn't demand that you move out of here immediately. He tried so hard to trap me today, all the while knowing that I'd already won and knowing that there were extenuating circumstances here last week where life and death were at stake. The son-of-a-bitch." His voice grew more hoarse as he talked. He swallowed with a wince. "That's all right. I've got a call in to Basil Glenn from the Department of Justice and to a judge I'm friendly with. Barrett is pushing me. Let's see what he thinks of me pushing back."

"Bryn, you better be careful."

"Fortune favors the brave," he said with a wry smile.

"Not always. Sometimes all the brave guy gets is a real nice headstone."

"This warning from the girl who never backs down," he said, walking to me and going down on one knee. "How's your leg?"

"Patched up."

"Can I look?"

I nodded and raised the hem so he could see my calf.

"Looks a lot better. Does it hurt badly?"

"No, it's okay. Where's your tie?" I asked, looking at his open collar and the bruised skin.

"My pocket. Couldn't take it anymore."

I touched the skin gently. "Did you overhear anything at the police station? Do they know any more about the gunmen?"

"No, it was pretty chaotic. People were upset. But whatever the gunmen's connection to the town is, I'm sure Hobbs will find it. The mayor and the town council were there and one of his deputies was held at gunpoint; the sheriff's department will be highly motivated to investigate and bring everyone involved to justice."

"What did people say about me? Anybody take what the gunmen said seriously?"

"No. It was heroic of you to offer to go with them to defuse the situation so other people wouldn't get hurt. People realize that. Hobbs read the statement you gave Smith and said he'll be in touch about interviewing you himself."

I nodded. "I just wish the gunmen hadn't blamed me for the supernatural stuff that's happened. Hear something often enough, and you start to believe it. Hate to see that happen; for the truth to start to sound true," I said with a sigh.

"I've got the largest account at the bank. Under threat of closing it, I'll put some pressure on Boyd Reitgarten to get his family to settle down."

I frowned, not sure that was a good idea. Maybe they'd just start targeting Bryn, too.

"Though I'm not sure Jenna and Lucy were directly involved in tonight's plan. They looked pretty shell-shocked at the station."

"Well, Sue and Mindy didn't seem shocked while they were dumping water on my head."

Bryn shrugged. "When I was at the police station, I talked to some of my neighbors. John Barrett's been to

Macon Hill several times since he's been here." He set my leg down. "Right about now, I'm sure he's trying to figure out a way to claim a piece of it."

I raised my brows. I didn't want Barrett to get too interested in any part of Duvall. I wanted him and the Conclave to hurry up and leave.

"I was at the tor today," I said. "Good thing Barrett didn't come to visit it while I was there. You know what else? Someone stole jewelry out of my trunk, along with my medieval spellbook."

Bryn sat down next to me. "When?"

"Tonight." I tucked a strand of hair behind my ear. My upswept hair had partially fallen down and was hanging haphazardly. I could feel that my makeup was smudged, too. It was a goal of mine to avoid mirrors until I'd gotten cleaned up. "Think it was the Conclave?"

In some ways I hoped it was. I didn't want the spellbook to have ended up in DeeDAW's hands. I could just see them passing it around at coffee-and-donut social hour at church, saying: "Look here what we found in the trunk of Tammy Jo Trask's car. Something's gotta be done about that girl." I frowned.

"Possibly, but not likely. The Conclave might have wanted to see what spells you're using and how much of your power's accumulated in the book, but they wouldn't take jewelry."

"Not even if it had a vision attached to it and maybe a dead spirit?"

"Whose dead spirit?"

"I don't know. Someone from my family I think. I wish Edie was still here. I should've shown it to her."

"I really wish you wouldn't have contact with disenfranchised spirits. I know having a family ghost has convinced you that they're benign, but they can be dangerous."

"You know that from experience?"

"I do, but it's a long story, and it's already been a long day." He stood. "Do you need help taking a shower? I promise not to take advantage of the situation."

"That's a real sweet offer, but I can do it myself. Except

I think maybe I should take a bath, so I can keep my leg out of the water and won't have to be standing up."

He carried me upstairs and set me on the bed in a guest room that's a few doors down from his bedroom. The room was fern green with a potted tree in the corner and sage-colored carpeting. There were blooming vines on the wallpaper. It appealed to the part of my nature that loves nature.

In the attached bath, Bryn filled the Jacuzzi tub partway, setting everything I'd need on the ledges.

"There's a bathrobe hanging on the back of the door. You should sleep here tonight, so you don't have to go up and down the stairs."

"Okay." I stood and turned. "Unzip me."

His fingers were light and didn't linger. I held the dress together until I got into the bathroom and closed the door.

It wasn't too hard to manage, and I sank down into the warm water with a sigh. I nearly fell asleep, but since I'm not drown-proof like Bryn, I thought I'd better get moving. After washing my body, I drained all the water so I wouldn't soak my leg while I washed my hair under the tap. I wrapped myself in the thick white bathrobe and shuffled out.

Bryn, who'd obviously showered, too, since he had wet hair and wore a bathrobe, was leaning against the bedroom doorway.

"What're you doing?"

"I brought you a hairbrush and Motrin."

"Oh," I said, pulling back the bedspread. He could've left them on the nightstand. "But what're you really doing?" I got in and smoothed the covers over me.

He walked to the bed and sat on the edge, handing me a glass and a pill, then he pulled the hairbrush from the pocket of his robe and set it on the bedside table. "Avoiding the part where I leave you."

I like it when he's honest. And when he's sweet. "If you stay on top of the covers, you can lie down here for a while."

"Not the best offer I've had from you," he said with a smile. He walked around the bed and lay down on his back next to me.

I reached over and tugged his arm to my side, then intertwined our fingers. The magic thrummed against our palms. "That better?"

"Always," he said.

"Let's rest," I said, turning off the lamp.

"Quite a roller coaster today." In the darkness, his voice was a soft rasp, so intimate it made me shiver.

"Mmm hmm."

"After the interrogation, all I wanted to do was stay home and coat my throat with half a bottle of whiskey." I heard that trace of an Irish lilt that I loved and was always listening for. "Then I walked into City Hall and saw you in that dress. Better than whiskey, Tamara. A lot better."

I smiled in the darkness.

"Then the gunmen came," he said, his voice like gravel under bike tires. "They thought they would just drag you out. You went along; I knew you would."

"I figured maybe I'd get away, maybe not, but no point in more people getting hurt when they only wanted me."

"And I was supposed to stand by and watch them take you?" His breath came out slowly, thoughtfully. "If we hadn't been able to overtake them with guns, I would have lit up that place like it was Samhain all over again."

"Lucky you didn't. That much magic, people would've noticed."

"Yeah, it would've compromised my cover somewhat."

"Somewhat," I said, laughing softly. It was nice to hear that he cared about me. Even as confusing as things were between us, I liked it. I rolled onto my side and felt for his face with my hand. I pressed a kiss onto his cheek. "Now, go to sleep. I'm pretty sure there won't be any kidnappings or shootings going on tomorrow, but sometimes things around here get worse before they get better."

17

ON SUNDAY MORNING, I woke with Mercutio purring in my ear. I was curled up next to Bryn with my head on his arm, and Merc was standing behind me on the edge of the bed. When I rolled toward Merc, he hopped silently down to the carpeted floor and waited.

"I'm up." I rubbed my eyes. "Why am I up?"

I climbed out of bed, tightening the sash on the bathrobe, and padded out of the room after him. We went downstairs, and I followed Merc to the kitchen windows. I peeked outside. With the outdoor floodlights, I could make out the landscape. Trees and bushes. The Amanos River snaking behind the property. I didn't see anything unusual.

"The police took my gun, Merc. I don't think I should go out in the dark without one. You want me to wake Bryn up and get him to give me a new one?"

Mercutio stood with his hind legs in the sink and his front paws on the windowsill. With his head next to mine, he looked back and forth.

The security phone on the wall rang, and I nearly jumped out of my skin.

"Jiminy Crickets, I'm going to get a heart attack before I turn twenty-four." I picked up the phone. "Hello?"

"Hey, it's Steve. What are you looking for?"

I looked around me, trying to find the hidden cameras. Reportedly, there were cameras downstairs and in the upstairs hallway, but not, Bryn promised, in any of the bathrooms or bedrooms. Also, he'd said there weren't cameras in his study, which gave me ideas.

"I'm not sure. Mercutio, you know, my cat—?"

"Yes, I do."

"Well, he got me up. You see anything suspicious on your cameras of the grounds?"

A bunch more floodlights blinked on, so I could see quite a bit better. I remembered that some of the lights were motion-activated.

"Did you turn those on?" I asked sharply.

"Yeah, so I could get a better look. Still don't see anything."

"Well, Merc senses something, and he's better than all your high-tech gadgets put together."

Merc hopped out of the sink and walked to the fridge, putting a paw on it.

"Although, now he's gotten interested in food, so maybe whatever it was is gone."

"I'll keep an eye out."

I hung up the phone and opened the fridge, finding that Mr. Jenson had left a raw game hen, a whole trout with its head still intact, and a chunk of ham next to a carton of heavy cream.

"I think you've got your own shelf, Merc." I set the hen on a plate on the floor. Mercutio yowled softly and went to work.

"Meet me in Bryn's library when you're done."

I walked down the hall, spine straight, not shifty. Didn't want to look guilty for the cameras. I opened the door and strolled in.

Like most things in Bryn's house, the study's pretty amazing. Floor-to-ceiling bookshelves with a ladder on wheels to get stuff off the higher-up shelves. Some of the books are locked behind custom-made stained-glass doors with images of the cosmos.

There's a brown leather couch, matching chair, and big square ottoman across from a stone fireplace. On the opposite side of the room, there's a heavy wood desk with carved legs. I rolled the ladder to the far left of the bookshelves and climbed up.

Just as I'd suspected, there were magical textbooks. Bryn's superorganized, so they were just where I'd expected them to be—at the beginning. Normally they were probably glamoured, but since he was just building his power back up, he probably wasn't wasting any magic for the smaller stuff.

I was hoping to find an "Introduction to Magic" book, but didn't. I was ready to take down one called *Prometheus's Domain: Foresight & Divination*, but then a black book with old-style lettering caught my eye. It had a single word etched on the spine in silver. *Death.*

I clutched it to my chest and climbed down. I sat on the Chinese rug and opened the book on the ottoman. I skimmed the introduction, which said that because of the topic's dangerous nature, there were not going to be any example spells in the book.

I scanned the table of contents, my pulse speeding up.

Chapter 1—The Energy of the Earth
Chapter 2—The Energy of the Universe
Chapter 3—Blood & Bones Magic
Chapter 4—Premorbid Metaphysics
Chapter 5—Crossing the Threshold
Chapter 6—Journey of the Soul
Chapter 7—The Afterlife: Current Debates
Chapter 8—The Undead
Chapter 9—Death, Ethics, & Law

I flipped the page and scanned the chapter descriptions. Blood & Bones magic pertained to healing spells and hexes that caused disease. Journey of the Soul was about what happened to the spirit after the body died, which was exactly what I wanted to know. I turned to page 254. The chapter started with a lot of stuff that didn't make sense, and I guessed I'd have needed to start at the beginning to understand all the energy talk. I flipped to the next page.

The majority of souls cross into the afterlife, which will be covered in Chapter 7. Of those souls who do not cross over, there can be two causes. In the first, it is the spirit itself that misses the opportunity to pass into the afterlife, giving rise to the term *lost soul*, and it occurs most often in cases when the body dies by violence, as is the case in murder, suicide, war, and martyrdom. The other reason a spirit is unable to pass the gate from one metaphysical plane (namely that of Earth) to the next (the afterlife) is that the soul becomes trapped by the magical nature of the death. This is seen in the case of someone dying by magical rites or when the person was the subject of a human sacrifice.

There could also be a combination of circumstances. A death by murder or suicide, for example, wherein a person has a spell acted upon them either in the moment of death or shortly thereafter. Historically, the best-known spell used for this purpose was called Purgatory, written by Morton Dunby in 1374. The spell was deemed illegal and immoral, and a coven of selected white witches studied Dunby's spellbooks in order to write counterspells. These reverse rites were performed to free the trapped souls, which Dunby had kept inside hollowed-out animal bones that he sealed on either end with wax.

My stomach churned at the thought, and I put a hand over my mouth while I shook my head.

The coven who carried out the original counterspells favored burning Dunby's journals and spellbooks in a cleansing fire, but the wizard magistrate for the region disagreed, citing a concern that the books might later be needed to generate other counterspells if further victims of Dunby's hexes were found. This decision, though considered practical at the time, allowed for the theft of Dunby's books and the widespread reproduction of his spells, which were sold on the black market. In the late 1800s, a bastardized form of the spell was used to trap souls that were then used as a tithe for demons by those seeking power through black magic. This selling of souls is covered more extensively in Chapter 9, but has always carried a death sentence with or without torture tender.

"What are you reading?"

I jumped at the sound of Bryn's voice. I hadn't heard him come in. He bent forward and closed the book, shaking his head when he saw the cover.

I bent my legs, feeling my wounded skin stretch against the stitches. I eased my legs a little straighter, resting my elbows on my knees. "What's a 'torture tender'?" I asked softly.

"Tender in that context means currency, as in how you pay for your crimes. It means they torture you as punishment. Usually before they kill you."

I rested my chin in my palms, my fingers splayed over my cheeks. "It said witches and wizards used magic to kill people and to trap and sell their souls. To demons. How could anybody do that and live with themselves?"

"I don't know, but that wouldn't be a problem for long if they got caught."

"Purgatory spell, it's called. Edie's been trapped, and we've been wearing that locket for years. How could they just—"

"Tamara, your family ghost isn't under a Purgatory spell. She's connected to the locket, but she roams freely, doesn't she?"

I nodded.

"Yeah, that's different. It was probably . . ." He tipped his head back, thinking. "Maybe a Dearly Departed spell. That's when a witch who's close to the spirit knows the soul can't cross over. The witch does a spell to link the spirit to some object that's kept close to the loved one and is passed down. It protects the spirit."

"From what?"

Bryn rubbed his jaw. "From deteriorating into a ghoul. After generations, as people who know a ghost die, their recollection of the spirit is lost, and the ghost loses its memories and changes. No one really understands the exact nature of the metaphysical disintegration or energy dispersal. There are a couple of interesting theories. There's a witch named—" He paused and smiled, deciding, I guess, that I wasn't ready for all the details. "Your aunt Edie hasn't been cursed, at least not by the spell that connects her to the locket."

"You said that her being connected to the locket helps preserve her memory."

"Right."

"All her memories? Even ones that aren't on the tip of her tongue or whatever?"

"You mean does she have a metaphysical subconscious where memories are stored but which she can't access normally?"

"Exactly."

Bryn shrugged. "It's possible. There's been research in that area, but I haven't read anything about it since I was maybe seventeen or eighteen. Witches and wizards who have family ghosts are notoriously protective. They generally refuse to turn them over to be studied."

"Of course they do," I said.

"So then it's hard for academics to do practical research, isn't it? Andre may know the current theories. The more esoteric a topic, the better he likes it."

"Can we get him in the mirror to ask him?"

Bryn chuckled. "Get him in the mirror? He'll love that expression." Bryn ran a hand through his shiny dark hair, which was mussed in a sexy way. "Andre's lying low right now, remember? The less contact I have with him while I'm under Conclave investigation, the safer he'll be. Why are you so interested in that research?"

When I didn't immediately answer, he sighed. "Let me guess. You think Edie knows the prophecy about our two families."

"We could prove it doesn't have anything to do with you and me," I said, my voice full of optimism.

"Even if it were theoretically possible to access the lost memories of lost souls, being able to draw out a specific memory? Extremely unlikely. The complexities of that kind of spell . . ."

"Right, but you're brilliant, so you could probably write one that would work. Wouldn't it be an interesting challenge for you?"

He laughed. "You're about as subtle as a hurricane."

"But what I lack in subtlety, I make up for in charm?" I asked with wide eyes.

"I'll tell you what, I'll do some research and I'll think about it. If I decide it's possible, we can negotiate what you'll do for me in exchange for me writing the spell."

"I could write recipes for thirty amazing desserts, better than anything you've ever tasted, and bring them over every day for a month."

Bryn picked up the book. "That sounds very tempting, and yet somehow not likely to be what I'll choose." As he went up the ladder, I frowned at his back.

"I hope you're not planning to—What's the word I want?"

"Extort?" he offered innocently.

"Yes, actually."

He smiled and put the *Death* book back on the shelf.

"I hope you're not planning to extort things that shouldn't be extorted," I said.

He laughed. "What things *are* fair game for extortion?" he asked with mock curiosity.

"You know what I mean. Don't pretend you don't."

When he came back down the ladder, he held out a hand. "Come on. You don't belong in my library when I'm not here."

"Just doing a little reading. You said yourself I need training."

"When I walked in, the expression on your face was so forlorn you would've thought you'd lost your cat."

"Well, selling souls to demons, who wouldn't be sad about that?"

"Right," he said, tugging my arm to pull me to my feet. "But it's dangerous to give yourself a piecemeal education, especially when it involves reading and casting actual spells. Plus, it's illegal and the Conclave's in town, and I've got this odd objection to giving them more reasons to stick needles in my throat."

I paled. "They're not going to know."

"Don't assume that it's easy to keep things from them. I promise you, it's not."

18

SCRYING TO FIND something isn't what I'd call easy magic, but to recover the brooch, first I'd have to figure out who'd stolen it.

I couldn't ask Bryn to help me directly since the Conclave was snooping around, because even though it was okay for us to see each other, he wasn't allowed to give me spells unless I agreed to be his apprentice or something.

On the other hand, Bryn could give my magic a boost without even trying, so just before I went down the hall, I stole a kiss. It surprised him for about a second, then his arms snaked around me and the kiss lasted way longer than I'd originally intended. I felt his magic tracing patterns over my skin, leaving tingling tattoos in its wake.

I pulled back, but he didn't immediately let me go, so it became a tug-of-war to untangle his fingers and get out of his arms. By the end, I was breathless with my hair tangled in front of my eyes. I pushed it back and glared at him. He only smiled, and I wondered if he'd guessed that I'd wanted that kiss for magical reasons.

"I'm going to take a walk before I make breakfast," I announced and hurried into the kitchen.

Merc was standing near the kitchen door. I grabbed a mixing bowl and said, "C'mon, Merc. Let's see if we can find anything out about the robbery." I opened the door, and he followed me out. "Here's the thing. I'm best when my feet are in the dirt, but for scrying, Momma and Aunt Mel used to look into a bowl of water. The water bowl didn't work for me last time, but wouldn't the Amanos River be more powerful than tap water? Plus, Bryn's got a connection to it, and I've got connections to him."

I went to the river and scooped up some water, then went back to the dock's edge where the grass had been worn away, leaving bare dirt. I dug my toes in and stood staring down into the bowl resting in my hands.

I'm not sure how much time passed. My eyes crossed and uncrossed as I stared into the water. At times I saw my own reflection. At others, someone else's image tried to take shape, but didn't. "It's there, Merc," I grumbled. "I can almost make him or her out."

I bent my face closer.

You who robbed my car.
Show yourself unmarred.

There was a face under the depths, so I shoved my face into the water, banging my nose on the bottom of the bowl. The watery vision didn't clear, and I lost my balance. I dropped the bowl, which splashed into the river as I fell. I landed half on the dock, with my feet still touching dirt.

Twisting my body over the water nearest the bank, I saw a face taking shape. I crawled farther over the edge, stretching to keep my toes in the dirt. The face was too far away. I had to get closer.

I slid my lower body off the dock into the freezing water and planted my feet into the slimy mud. An icy chill shot up my legs, and Merc yowled. "Just a minute," I mumbled.

The current pushed against my legs, trying to knock me over. I wrapped my arms around the slippery moss-covered struts of the dock and bent forward, my face nearly to the water.

"Show yourself," I demanded.

The current shoved me like it had hands. I landed on my knees, my face underwater, the metal of the dock scratching my arms that were locked around it. I opened my eyes and the water swirled around me, taking shape. Gwen's face appeared just in front of my own, her lips pursed almost in a kiss.

"You!" I said, realizing a moment too late that I was underwater. I choked on a gush of river water, and the current dragged my legs away from shore. Water soaked the robe, and it felt like ten tons of fabric weighing me down. I needed to breathe. I tried to get my feet under me, but couldn't.

I heard a muffled keening sound and felt something tearing at my hair.

I have to breathe!

I tried to push my head above the water, but couldn't make it. My whole body seemed to sink down to the riverbed. I bent my arm so the strut was in the crick of my elbow and let go with my right hand. The current dragged the robe off my shoulder. I grabbed the strut with my right hand again, then hooked my right elbow around it. Releasing my left, the robe slid down and off me.

Slippery as a fish and pounds lighter than I had been, I scraped my way to the surface for a few sips of air. Mercutio's paws wound in my hair and helped give me leverage. Everything was so slick and slimy. I might slip any second.

My heart pounded and my stomach churned. I found the dock's metal struts with my flailing feet and pressed against the slats, using them like ladder rungs, then clawed my way up the bank.

I rolled onto my side, coughing and sputtering. The air nipped my wet skin.

"That was way too close. I think that water's possessed!" I said, shaking. "That's how many times it's tried to kill us so far?"

Merc yowled softly.

"Yeah, too many." I shuddered, rubbing the gooseflesh on my arms. "It's so cold out here." I looked over my shoulder toward the river. The borrowed robe was long gone.

I glanced down at my body. I was dirty, wet, and nearly naked. I looked like I was one of those mud wrestler girls. My cheeks burned. I needed to get back into the house unseen. But Bryn had those blasted security cameras.

I got up and arranged my hair over my chest, mermaid-like, then crossed my arms over it. I tried to reason that my undies covered as much as a bikini bottom, but I wasn't at all sure they actually did. Probably too sheer and lacy.

"Merc, can you go get Bryn?" He could at least bring me another bathrobe, if I didn't die of exposure first.

Merc started toward the house, but then stopped and looked to the right.

"Merc! Hurry up. I'm freezing!"

Mercutio didn't pay attention to me. His head was turned firmly upriver. My gaze darted there and movement caught my eyes. I stood very still, squinting. There was a spot near the woods where the ground darkened and undulated like it was alive. Merc crept toward it.

"Uh-oh."

I rushed to catch him.

"Merc, wait!"

He didn't wait, and then I heard a clicking sound. I looked up and saw a swarm of insects emerging from the woods. The insecty mass was funnel-shaped, like a huge inverted pine tree.

"What?"

I stumbled back and turned to run. The noise of their legs got louder and then the cloud of them surrounded me, whirring over my skin with their skittering legs and clicking wings. I screamed, then clamped my mouth shut for fear of swallowing them. I flailed my arms and ran, trying to get out of their creepy-crawly cloud.

Nothing stung me. *Not bees*, I thought, as the noise receded. I stilled and opened my eyes, panting for breath. The insect tornado moved toward the house. There were a few tangled in my hair, and I shook my head very hard, trying to get them out. I clasped one in my hands, then separated my palms carefully. A big brown locust.

"Holy moly," I mumbled as it flew off. I turned to tell Mercutio, but the words stuck in my throat when I saw him hopping up and down on the ground, doing some sort of predator dance.

I hurried to him and realized it wasn't the ground that was moving.

Frogs!

"What in the Sam Houston is going on here, Merc?"

Large frogs hopped from the river in five single-file rows. There were hundreds of them.

I slapped a hand over my mouth for a moment, then let the hand drop, shaking my head. "Oh my old-testament-two-of-the-ten-plagues gosh!"

The frogs didn't scatter at Merc's pawing or biting them. They just hopped forward, in a creepy and unnatural way.

This is no good! What will people think?

These frogs had to be stopped. I couldn't let them get off Bryn's property where folks might see them. I ran. By the time I got to the front of the rows, I was at the edge of Bryn's house.

"Stop!" I said, trying to divert them. They ignored me, and I looked around helplessly. I needed a trap. I needed a whole lot of traps.

They went over and around my feet.

"Don't!" I said, scooping them up and tossing them back. The frogs I threw just got back in formation, like some lunatic frog army on the march. I couldn't scoop fast enough.

"Where are you going?" I snapped at them, but they didn't speak human and I didn't speak frog, so I supposed I couldn't really expect an answer. I rushed to the house, knowing we had to stop them before they got to the street.

I opened the back door to the kitchen and dashed in. "Bryn!" I shouted before I realized he was sitting at the kitchen table with a cup of coffee.

He turned his head and raised his eyebrows.

I remembered I was half naked and covered my chest with my arms. "Give me your shirt and come on!" I said.

He stood and unbuttoned the first couple buttons of his

shirt, then hauled it over his head and handed it to me. I turned my back to him and dragged it over my head as I went back out the door.

Then I heard tires squealing and jerked to a halt.

"Uh-oh."

I ran around the house and down the front drive to the gates. The frog army was well out into the street. A few houses down, Bryn's neighbor Cecily, aka Cruella de Vil, had gotten out of her silver Lexus, leaving the door ajar to stare at the frogs. Without warning, a splinter group from the locust twister appeared and swarmed around her and into the open car.

The sound of her screeches is something I will never forget as long as I live.

"We have to do something," I whispered when I felt Bryn at my back. His other neighbors were opening their doors and coming out. Most of them stared at Cecily, but one of them walked along the frog rows until he saw they were coming from under Bryn's gate.

"Morning," I said. "What's going on?"

The man peered at me, then at the frogs hopping out next to my feet. He didn't say a word, only frowned, turned, and walked away.

"C'mon," Bryn said, taking my arm. "Come inside before you get pneumonia."

"We have to stop those frogs before they get out of the neighborhood."

"Someone's calling them. The magic isn't complex, but it's strong. I'd have to concentrate power to stop it, and it doesn't seem worth it. Frogs and insects will be a nuisance, but no one will really get hurt."

"Except me! I've been seen out here, right where they're coming from. Who do you think Duvall is going to blame for this?"

"Some people will speculate, but they won't be able to prove anything."

"They don't need proof. I'll be convicted in the court of public opinion."

"Come inside. Your skin is like ice."

My feet, numb with cold, wouldn't move. "I need to stop this. Don't you see?"

Bryn didn't answer. He just pulled me to the front door.

"Jenna will use this to run me out of town," I said, my teeth chattering. "Duvall's more than my home. The people—most of them—are family to me."

"Jenna can try, but it won't work. We'll make sure it doesn't."

"What about the Conclave? You know they're doing this, right? Out of spite. It's not fair."

He wrapped his arms around me. I struggled for a moment, but then finally relaxed, letting the warmth seep back into my body.

"Of course, I don't agree with casting spells that will terrorize the town, but the Conclave doesn't take it well when humans start exposing and threatening witches. The association will always send Conclave operatives if a witch comes under fire."

"Yeah, but marching frogs and swarms of bugs will just make people more scared and likely to act crazy. Doesn't it make more sense to let things die down instead of conjuring up a couple of plagues?"

"Yes, it does."

"So what are they doing?" I demanded. "Could they be doing this stuff to make it so we can't live here? John Barrett told me that he wants us to move to England."

"Both of us?"

"Yes. He wants me to move to get training. And to be bait to draw you there."

He smiled. "I might not like the man, but he does have great taste in bait."

"Oh, c'mon! You wouldn't leave Duvall to chase after a girl. You work here. You live here. You've got this great mansion on the river—even though the river is kind of dangerous to ordinary people . . . but not to you though, so that works out. Anyway, it's a nice view, and it's Duvall. It's your home, right?"

"There are two things in this town that interest me, and the view isn't one of them."

"Two things?"

"Macon Hill and you."

The tor. And me. Oh boy. "Well, we've—"

"Wait a minute," he murmured, drawing his brows together thoughtfully and glancing toward the front of the house. A moment later, he grimaced. "God damn him. I know what he's doing."

Bryn's disgusted tone sent a chill down my spine. "Who? John Barrett? What? What's he doing?"

"He wants the town."

"What?"

"They aren't trying to shake things up in some act of petty revenge. Before the Conclave came to town, WAM wasn't aware of how powerful the Duvall tor was because most of the magic is insulated from the outside world. It's fae territory, so the central core of power is masked. The ley lines were the only indication that a tor was here, but now that Barrett has discovered what a significant source of power Macon Hill is, he wants to claim it for the World Association of Magic. But for a bunch of witches and wizards to move in and take over, what does WAM need to do first?"

Blood roared through my ears. "To run the people out?"

"Yes."

"They can't. I mean they're from England. That's where they live." I pointed forcefully in the general direction of Europe. "Over there."

"That's true, and WAM won't move here, but settling the town in the name of the World Association . . ."

"They can't do that!"

"They can," he said with a frustrated sigh. "They've done it before with a town called Revelworth."

19

ONCE THE INITIAL shock wore off, I squared my shoulders. "That's not happening. They think they can just come in here and take whatever they want? My brooch? My town? I don't think so." I narrowed my eyes and grabbed Bryn's arm. "C'mon, help me cast a spell to get those frogs and bugs back."

Bryn blew out a slow breath and nodded. "I'll do it. You take a shower and get dressed."

"You don't need extra power from me?"

He shook his head.

"Okay then." I marched into the bedroom. "Taking over Duvall? Not happening!"

I took a hot shower, and when I came out I found Bryn sitting on the sun porch. He had his elbows on his knees and his head in his hands.

"What happened? Didn't work?" I looked outside.

"It worked," he said in a hoarse voice. "I used a spell to shatter the one that was gathering them. I couldn't drive them back into the water, but they'll disperse, so it won't look so unnatural."

"Why are you holding your head? You have a headache?"

"Yes."

"I'm sorry." I sat down next to him and put a hand on his back, rubbing in small circles. "We need help fighting the Conclave. Who can we call? Can we ask the people from the Wizard's Underground to come to Duvall?"

"Barrett would love that. To draw the Underground members out in the open. Then Conclave assassins could pick them off one by one. No."

"Well, what can we do?"

"Barrett will try to scare the townspeople. When people decide the town is cursed, they'll want to move. Right now, he's probably lining up some loyal association members who are U.S. citizens to be ready to buy property in the town."

"Okay, so what we have to do is to keep people from selling. We'll come up with a story. You can talk to the mayor and the town council. I'll talk to the regular people. Now what kind of story—"

Bryn held out a hand.

"What?"

He didn't answer, and I realized his head must be hurting him really bad. I massaged the back of his neck, putting gentle pressure at the base of his skull. He exhaled slowly.

"It was the magic. I think somehow the original spell was mingled with a kind of kickback spell. So that if someone were to interfere with it using a counterspell, he'd get a nasty surprise. It felt like a lightning bolt shattering my skull."

I sucked in a small gasp at the image.

"It was almost like having my own power backlash on me, but there's no spell I know of that could do that. I think I've underestimated Barrett."

I stood and kissed the top of his head. "Yeah, well you've beat him before, and we'll beat him again," I said. "I'll be right back."

I went in the house and found Motrin, Tylenol, and some squares of dark chocolate. Hey, chocolate always makes me feel better.

Bryn took all that I gave him, and I tried not to grimace at his bloodshot eyes. I put a blanket around his shoulders.

"You rest until that choc—medicine kicks in."

"What are you going to do?"

"Nothing much," I lied.

"Stay inside the house for now." He leaned against the thick cushions, tipping his head back. "I'm sure this headache will ease off soon, and we'll need to plan our strategy." He closed his eyes.

"Sure thing," I said softly and pressed a kiss onto each of his eyelids.

As I walked to the door, I felt a whisper of magic raise the hair on my arms. I glanced at Bryn and saw that his lips were moving wordlessly. Was he dreaming or spell-casting? Whatever he was doing, I hoped it made him feel better.

I went into the house and whistled. Mercutio darted into the kitchen.

"Well, Merc, hope you ate plenty of frog legs to get your strength up. Turns out, we're going to war."

Merc yowled.

"Glad someone's happy about it."

I marched into Bryn's study and turned on his computer. A minute later, a short muscular guy appeared in the doorway. He had a crop of bleached blond hair and a dark blue security guy blazer. *Pete*.

"Mr. Lyons said you're not supposed to be in here on your own."

"Mmm-hmm."

"So come out," he said, waving a hand to beckon me into the hall.

"He doesn't want me reading his books. See how I'm not reading his books?" I said with a wave of my hand. I found the website for the Savoy in London and dialed the phone. My heart kicked into a faster rhythm. I'd never called England before. It was kind of exciting.

Pete strode in and pressed the button, hanging up the phone, then he grabbed my arm and pulled me out of the seat. Merc hissed and swiped a paw over his leg, tearing his trousers.

"Easy, Merc," I said, trying to defuse the situation.

Pete hauled me out of the room and set me outside the library door.

Merc snarled at him, menacingly. Pete snarled back.

"I can see we're going to need to settle this. C'mon," I said, waving a hand for Pete to follow me. We went to the screened-in porch. Far be it from me to take advantage of a position that I haven't even agreed to be in, but I couldn't have Pete—or anyone—getting in my way when I needed to get things done.

I nudged Bryn's shoulder. "I'm so sorry to bug you."

He rubbed his eyes and opened them. "What is it?"

"You want me to live here with you for a while, right? Or should I leave?"

Bryn drew his brows together in confusion. "Is this a trick question?"

"She was in your study, Mr. Lyons. I got her out of there."

"He dragged me out. By force," I added. "I was only on the computer getting a phone number."

Bryn sighed. "Tamara—"

"Okay, then I'll move out."

Bryn clenched his jaw, catching my wrist before I had a chance to move away. "Stay."

"Well, that depends on what the house policy is on the security guards manhandling me."

Bryn turned his gaze to Pete, studying him.

"I didn't hurt her," Pete said.

"Don't ever touch her," Bryn said, his voice snow-cone cool.

"You said she wasn't supposed—"

"You ask her to leave a room. If she doesn't, you let me know. Don't *ever* touch her." Bryn's eyes had gone the dark blue-gray of storm clouds, and his voice carried an edge that was like a switchblade slicing. I felt a wave of that dark magic roll off him and shivered.

Yikes.

"I misunderstood," Pete said.

"An honest mistake," I said, suddenly anxious to smooth things over. Bryn was kind of quick to fire people, and I didn't want things to go that far—or further, since he seemed to be calling up the magic that I didn't trust.

"Go back to work," Bryn said.

Pete nodded and walked out.

Bryn looked me over. "You can't have it both ways, Tamara. Not forever. You want them to treat you like you belong here, then maybe you'd better make the move permanent."

"Permanent? We're not even sure we're going to survive the week," I said lightly. And I sure wasn't committing to anything until I knew the nature of Grandma Lenore's prophecy, which I'd already told him more than once.

Bryn moved so quick it caught me off guard. One moment I was standing next to him. The next, I was lying on the couch under him. The kiss bruised my lips, and a blaze of magic curled down my throat and pooled in my lower belly, making it clench. I felt him suck a little of my magic into him along with my tongue. Then he tugged my shirt up, so he could touch my bare skin. My fingers twisted in his hair like they had a mind of their own.

As the dizzying lust pitched higher, his hand went to the button of my jeans. I knew if I didn't stop us soon, there'd be no stopping.

I pulled my mouth away, breathlessly. "What about your headache?"

"Why don't you help me forget it?"

I noticed that the red of his eyes had faded.

"In the middle of the day? When you've got security cameras all over? I don't think so." I shoved his shoulder until he let me go.

He rubbed the back of his neck with a slight smile. "When you move in for good, I'll have to reconsider where the cameras are."

"When I move in for good," I muttered as I stood on shaky legs. Getting involved with Bryn was like jogging in quicksand. Even when I wasn't moving, I just kept getting in deeper.

I CALLED THE Savoy in London, hoping to reach Aunt Melanie, but the phone lines to her room weren't working. I left a message with the front desk, saying it was urgent that I get in touch with her and asking her to call me.

Then I called Marsha, the most popular real estate agent in town. Sure enough, Gwen had been by to talk to her and to buy her a cup of coffee. Obviously Gwen was making nice with the locals before she stabbed us in the back and stole our land. Different century, same old story. Well, Duvall wasn't going to become some Brit-witch colony. We were staying independent and human—well, mostly human.

I drove to my friend Johnny Nguyen's place. Johnny's a fantastic hairdresser and, before Jenna and DeeDAW got wise, Johnny was the only regular person in town who knew about ghosts and witches. Unlike DeeDAW, he never held having ties to the supernatural against me. Not that he really could, since he'd fallen for a cross-dressing vampire named Rollie.

Merc was asleep in the passenger seat, so I left him there while I rung the bell to Johnny's. Johnny opened the door, and my eyebrows shot up. He wore black Lycra bike shorts with neon yellow piping that matched the zip-up neon yellow Lycra shirt.

"Hi there, Tammy Jo. How it going?" he asked cheerfully.

"Um, are you fixin' to go biking?"

He smiled. "No. I doing dance-workout video." He illustrated some leap-and-twist-in-the-air moves that made my jaw drop.

"I'm not normally clumsy, but I don't think I'd try that workout without a safety harness," I said.

"Well, I add a little extra to the moves myself. Johnny Nguyen signature."

"Oh, right," I said with a smile. "Well, I hate to interrupt your fitness routine. Wanna burn some calories helping me create a diversion so I can search a witch's hotel room?"

"I always up for Tammy Jo adventure," he said, pumping his small fist. "What I need to wear for this? Probably not Lycra stretch. What I going to be doing?"

"I thought you could present the witch, Gwen, with a complimentary spa treatment. Get her out of the room and to the salon. She might not go for it, but I have reason to believe that these out-of-town witches are trying to dig their heels in here in Duvall, so she might. I want you to say that the gift certificate's a present from Crane Realty."

"Okay then. I definitely need outfit change. Form of: Johnny Nguyen, exclusive salon owner. Shape of: God of Hair," he mumbled as he hurried down the hall to his bedroom.

I laughed softly. Ever since Johnny had started dating Rollie, he'd been incorporating some real interesting turns of phrase into his life.

When Johnny came out from changing clothes, he wore black trousers, a black smock shirt, shiny patent leather slipper shoes, and blue mousse in his hair. He looked like a punk ninja.

Armed with a salon gift certificate and a Color Me Badd key chain, Johnny bounced down to his BMW and followed me across town to the motel. He parked in the lot while I went around the corner to leave my car where the witch-spies wouldn't spot it.

Johnny went to the office and found out Gwen's room number and texted it to me: *She is in Finch room—Room 5.*

I glanced at the hotel. A couple years earlier, it had been pretty run-down, but new siding and paint had brightened it up. Now it wasn't exactly cheerful or pretty, but at least it didn't look like it would fall down during the next hard rain.

I walked to the tall grass at the edge of the property. Gwen was in a ground-floor room. If the plan went perfectly, Johnny would draw Gwen out of the hotel to the salon. If it went okay but not perfectly, he would make an appointment for her to come to the salon, leaving her room unguarded at some point in the future that I'd know about. If it didn't work at all, she'd tell him to forget it. Then I'd have to stake the place out until she left, never knowing when she'd be back.

I waited patiently to get one of the three preprogrammed texts that Johnny had ready. When my phone vibrated, I flipped it open and pressed the button to open the message. Then I smiled.

We going. Do that thing!

That sweet-talking black-and-blue-haired charmer! Johnny might not have been from Duvall, but he could pour on the sugar with the best of them.

I counted one-one-thousand, two-one-thousand, all the way up to one-hundred-one-thousand to give them time to clear the parking lot.

I crept to the back windows. I'd brought my tire-iron from the trunk, and I'd wrapped it in my jacket, hoping to muffle the sound when I used it. But that didn't turn out to be a problem. She'd left the back window unlocked. I shook my head. Some superspy.

I crawled in and looked around. The brown-and-white striped wallpaper was covered with finches. It was a weird combination, but I'd seen pictures of the insides of English castles and when it comes to busy patterns, we've got nothing on them, so blue-blood Gwen probably felt right at home.

There were locked file boxes on the floor. They were kind of heavy, but I thought that I might be able to carry them back to my car one at a time. Then I'd really find out what WAM and the Conclave were up to. I found a jewelry pouch, and dumped the contents out onto the bedside table. All delicate little chains and tiny charms. No stolen brooch.

The longer I searched, the more worried I got. Did she have it with her? So unfair after getting my hopes up with the open window. I'd just finished looking under the mattress when I felt a sharp pinch in my thigh and pain spread out, flash-fire style.

I crumpled to my knees, turning my head just in time to see the gun in Gwen's hand. I arched back, but not fast enough. The butt of the gun cracked my skull, and everything went black before my head hit the carpet.

20

MY EARS FELT like someone had filled them with cotton, but I still heard her voice when I woke up.

". . . him getting involved with a well-controlled, politically savvy low-level witch with potential, I could see. Or even a human being with exceptional intellect and magical leanings. But you?" she scoffed.

My wrists ached from being pinned under me. I was lying on the grass, and Miss Spy-Perfect Wardrobe had taken off her tailored jacket and rolled up her silk sleeves, so she wouldn't get dirty while she shoveled.

Shoveled? Uh-oh!

She dumped new dirt on the pile next to me and some of it rolled down the mound onto my legs.

"Why are you digging?" I asked, rolling from side to side, trying to get into a sitting position.

She glanced at me with an ice-water look. "If you try to get to your feet to run, I'll decapitate you with this shovel," she said calmly.

I froze. Decapitate? No matter what else happened, I was determined to keep my head and my body together. Even if

I was going to die. I had come into the world in one piece and that's how I planned to leave it.

When I was sitting up, I spotted Mercutio's body lying next to mine. I let out a cry of fury and half-rolled, half-crawled to him. I was rewarded with a sharp whack across my shoulder blades, which knocked me face-first to the ground. The good news was that, lying across Merc, I could feel that he was still warm and breathing. Something sharp was jabbing me in the belly and I moved slowly to get off it.

I realized it was a tranquilizer dart stuck in Mercutio's side. Had that been what she'd shot me with, too? A tranquilizer dart? Just like Scarface? Were they working together?

"Can I sit up?" I asked. "I won't try to stand."

"Yes, you may sit, if you like."

I positioned myself so that Mercutio's body was behind mine.

"So how come you're going to kill me? Isn't that kind of a stiff penalty for breaking into your room?"

I used my cuffed hands to pull the dart out of Merc.

She flung dirt onto the mound. "It's nothing personal."

She tossed the shovel on the ground and marched over to me. She grabbed Mercutio by the scruff of the neck and pulled him away from me, then stabbed him with the dart again.

I spewed a string of curses that would've made a sailor blush.

She smiled at me. "Look at you," she said with a sniff. "You tripped the wards on my motel room and then hung around waiting for me to show up and find you. Pathetic. Couldn't even recognize simple protective wards."

Wards. Of course. A witch's magical security system. Except I couldn't feel magic, so I hadn't felt a thing when I'd crossed them.

"Where's Johnny?"

"Nursing a headache. He'll never even remember coming to the hotel."

At least he was okay.

"Isn't killing me kind of extreme? John Barrett offered

me like a scholarship to go to school in London. Weren't you supposed to wait for me to say 'no' before you killed me?"

She waved off the suggestion, like killing me was no worse than shoplifting a pack of gum. "Do you know what Bryn said when we spoke about you?" she asked, hopping down into the hole and dragging the shovel in.

"If I had to guess, I'd put my money on something other than 'Kill Tammy Jo.'"

"You know . . . never mind what he said," she murmured. "Suffice to say that you have to die."

"He probably said that he likes me because I would never sit around and let my boss put a needle necklace on him."

She smiled. "Actually, that is fairly close to what he said." Dirt flew out of the hole.

I wriggled hard to get the chain connecting my wrists under my backside. I had to get my arms in front of me.

"He thinks you're incorruptible," she continued. The shovel paused as she laughed. "As if such a thing were possible. Everyone is corruptible. Sometimes it's necessary to dabble in darkness. Look at Bryn. He finally tapped into the black magic cache he got from outsmarting a demon. For years, he resisted using that power, which was free for the taking. His by rights. Until recently. He seems to be running a bit wild now that you've come into his life."

"His by rights?"

"Usually, when one taps into black magic, one has to pay a price. But Bryn has a source of black magic that he earned with his wits a long time ago. So far as I know, he's never used it before now. Maybe he thinks you're such sweetness and light that you'll ward off any dark powers that might take an interest."

"Why do you care what Bryn thinks or does? You guys broke up." I bent my knees to my chest and inched the chain under my feet. I could barely breathe while I did it, but I got my bound wrists in front of me.

"We didn't really break up. We took a break. Temporarily. He left to spend some time with his father. I never expected him to actually stay in this ridiculous town. Our lives were perfect when we lived together. When you're out of the way, I'll have him again. And it's for his own good. Someone has to get him out of here before evidence of his connection to the Underground is uncovered."

I kept my eyes on the hole as I knee-walked to Mercutio. I pulled the dart out of him and tossed it into the grass, then looked around for a weapon. Where was her gun?

With a whoosh of air, she was out of the hole and advancing on us. I jumped to my feet and crashed into her. We flew across the dirt and tumbled into the hole. The landing jarred me, but I didn't let it stop me. We fought like our lives depended on it, which in my case it did, of course.

I slammed my palm into her nose, and her blood sprayed all over us. The noise she made was half-scream, half-banshee wail. I got the shovel away from her, but she was fast and before I could crack her in the head with it, I felt a sharp slice along my side. She'd gotten her gun out and shot me again! I was only grazed by the dart, but I could feel that it had broken the skin.

Damn her!

My bloody hands slid along the handle of the shovel. I tried to knock her out, hoping I might wake up first, but my hands got wobbly too soon. The last thing I remember was her big swollen nose in my face while her hands choked my throat.

I WOKE WITH the weight of the world pressing down on me. It felt heavy and kind of soft actually—at least the part on my face, which I realized a moment later was Mercutio. I inhaled kitty fur and fought the urge to sneeze.

I was groggy and suffocating, maybe hallucinating, but being cocooned in the earth with my blood seeping into the dirt wasn't nearly as scary as it should have been.

I tried to move my arms, but couldn't. I needed to reach into a pocket of power with my mind, not my hands.

H'llo Earth, it'sssme. Tammel. Tammy Jo, I said in my head, as I fought the urge to take a deep breath. I needed air. The more alert I became, the more I needed it. I tried to concentrate on a spell. *Any spell*, I thought frantically.

My heart throbbed in my chest, and I choked on dirt and Merc's fur.

> *I know I'm a mess, and I don't have much clout.*
> *But I'd really appreciate it, if you'd just spit me out.*

I felt the ground move. I clamped my fists until they cramped.

> *Don't have much clout.*
> *Please, spit me out!*
> *Don't have much clout.*
> *PLEASE! Spit! Me! OUT!*

There was a horrible wrenching, like my arms and legs were being pulled from their sockets. Then the ground exploded and flung me out of the hole.

I landed on the ground with a rib-cracking thud. I sobbed out a groan and grabbed my side. Every breath hurt.

I tasted dirt in the back of my throat and coughed, sending spikes of pain through me.

"Uh," I moaned, trying to stabiiize the pieces of my ribs that were grinding against each other.

"Mer?" It was as much as I could manage. As I forced myself to roll onto my uninjured side, tears trickled from my eyes. I kept my arm pinned to my left side, trying to keep it as still as possible, but every centimeter of movement was a knife, every breath like a shard of glass shoved into my flesh. I saw Merc lying in the dirt.

The sound I made was barely human. I moved faster than I could stand and shrieked in pain. By the time I leaned over him, I was crying outright.

I scooped dirt from his mouth and banged his limp body. She'd put another damn dart back in him, and I yanked it free. I pressed his chest and blew air into his mouth and sobbed.

I don't know when he started breathing again. Maybe he was breathing the whole time, but too shallow for me to realize. I only know that when he started to retch up dirt, it was the best awful sound I'd ever heard.

I leaned on my right arm, held my side with my left, and asked God for forgiveness. In advance.

"I was just gonna be a pastry chef. You know I was," I said as I picked Merc up and arranged him over my shoulders like a shawl. "But here I am." I ground my teeth together ～～～～ of pain tearing through my side.

"She buried Mercutio and me alive. If I weren't half faery, I'm sure I'd be dead." I panted shallow breaths, trying to steady myself. "I think You understand," I rasped and then clenched my teeth in pain and fury.

"Some folks—" I wheezed out a breath. "Some folks just need killing." I felt the tears drip off my jaw as I started forward. "That's all I'm gonna say about it."

BY THE TIME I got out of the woods, I was slightly less homicidal. I was surprised to find myself at Macon Hill. She'd brought me to the tor and to the woods where I'd almost been killed the week before. What was it with these Conclave jerks? Did they all carry the same playbook?

Merc had woken up. He stumbled along groggily, but I didn't fill him in on anything. I figured he was still too full of tranquilizers to concentrate.

Bryn lived near the tor, but I was in too much pain to walk all the way there. Instead, I stopped at Magnolia Park and waited for someone to drive by that I could flag down. Ironically, the first person to show up was Edie, but, being a ghost, she doesn't have her own car.

"What in the world happened to you? You're covered in dirt."

"Could you go get Bryn?"

"No, I won't! You're not supposed to be seeing him. Why don't I get Johnny Nguyen? Of course, I'm not sure he'll want you in his car like that. I'll tell him to cover the passenger seat with a sheet."

"Not Johnny. Things are too dangerous for him to be

around me right now. Why don't you get Bryn? Being involved with me is pretty likely to get him killed."

"Really?" she asked.

"Really," I said, lying down on the bench.

"All right then. I'll appear to Johnny and ask him to call that son-of-a-bastard, Lyons. First tell me what you wanted to tell Melanie. I'm not sure how long I'll last over here with the locket there."

"I need her to come home. This trouble is pretty big. I need her help."

There was dead silence. I turned my head to see if Edie was still in the park. She was.

"I don't think that's possible," she said.

"Why not?" I asked, frowning at her.

"Well, her powers diminished while she was underhill and . . ."

"And?" I demanded.

"She's stuck in the UK. There's some sort of curse trapping her there. If she wants to restore her power, she'll have to find a way to lift it."

"A curse. Of course there is." I put an arm across my forehead. The dirty grit on my arm rubbed across the dirty grit on my face. I grimaced.

"Is my grandmother alive?"

"What?" Edie asked sharply.

"My grandma. Momma and Aunt Mel's momma? Alive or dead?"

"I'm going to get the candylegger." With that she was gone.

I sighed. *Alive then. Darn them.*

"FOR THE LOVE of St. Patrick," Bryn sputtered. "What happened?"

"You want the good news or the bad news?" I asked, sitting up with a terrible grimace.

"Bad, first," he said, grasping my shoulders to steady me.

"Your ex-girlfriend tried to kill me because she thinks I'm in the way of her getting you back."

"Gwen? Gwen did this?"

I nodded. "Carry me," I said, putting my arms out.

He picked me up and I groaned when his hands pressed my broken side.

"Stop! Put me down!" I rasped.

"What? Why?"

"You can't squeeze my left side. Nobody can. I'd rather stay here—live here, if I have to."

Bryn knelt down in front of me and lifted my shirt. "God damn it."

I looked down and saw the mass of swollen red and purple bruises covering my lower ribs.

"I'm sorry," he said.

"Me, too."

"All right, put your arms around my neck." I followed his instructions, and, in the end, he cradled me kind of like I was sitting in a chair. We got to his car and I climbed in. Merc sat on Bryn's lap instead of mine. That's why Merc and I are best friends.

"What's the good news?"

"Turns out I'm hard to kill. Shot, choked, and buried alive. Then shot like a cannonball out of the ground, and, so far as I can tell, not dead. Pretty sure being dead doesn't hurt this bad."

Bryn reached over and stroked my hair.

"This is . . . worse than I thought," he said. "You can leave. I'll take you to some Underground members. It'll be dangerous, but—"

"Let's talk about it after you wash the dirt out of my hair."

IT WAS THE oddest shower ever. Mercutio walked around Bryn and me in circles, hissing whenever the jets of water splashed on him. Motrin and Tylenol weren't nearly strong enough painkillers, so I drank rum mixed with pineapple juice from a squeeze bottle while Bryn soaped up my skin.

I stood under the warm spray facing Bryn as he massaged my scalp. Yep, there was definitely magic in those fingers.

I tipped my head back to rinse the shampoo away, and Bryn kissed my shoulder.

"I'm too hurt," I said as his hand slid down my spine to the curve of my back. He drew me to him, so our bodies touched, cool and slick from the water.

"I'll ease the pain," he whispered against my mouth. His black lashes were spiked together, framing those intense blue eyes.

"Nobody tells prettier lies than you," I whispered back.

His mouth caught mine, and his kiss was gentle, just a caress really, as the tip of his tongue touched mine questioningly.

He mumbled against my mouth in Gaelic, and I felt the magic, rich and complex, spinning out of him.

"Speak English," I said, and he did.

> She comes down from the mountain
> Through mists of dawn;
> I look and the star of morning
> From the sky is gone.
> The misty mountain is burning
> In the sun's red fire,
> And the heart in my breast is burning
> And lost in desire.
> I follow you into the valley
> But no word can I say;
> To the East or the West will I follow
> Till the dusk of my day.

"That's beautiful," I whispered.

"From a Celtic poem by Thomas Boyd."

I slipped my fingers into his hair and drew his mouth to mine. The kiss was more than a caress.

Maybe it was the liquor buzzing in my head. Maybe it was the magic. Or his sexy voice whispering pretty poetry, but the pain dampened.

"I'm not sure about this. I want . . . but you'd have to be so careful with me. So careful it might not be good. Probably wouldn't, but I couldn't take—"

He brushed his lips over mine. "I'll be more than careful. I'll be what you need."

Arms around his neck, legs around his hips, our tongues tangled together, he carried me to the bed and sat on the edge with me on his lap facing him. He had his hands on my hips, holding me just away from the part of him that wanted me most.

He glanced to the cut-glass skylight then back to my eyes. "Give me your body, and I'll give you mine."

"Isn't that what we were doing?"

He smiled and kissed me, but briefly. Too briefly.

Blood of my blood. Bone of my bone.
Two bodies, one. Never alone.

"Blood of my—" I started to repeat what he'd said, but he stopped me, touching a finger to my lips.

He stared into my eyes, and I could see the universe there, just behind his half-lowered lids.

"That spell is a circle that would bind us together. If you say the words too, you'll close the circle," he said.

I was so tempted, but stayed silent.

"Blood of my blood," he said against my mouth, and the words wound together like our bodies. He pulled me onto him, connecting us with the last word. The magic swallowed us both.

It wasn't that the pain was gone. It was only that I didn't care about it. The rhythm was slow, agonizingly so. The corded muscles in his arms were taut, his control absolute. Only when I dug my nails into his shoulders and moved back and forth faster did he match me.

Then the kaleidoscope of sensation started, and he sucked my magic into him, dragging my hand to his side while he touched mine. The sharp pain dulled, and I felt him stiffen and bite my lip. I gasped into his mouth and dissolved into pulsing tingling flesh. When the blood stopped rushing in my ears, I opened my eyes and looked at his face. Agony and ecstasy in one.

Finally, he closed his eyes and fell back onto the bed, breathing hard. He fisted his right hand. I studied him, realizing what he'd done. There, a mirror image to mine, the side of his chest was scuffed and bruised a reddish purple.

I shook my head. "Is there anything men won't do for sex?" I mumbled, tracing a finger around the edge of his warm, wounded flesh.

"That's the wrong question, Tamara."

"What's the right question, Bryn?" I whispered.

"I'll tell you when you're ready to hear it."

His cell phone was sitting on the nightstand, and when it rang, it startled us both. I climbed off him gingerly, but he caught my arm.

"Leave it," he said.

"I'll just see who it is. Maybe someone you care about needs you," I said, thinking of Mr. Jenson tucked away out of town and his friend Andre on the run. I tugged my wrist free of his grip and went to the phone. I looked at the display and froze.

Gwendolyn Vaughn.

You have got to be kidding me!

I clutched the phone and sat down on the bed. "Say hello."

Bryn, who was already half asleep, mumbled, "What?"

"Say hello," I said sharply, not wanting the call to go to voicemail.

"Hello," he murmured when I picked up. Then I put the phone to my ear and listened to her lie. She was world-class. The tears. The way her voice caught as she claimed that I'd attacked her. I almost believed her myself, and I'd been there.

"It was self-defense," she sobbed. "But I—I'm not sure if she's even still alive. I need you to come to me right now. Please."

I wished I knew as many languages as Bryn so I could curse at Gwen in all of them. Instead, I hung up on her.

The phone began ringing again immediately.

"What?" Bryn said, opening his eyes and reaching for the phone.

I slid it away from him. "It's the spy who shoved me. She wants to tell you that she was only defending herself when she killed me."

Bryn struggled to alertness. "Give it here."

"If you agree to meet her *ever again*, I might lose my mind and stab you through the heart or something."

The corner of Bryn's mouth curved up.

"But you know," I said with a mock casual shrug. "Do whatever you want." I slapped the phone into his hand and walked to his dresser.

"Hello," Bryn said.

I dug through Bryn's T-shirts until I found a well-worn one in his Yale Law School colors. Printed on it in bold letters were the words: *You have the right to remain silent. Please use it.*

I slipped it on just as he said, "Thanks, Gwen."

I went still, trying to imagine whether I was hallucinating. What reason in the known universe could there be for Bryn to thank Gwen? I turned slowly and glared at him.

"I'm sorry," he said to her, but shook his head so I'd know he wasn't being sincere. "What's that?" He paused, frowning. "Tomorrow morning will be soon enough." He stopped and I knew that she was arguing. "Well, it'll have to be." He hung up the phone and turned it off.

"Why did you say thank you?"

"She told me I was remarkably composed. Just like my old self. She's proud of me."

"For being completely emotionless about me being murdered?"

"Apparently."

"That bitch!" A sharp cramp of pain reminded me that even though Bryn had taken half the injury, there was still some left. I rubbed my side.

Bryn pulled the covers back and crawled under them. He held out a hand to me.

"I was thinking of sleeping downstairs," I said.

"No."

"What are we doing here?" I ran a hand through my hair. "There's the prophecy thing. Plus, I broke my promise to Zach," I said with a sigh.

"No, you didn't. You told him you wouldn't decide between us. I'm not asking you for the rest of your life. I'm just asking you for tonight."

"Loopholes and technicalities," I mumbled, then chewed the inside of my cheek and stared up at the sky through the panes of glass. "I don't know if I can do it. Getting caught up in the moment, that's one thing. I was naked. You were—you."

I looked back at him and found he was smiling.

"Okay, sleep downstairs," he said, setting his arm down.

The tension eased out of me. I was off the hook. Wasn't that nice of Bryn?

"Good," I said, exhaling in relief as I walked toward the door.

"Two things," he said.

"Yes?"

"That T-shirt's not long enough. You'd better wear something more unless you don't care about the security cameras."

I blushed. Of course, I cared. I'd just forgotten about the darn cameras. I went back through his drawers until I found some drawstring pajama pants.

"What was the second thing?" I asked, moseying back toward the door.

"Sleep on the left side of the bed."

I cocked my head. "Why?"

"Because when I crawl into bed with you, I don't want to accidentally bump into your injured side."

My jaw dropped. "I'm—The point of me going downstairs is for me to sleep alone."

"That's your point."

I glared at him. "This is how you are. Give you an inch and you try to take a mile. You're just like a lawyer!"

"I am a lawyer."

"See!"

"Come to bed."

I stood between the bed and the door trying to decide what to do until I started to feel ridiculous. Finally, I padded over to the bed and climbed in.

"It doesn't mean anything," I mumbled stubbornly.

"No," Bryn said, pulling me closer to him and pressing a kiss to my hair. "Doesn't mean a thing."

21

I WOKE TO the sound of Bryn's voice. He was talking quietly into the bedside phone.

"I have meetings, but I'll try to make it to your office before five," Bryn said and hung up.

"Who was that?"

He rolled so that his body was pressed along my right side. His dark blue eyes scanned my face. "Why are you awake?"

"Light sleeper. Who was on the phone?"

"The mayor."

I turned my head to look at the clock. "He calls you at midnight?"

"My side feels better. How about yours?" he asked.

"Yeah, it's way better," I said, moving gingerly. A faint ache, a little throbbing. Nothing terrible. It made me wonder: how could being involved with Bryn be wrong when it always seemed to do me such good? Also, how could I trust what my family said about him when they'd lied to me about the most basic and important stuff, like who I was and who in my family was alive and wanted to meet me? Maybe Lenore's list was a lie, too.

He bent his head and ran his tongue over my lower lip,

making my belly tighten and goose bumps rise along my arms.

"Does every inch of you taste like honey?"

"Not that I know of," I said, trying too late to catch his hand before he pulled my T-shirt up. "Doubt it," I added, exhaling slowly as he ran his tongue along my right ribs. I shivered, gripping his shoulder as I arched.

His mouth closed on my breast, teasing me slowly. It was as if he were saying, "Let me show you how it can be between us."

I didn't stop him. I didn't want to.

He treated foreplay like it was the main event. Well, I guess he turned it into the main event for me . . . more than once.

Sometime later, I stretched, his hair brushing my thigh as he moved up. He bit my earlobe, his breath coarse and full of need.

"Is it finally your turn?" I murmured.

He answered with his body, and the magic that he'd been holding back broke over us in waves. We were more than flesh and bone. The night and the dawn seemed to crack open, pulses of light, then falling shadows, in an ancient rhythm that was human . . . and not.

Afterward, he made no attempt to untangle us, and neither did I.

I stroked his hair, so irresistibly silky. "It's no wonder."

"What?"

"That Gwen's so determined to get you back." There was an edge to my voice, something vulnerable.

He raised his head to look at me. "Is that a question, Tamara? Are you asking me if it was like that with her?"

"No. I mean—that's none of my business." I shrugged, but that didn't mean I wasn't holding my breath, waiting to hear what he'd say next.

Bryn smiled. "But you wouldn't mind me telling you?"

Was he reading my mind? If so, why couldn't I read his? "No, I wouldn't mind. At least I don't think I would."

"Gwen was—adventurous in bed. It was—"

Adventurous?! Translation: slutty.

"Never mind," I said, suddenly trying to untangle my legs from his.

He grabbed me to keep me from slipping away. "What I had with her will never compare to what I'll have with you."

I went still. "How do you know?"

"Because I was here tonight. You and I cross the boundaries between the physical and metaphysical worlds. Effortlessly and without words. We haven't done any rituals or special ceremonies, no elaborate spells." His hand found mine, and he laced our fingers together. "The way we are together transcends will. It just is."

I smiled. Yeah, what we had felt pretty special.

Then a faint sound, or maybe just the echo of a sound, made me turn my head toward it. Prickly magic poked my fingertips. I jumped.

"What's that?" I squirmed, untangling us.

Bryn had turned his head, too. "You felt it?" he asked, climbing out of bed.

I flicked on the light. "I felt something."

"Someone's crossed the wards."

We both pulled clothes on, and he took a gun out of the nightstand.

"Only one gun in there?" I asked.

"Yes," he said and held it out to me.

I raised my eyebrows as I took it.

"I'm better with magic than guns. You're better with guns than magic." He took my free hand and led me to the door.

I smiled to myself. Two weeks ago when the town was under attack by werewolves, he'd wanted to put me in a vault for safekeeping. Now, he was taking me with him. This was another taste of what I could have with Bryn. Well, what I could have with him if we survived.

My heart thumped faster in my chest as we hurried down the stairs. I could see that the front door was open. I looked to the right toward the kitchen and then left to the long hallway that led to many rooms. There were so many places for an intruder to hide.

Bryn tugged my hand, signaling that we were heading

to the kitchen. Even with some of his magic still coursing through my body, I couldn't sense whatever it was that he felt. I stayed light on my toes, trying to be silent.

Blood raced through my veins. I nodded at the light switch, but Bryn shook his head. He drew me to the wall where a security phone hung. He picked it up and waited. I could hear the ringing. Where was Steve?

A clicking of footsteps made me whirl to the kitchen door. It took me a moment to realize that the woman in the doorway was Gwen. Her nose was double its normal size, her whole face bruised and swollen.

"Bryn, I needed to see you. I have something for you," she said, her voice muffled from her nose being plugged. She turned on the light, and the moment she saw me, she went rigid.

"No," she said. "How? What are you doing here?" Whatever she'd had in her hand, she dropped into her pocket. When she brought her hand back out, she raised it toward me. Bryn moved in front of me.

"What is it, Gwen?" he asked, calm, as if I hadn't thrown on his clothes to cover the fact that I'd been naked five minutes ago. I maneuvered the gun so the barrel peeked out from next to Bryn's body.

"Look," she said, then she shook her head. "I have something you've always wanted, but to get it, you have to give her up. That's the bargain."

"You don't have anything that I want more than her," Bryn said.

I smiled. Sometimes he says the exact right thing at the exact right time. Must have been the lawyer in him, and, for once, I didn't mind.

"Is that so," she asked in a venomous voice. "She's more important than heritage, than family? More important than what you destroyed your life for?"

"What are you talking about?" he asked slowly.

"Your plaything doesn't know anything about it, does she? You can't confide in her. Good for a quick shag, but the brilliant Bryn Lyons with a brainless twit? Who are you kidding?"

I flinched, reeling from the insecurities that came bubbling up.

"*Tammy Jo?* Even her name is ridiculous. I notice you don't call her by it."

I glared at her, thinking I'd liked it better when she was just trying to kill me.

Bryn shook his head. "I can't make you understand it."

"Clearly." She licked her lips. "I've made a report, Bryn, about how she attacked me. Not the first Conclave member she's tried to kill, am I? You know how it'll end for her. Badly."

My finger itched to pull the trigger. I gritted my teeth against the urge. I didn't want to kill her in cold blood. If she would just attack me with something besides words, I'd be all set . . .

"She's marked now." Gwen turned.

"We'll see. Now, what about the past?" Bryn asked and I hated that he cared about whatever she was talking about. I hated that he was still talking to her, period.

"I'll give it to you when she's dead," she said before she walked casually out the door.

I lowered the gun, although my legs twitched, anxious to chase her down the hall so my arm could shoot her in the back. Or the front. My fury wasn't too picky.

Mercutio's yowl from outside the kitchen made me snap my head to the left, toward the back lawn. I saw a figure outside and the glint of light off of the gun that was pointed at us through the back window. I swung my gun around and shoved Bryn aside. The window shattered, and Bryn's body jerked when the bullet hit him.

I squeezed the trigger and saw the figure on the lawn stumble and turn to run. It wasn't Gwen.

I leaned over Bryn.

"I'm all right," he said, holding his arm. Blood streamed down the back of it. I pried his fingers away, so I could see the wound. The bullet had made a centimeter-deep channel through his flesh, but it was just a nasty graze.

I crossed the kitchen and yanked the back door open. I charged outside, tripping the motion detectors so that the extra floodlights blazed on. I surveyed the area, not seeing him. My eyes studied the woods, looking for any movement.

"What the hell?"

Several feet away, Merc yowled at me and then turned and ran toward the water. I rushed after him. A boat's motor buzzed to life. I raced to the dock as it pulled away. I saw Scarface leaning over the wheel and raised my gun, shooting at the boat and hitting it, but not slowing it down. In seconds, I was out of bullets and he was out of range.

My hot breath fogged the cold air as I panted and walked back to the house. I saw Bryn kneeling in the sunroom. What was he doing?

I pulled the door open and realized he was leaning over a body. A body in navy blue dress slacks and blazer.

"Oh, no! Steve!"

22

I DROPPED TO my knees, slamming the gun on the ground as my heart hammered. "Where? Where's he shot? Damn them."

Bryn held up a tranquilizer dart. "This was in his shoulder."

"Oh," I said, melting with relief. "I've been shot with a couple of those. He'll be all right. It's a knockout drug is all."

Bryn stared at me.

"He'll be all right," I repeated, standing up. "Help me put him on the couch. We'll cover him with blankets. He can sleep here until it wears off."

"He's barely breathing."

"Yeah, that happens. It's actually kind of helpful if you're buried alive." I put a hand under one of Steve's bulky arms. Bryn did the same and we hauled him onto the softer surface. I covered him with the throw blankets, then looked Bryn over. There was still blood dripping from his wound and his skin had taken on a faint bluish cast from the cold.

"Let's get you inside," I said.

Bryn studied Steve and rechecked his pulse. "I'm going to call the paramedics."

"Okay. You'll have to think up a story then. And you'll have to make a police report since you've been shot."

"I'll say it was an intruder. Didn't get a good look at him."

"Shot you with bullets, but your security guard with a tranquilizer dart? That'll seem odd."

"That *is* odd."

"For a regular kidnapper or thief, yes. For a Conclave minion?" I said, shrugging. "Knock out the human. Kill the wizard. It was Scarface. Before, I thought he might've been hired by DeeDAW even though he seemed too polished for them, but now I know he doesn't work for them."

"You think he was with Gwen?"

"Nope. He shot you, not me."

"He might have been aiming for you."

"No, I saw him. You were his target. Plus he could've killed me twice before if he'd wanted to. He tranquilized me. Why? Has to be that I'm not his target. Maybe he just wanted me out of the way."

"So he's Barrett's man then. The president brought an official entourage and an unofficial one." Bryn rubbed his arm, and I grabbed his elbow and tugged him to the door. The house was nice and warm. I took him to the kitchen and scrubbed his wound with soap and water, then wrapped a towel around it. He winced, but didn't complain.

"Sorry," I said, pressing a kiss on his jaw when I finished.

"Thanks," he said, seeming distracted. He glanced in the direction of the porch. "You know, Steve's young and healthy, but he's also human. Maybe that tranquilizer will affect him more than it affected you."

"He's a pretty big guy, but maybe so."

Bryn walked to the phone and called nine-one-one. When he hung up, I said, "Don't tell them I was here. Also, I need a few more clips for this gun."

"Where are you going?"

"I'm going to have a look around."

"A look around?" he echoed skeptically. "If you really are marked for death, you'll have to go underground."

I wasn't doing that, but I wasn't in the mood to argue

about it. "And what about you? If I went underground, you'd stay here alone?"

"I could come with you," he said thoughtfully.

"You said if we started running, it would be hard to stop, hard to clear our names."

"Right, but it'll be even harder to clear our names if we're dead."

"As usual, you've got a point. I'm sure gonna think that over when I get a minute. In the meantime, can you give me some more bullets for this gun?"

He folded his arms across his chest.

"I can go without them, but I'll be a lot more likely to end up dead," I pointed out.

Bryn scowled, but he went down the hall and opened a drawer in the bureau. He handed me several loaded clips.

"My car?" I'd told Bryn where it was and that we needed to get it, but he'd said he'd take care of it.

"It's in the driveway. Steve and Pete picked it up from behind the motel."

I gave Bryn a quick thank-you kiss, then went to change into my clothes. Afterward, I whistled for Mercutio.

We went out and sat in my darkened car at the end of the drive. When the ambulance was halfway to the house I started my car and we slipped off Bryn's property.

"It's time to deal with Gwen," I said. "She's got my stuff. And she's got something of Bryn's. She's like a darn kleptomaniac. A homicidal kleptomaniac. I'm going to get our stuff back. While I'm at it, I'll get her to sign a confession that she attacked me." I took a deep breath and blew it out. "Think that'll work?"

Merc licked his paw.

"Yeah, I've got a few doubts, too, but we can't just sit around while they try to kill us and steal our town. Right?"

Merc meowed his agreement.

"Right." Of course, I'd known Mercutio would agree to fight back because if there's fighting involved in a plan, he's in favor of it.

I drove to the motel and parked on the street where I'd

parked earlier in the day. Mercutio and I crept to the back window. She'd feel me crossing her wards, so I needed to be sure I was ready. I'd need to get inside fast.

Mercutio didn't wait for me. He went through first, which I hoped would be a good diversion. I climbed in quickly, but slipped, landing hard. Luckily the gun's safety was on or I'd have shot something. The carpet squelched under my feet as I stood.

Uh-oh. Why is the carpet wet?

The eerie silence seemed to close around me.

Uh-oh.

I grimaced, moving to the door, searching for the light switch as a voice in my head yelled that something was very wrong and that I should get out. My fingers didn't listen though. I flipped the switch and in an instant, I regretted it.

Gwen lay on the floor dead. I slapped a hand over my mouth. Sliced throat. Blood spray everywhere. I shuddered, frozen in place.

Mercutio stood on the bed looking down at her. I looked at everything but her. The finches on the wallpaper were speckled with blood. Biblical passages had been spray-painted in black.

I stared at the most prominent one. THOU SHALL NOT SUFFER A WITCH

Oh my gosh. Had DeeDAW brought in more crazy, violent out-of-towners? Had they seen Gwen doing something suspicious? Confronted her? She could've tried to use magic to defend herself, and they killed her for it.

I looked at the place where the locked file boxes had been. There were grooves on the carpet from the weight of them. I hated to think that DeeDAW had the WAM files, which were sure to be incriminating.

I scanned the room and toed open the door to the closet. There were clothes hanging inside, including her coat. I checked the pockets. Empty. The brooch and the medieval spellbook would have my fingerprints on them. It would be bad if they were found in the room of a murder victim, but I didn't want them in the hands of her killer or killers either.

I used a shirt to wipe my prints from the light switch. I'd been in the room earlier. What had I touched? Were there strands of my hair in the room? I cringed, but forced myself to look at her body lying at the foot of the bed. There was a bloody paw print from where Merc had walked, plus a couple of my boot prints. I picked Merc up.

"You go back to the car. I'll meet you there in a minute." I dropped him out the open window and turned. I should've worn gloves. Both times, I should've worn gloves. If I tried to wipe away my prints, would I also wipe away evidence that the real killer had left behind? Just because I'd been prepared to shoot Gwen didn't mean I thought everyday murderers should go free.

I spotted her keys on the nightstand. My brooch and book hadn't been in the room earlier. Might they be in her car? I picked up the keys and shoved them in my pocket.

I tucked the gun into the back of my jeans as I smudged Merc's paw print as well as the ones I'd made. I was careful to rub my boot's toe back and forth until I was sure I wouldn't leave a new print. Then I turned out the light using the shirt and did the same to open the door. Most of the hotel rooms were dark and the cement walkway was clear. I dropped Gwen's shirt, stepped outside, and closed the door with my forearm.

I was two feet from the room when the door to Room 6 opened. I froze and wished I knew a spell to become invisible. Mrs. Thornton's silver hair sparkled in the moonlight as she stepped out.

"What are you doing there?" she asked.

"I came to talk to Gwen. I think she took something of mine the night of the benefit and I want it back."

"What do you think she took?"

"A piece of jewelry and a book."

"This seems an odd time to come looking for it. Why not earlier? Or later today?" Her cool green eyes sized me up. I felt like I had a big "I'm guilty!" stamp on my forehead and willed my cheeks not to flush.

"She didn't answer," I said. "I'll come back later."

"Is that why you attacked her earlier? Because you thought she stole something from you?"

"I didn't attack her. I wouldn't do that to someone out of the blue. On the other hand, if someone attacks me first, I do mostly fight back."

"There are occasions when you draw your weapon first. For example, if someone threatens Bryn Lyons," she said, her tone mild as milk.

"It's not only Bryn. There are quite a few people in town—and, in fact, the whole town itself—that I'd protect if it came down to it."

"And how far would you go to protect it?"

"Far enough."

"Hmm. We'll see. As far as Gwendolyn Vaughn's story goes, we'll discuss that later. You can tell us your side of what happened, and we'll see what President Barrett thinks of it. I warn you though, this is no game. Lie at your own peril."

I nodded and didn't exhale until she went back into her room and closed the door.

Great. Now when the police questioned her, Mrs. Thornton would have to tell them that she saw me lurking around outside Gwen's room at two a.m., only hours after Gwen had alleged that I'd assaulted her. Going on the run was starting to look kind of good.

I crept through the parking lot, aware that with every step I was risking being seen again and that I was getting farther and farther from my car.

Finally, I spotted her rental. With a heart that was slam-dancing in my chest, I unlocked it. I checked the front and backseats and the glove box. Nothing. Then I opened the trunk. Empty as well.

How does that saying go? If not for bad luck, I wouldn't have any luck at all. I wiped off Gwen's keys and dropped them on the front seat. Then I closed the door and walked away.

Yep, running away from home was looking kind of good.

ALL THE WAY back to Bryn's house, I couldn't stop picturing the body. I gripped the steering wheel tight to keep my hands from shaking.

"You know when Gwen tried to kill us, Merc, I thought maybe I could kill her back." I shook my head. "If you would've died, I guess I might've been crazy bent on revenge. But seeing her like that . . ." I pursed my lips. "Put me down for self-defense, but the premeditated stuff? No. No way."

Mercutio licked my arm.

"Thanks, Merc. You being a predator, I wasn't sure you'd really support me on that." I rubbed his fur.

Bryn opened the gate and was standing in the doorway when I pulled up.

"How's Steve?"

"Awake. He was pretty sick when he woke up, but he's all right now. The paramedics came. We both declined transport to the nearest hospital, so they rebandaged my arm and left.

"How is your arm?"

He shrugged. "Hurts, but pain is sort of par for the course the past few weeks."

"Yeah, I guess so. You know what else is par for the course lately?"

"What?"

"Dead bodies."

His eyebrows rose. "What's happened?"

"I didn't kill her."

"Who? Gwen?"

"She was already dead when I found her."

"Gwen is dead?"

I nodded. He looked around as if the answers to everything that had happened were floating somewhere around the room and if he looked hard enough, he'd spot them.

"So you found her. In her hotel room?"

I nodded again.

"What were you doing there?"

"Looking for my stuff that she stole."

"Why are you so determined to get it back? You've said the spellbook's instructions are often impractical, and you're not even sure the jewelry's yours. Besides, what makes you so certain that Gwen took them?"

"A hunch." *That I got from casting a spell that nearly drowned me.*

"Uh-huh." Bryn sighed. "Did you touch the body?"

"No way."

We talked for a few minutes more, but the nagging irritation about having lost the brooch was still there. I had to get it back.

I glanced at Bryn's profile, and a tingling sensation crawled over my skin. I was inexplicably attached to that brooch the same way I was connected to Bryn's magic. To Bryn himself. The woman in the brooch . . . why did I want to help her so much? What if she wasn't important to my family? What if she was important to Bryn? My mind tripped back through the things that everyone had said over the past couple days.

"Bryn, why did you get kicked out of school?"

"What?"

I reached out and touched his forearm. "It keeps coming up. I heard that it changed your life, and Gwen mentioned it when she was here."

His eyes narrowed. "It doesn't have anything to do with what's going on now. Nothing to do with Gwen's murder."

"What were you chasing that summer? Was it a girl?" There was a knot in my stomach that made it hard to look at him. Something about the memory haunted him. I could see it in his eyes, in the tightness of his mouth.

He didn't answer at first. It was unsettling since he's not usually at a loss for words. I waited, muscles clenched.

"My mother died before I really knew her. I wanted to meet her." He glanced around, a faraway look in his eyes. "Wanted to talk to her. Just once." It was only a few words, but they captured a heap of carefully guarded emotions.

"What did you do?" I asked softly.

"I called the dead."

"Did it work?"

"No. And yes." He rubbed the back of his neck like it exhausted him to think about it. "When she didn't come at first, we fed more and more power into the spell and opened the incantation, casting it farther, beyond the place she died. A lot of souls returned. Some good. Those were gone in an instant. Some that were stuck on Earth. They were confused or begged for help. And finally there were some spirits that were darker than anything I've ever felt. They didn't want to go back to Hell or wherever they'd been. Those souls wanted to stay. I'd used everything I had in me to bring them. So once they were out, I couldn't force them back."

"Oh my gosh."

"Exactly. That prejudice I have against disenfranchised spirits, I earned it."

"Why do you think she didn't come?"

"She died young and innocent. A lot of people described her as being . . ." His jaw muscles worked, and his eyes shone unnaturally bright. "Angelic. I suppose she's too far inside to be called back by any magic, even to a son who was desperate to know her."

I wrapped my arms around him and hugged him tight. Tears dripped from my eyes. "I'm so sorry."

"It's all right," he murmured, clearing his throat. "It was a long time ago."

If Bryn hadn't been able to call her to him, with all his magic and his bond to her, then there was no way that the woman attached to the brooch was related to him. But the idea that she could be needled me. His magic was the kind I felt best. Better even than my own.

What color were the woman's eyes? I'd been so focused on her pain that I hadn't been paying attention to her eye color, but thinking back . . . I pictured her face. Blue, I realized. I was pretty sure they were a familiar deep blue.

I pulled back, wiping my face. "Are you okay?"

"You're the one who's crying," he pointed out mildly, but I noted the flush in his cheeks and the blanched skin of his knuckles where he'd been clenching his fists.

"Can I ask you something else? Unless it's too hard for you to talk about," I added.

"Ask."

"Do you have any pictures of your mom?"

There was a hint of a wry smile. "One or two," he said. He hesitated, then waved for me to follow him. When he spoke again, his voice was utterly calm, like he was talking about someone else. "I don't remember when I started collecting them. Lennox thinks I was about five."

He led me to the library and booted up his computer. He clicked open folders until he reached the one called Cassandra Lyons.

"I'm pretty sure I have the original or a copy of every picture that was ever taken of her. A few years ago, I scanned them all in."

"To protect the photographs from damage," I said matter-of-factly. "I bet you keep the actual pictures in your impenetrable vault."

He glanced past me to the door and nodded. "Yes. I keep the originals in the vault."

I bit my lip, my eyes filling, but I blinked away the tears. He looked at me for a second, then at the screen. Perfect rows of icons. Hundreds—maybe thousands—of hours of work must have gone into getting all of them.

"If I ever have a little boy, that's how I want him to love me," I whispered.

His gaze stayed fixed on the monitor, as though he would've gladly joined her inside it. His voice came out soft and rough. "That button will play a slideshow or just click to open the individual pictures." He walked away, going to the far windows, his back to me.

I took a few slow breaths, staring at the keys. *Don't let it be her.*

My fingers trembled, hovering over the buttons. I wanted Cassandra Lyons to be in Heaven, knee-deep in angels and untouchable.

I clenched my jaw to brace myself and clicked the slideshow icon.

There she was. The beautiful brunette from the brooch, the one who'd been running for her life, the one who needed my help. Sparkling cobalt eyes. A tiny dimple in her right cheek

when she smiled. Once upon a time—before the brooch—
she'd been happy.

My heart squeezed painfully. Why did it have to be her?

I covered my mouth, got up, and walked silently from the
room.

Down the hall. Through the kitchen. Out the back door.

I wilted against the gray brick, my shoulders sagging. I
bit my lip and closed the door to be sure Bryn wouldn't hear
me when I started crying again.

23

IT TOOK ME a few minutes to pull myself together. I couldn't decide whether to tell Bryn about the brooch. On one hand, he might be able to help me get it back. On the other, I would shatter his peace of mind. He thought her soul was safe and happy. I didn't want to take that away from him.

A thick fog made it impossible to see the river. I blew out my breath slowly and shuffled through the grass toward the path that led to the guesthouse.

I wouldn't call Lennox and me friends, but we did have caring about Bryn in common. And he'd certainly want to know that his wife was trapped in a brooch and needed help. My feet crunched the gravel until I stopped walking. I didn't know how she'd died. Foul play seemed likely.

"When a woman is killed, the number one suspect is the husband," I mumbled. That much I knew from being married to a sheriff's deputy. Plus, I watch television.

I chewed on my lip, deciding that I'd gather information before giving any away. Assuming that he cooperated, which actually wasn't all that likely.

I stumbled along. The fog was as thick as cream of mushroom soup. I frowned. We never got much fog in Duvall. Fog was something I associated with places like London. I frowned. Had WAM brought fog with them?

I finally got to the guesthouse and could see that there were lights on inside. I knocked. No one answered, so I knocked again harder.

Finally, the front door opened. Lennox wore a thick black bathrobe and looked like he'd just gotten out of the shower.

"Hello," I said.

"What do you want?" he asked.

"Can I come in?"

He glanced over my shoulder, though unless his eyes doubled as fog lights, there was no way he could see if someone was lurking behind me.

"I'm alone," I said.

"What do you want?" he asked again impatiently.

"I need some information."

He looked me over and then ushered me inside. "Sit there," he said, pointing to the couch. "If you stray an inch, you're out."

I wondered what in the world was going on with him. As I sat down, I noticed that there was brownish grit under his nails. Had he been digging?

He caught me looking and glared. Then he left the room and I heard a heavy door open and close.

I hopped up and crept through the house. Like at Bryn's, the kitchen faced the water. I jumped when light suddenly cut through the fog. A moment later, I smelled smoke. Lennox was burning something.

My fingers itched to open the door, but if I went outside, I wouldn't get the information I'd come for. I heard a noise and that decided it. I rushed back to the front room and dove onto the couch.

I positioned myself just in time.

I smelled lighter fluid when he came back into the room.

"Well?" he asked.

"Um, what happened to your wife?"

He blinked. "Come again."

"You were married to her, right—Bryn's mother? I want to know how she died."

"Why didn't you ask him?"

"Because I thought talking about it might upset him."

"And you didn't think it would upset me?" he asked.

"Well—"

"Ah. You did think it would upset me, but you didn't care."

"I didn't say that. I'm not out to upset anyone. But if someone has to be upset, well, better someone who stole something from me and nearly got me killed than someone who didn't."

"My wife was murdered."

"Where? How? Who did it?"

"She was stabbed to death in Revelworth, England, by a man named Simon Pritchard."

"Why did he kill her?"

"He lost his mind."

"Did he have any magic? Was he a wizard?"

Lennox crossed his arms over his chest. "Of course. Everyone in Revelworth is a witch or wizard."

"Oh, right. That's the town the World Association of Magic took over. The one they ran all the regular nonmagical people out of?"

"Yes."

"That's the same place where Bryn got in trouble for trying to raise her ghost?"

He frowned. "Who told you that he tried to call her ghost?"

"He did."

He cocked an eyebrow. "And what did you do for him that made him inclined to confide in you?"

I glared at him. "We're friends."

"Sure you are. Now if that's all—" He yanked open the front door and pointed toward the fog-laden path.

"One more thing," I blurted, as he took my arm and helped me to my feet with more enthusiasm than was strictly polite. "What happened to Simon Pritchard?"

Lennox pushed me firmly onto the front step before he answered coldly, "He died for his crime."

The front door closed, and I stood for a moment, thinking things over. If Simon Pritchard had killed Cassandra Lyons, had he tied her to the brooch? And when he died, who had taken possession of the brooch? Who had mailed it to me?

I needed more answers. I closed my hand around the front door handle and tried to turn it. It didn't budge, and, what's more, it was dirty. I lifted my gritty hand to my eyes, but it was too dark to see. Uneasiness oozed through me.

I walked down the path to where there was a small gas lamp. I held my hand near it. Tiny rust-colored flecks marked my palm.

Lennox had been freshly showered, burning something in the backyard, with brownish grit on the door handle and under his nails. *Uh-oh*, I thought. I closed my hand to protect the possible evidence and hurried away from the house.

The fog was like a living thing, its cool breath chilling my arms. I rushed toward the main house, relying on memory and following the pulse of Bryn's magic. I stumbled a couple of times, but didn't fall. When I reached the front door, I had to knock because it was locked.

Bryn opened it. "What are you doing out there? I was looking for you."

"Do you have any more peroxide?"

"Are you hurt?"

"Just a scratch," I lied. "I'd better clean it."

He took me upstairs and into the master bathroom. "I don't normally have such a stash of first aid supplies, but Jenson decided to stock up after last week."

"Mr. Jenson's the best," I said brightly.

Bryn's hand full of gauze pads paused as he looked at me. "What's going on?"

"Nothing," I said, trying to look innocent. I kept my right hand firmly closed and held out my left. "I don't need gauze. Just the peroxide bottle please."

Bryn grabbed the bottle and uncapped it. "I'll pour."

I opened my hand, revealing perfectly intact skin and

minute reddish brown flecks. "Go ahead and pour a little of that onto my palm."

He tipped the bottle and a few drops splashed onto my hand. The flecks burst into bubbles the way blood always does when mixed with peroxide.

"Okay," I said, turning on the tap and washing and rinsing both my hands.

"Okay what?" he asked, his gaze trapping me.

Okay, your mom's trapped in a missing brooch, and your dad might've killed your ex-girlfriend tonight. I dried my hands on the towel and couldn't escape the feeling that things were spinning out of control. *As usual.* I put my arms around his neck, hugging him.

"What's going on?" he demanded.

"Nothing, but, you know, I think we should stay somewhere other than here."

"Like where?"

"Oh, you know," I said with a casual shrug. "Anywhere."

"Tamara, trust me. Tell me what's on your mind."

"The Conclave and Scarface are after us. Gwen's been murdered, and we'll both be suspects, especially me. Plus, DeeDAW hasn't given up. I just think it would be good if we were hard to find for a little while."

Bryn frowned. I didn't blame him. A fancy mansion with a library, a vault, and a security detail. Who'd want to leave all that behind?

With my arms around his neck, I pulled his face closer to mine. "I'm going." I brushed my lips over his. "Come with me," I whispered.

"There it is," he said, glancing at my mouth. "The offer he couldn't refuse."

WHEN I HAD my suitcase packed and Mercutio in tow, it occurred to me that there was nowhere in Duvall we could hide. Friends, enemies, potential gossips. They were everywhere these days.

When Bryn came downstairs with his fancy suitcase,

garment bag, and duffle, I was sitting on the edge of the bed in the guest room.

"Ready?" he asked.

"Where will we go? Not Zach's house—"

"Definitely not."

"Not my house, with the workmen coming and going. Not Georgia Sue's. She couldn't keep a secret if my life depended on it. Johnny's neighbors are right on top of his front door."

"I've got a cottage. It's outside Duvall. We can stay there."

My jaw dropped. "You've got another house?"

"I've got other *houses*."

"A mansion in Duvall's not enough, huh? You have to keep your options open?" I demanded. I was being ridiculous, of course. It wasn't like he said he had other girlfriends or something. It's just that I'm part of the town, and it's part of me, and Bryn was supposed to be part of us, too.

He smiled. "I solved the problem of where to stay. You're supposed to say, 'Bryn, that's wonderful. I'm so glad to have you in my life.'"

I rolled my eyes. "Just 'cause you've got a good solution to a serious problem doesn't mean I have to be happy about it."

"Of course not," he said mildly.

I got up and tipped my bag to roll it through the house when a thought occurred to me that stopped me dead in my tracks. I turned to face him, sharply pointing my finger. "You've got other houses, but there are no girlfriends or wives living in them, right?"

The corner of his mouth turned up. "Careful, Tamara, you're crossing into dangerous territory with that question. Are you acknowledging that you're entitled to that information, that you and I are involved?"

"Don't get lawyerly. Just answer the question."

He smirked. "No. No wives. No other girlfriends. Honestly, at the rate your life explodes into chaos, you're about all I can handle these days."

Mercutio sniffed, like he found that amusing.

I bit off a smart remark, knowing there was some—okay,

a lot—of truth to that. I glanced down at Merc and grumbled, "I guess he does kind of have a point."

THE DRIVE WAS slow and scary. I kept clicking the high beams on and off. I couldn't tell if they helped me see through the fog better than regular lights or not.

And of course, Bryn's sports car would have to be black, all the harder to follow in the dark and fog. He'd given me directions, but he'd said that the road to turn off onto wasn't marked and was partially cloaked by bushes. Just what I needed. But I guess the fog had let us drive out of town unnoticed.

When Bryn slowed down to about two miles per hour, I knew the turn must be close. I also thought that his car must've been furious. Cars that can go from zero to a hundred in three seconds aren't meant to be driven at speeds that nonjoggers can jog faster than.

It was lucky that I was right behind him because I couldn't see the way even after I'd made the turn. For all I knew, I was following Bryn into a ditch.

We bumped along on uneven ground.

"Is this a road?" I asked Mercutio who was standing on the passenger seat with his front paws on the dash.

He gave a soft yowl that I took to mean yes. I chewed my lip and tried to stay centered behind Bryn, hoping his night vision was as good as Mercutio's.

Finally, Bryn pulled sideways into a makeshift parking spot, his headlights casting some light on a small brown brick house with white trim.

By the time Merc and I got out, Bryn already had the front door open and was transferring bags to the entryway.

As Bryn came to my car, another light blinked on inside the house. I froze for a second, then pulled out my gun.

"Don't shoot my butler," Bryn said from behind me, my suitcase in his hand.

Sure enough, Mr. Jenson appeared in the doorway. He

wore a white monogrammed terry cloth robe over his striped pajamas, and despite the fact that we'd obviously just woken him up, his hair was neatly combed.

"This house comes with a Mr. Jenson! Why didn't you say so? I would've made a break for it so much sooner!" I said.

"Good morning, Miss Tamara. Mr. Lyons."

"Sorry we woke you up," I said.

"Think nothing of it," Mr. Jenson said, bending to pat Mercutio who was circling him in a way that said, "Have you got any raw chicken for me?"

"Go back to bed, Jenson. We are," Bryn said.

"Yeah, go back to bed, Mr. Jenson. Bryn's going to bed, and Merc and I can find our own way around the kitchen. You know us."

Bryn gave me a look that said he wasn't too happy about me revising the plan, but I had stuff to do, plus I was hungry.

"I shall vacate the second bedroom for Miss Tamara," Mr. Jenson said.

"No," Bryn and I both said at the same time.

"I'll find somewhere to sleep. The couch . . ." I mumbled, my cheeks pinking up, aware that Bryn looked ready to contradict me any second. "Or, you know, somewhere."

"Very good," Mr. Jenson said without turning a hair. "I shall be up promptly at six. Please don't hesitate to knock sooner should you require assistance with anything."

With that Mr. Jenson went back down the hall. I glared at Bryn, but he just grabbed our bags.

"Gentlemen don't kiss and tell," I said.

"I didn't tell him anything."

"You told him plenty," I snapped, following him into the bedroom. "We don't need everyone knowing, you know. We're not even sure where this is going."

"One of us isn't sure," he said, toeing off his shoes. I looked around the small room. There was a black-and-white quilt on the bed and a matching black-and-white rug over the hardwood floor.

Bryn stripped down and climbed in bed. Mercutio batted my leg to try to get my attention, but I was still focused on Bryn who'd lain back on the soft white pillows.

"Why'd you get a second house so close to your regular house?"

"I wanted property on another of the tor's ley lines."

"Oh. Well, it's not as fancy as your regular place, but I like it," I said as Bryn closed his eyes.

"I like it, too, now that you're here," he said without opening his eyes.

I silently scolded my limbs, which were itching to crawl into bed with him. "You've got to watch out for the charming ones. They're really hard to resist," I whispered to Mercutio as I turned off the light and closed the door.

Merc dashed down the hallway with the kind of zero-to-something-fast speed that Bryn's car would've admired. Plus, Merc was silent in a way that nothing man-made would ever be. You gotta hand it to whoever designed kitties.

I stretched. "You ready to do some magic, Merc?"

Merc yowled softly.

"What?"

He put a paw on the fridge.

"Okay, okay. Breakfast first."

I HAD APPLEWOOD bacon and biscuits with orange marmalade. Mercutio had his bacon with a side of smoked ham. He's mostly a carnivore, though he doesn't say no to heavy cream very often.

I got out a large bowl and filled it with water. "I've gotta find that brooch, Mercutio. You're here. Bryn's right down the hall. That's sure to give my power a boost, don't you think?"

I sat at the table and stared down into the bowl. I gave the water a swirl with my finger and watched it move. When my eyes lost their focus, I began to see dancing shapes, but when I concentrated on the brooch or on Bryn's mom's face, they dissolved.

"Maybe I need some dirt?" I took off my boots, tucking

my socks neatly inside them so I was left with bare feet. Then I grabbed a dish towel and put it near the kitchen door. No need for me to track in muddy footprints when Mr. Jenson had the kitchen tile so clean.

I opened the door and shivered. It was extremely cold out. I carried the glass bowl as the fog wrapped around me. The cement steps led to the woods that surrounded the house. I sat sideways on the steps with my legs dangling to the ground. I dug my toes in the damp earth and stared down into the bowl again.

Mercutio sat next to me and pawed the door closed, which plunged us into darkness.

"Now I can't even see the bowl, Merc," I complained, but my voice trailed off as my eyes adjusted. The mist rose from the grass, and so did a vaporous image of Cassandra Lyons. Even made of fog she was really, really pretty. Then more images began to rise. Two scowling men. I cocked my head. The first looked like Bryn, but I realized that it was a younger Lennox. The other man looked familiar, too. His eyes stared through her and focused on me. His body was solid, robust, and appealing, but his eyes were cold, like icicles scraping my skin.

Cassandra's image shifted, melting in fear, just as I recognized him. A younger, clean-shaven John Barrett.

The moment I realized who he was, a gust of wind knocked me back. As I tried to catch myself, the bowl tipped off my lap and crashed onto the steps. I tumbled down, rolling over the broken glass and landing hard on the ground, banging my elbow and hip, scraping my palms and scuffing my knee.

I caught my breath and a sharp spike of pain dug into my eyes. I groaned, grabbing my head. The bacon and biscuits churned in my belly. I didn't understand. I hadn't even hit my head, but it hurt more than anything. My stomach heaved and a disgusting acid taste burned up my throat.

I hung my splitting head, breathing deep through my mouth, the curtain of my hair seeming to block the fresh air. Sweat popped up on the back of my neck and between my breasts. I opened my jaws wider, gasping.

"Just what do you think you're doing?" a female voice asked.

The rushing sound in my ears quieted as the pain slowly eased.

"Tammy," Edie said sharply. "Can you hear me?"

"Kind of." I raised my right hand and rubbed my palm against my jeans. "What's up?"

"What are you doing?" she asked.

I ignored her question at first, trying to concentrate. I remembered Bryn saying magic had backlashed and given him a terrible headache when he'd cast the two-plagues counterspell. Was my headache John Barrett's doing? Because I'd seen him?

"I was looking for that brooch I told you about. I think someone powerful is trying to block me from finding it."

"Melanie didn't send it, but she did send you spellbooks by overnight mail. They should be at the house."

"Good," I said, standing up with chattering teeth.

"Whose house is this?"

"Bryn Lyons's."

"Haven't you heard anything we've said? Lenore didn't put that family on the forbidden list for no reason."

"Prove it," I said. I walked carefully up the stairs, hissing in pain as a shard of glass cut my foot.

"I don't have to prove it. You shouldn't need me to prove it."

I looked over my shoulder at her, narrowing my eyes. "Oh really? I should just take everything that you and Momma and Aunt Mel say at face value, huh? Because you guys would never lie to me about anything important, right? Like what I am? Or the fact that you're not my only living—and dead—family?"

I hobbled into the kitchen.

"What's happening?" Bryn asked. "Were you spell-casting? I was just falling asleep when I felt your magic flare and then got another killer headache."

"I'm sorry," I said, feathering my fingers over his temple. "I didn't know it would wake you up or hurt your head, too."

"Are you bleeding?" Bryn asked sharply, putting me in a chair and lifting my wounded foot.

"That's enough!" Edie snapped. "Don't let him touch your blood."

I stared at her defiantly, not saying a word to stop him.

"There's a piece of glass. I can't get a good enough grip. Hang on. I'll grab some tweezers," he said.

"Thank you."

Bryn started to move away, but paused when he passed Edie. He spun and squinted. "She's here. Your aunt." He took a step forward, and Edie floated back, away from him. He put his thumb to his mouth and licked my blood off it very deliberately.

"Yuck!" I said, but the power arced between us with a sizzling energy that stole my breath.

"What do you want?" he demanded, staring at Edie now that he could see her using my magic.

"You'll leave her alone, Lyons," she said. "Or you'll pay the price." A funnel of icy air spun around us.

I reached for Bryn's arm, but was too late to stop him.

"*Dead to rights,*" Bryn snapped, clenching his fist on the air.

Edie's scream shattered the quiet and then the green light that usually formed an orb faded in shreds.

"Bryn, no!"

He looked at me with dark blue-gray eyes. "She'd be wise not to threaten me. She's a powerful spirit, but she's dead, and I know death magic. I learned my lesson the hard way, but I learned it well."

"Bryn, she's my family. Whatever else she is, she's watched over me since I was a baby. I can't let you hurt her."

He didn't respond.

"Please don't make me choose," I said.

"I'm not the one who's making you choose. I'll share you with your family. They need to learn to share you with me." He walked away. "I'll be back."

Merc licked up a bloody smudge from the tile.

"Merc, don't. That's all mixed with dirt."

He looked between the smudges and me, clearly unde-
cided. Since he ate dirty rodents, lizards, and birds all the
time and used his tongue to give himself a bath, I guess I
could see his point.

Bryn returned, and I said, "Can I ask you something
about your mom?"

"Yeah," he said, pulling a chair over so that he was sitting
in front of me with my foot on his lap.

"Did she know John Barrett?"

"John Barrett? Not that I know of." He held my ankle
firmly, which was good because I tried to jerk it back when
he dug the glass out with the tweezers. The sharp pain died
down to a throb when he finished.

"That hurt!"

"Sorry." He bent forward and kissed the top of my foot,
sending a warm swirl of magic up my leg. He held up the
shard, which was at least an inch thick. "Had to get it out."
He tossed the piece of glass into the trash. "You want a
couple swallows of whiskey before we wash out the wound?"

I wrinkled my nose at the thought of the stinging pain
that would go along with cleaning the cut.

Bryn opened a cupboard and took down a crystal decanter.
He set two glasses on the counter and put a double shot in
each. He handed me a glass and swallowed his in a couple
of gulps.

When he turned to the counter, he set the glass in the sink
and braced himself there for a moment. "I know family's
important, Tamara. I promise you, no one understands that
better than I do." His breath came out in a ragged sigh. "But
where is yours when you need them?"

I took a swallow of the smooth woodsy scotch, and it
made me cough a little. "Gone," I said. I didn't bother to tell
him that Aunt Melanie couldn't come because she was
trapped and Momma couldn't come because she was underhill with the faeries.

When they'd left, I was still living a normal human life.
They didn't know that I'd get my powers and have to face

werewolves and warlocks and all. On the other hand, they'd left me alone.

"Gone," he echoed. "You're supposed to face the Conclave alone. And I'm supposed to give up what I want without a fight."

I drank the rest of the scotch. "Yeah, I guess." I licked my lips, which were numb from the liquor.

"Giving up what I want is not something I do."

24

I KEPT EXPECTING dawn to burn through the fog, but it didn't. I sat on the bed, looking out the window, uneasiness tickling my bones. It was like the sun hadn't risen at all.

"Darkness," Bryn said. "One of the ten plagues of Egypt, if memory serves."

I clucked my tongue. "People in Duvall aren't going to handle this well. They're going to need reassurance. You should tell the mayor and the city council to start calling folks, to tell them everything's going to be okay."

"If I call them and they tell me that I'm wanted for questioning in Gwen's murder, I'll have to go in to the police station. But if I keep my cell phone off, I can say the battery died so I missed my messages. It's called plausible deniability."

"Right, good lawyer thinking." I chewed my lip. "My cell phone's in a grave or a pile of dirt in the Macon Hill Woods where Gwen buried me. If anybody's trying to reach me, I've got plausible denial-ability, too. I also have plausible missing-my-important-messages-ability. What if someone needs me?"

He smiled. "The mayor, the city council, the police, and the volunteer firefighters are all still in town, Tamara."

"Yeah, but they were all in town last week, and who had to fight the werewolves and faeries?" I demanded. "You and me, that's who," I said as if he needed reminding.

He picked up the house phone from the dresser and set it on the bed next to me.

"Keep it short, and don't call anyone who could trace the call."

"The second part's no problem," I said, punching in my friend Georgia Sue's number. "But Georgia Sue never had a long conversation that wouldn't have been better if it'd gone on for another forty minutes."

"Hello?" Georgia said hesitantly.

"It's Tammy Jo," I said.

"Tammy Jo? I been callin' you! Everyone has! Girl, where's your phone?"

"I lost it."

"Tammy Jo, you can't believe what people are saying. It's just silly is what it is. Of course, you're not a Satanworshipper! Everybody knows on Horror Movie Weekend, you closed your eyes through every minute of *Halloween*. And that Freddy Jooger from *A Nightmare on Elm Street* nearly scared you to death."

"Freddy Krueger."

"Whatever. I'm just sayin'. After that, am I really supposed to believe you'd give Satan, of all people, a jingle? Please! I told Jenna and her friends that I've known you since we were two years old and that I was your maid of honor for heaven's sake. You got married in a church. Well, I guess the marriage didn't work out in the end, but it's not like you'd thumb your nose at God on purpose. I just don't believe that for a minute." She finally took a breath. "Now, you haven't gotten mixed up with Satan, have you?"

"Of course not."

"Now see, I knew that. All right, so come on over to my house. We'll get Kenny and Zach's brother to take us over to set the record straight with Reverend Fuller."

"That's a really good idea. Maybe later today or first thing tomorrow, I can fit that in."

"Oh, Tammy Jo, I really think we need to clear things up right away. You know how some people can get. Not everyone mind you, but some people are quick to think the worst. Do you know that Miss Cookie hung a cross in the window of the bakery just to prove that her Devil's Food Cake isn't really the work of you-know-who?"

"For the love of Hershey."

"You know how people can be. They get carried away, and that Jenna's a real pistol, loaded for gossip and firing with both barrels."

"What are people saying about the fog?"

"Well, that it's a sign that the world's coming to an end, of course. You know that group on Sycamore always says that. The car wash machine breaks down. It's a sign. A couple of flowerbeds die. It's a sign. At this rate, the world would've ended twenty-seven times since August. This fog is just weather, that's all. It can't always be sunny. That's not normal. This is Texas, not California. We go in for a little rain and fog now and again. I'll tell you what else: Kenny's been telling people flat out, 'Look if it's the end days, you'd better get to praying instead of spreading gossip about a girl who's never done any harm to you and yours.'"

I smiled. Georgia's husband, Kenny, was a good friend to me. After we got past the Conclave and their plagues, I'd have to take him a blackberry pie, his favorite.

"Besides, we all read Revelations. If it's the end times, where are the four cowboys of the apocalypse? Shouldn't they be trotting down Main Street? I'll tell you, I'm getting so sick of people quoting scripture willy-nilly. The Bible ain't a country song with twenty-five lines. It's complicated and we'd better be careful about how we interpret it. Maybe God'll hear those Sycamore folks calling everything a sign, and He'll start thinking Duvall's ready for the end when there's plenty of us who aren't. We just got that brand-new jukebox for Jammers, and people are enjoying the heck out of it. All I'm saying is, I don't think we should give God any ideas about ending things. Just let Him take His time. He'll do it when He's ready."

I smiled. "When you're right, you're right," I said.

Bryn tapped his wrist to remind me that I was supposed to keep it short.

"Georgia Sue, I've got to go, but let me ask you one more quick thing."

"What's that, sugar?"

"Is everything quiet at the police station? They've seemed kind of out of sorts and strapped for help lately. I'd hate to think of them being overwhelmed with Zach gone and some of the guys on light duty after last week."

"So far as I know everything's fine. They're still investigating that shootout at the benefit, but they seem to be handling it just fine. They're sure mad. Wouldn't want to be anyone who was involved in planning that disaster. They say one of those gunmen was kin to Mindy Glusky who's from Dyson. He's part of some nutty survivalist group that spends every weekend in the woods training for a war against the government or, you know, whoever turns up. I guess they had a whole arsenal out there! Mindy says she might have mentioned all the strange goings-on around Duvall to some people from Dyson, but that she never expected anyone to come to Duvall to check things out, let alone to bust in on our benefit with guns. I'm not sure that the sheriff believes her though."

I definitely don't! Maybe Mindy hadn't expected the gunmen to crash the benefit so violently, but she had definitely given them my name and told them I was a witch or they wouldn't have been looking for me in the first place. I wondered if Jenna and Lucy had been in on the plan to involve the militia guys.

"Well, I hope they solve it. I have to go, so I'll talk to you later," I said and hung up. I looked at Bryn. "They haven't found Gwen's body yet."

TURNS OUT HAVING the sky totally obscured is unsettling to someone with celestial magic, so Bryn spent the morning working on a spell that wouldn't drain his power, but would be powerful enough to overcome the fog. He also wanted to avoid getting a whopper headache from Barrett's magical backlash when he cast it. A pretty tall order.

Bryn being busy was actually a good thing because it meant I could slip out without him noticing. I'd decided that I was going to get the Cassandra brooch back before the end of the day. I hadn't figured out how yet, but I had never let lack of a firm plan stop me. The trouble was that even if I got someone to get John Barrett out of his room, where I suspected I'd find the brooch, Barrett would feel me cross the wards on the room and come rushing back like Gwen had. And even though I didn't have a set plan, not getting caught in the middle of a burglary was sort of a standing goal of mine.

I drove to my house. The midday darkness was eerie, even with the streetlights still on. I spotted a couple of fender benders in my neighborhood.

The construction guys were busy working. Apparently they weren't going to let a little thing like a plague of darkness get in the way of a paycheck. I decided they were right about the fact that we should all keep to our usual routine, so I ate half a bag of Hershey's miniatures to raise my blood chocolate level.

Despite the fact that I was limping on my sore foot, they didn't pay me much mind as I found the package from Aunt Melanie, which was far heavier than I'd expected. I loaded it into my trunk, then went back in and cleaned out my cupboards of all Aunt Mel's herbs. I carried the two shopping bags full of plant extracts and essential oils to my car and placed them carefully in the trunk surrounded with a couple of extra bags of my clothes.

Just as I shut the trunk, a flashlight beam caught me in the eyes. I jumped and reached for my gun, but stopped when a woman's voice said, "Hey there, Tammy Jo. I'm so glad I ran into you!"

My hand hovered at the small of my back as I squinted. Was this a new DeeDAW member?

"Marsha Crane of Crane Realty. Your friends from England mentioned that you've been thinking about moving, and, with their interest in Duvall properties, I thought I'd have a look at your house."

What the Sam Houston? "The house isn't for sale, and it's not going to be for sale."

"Okay," she said cheerfully, "but just remember that if your property goes on the market late, the buying frenzy may be over, and you won't be able to get the best price. Just today I've gotten two new listings. It's going to become a buyers' market soon, and I just want you to have all the information you need. They were specifically interested in your house, or I wouldn't be here. It's a good opportunity for you to get—"

"Not. For. Sale. And you shouldn't be rushing into any sales between townspeople and out-of-town visitors. I've heard those out-of-towners don't have nearly the capital they pretend to," I said, though I hadn't heard any such thing. I figured that since she was in sales, she wouldn't want buyers who couldn't buy.

"Uh-huh. Well, I don't know where you're getting your information, but the bank they're using in Dallas confirmed that ten million dollars was wired from London. Now, would you mind if I took a quick peek inside your house? I'm interested in how the renovations are coming along."

"Yes, I would mind," I said, blocking her way. I gave her arm a tug to turn her around. I pointed down the driveway to where I assumed she'd parked her car. "Go on now."

She clucked her tongue in disappointment and stalked off.

I climbed in my car and had just about made it off my street when someone tapped my back bumper with their car. Probably Marsha. I knew there couldn't be much damage, so I just waved a hand out the window in a "Don't worry about it" gesture. Apparently though whoever it was did want to worry about it because she followed me. Not an easy task in the foggy dark.

When I finally pulled over, I kept a sharp eye on the

rearview mirror. The moment I saw Lucy and Jenna Reitgarten emerge, I put my foot back on the gas pedal. I zoomed around the corner with a white-knuckle grip.

Flipping my high beams on and off, I barreled along to the main intersection. I couldn't see anyone coming in the crosswise traffic, but then I couldn't see ten feet in front of me. I held my breath and made the turn.

I exhaled and slowed down, not wanting to come up on another car too fast to stop. I shook my head. It was hard having a high-speed chase while going only five miles per hour, but there it was.

I looked in my rearview for headlights, but didn't see any. Then I heard metal crumpling. I jumped at the sound, but my car kept driving smoothly ahead. The crash was behind me.

Lucy and Jenna. Well, that's what they got for coming after me.

I wondered who they'd run into. For some reason, I pictured it being a police car full of deputies coming to get me for questioning. I pictured them comparing notes with the Reitgartens and coming to the conclusion that I was a public menace. I shuddered. A vivid imagination . . . not always a good thing.

I only went down a few blocks on Main Street before pulling into the parking lot of the ice cream shop, which was closed for winter. I maneuvered my car behind a Dumpster for maximum camouflage and popped the trunk. Retrieving the big box, I opened it and peered inside. A pair of old spellbooks. My heart raced. Family spellbooks. Finally!

I took out the top one, fingering the brown leather cover with the gold *M* embossed on it in fancy script. I opened it and scanned the pages. There were recipes and spells for truth serum, sleep serum, and memory-enhancement serum. Spells for finding things and for cloaking things. Potions for good luck, bad luck, a flawless complexion, silky hair, and seventeen different protection spells to guard against all kinds of dangers. And not once did a spell call for anything impossible to come by like the tooth of a beheaded monarch or a chunk of chain mail as my medieval spellbook often did. At the top of each page was the name of the spell and the initials of the witch who'd written and perfected it. Occasionally there were handwritten notations and addendums.

I set the book on the passenger seat and looked in the box at the other book. The custom cover had two large letters in fancy script. They were intertwined. *L* and *E*. Lenore and Edie. My heart sped up. Aunt Mel had sent me Edie's very own book. Edie must have known, must have agreed to let me use it. That made me feel as good as Merc with a mouthful of lizard.

I flipped it open and found flowers pressed into the opening pages. Poetry and verses from their favorite writers. Photographs. At first I thought it was just a scrapbook, but then I realized that each page contained a concealed pocket. I drew out the hidden contents, one by one.

All sorts of spells for generating power and doing various things . . . the most important of which were the ones for conjuring spirits, doing glamours, seeing into the future, and attaching a soul to a beloved object.

I hugged the book to me. Getting family spells was as exciting as finding buried treasure, and I suddenly knew how I was going to search John Barrett's room without tripping the security wards. I was going to get him to invite me in.

25

A NAGGING LITTLE voice reminded me that I'd seen Lennox Lyons in that last vision, too, and that there had been blood on his door handle. A part of me argued that searching his place would be easier. I could probably find a spare key to the guesthouse somewhere in the main one, and if the security guys caught me, I could always just tell Bryn the truth. I winced. That was the problem. I didn't want Lennox to be guilty of killing Gwen or, worse, of having something to do with Cassandra's death. How much would that hurt Bryn? So maybe I'd come up with some other excuse, but at least I needed to know the truth myself.

I went to Bryn's mansion. Security Pete told me that John Barrett and Mrs. Thornton had been by, but when he'd told them that we weren't home, they'd left.

I found spare keys for the guesthouse in a kitchen drawer and slipped them into my pocket. I picked up the security phone and got the phone number for the guesthouse from Pete. I didn't tell him why I wanted it, and he didn't ask. It was pretty convenient, his seeming to be willing to let me do whatever I wanted.

When I called, Lennox answered on the third ring.

"Hello? Lennox?"

"Speaking," he said.

"It's Tammy Jo Trask."

"And?"

"Bryn needs your help at the Corsic Creek Bridge." I hoped sending him across town would give me enough time to do a proper search.

"What sort of help? And why there?"

I chewed on my lip. "He didn't tell me."

"And you have no idea what's happening?"

"Nope."

"Hmm."

"So are you going to help him or what?" I asked impatiently.

"I suppose I will."

"Don't sound worried or anything. He's just your son, after all."

Lennox hung up on me.

"Jerk," I mumbled, putting the receiver down a little too hard. "Sorry, phone. Shouldn't bang the messenger."

I waited until I saw Lennox's car leave the property before I hurried along the path with a flashlight. The fog would delay his progress to the bridge. I'd have plenty of time. And luckily Bryn was the one who did the wards on the property, not Lennox, so I wouldn't have to worry about tripping them.

I got to the house and unlocked the door, going inside. It smelled faintly of chicory and woodsmoke. He'd had another fire burning recently and this one in the house. I checked through the fireplace ashes, but didn't find anything.

I started with Lennox's room. If I were going to hide a brooch with my dead wife in it, I'd keep it as close to me as possible. His bed linens were rumpled. I pulled them off and made the bed piece by piece to be sure that the brooch wasn't hidden in the covers.

Then I rifled through the drawers. Nada. On the bedside table, there was an empty glass with a little whiskey left in it and a framed wedding picture lying on its back. I picked it up. Lennox in a black tuxedo and Cassandra in a white wedding gown with tons of lace. They looked really young and really happy, each with beaming white smiles.

"Find what you're looking for, Nancy Drew?"

I jumped and spun around to find Lennox in the doorway.

"What are you doing here?" I demanded, standing the picture on the bedside table.

"Shouldn't that be my line?" he asked.

"I'm searching this house," I said. "I thought it would be less awkward if you were gone, but whatever." I wasn't going to act embarrassed or guilty. Lennox Lyons was a half-assed father and a thief. It had only been a couple of weeks since he'd almost gotten me killed. What's more, I'd helped save his life. "You didn't even want to check to see if Bryn needed you? You don't even care?"

"If Bryn needed me, he would've called himself or given you a code word that would've let me know what was needed."

"Oh," I said, going to the closet and opening the door. Lennox put a hand out and shut it forcefully.

"Last night, you had blood on your hands and probably burned bloody clothes. Did you kill Gwen?"

He looked surprised for a moment and then said, "Did you?"

"No, why would I?"

"Why would I?"

"I think you wanted something that she had. Something that used to belong to Cassandra."

"What are you talking about?"

"Either you know, and I don't need to tell you. Or you don't know, and you're better off not knowing."

He grabbed my arms and squeezed them tight. "You will tell me what you're talking about."

"Did you kill Gwen?"

"No. When I got there, she was already dead. Your turn," he said.

"I think she had a brooch that used to belong to your wife."

He let go of my arms with a little shove to push me away from him. "How?"

"Nope, your turn first. Why did you go to see Gwen?"

Lennox rolled his eyes. "To help my son. Gwen was still in love with him. That could've been an advantage during the investigation, but I knew he wouldn't seduce her with you turning up like a bad penny every five minutes."

"So what were you going to do? Promise to help her get rid of me?"

He clucked his tongue. "My turn to ask a question. Where would Gwen have gotten Cassie's brooch from?"

"She stole it from me, and before you ask, I don't know who sent it to me. It came from London. Did Cassandra know John Barrett?"

Lennox shrugged. "Sure. Her family was well connected and so was his, but after she met me, she didn't spend much time with her old set."

"Why not?"

"Because I wanted her all to myself."

Selfish, that sounded like the Lennox I knew. "How did you meet?"

"We were both musicians."

I raised my eyebrows.

"She was classically trained as a cellist and was an excellent composer. She had broad tastes in music and came to a club where my band was playing. A witch and a wizard in a small space. We couldn't help but notice each other."

"Did you fall in love right away?"

"No, of course not. I was a cynic and an up-and-coming rock star. She said at least eight words before I made up my mind about her."

I smiled. "What were they?"

"That's a lovely guitar. Must you mistreat it?"

I laughed softly. "She was wonderful?"

Pain crinkled the skin around his eyes. "She was . . . none of your business," he said.

"She's my business. I didn't ask for her to be, but she is." I paused, then added, "I saw her ghost, and she asked for my help."

"Bollocks."

I drew my brows together in confusion.

"That means I don't believe you. You didn't see her. No one has seen her spirit since the night it left her body."

In that moment, I knew that Bryn wasn't the only Lyons who'd tried to see Cassandra again. "I think that's because someone bound her spirit. Probably with a spell that specifically blocks the people that loved her from finding her."

"Bryn would've broken through it. You have no idea the kind of things he was willing to do to get to her."

"So whoever did the binding was really powerful. Like maybe John Barrett. Did Barrett live in Revelworth at the time that she was murdered there?"

"The murder was solved. There was a magical trail, thick as paste. She'd been there seeing her family and her former teachers. Extremely brilliant and powerful people. If there had been any doubt, any possibility of another person being involved, it would've been found. They loved her, and they were bloodthirsty in their pursuit of justice."

"Where were you when she died?"

There was a haunted look in his eyes. "What does it matter where I was? Not there," he spat. "But I don't take responsibility for her dying alone. It was Cassie and her family who decided she would visit while I was on the road. We fought about it, but she insisted on the timing. She could be so stubborn. I think she thought it would be easier to go on her own. So I finally agreed. I sent them my wife, and they let her get butchered." His voice was raw, like someone had dragged a grater down his throat.

"It must have been very hard for you," I whispered.

He walked down the hall to the liquor cabinet and swigged from a bottle. I trailed after him.

"Lennox, I'm sorry."

"Just go away."

He was in pain. Since I couldn't help, I left him alone with it.

26

BACK AT THE main house, I went to the kitchen and mixed a sleeping serum from the spellbook. Valerian, whiskey, cider, and a dash of nutmeg. I whispered the spell over it and poured it into a vial I'd borrowed from Bryn's potion-making closet.

Then I brewed some tea and filled a basket with patterned teacups and saucers, a large thermos of hot tea, and some scones and small cakes. English people in movies can never resist tea and cakes. With cakes involved, who can blame them?

When I passed the gates at the end of Bryn's property on my way out, two pairs of headlights blinked on. Cars lying in wait.

"Now what?"

I spotted Jenna and Lucy in one of the cars.

"You again," I muttered. I didn't have time to mess around. I wanted to get my burglary over with before the police discovered the dead body. And before the tea in the thermos got cold.

My car jerked as they bumped into it. I blasted my horn to warn them off. A second big bump told me they were doing it on purpose to rattle me. With it too dark for anyone to witness what was happening and with it dark enough for them to claim it was an accident, they were getting bolder.

The other car drew up alongside me. The interior light was on, and I spotted Sue, who was driving. I rolled down my window. Jenna bumped the back of my car again, making me lurch against my seat belt and bite my tongue. I shook my fist out the window, not that they'd be able to see it.

Sue's car swerved again, but I managed to avoid getting hit by moving all the way to the left and scraping my tires against the curb. This was crazy. What if there had been a parked car? I'd have sideswiped it and felt compelled to leave a note. Could I afford higher insurance premiums? No, I could not.

Sue's car rolled along beside me, not giving me an inch of room, and I realized it was only a matter of time until a parked car popped up in front of me. Then they'd have me boxed in on all sides.

"I don't think so." I pressed my foot down and sped up. My lights flashed on the back of a parked car and I swung my wheel to keep from hitting it.

Unfortunately for Sue, she had sped up with me and I rammed the edge of her car when I'd darted out to avoid the parked one. She careened sideways, jumped the opposite curb, and ran into a tree. Poor tree.

I drove farther to see if Jenna and Lucy would help their friend or stay in pursuit. Jenna didn't even slow down. I should've known. Jenna doesn't know the meaning of friendship.

I sped up after the stop sign, drawing her forward. Then I hit the brakes, and she banged into me. I threw my car into park, then jumped out and raced back to Jenna's. I slammed the butt of my gun twice against the driver's side window. Both she and Lucy shrieked. Lucy with fear. Jenna with fury.

The window shattered, and I socked Jenna in the cheek to stun her. Then I reached in, turned off the car, and yanked out her keys.

"I don't have time for this. You need to go on home."

Jenna held her cheek and glared at me.

"Y'all started it," I said, my knuckles smarting. As I

walked away, I opened and closed my fist. I'm not usually violent. For a lot of years, the only thing I whipped was cream. Actually, before I'd come into my powers a couple weeks earlier, I'd never been in a real fight in my whole life. Mostly I got along with people, and any tiffs at school had been minor. Plus, Zach had always been around. Zach and his brothers didn't put up with bullies. I had a small pang of missing Zach, but pushed him from my mind.

A close look at my crumpled back bumper made me shake my head and frown. I needed to send the Reitgartens a bill. I guess I'd shocked them with my window-smashing, cheek-socking routine, because instead of getting out of their car to come after me, Jenna and Lucy just screamed out their windows at me. It was real unusual hearing the psalms mixed with four-letter words.

"My herbs and oils better be okay," I grumbled as I got behind the wheel.

I drove to the hotel and circled the parking lot to be sure there were no police cars. Actually, the place looked almost deserted.

I parked on a street a block away from the hotel and hefted my picnic basket. I passed through the wooded lot behind the hotel's property.

Gwen had been in Room 5. Mrs. Thornton was next to her in Room 6. Room 4 was around the corner, so I thought it was more likely that John Barrett would be next door to Mrs. Thornton in Room 7.

I couldn't resist trying to look in Gwen's room, but it was too dark to see the body. Of course, nothing would've changed. If the body had been found, there would've been crime scene tape and flashing lights.

I went to the front door of Room 7 and noted that the light was on inside. I tapped several times. I was just beginning to wonder whether he'd gone out and left the light on, when he opened the door.

His eyebrows rose in surprise, then he smiled, his eyes twinkling. I had to remind myself that he was a homicidal maniac.

"Well, Tammy, please come in," he said. "Mrs. Thornton was worried that you and Bryn had absconded. I didn't think it likely, but when we didn't find you at home . . ."

I glanced around the room. Fish everywhere! On the wallpaper, bedspread, and the tablecloth on the small round table.

"Yes, Bryn and I went out early this morning. We should've called to let you know, but things were kind of hectic. Anyway, I wanted to talk some things over with you. I brought tea and cakes. May I?" I asked, pointing to the table where there were a couple of open files. The file boxes under the table looked exactly like the ones that had been in Gwen's room.

"Yes, please," he said, closing the files and setting them on the edge of the bed, which was neatly made. That seemed weird. If the maid had cleaned the rooms, why hadn't she called the police? If the maid hadn't been, then Mr. Barrett was really neat for a world leader/psycho killer.

I laid out the cakes and poured tea, putting some of the serum into his tea when his back was turned.

I really wanted to know if Mrs. Thornton was in her room. I would've mentioned her and told him to invite her over for tea, too, so I could drug her and search her room as well, but I didn't trust that I could put anything over on the Winterhawk. She'd probably see right through me. Plus, it was my first poisoning. Starting with one victim seemed more sensible.

I'd made sure that I brought cups with different floral patterns. I took a sip from the yellow rose cup and left the poisoned purple rose cup for Mr. Barrett. I put scones and double chocolate pecan cookies on small plates.

He moved a piece of rolled paper off his chair and set it on the bed. It partway unrolled, and I could see it was a map of Duvall.

"It's the town?" I asked, walking over.

"Indeed," he said, sitting down and taking a bite of an iced cranberry-orange scone.

I unrolled the map further, cocking my head at the high-lighted sections of town. I looked up at the legend, but there wasn't any explanation of the highlighter colors. I leaned closer and realized that the map hadn't come that way. Mr. Barrett had done the highlighting himself.

"What do these colors mean?"

"Oh, just some planning we're doing. You said that you wanted to talk to me about some things?"

I went back to the table, gratified that he'd drunk half of his cup of tea and poured some more.

I took a few swallows myself and had a cookie. "Bryn said there are whole towns in England with magical people."

"Yes. Revelworth being the most famous," he said with a smile. "Completely inhabited by witches and wizards, a place of collected wisdom and power. There's a very long waiting list of people who would dearly like to live there."

"Well, Duvall's a long way from England."

"Yes, it is. Revelworth is where your grandmother lives. Did you know? You could stay in the village in your family house. Such an incredible opportunity. Many would envy you." He yawned, and so did I. In fact, my throat felt strange, kind of prickly. I looked sharply at my cup. Definitely the yellow rose. Definitely not the one I'd poured the serum into.

"A wise witch would use any advantages she was given in life, especially foretelling that never fails," he said.

"What?"

"Your great-great-grandmother Lenore was a seer whose every prophecy has come true. She left your family instructions that you choose to ignore."

I paled. "Who says she was never wrong?"

"It's known. Her chronicles about the wizarding world—all completely accurate. I understand that those about your family have never been inaccurate either."

"Maybe not yet. There's always a chance, and fortune favors the brave," I mumbled, Bryn's words tumbling out unintentionally.

"Sometimes. At others, fortune finishes the fool."

"I thought you wanted me to be with Bryn? To be bet—bait—to lure him to Engle—England?" My tongue felt slippery. I smacked it against the roof of my mouth. Something was definitely wrong. Had a drop of the potion dripped into my cup? It shouldn't have; I hadn't reached over it with the vial.

"Mmm." He smiled, his eyes twinkling again. "Yes, there's a sweet, silly girl. Ignore that which will protect you to win the approval of strangers." His lids drifted half closed and he forced them back up. "Unimpressive."

"I'm not trying to win your approval." My chest tightened. I needed to keep my mouth shut and I wanted to, but suppressing my words was like trickling acid down my throat. It burned until I couldn't stand it. "Bryn risked everything for me. Plus, he's ten flavors of amazing and more delicious than wedding cake. So no, I don't want to believe that Bryn's bad for me. I won't until I see some proof."

"When someone shows you proof, you'll still refuse to see it." He closed his eyes and licked his lips. "Blinded by love. A story as old as magic. I know it too well." Mr. Barrett's head plunked down on the table.

I took a couple of breaths, shivering at what he'd said. "Sure it's an old stairwell—story. People want love to work out. Why wouldn't they? What's better than love? Nothing, that's what." I rubbed my throat, not able to keep myself from talking. "Truth serum. You poisoned me, too, didn't you?" I ran a hand through my hair, my scalp damp with sweat. "It's wrong for you to look so much like Santa Claus. He'd never poison his elves. Or his reindeer. Or the people who live in the houses he visits." My head buzzed, and I stumbled from the chair.

The fish on the wallpaper seemed to swish toward the stripes. I picked up the phone and called the front desk. "Hello?"

"Yes, can I help you?"

"I like fish and all, but don't you think you've gone a bit far with it? Wallpaper, plus bedspreads, plus tablecloths? It's too much." I hung up. Several catfish flopped off the wall while others swam around the light and then dove toward my head. "Don't get too rowdy, you fishes. Stop that swimming off the wallpaper. I have a gun, you know."

I tripped, over my foot I think, and landed hard on the carpet. I stared at the file boxes.

"I came here for you," I murmured. "That's why I brought him tea. I don't like him. I don't trust him. He's dangerous. Right now he's sleeping," I babbled. I pulled out the boxes. They were locked, of course, but I dug through John Barrett's pockets and found several small keys. "You Conclave types are always underestimating me. That's your big mistake." I unlocked the boxes and pulled out the files.

The letters swam before me. "Just you stop that moving. You're not fish. You don't have fins. It's one thing for the wallpaper to dance around, but letters are supposed to stay still."

I dumped the boxes out and, in the box that had been under two others, I found a small velvet case. I opened it, and there she was.

"Here you are, Nassandra. Cassandra. Bryn's mom."

There was a sharp rap on the door.

"John?" a voice called.

"Oh no!" I whispered. "Somebody's here." I closed the cover on the brooch and clutched it tighter. "Sounds like the winnerhawk."

"John, open the door."

"He can't. He's asleep!" I called. "Well, he's drugged asleep." I giggled. "Gotcha," I said, giving John Barrett a pinch as I stood up. I staggered into the bathroom, slamming the door closed. I locked the door as I heard the front door banging open.

"Probably picked the lock. Standard spy stuff." I unlocked the bathroom window and shoved it open. "I'd like to pick locks. Not all locks. Not wanting to be a spy or anything."

The bathroom door rattled.

I cocked my head. The window was really too small for me unless I could turn myself into a pixie or something. Only I didn't know how.

"Shh. Be very quiet." I stepped into the shower and closed the curtain.

A moment later the door opened. I heard her pass the tub, and I couldn't stay quiet. I yanked the curtain back.

"I'm here," I announced.

She spun very quickly, but not quickly enough for her to stop me from running into her when I tripped on the tub's lip. We crashed to the floor, my knees slamming the tile and searing with pain.

"Sorry. Sorry about that." I got up with throbbing knees and ran from the room, banging into the bed and then the door frame as I fled.

Something struck my back and knocked me down. I scrambled to my feet, ran around the corner of the building, and dashed into the woods.

I heard footfalls. She would catch up. She would get me!

"Help me, tree," I called, running straight for a trunk. I couldn't stop. I closed my eyes, expecting an impact, but it didn't come. Someone grabbed my waist and pulled me off the ground.

I was too scared to move or open my eyes. Was it the kidnapper? Scarface? I had to know. In the distance, I heard crunching leaves. I was lying on something hard and narrow. I couldn't figure that out. What was happening?

I opened my eyes and a thick layer of fog was all around me. So was a thick tree branch. The tree had picked me up.

"She'll never find me up here," I whispered with a smile, patting the branch. "Never."

I turned my head from side to side and spotted a small salmon-pink light. A firefly? A dancing bug?

The light landed on my nose. The blurred image was hard to focus on, but I saw a silvery figure with green speckled wings. I also heard a very high-pitched voice, almost unrecognizable. Faery. A tiny one.

"I'm one of you," I whispered. "It's how come I can talk to the trees sometimes." Then I told her all about my life, from as far back as I could remember.

27

THE OVERWHELMING BUZZ wore off, but I knew I wasn't back to normal, and I was terrified of climbing down the forty feet to the ground. I marveled at the fact that a tree had swept me up at my request. I couldn't normally communicate with the plants and trees, but sometimes the fae in me seemed to rise up and communicate. Mostly when something disrupted my ability to think. Get me drunk or bespelled, and I can do Scary Faery with the best of them.

I had no idea how much time had passed. Was John Barrett awake? Were he and the Winterhawk looking for me? Had the police come? The need to talk burned in my throat. I wanted to call the police and report the murder. I wanted to make a statement about everything that had happened and was still happening around town, but at least a part of me knew that that would be a disaster, so I whispered a statement under my breath.

I tucked the velvet brooch case into my bra to secure it and then began to climb down. Stretching my foot made the wound in my foot hurt. I muttered in annoyance, but didn't slow.

I was almost to the ground when I realized with a start that

I could see it. The fog had lifted. It was still overcast, like there'd been rain, but it wasn't black-as-night out. I wondered if that was because the magic had dissipated when I knocked out John Barrett or if Bryn had done a spell to make it happen.

I hobbled through the wooded area to the street where I'd parked. I held my breath until I saw my car. Banged up, but still there. I hurried to it and got in. Just as I put the key in the ignition, I heard a child crying. I looked around. Where had it come from?

I started the car and rolled down my windows. I wasn't very far from the school.

"Which way? Which way?" I whispered. Another high-pitched cry that chilled me worse than the wind. I swung the wheel and turned toward where I thought the sound had come from. Vines swayed in the breeze, like they were beckoning me west.

"This way," I murmured, inexplicably drawn. Straight, left, then left again.

I spotted a flash of a blue sweater moving behind a circle of lawn furniture in the deserted corner of a yard on a dead-end street. I parked my car and climbed out, hurrying over. There were six little girls, probably kindergartners, huddling under a plastic table.

I bent down.

"Hi." I pushed my hair over my shoulder. "Hi there. What happened?"

"We got lost," a little blond girl said.

Another girl with very mussed brown hair and big eyes sniffled as tears spilled down her pudgy cheeks.

"We were walking in a chain, and she let go!" a dark-haired girl said, pointing at a wide-eyed little girl with a short brown bob. I cocked my head. I knew her. She was from my neighborhood. Paige.

"Hi, Miss Tammy," Paige whispered.

"Mrs. Beech is gonna be so mad," the dark-haired girl said.

"No, she won't. She'll be glad you're okay," I said. "She probably feels guilty. Who takes a whole bunch of five-year-olds out for a walk in the pitch dark? I mean I might've last week when I was faeryfied." I clamped my lips closed.

Be quiet. Be careful what you say!

"Come on. I'll take you back to school," I said.

"I'm not going with you. You're a stranger," the dark-haired girl said.

"I don't blame you," I said. "It's good to be careful. But Paige knows me. C'mon," I said, holding out a hand to the crying girl. She crawled to me, and I picked her up. "When I was little, I went to your school. Did you know that?"

I chatted on about my time in kindergarten, and they all decided to follow me. I put them in the backseat, buckling them in as best I could. It was only a couple blocks away.

I started the car and drove around the corner. Then I spotted Jenna's Lexus coming down the block.

"Not again!"

Six little heads jerked to look out the back window.

"They're after me," I said, and then gasped, realizing that Jenna might ram my car again while the backseat was full of little girls. I pulled over sharply. "Everything's going to be okay. I think. I hope. Well, I don't want you to worry. Just stay in the car."

I climbed out and walked a few feet past my trunk and onto the sidewalk. Jenna needed to pull over and park. Then we could talk woman to witch, like normal people. I placed my feet shoulder-width apart and put my fists on my hips in a way I hoped was imposing.

Jenna revved her engine and drove straight for me.

She couldn't be thinking of hopping the curb. She'd bust a tire and crack her axle, or at the very least, mess up her alignment. Plus, her insurance company was sure to have a policy against running over pedestrians.

Jenna didn't slow down. I stood my ground nervously.

The little girls screamed, and the car barreled toward me. I dove out of the way just seconds before the car rammed the curb and jerked over the sidewalk and onto the grass.

I got up and dusted myself off as Jenna and Lucy got out of

the car. Lucy had a length of rope, and, oh my gosh, Jenna had a rifle.

> *She's a danger with that gun*
> *Take it from her, number one!*

I yanked off my boots and socks as I backed up, repeating the incantation. My bare feet touched the grass and I dragged my foot across a tree root, hissing for a moment at the pain as the bandage was wrenched off and the wound reopened.

My blood trickled into the earth.

> *She's a danger with that gun.*
> *Take it from her. number one.*

A tree limb swished down, knocking into Jenna's side. She fell and the gun flew out of her hands when she landed. I heard the girls gasp.

"Close your eyes," I said, covering my eyes for a second to illustrate. "Close them. I don't want you watching."

"We didn't want to resort to weapons," Lucy said. "Especially after Mindy's people got so carried away. They took things too far at City Hall. We never expected that. Mindy's out of the group. But you're sure a gun-toting little miss these days, Tammy Jo, and we have to fight fire with fire."

Jenna reached toward the gun, but the branch whizzed toward the ground, and she had to roll away to keep from getting smacked.

"She's doing it! Did you see that! It's proof!" Jenna screamed, getting to her feet.

Lucy started quoting scripture in a ready-to-rumble voice that sounded like she was about to begin a WWF bout.

"We want you out of this town!" Jenna screeched, rushing toward me.

I put my hands out in front of me, wincing. Without time to think, I just spewed out a spell.

You're dangerous and full of gall
Bottle that rage and make it small.

Jenna disappeared. One minute, she was about to crash into me. The next . . . gone.

My jaw dropped open. The little girls in my car cheered. Lucy trailed off, staring at the spot where Jenna had been.

"Where is she? What have you done with her?" Lucy demanded.

"I—I don't know." I looked around. "She's probably around here somewhere. I don't think I disintegrated her or anything. Pretty sure I didn't."

"You bring her back. You bring her back *right now*!"

"I don't even know where she is. I'm sure she'll turn up though," I said, walking to the rifle. I cocked it open and removed the live shells, then tossed the gun back down. I went to the Lexus and checked the ignition. The keys must've been Jenna's spare set.

"I'll throw these out the window when I get to the end of the block. Don't follow me or I'll have to do a spell on you." I clamped a hand over my mouth. *Don't tell her that! Don't admit anything!*

I grabbed my socks and boots and hustled back to the car. When I opened the door, the little girls smiled and clapped. I tossed my boots onto the passenger seat and got in.

"Told you she was magic," Paige said.

"Will you teach us some magic, Witch Tammy?" the dark-haired girl asked.

"Oh, no. That's—"

"She's not a witch. She's a faery princess!" Paige exclaimed. "Will you show us your pointed ears, Princess Tammy?"

"Oh, honey, I'm not royalty. Princesses don't wear cowboy boots or carry pistols or disintegrate their enemies."

"What do princesses do?"

"Do?" Did they really do anything? I ran through the fairy princesses. Snow White. Gets poisoned and rescued. Sleeping beauty. Gets poisoned and rescued. Cinderella.

Gets locked up on the night of the ball and gets rescued.
"Well, they wear fancy dresses, and people admire them for
their beauty and poise. They're kind of like supermodels.
Real nice to look at, but not doing too much real work once
they become princesses. Being pretty is their job, I guess."

"Well, you're pretty," Paige said, and they all agreed.

"You're pretty and you cast spells! That rocks."

"And sure *you're* going to have cowboy boots. You're
from Texas! Maybe you should get pink cowboy boots."

"With pink glitter!"

"And a pink wand!"

"That sparkles!"

"Magic wands are for wimps. The best witches don't need
them, Bryn told me." I bit my tongue. Literally. I had to stop
talking! The last thing they needed was encouragement or
to learn secrets about real witches and wizards. Stupid truth
serum. How was I supposed to keep a low profile when I kept
having to blurt out the darned truth all the time?

"No wands? Not even just to go with your outfit?" the
blond girl asked.

"Hey, look, here's the school."

"We don't have to go back right now," the dark-haired
girl said. "We could stay with you."

"Yes. We want to!" Paige said.

"Maybe another day." *When I'm not being hunted all over
town, or stuck with the truth as my only conversational option.*
"Mrs. Beech must be real worried," I said, getting out.

A chorus of chirpy arguments rose from the backseat.

"C'mon now. I could get in a lot of trouble for not returning you. You wouldn't want that when I've got bad wizards
to fight."

"Bad wizards," they gasped.

I tugged them out of the car.

"Yes, it's a secret. Can I trust you?" I asked.

They all nodded and crossed their little hearts. I smiled
and gave them each a kiss on the top of the head. "Go on
now. And remember it's our secret!"

When they were safe inside, I leaned up against my car

and cupped my forehead in my hand for a few seconds. Poisoning people and making other people disappear was tiring as all get-out.

I put on my socks and boots before I drove back to Bryn's. I turned into my parking spot a little too fast, fishtailing. I patted the car in apology.

"Hi, Mr. Jenson!" I called when I went into the cottage.

"Miss Tamara," Mr. Jenson said, coming out of the kitchen. He put his finger to his lips to quiet me down.

"Sorry. I've just had the craziest morning. I got in a poisoning contest with the leader of the World Association of Magic and I'm pretty sure I won! Also—"

"There's a situation," he said gravely.

"Another one?" I asked, heaving a sigh. "Bigger than me drugging John Barrett?"

I followed him into the kitchen where Bryn was talking quietly into the phone. I sat down next to him, fidgeting in my chair until he finally hung up.

"Well?" I demanded. "What's happening?"

"Andre's missing."

"Wasn't he trying to be missing? He said—"

"Apparently, he was on his way here. Even though we agreed that he wouldn't come." Bryn rapped his knuckles on the table. "I told him not to."

"Well, you're not the boss of everyone. Maybe he wanted to help you. That's what friends do. Wouldn't you want to help him if he was in trouble? I'd help Georgia Sue. Or Johnny. Or you. Or Zach or Mercutio. Or Mr. Jenson or Steve—"

"Miss Tamara," Mr. Jenson interrupted. Bryn was staring at me like I'd lost my mind, which was halfway true.

"Sorry. I tangled with John Barrett, and, even though I won, I'm not quite myself. You were right about him being sneaky."

"You saw Barrett? Where?"

"At the hotel. Andre wasn't there, by the way, so Barrett doesn't have him, if that's what you're wondering. Also, I don't think Andre was tied up in Mrs. Thornton's room since she came chasing after me. Would she leave a prisoner tied up in a hotel room with flimsy walls and doors? The Duvall Motor Inn's not exactly a secure holding place for kidnap victims. Although dead bodies can apparently lie around there for hours and hours without anybody finding them. It's ridiculous! Not that I'm saying that Andre's dead. I'm sure—well, I sure hope he's not."

"Tell me what happened," Bryn said calmly.

My explanation was a bit scattered, and Bryn seemed more than a little impatient until I reached into my shirt and came out with the velvet box. When I opened it, he paled.

"I know that brooch."

"You've got all her pictures, so I bet you do."

He leaned closer. "My mother was wearing it the night she was murdered. It was never recovered. How can . . . How can you have this?"

I explained about getting it in the mail, seeing the visions, and how it had disappeared from my trunk and then turned up in John Barrett's hotel room.

Bryn lifted the brooch and cupped it in his hands. Nothing happened. "You said you saw her. Show me," he said, holding it out to me.

I touched it with my fingertip. Nothing happened, so I took it from him and pressed it between my palms. She didn't appear.

"What about an incantation? Or something you did?" Bryn said. "Think, Tamara."

I reached my hand over and gripped his arm. "It's okay. She doesn't come out every time, but she's in there. And now that I have the brooch again, we'll save her. Don't worry."

Bryn ran a hand through his gleaming black hair and stood up, taking the brooch back from me. "I don't understand why you'd see the vision the first time you touched it and I wouldn't."

"I don't know."

He stared at it and rubbed his thumb over the girl. "I'll keep it," he said finally. Then he looked at me, as if he expected me to argue.

"Yeah, she's your mom. I think you should keep it."

He blinked, as if emerging from a daze. "If her soul really is attached to this brooch, nothing can happen to her so long as we have it. Andre on the other hand may need help right now." He slid the brooch into his pocket. "Want to help me cast a spell?"

"Love to."

28

"DO YOU FEEL like a drink?" Bryn asked as I followed him down the hall.

"I'm not sure I should mix alcohol and truth serum. Never know what I might say or do."

Bryn smiled. "I'll take my chances."

"You say that now," I murmured, pausing in the doorway of the bathroom. Bryn went inside and yanked the clear plastic shower curtain, cracking the plastic rings and bending the shower rod.

"Wow. Next time someone takes a shower, the water's gonna go all over the floor," I pointed out.

"So be it," Bryn said.

"Spoken like someone who doesn't mop."

"Spoken like someone who cares more about his best friend than a house. Besides," Bryn said with a shrug, like that finished the sentence.

"Besides what?"

"I can afford new floors."

He went to the kitchen and opened a drawer full of pens and scrap paper. He pulled out a Sharpie marker and laid the shower curtain over the table.

"I couldn't reach the mayor today. Or anyone from the city council. They must be tied up trying to calm the masses," he said.

"I guess. I actually didn't see very many people. Not that I could've seen them anyway with the fog and dark, but I didn't hear many cars or people outside."

"Well, I warned the mayor to try to stall any property sales. He was supposed to meet with the real estate agents this morning."

"Not sure that worked out," I said, telling him about Marsha. "And how come they want my house? We're a family of witches. Shouldn't we be on their list of desirable residents?"

"Yes, but Barrett probably wants the property because it's on a spoke."

"A spoke?" I said, watching him draw a line down the middle of the clear curtain.

"Yeah. It's on one of the ley lines coming from the tor. Just like my place. I'm on the east meridian."

Bryn drew long curved lines on the clear plastic and then filled in some continent-shaped blobs.

"Grab me a drink, sweetheart."

"You sure you should drink before spell-casting?"

"I'm not planning to get drunk. I just want to pretreat myself. If there's one of Barrett's counterspell backwashes when I cast this, I want to be ready for the ensuing headache."

"Oh, those headaches. Maybe I'll have a little sip of scotch, too."

I went to the cupboard and opened it. I lifted the decanter, then dropped it the half-inch back to the shelf. Standing inside in the amber liquor was a five-inch-tall scotch-soaked and furious Jenna Reitgarten.

"Holy moly!" I said with a gasp.

"What?" Bryn asked, bisecting the empty half of the shower curtain in half again with another black line.

"There's something I forgot to mention earlier," I said, taking the bottle down. I kept it mostly level, but having the bottle tipped even a little made Jenna fall against the glass wall. It probably wasn't only the movement. I'm sure it was plenty slippery in there. She sloshed around, lost her footing and went under. I winced and paused until her head popped up above the surface.

"Sorry," I said. "Sorry about that."

"About what?" Bryn asked.

I set the decanter in the middle of the table.

"Tamara," he complained, reaching to move it away from where he was drawing a map of the U.S.

I grabbed his hand to stop him touching the bottle. "Here's the thing," I said, using my free hand to remove the stopper from the decanter. I could tell from her face that she was screaming, but it was just a barely audible squeak. I guessed that her rage was bottled up and, from a certain point of view, small.

Bryn stared. "Is that a pixie? How did she get in there?"

"Not a pixie."

Bryn leaned down to peer closer. Jenna was shaking her fist, her eyes tearing, mascara running, scotch dripping.

I cleared my throat. "She's Jenna . . . in a bottle."

The corner of Bryn's mouth curved up. Then he chuckled.

I chuckled a little, too. "Probably we shouldn't laugh. It's not very nice."

"Probably not." Then he laughed.

And I laughed.

He walked away from the table, putting his hands on the countertop while he kept laughing, which made me laugh harder.

When he turned around, he'd gotten hold of himself. "Tamara, what's Jenna Reitgarten doing in my scotch?"

"How should I know?" I asked with mock innocence, then I realized that my throat hadn't burned. I could lie again. Progress! "Maybe God did it," I said. "They were quoting scripture and screaming and cursing in front of lost children that I was trying to save! He could've decided to smite them."

"Did you help Him smite them with say—a spell?"

"God doesn't need my help."

"That wasn't the question."

"I might've said a few words about bottling up her rage and making it small."

Bryn laughed again.

"She started it!"

"I'm sure."

Bryn took out a piece of scrap paper and a pen. "Write down the spell before you forget what you said. We'll need it for a counterspell later."

I sat down at the table, my gaze shifting on and off to Jenna. "Calm down, little Jenna," I said. "We're going to get you out of there." I looked down at the paper and smiled. "Sooner *or later.*" I cleared my throat and handed the paper to Bryn.

He looked at it. "*This* is the verse you used?"

"Yep. I said that and then, poof, she disappeared. Well, there wasn't really a poof sound. She was just gone. And then here."

Bryn smiled. "You're like a force of nature."

I couldn't tell from his tone whether I should be flattered or insulted. "Is that a good thing? Or a bad thing?"

"Causing a human to shift into a different form—smaller, bigger, whatever, that takes an unbelievable amount of power."

"Felt easy to me."

"Yes," he said with a wry smile. "That's the irony of you, sweetheart. You can't do spells I could do when I was six years old. But then most of the world of magic can't do spells that you can do without even trying."

Kind of a backhanded compliment, I decided. I glanced down at the bottle where Jenna was leaning against one of the glass walls, catching her breath after her tirade. "Well, Jenna, I'm pretty sure there's a lesson to be learned from all this. When I figure out what it is, I'll let you know."

AFTER POURING OUT the scotch, rinsing Jenna and the bottle with some tap water, and pouring that out, Jenna was sitting on the floor of the unstoppered bottle wiping her face and hands with a piece of fabric I'd cut from a wash-cloth and dropped inside for her.

I took it as a good sign that she wasn't red-faced and screaming anymore. I left her on the table while I swept the stairs where I'd dropped the glass bowl because Bryn said we were going out behind the house.

Once the sweeping was finished, Bryn carried the markered shower curtain, and I carried a bedspread that he'd asked me to bring.

He smoothed out the shower curtain and put rocks around the edges to keep it from blowing away. Then he took off his shirt and set it on the steps. He glanced at the sky and then at the house, then back up at the sky.

"A lot of cloud cover," he said, cocking his head. He moved around the shower curtain, back and forth, until stopping at the left side and taking a few steps back. He glanced up again and at the house. "I know the position of the house, where we are on the earth, and our relationship to the constellations, but there's no way to do exact measurements without a telescope, which I couldn't use with my view obscured anyway."

"Do we need things to be exact to find him?" I asked. Bryn's way of scrying seemed a lot more scientific than anything Momma or Aunt Mel had ever done.

"Maybe. Maybe not." He glanced one last time up at the sky, then waved me over to him. He took the blanket from me. "Take off your shirt and socks and shoes."

This was a normal part of the process for us sharing power. We were usually skin-to-skin—at least from the waist up—and I was barefoot with my toes in the dirt.

Unfortunately, any work you do that involves taking off clothes feels kind of dicey. Strippers. Adult films stars. Prostitutes. Not exactly the kind of company I want to be in.

Still, Andre was missing and doing magic was our best chance of finding him fast if he needed our help.

I took off my socks and boots, the wound on my foot stinging. "That cut on my foot's not healed yet. I bet if Dr.

Suri knew I was rubbing my cut in the dirt, he'd give me a really long lecture."

"And a tetanus shot, I'd imagine."

"You don't think I'll get a bad infection and have to get my leg cut off, do you?" I asked, removing my shirt and folding it up.

"Last week, I pulled an arrow out of your chest. This week, I'd be hard-pressed to find the scar. I doubt garden-variety bacteria stands a chance against your body's ability to heal. Your fae blood, no doubt."

I smiled. "I think so, too. Maybe my family shouldn't have been so quick to condemn my half-fae status." I walked to Bryn, and he wrapped the blanket around us, drawing me up against him. My skin prickled immediately with magical energy.

"Hold this," he said, giving me the edges of the blanket.

I kept it around us and felt him fiddle with the clasp of my bra a second before it sprung open.

"You didn't need to do that," I admonished.

"Not for the spell," he said a moment before he kissed me.

The power arced between us as we tasted each other. His fingers in my hair, skin sliding against skin. Before I knew it, he'd lowered us to the ground, and we were tangled up together.

"Bryn," I gasped as he unzipped my jeans.

"Later," he said, licking my throat.

"Andre is your best friend."

"Which is why he'd understand."

"Wow that feels good," I mumbled, dizzy and breathless, before tugging his hand away from the inside of my thigh. "Bryn!"

He pulled me closer and sucked my tongue and plenty of magic into himself. When he exhaled, he shoved his hand out of the cocoon of the blanket and whispered a spell in Gaelic. Needles of bright light pierced his hand and bent off it to light up the shower curtain.

"Beautiful," I whispered.

He rolled us closer and moved his hand slowly, watching

the light dance over the surface. North America, Texas, and a place somewhere to the southeast of Dallas lit up brighter than the other parts of the map.

He whispered another spell and closed his eyes. "I recognize the spell that's cloaking him. It's one I wrote. He's doing magic, so he must be all right."

Bryn pulled his hand back inside the blanket and bent his head to kiss me again. His blue eyes glittered as if lit by the starlight, too. I stared into them, feeling caught up in the universe of Bryn as usual.

"Are you sure we have time for this?"

"I'm absolutely sure we have time for this," he murmured back, tugging on my lower lip with his teeth.

That was the last time we talked about anything for a while.

29

"ANDRE'S MILES OUTSIDE Duvall, but he's in Texas,"
Bryn said. We were still wrapped in the blanket and lying
on the hard ground, but somehow it didn't bother us, our
warm bodies pressed together under the night sky.

"Who told you Andre was missing?"

"His dad. Maybe the spell Andre's doing is shorting out
his phone. After all, Gwen's dead and you saw Barrett and
the Winterhawk this morning. If they'd taken him to get to the
rest of the underground or to me, he wouldn't be using my
spell to cloak his location. He'd want to be found."

"So he's okay?"

Bryn shrugged. "I don't know. He's trying to keep his
location secret and he's here, in the U.S., in Texas. He knows
things are precarious. There are plenty of places in the world
that would be safer for him. I wish he hadn't felt compelled
to come."

"Do you think we should track him down?"

"And possibly lead Barrett and the Winterhawk to him?
No. I hope he stays where he is."

I dug through our clothes until I found the brooch in

Bryn's pocket. "If he doesn't need us, then we can use the power we generated for something else."

"Like what?"

I opened my hands. "To call the dead."

Bryn sighed and shook his head. "I want to see her. I always have, but I've got to think long and hard about the spell I want to use to try to draw her out."

"I'm connected to her. I can feel it. And so are you as her son. Who better to call to her?"

"I need to be sure that I can control what happens," he said, taking the brooch and setting it away from me.

"It's your mom," I said, holding out my hands to show that I wouldn't interfere. "So that just leaves one really important thing that I need to use magic for."

"What?"

"To look into the past."

He laughed. "Time-walking. Even more dangerous than calling ghosts."

"I have Lenore and Edie's spellbooks. I have actual things that they touched, spells they wrote, possibly with remnants of their actual magic. There are spells in their book to enhance soothsaying. I could do a spell that's the opposite of that. I'll keep it simple." I thought of John Barrett lecturing me about being blinded by love. I needed to hear that prophecy for myself. Or better yet, to see it firsthand.

"You can't just change a few words and expect it to work the way you want it to," Bryn said.

"Then help me. Tell me what to say."

"No."

"You're afraid, aren't you? That I'll find out why we shouldn't be together. That it'll be something really horrible. But, look, how horrible can it be? It's probably not even about us."

"I'm sure it isn't. What worries me is what will happen if you try to send your mind on a time-walk and it goes wrong. It could damage your brain."

"I heal really well. You said so yourself."

"We're not talking about a cut. We're talking about

fracturing your mind. Sending a part of it out into the universe with an untested spell. I won't risk it."

"Ever?"

He didn't answer.

"Ever!? So before, when you said that you'd help me later, you didn't really mean it? You just wanted me to stop bugging you?"

"I wanted time to think about it. I've thought about it."

"I have to know."

"You don't. You've lived your whole life without knowing."

"But I wasn't sleeping with you then!"

"Your grandmother's premonition wasn't about us."

"Edie!" I called.

"What are you doing?"

I closed my eyes. "Edie, come to me." Edie's not the type to come when she's called, but I could feel Bryn's power coursing through me below the surface and knew that getting a taste of our mixed magical energy would infuriate her.

"Tamara, don't do that."

A bright green light flared and then Edie appeared. "Well, well. Still sleeping with the enemy, biscuit?"

"We want to know the nature of the prophecy. Lenore told it to you. Will you let us do a spell to try to retrieve the memory from you?"

"Let *him* do a spell on me? Have you lost your lust-addled mind?"

"If you don't help me, I'm going to try a time-travel spell."

"Those never work right."

"First time for everything," I said with a sweet smile.

"Witches who dabble in time travel usually end up in a mental institution afterward. But, of course, with your superior skills, there's no risk of that. A dangerous and complicated spell is sure to work out because your spells never go wrong," she said, her sarcasm martini-dry.

I glared at her. "At least I'd be doing something instead of following along like a good little sheep the way I did for years."

"You were far better off when we did the thinking for you. Every important decision you've ever made has ended badly. Marrying your first boyfriend when you were barely out of high school? Ahem. Divorce. Going away to work in Dallas at that restaurant? Too homesick and lonely to concentrate, you came back to work in Cookie's pathetic little bakery for a pittance. And now, left on your own, you're letting a Lyons ride you like a magical whore."

I gasped and felt Bryn's magic thrashing to get out of him. He wanted to smash her, but he sucked the power deeper into himself.

"Harsh, yes," Edie continued. "Welcome to the world of grown-up witches, where if you act like a fool, I'll call you one. And don't think your pretty boy is any different. His soul is as black as his father's. He just hides it better."

"Go away," I said, hearing the hitch in my voice.

"What did you expect—"

"I said go!"

Edie dissolved into a green orb and disappeared.

"I forgot how mean she can get whenever anyone challenges her. Momma says it's because Edie's father beat their mother and them. It made Grandma Lenore timid and Edie prone to rage. That's what Momma said . . ." My voice trailed off and I stared out at the trees. The sway of their branches comforted me a little. A very little. "The thing is, even though she says hurtful things, a lot of times she's right."

"She's not right. You're extremely bright and intuitive. Untrained, yes, but that's their fault. Not yours. As for you and me, we're amazing together on every level. She's not right about us being better off apart."

"You can't know that." I ran a hand through my hair. "Neither of us can know that without knowing what the prophecy says." I wiggled back into my clothes. "I think I'm going—"

Bryn caught my wrist. "Don't. Don't reward her for talking to you that way."

"It's not about her. It's about me. I need a little time."

He tightened his grip on my hand like I'd have to give him a way more convincing argument if I wanted him to let me go.

I leaned over and pressed a kiss on his cheek. "Thank you for not doing anything to her just then. I know how much you wanted to." I tried to pull my hand back, but he kept it.

"Show me your great-great-grandmother's book."

I stilled. "Why?"

"So I can prove that the prophecy has nothing to do with us."

"You'll help me do the spell?"

"Yes, and if we survive it with our sanity intact, the next time I see your aunt Edie, I'll take great pleasure in ramming the truth down her metaphysical throat."

I smiled. "If we get the chance, I'll be busy telling her off myself." As we got dressed, I added softly, "Thanks, Bryn, for helping me with this."

He paused, then finished tucking in his shirt. "Last night I told you that you hadn't asked the right question. Because yes, there are plenty of things I wouldn't do for sex. Rape and murder come to mind. The right question to ask me is what I wouldn't risk to be with you."

I stared at him. "What wouldn't you risk to be with me?" I whispered.

He took my face in his hands and pressed his lips to mine. "I don't know anymore. Apparently nothing."

I smiled. "On the outside, you can be like your dad, the cynic. But on the inside, you're a romantic. I wonder if you get that from your mom. Like your eyes." I brushed a thumb over his cheek along his lower lid.

"Obviously, I wouldn't know." He turned and walked toward the house. "I need to write some instructions for Jenson."

"Why do you need to write them down?" I said, trailing after him.

"In case we both go insane. He'll need something legal. I'm going to have you write something, too."

I raised my eyebrows. "Do you really think we'll end up insane?"

He shrugged. "If we do, I'm going to insist that they place us in the same sanitarium. We can eat Jell-O and play checkers together for the rest of our lives."

I laughed. "Edie would really hate that."

He smiled. "I know."

BRYN AND I drove back to his mansion, so he could get a spellbook out of his vault. There was a collection of gold pyramids on the book's cover.

"The summer we were nineteen, Andre and I went to see the pyramids at Giza. They were aligned with the stars, you know."

I stared at him.

He nodded. "We studied the sphinx and those pyramids day and night, Andre doing calculations and me writing spells. We were obsessed with the past and what it could mean for the future."

He paged through the book until he found the spell he wanted. There were numbers and equations and geometric drawings on the left-hand page, musical notes on the top margin, and foreign verse on the other.

Bryn went to his desk and set his spellbook next to the one from Lenore and Edie. "I'll need a little time." He smiled. "No pun intended."

I BUNDLED MYSELF into a quilt and went to sit on the sun porch. I was more than a little surprised when Edie appeared.

"I apologize," she said stiffly. "We kept quite a few things from you. It's natural that you wouldn't fully trust what we say now. In our defense, I can only say that we did everything in the interest of protecting you."

I stared at her.

"I know it's difficult to understand. Melanie thinks it would be best for you to come to England where she can talk things over with you face-to-face. I think that's a good idea as well. She has infinitely more patience than I do and won't alienate you."

"Did she send you here to make things up with me?"

"No one sends me anywhere. I go where I choose to go."

I folded my arms across my chest, thinking it was time for me to choose to go, too—away from Edie. I stood.

"What I said earlier was extremely crude. I wanted to shock you."

"You wanted to hurt me."

She sighed. "Look, I had far more lovers than you ever will. Some of them were dangerous, and those relationships cost me things."

"Like your life?"

"Marlee and Melanie have also both made bad choices. What I'm saying is that you're no different from us, but we'd rather that you learned from our mistakes instead of making your own. We do love you."

"Will you help me then?"

"Help you do what?"

"I'm going back to see Lenore."

She was silent for several long moments. "If I can't talk you out of it, then yes, though if something goes wrong, they'll never forgive me." She swayed and faded. "I've got to go back to the locket soon, but I'll tell you some things before I go. If you are going to time-walk, the most important thing is to not allow yourself to get disoriented. Lenore had great power and control when it came to dissociative states, but you have to rely on knowledge to help you. Let me tell you about the house. It's where you should go, and stay inside it until you return from the past. Whatever you do, don't venture out and get lost."

I nodded.

"All right," she said, and then described the house in detail. She might have forgotten the prophecy, but she hadn't forgotten a thing about the place where she'd lived.

I sat listening until she grew too weak and disappeared, then I chewed on my lip, lost in thought for a while.

Mercutio's sharp yowl startled me.

"What?" I asked.

He darted into the house.

"Okay," I said, getting up. "I'm coming."

I trailed through the house after him and found him in the foyer with his paw resting on the front door. Since he could've gone outside and around the house on his own, this was a sure sign that he wanted me to go out with him. Considering that Merc always seemed to tear off when he was on the trail of trouble or magic or both, the paw on the door worried me as much as running out of chocolate chips the night before the Duvall bake-off would.

30

I TOLD BRYN that I was going out with Mercutio for a little while. Bryn only looked up for a second to tell me to be careful and then he was back to flipping pages and writing notes.

The security phone rang as I was starting out of the room.

"I got it," I said, picking it up. "Hi, Steve. He's working. Can I help you?" I asked.

"There's a guy in a taxi at the front gate. Says his name is Andre Knobel. His name's on the admitting list, but I don't know what the guy is supposed to look like and with the way things have been, I didn't want to take a chance. I thought Mr. Lyons might want to look at the monitor before I opened the gate."

"I know what he looks like. I'll go see," I said. I wondered where the taxi had come from. We don't have a taxicab service in Duvall. If someone's car breaks down, he just walks or bums a ride from someone else.

Bryn wasn't paying attention. He was using a ruler and one of those protractor things that I hadn't used since high school geometry.

I slipped out of the room, checking my gun as I opened

the front door. Mercutio darted over to the car, so, whatever he sensed, it wasn't Andre.

"Hang on. Bryn's got a visitor."

I jogged down to the gate, checking the area for any suspicious movements. There didn't seem to be anyone lying in wait.

"Andre?" I said. "Get out of the car so I can see you."

The back door opened, and Andre got out. He looked a little bedraggled and moved kind of stiffly.

I pressed the intercom button. "Open the gate, Steve." To Andre, I asked, "Are you okay?"

Andre gave a wad of bills to the cab driver. "Thank you," he said to the man and closed the car door. As the taxi pulled away, he said, "They were waiting for me. They ran the first taxi off the road. I had to run very fast. It was lucky that I had a good cloaking amulet and knew a simple spell that I could remember at such a time." He exhaled, like it was an effort to breathe. "It gave me enough time to get out of the ditch and get away. Bryn always says I am not suited to fieldwork, but I was not quite so sure until tonight. My head is not so cool in a crisis. He was right about sacrificing power for simplicity with the spell."

I put a hand out to steady him and drew him toward the house. "Who was waiting for you?"

"Conclave. Certainly." He took a deep breath and exhaled, looking over his shoulder. "I should not have come here, but, you understand, I could not think what to do. I planned to come to America, but not to this town. I would just be close in case he should need my help. Instead, I have come straight here. No luggage. Not sure if I have been followed."

"Well, where else would you go when you're in trouble in a foreign country besides to your best friend's? He'll be totally glad to see you. He was worried about you because your dad said they hadn't heard from you."

"I did not dare call. I would have had to drop the cloaking spell to prevent the phones shorting out from the magic. Also, my parents' phones will be tapped surely."

I opened the front door and ushered him in. "Normally,

Mr. Jenson's here to welcome people, but he's staying at another house. If you're hungry, you can help yourself. There's plenty of food in the fridge. Tea, coffee, or hot chocolate with marshmallows, if you want, in the cupboards. I'd make you some, but my cat says we've got to go out."

I took him to the study. "Look who's here," I said.

Bryn looked up from the book and frowned. "Andre, what the hell? We talked about this."

I interrupted sharply. "Andre came to help us, and he had some trouble getting here. Aren't you glad to see that he's okay?"

Bryn got up and rounded the desk. "It can't have been too much trouble. I don't see any blood," Bryn said dryly, but I knew he was relieved to see his friend alive and well. Bryn put a hand on the side of Andre's neck to draw him in for a hug. I smiled.

"I was run off the road!" Andre said as Bryn walked back to his desk.

"That can be really rough! Rattles the teeth something fierce," I said.

"Well, you're here just in time," Bryn said, tossing the protractor to Andre.

"Why? What are we doing?" Andre said, shrugging off his tweed coat.

"A time-walk spell."

Andre cursed in German, then he smiled. "So lucky I came then," he told Bryn. "You'll need this math to be perfect. I trust you to measure, but to calculate the angles, my friend? This will take a genius."

I didn't know what they were talking about, plus Merc was still waiting outside, so I said, "Okay, have fun."

"You will go out alone?" Andre asked in surprise, looking from me to Bryn and adding something in German.

"Not alone. I have this cat—"

Andre spoke again in German, and I could tell by his tone that he was skeptical. Couldn't blame him. He didn't really know Mercutio. Bryn nodded, apparently understanding German just fine.

I looked at Bryn with raised eyebrows. "What do you have? The gift of tongues? How many languages do you speak?"

Bryn smiled and said, "A few." To Andre he said, "Yes, she's going out alone. Forces of nature don't believe in fear."

"Do they believe in strategy? Forethought?"

"Sure, as long as it can be done in the time it takes them to find their car keys."

I clucked my tongue and glared at Bryn. "I'm not that impatient! I'd plan a strategy if I knew what to strategize about, but how can I plan ahead, if I don't know where Merc's leading me to?" I demanded.

"The cat is in charge?" Andre exclaimed, bewildered.

"We're kind of equal partners," I explained. "I'll be back."

"I have no doubt," Bryn said.

"He always wants to get the last word in. It's very annoying," I said to Andre.

"I know," Andre agreed gravely. I smiled at Andre, and as I passed him, he took my hand and then pulled me to him and gave me a hug. "I hope you will take great care. We have only just met after all, and I must know you better."

"Well, I'll do my best to get back in one piece."

MERC YOWLED AT me the minute I came out the front door.

"Sorry! That was his best friend, and I was curious." I pulled up to the gate and gave Steve a buzz. "Andre's nice. You'll like him."

I rolled the window down a crack for some fresh air.

"It feels kind of muggy. Think it's gonna rain?"

Merc licked his paw.

"I didn't bring an umbrella. Are we going someplace that's outside?" I paused. "Or inside?"

Merc didn't answer. He might've been kind of annoyed at having been kept waiting. As I drove he occasionally tapped the dash or the windshield when he wanted me to turn. Having an ocelot navigator is actually a lot better than you'd think. Those GPS devices are amazing, bouncing up to space and back in a few seconds, but they can't follow a magical trail worth a darn.

I drove down Main Street, not sure what I should be looking out for. Then I saw Johnny Nguyen standing on the side of the street, flagging me down.

I swerved into the City Hall parking lot. "Hey, Johnny, what's up?"

"Tammy, I try to call you. Where your phone?"

"Lost it when I got buried alive. What's going on?" I asked, getting out of the car. Merc darted out, too.

"Shh!" Johnny said, glancing at the police station.

Uh-oh. "Why shush?"

"Come. I show you."

I followed him behind the building to the courtyard, surprised to see that there were a bunch of new marble statues amidst the old benches, bushes, and flowers.

"Wow. When did they get those? They're kind of modern, huh? Never saw any pictures of statues wearing cowboy boots or spiked heels." I moved closer to the one of a man in a suit and tilted my head.

"Is that . . . ?"

"Yes, it the mayor!" Johnny whispered frantically. He ran a finger over the statue and put it close to my lips. "Taste."

"Taste what?" I demanded. *Dirt? Dust?* Johnny wouldn't bother telling me to taste dust . . .

I turned my head to stare at the white crystalline statue, then stuck out the tip of my tongue. Johnny touched his finger to it.

"What in the Sam Houston?" I asked, my gaze darting around the garden.

"Yes! They pillars of salt, Tammy Jo. The mayor. The city council. Somebody want them out of the way. Who? Why? And who going to run our town now?"

"Oh my gosh!" I sure knew who wanted to run the town. "Hey, pillars of salt aren't one of the ten plagues. That's a whole other part of the Bible!" I snapped.

Johnny cocked his head in confusion.

"Okay, calm down. Let's not panic," I said, giving Johnny's

arm a squeeze. Then I felt a raindrop plop down on my cheek. *On second thought.*

Mercutio yowled softly. "I felt it, Merc."

"What?" Johnny said, looking up. A raindrop hit him between the eyebrows and he jumped. "That not good, Tammy Jo. Salt melt in rain."

"I know it. We've gotta move them inside. Help me," I said, hoping they weren't going to break apart. Together we tipped the mayor sideways, and each of us lifted an end. He was really heavy. We had to stop twice to catch our breath. "Wait a second," I said, winded. "We're gonna need help." I hadn't felt any more rain, but I knew the sky was threatening.

I jogged over to the police station and went in. Smitty looked at me and grimaced. Just past him I could see into Sheriff Hobbs's office where Lucy and Boyd Reitgarten were sitting across from the sheriff.

Uh-oh.

Smitty walked briskly to me and grabbed my arm. "Now ain't exactly a good time for you to be here," he whispered, maneuvering us outside the building.

"Why?" I asked innocently. "What's going on?" As if I didn't know.

"Lucy Reitgarten claims you kidnapped her sister-in-law."

"That's just silly. I don't have time to go around kidnapping people."

"Well, you have had kidnapping on the brain lately."

I waved my hand. "That was at least a couple days ago. I do need your help though. Are there some other guys on duty or are you it?"

He cocked an eyebrow and, at first, wouldn't agree to come with me, but finally I convinced him to walk the hundred feet it took to get to the courtyard.

"Someone carved these amazing statues of the mayor and city council, but they didn't finish putting sealant on them. I just know they're going to get damaged in the rain, and all that work will be lost, along with whatever taxpayer money went into the project."

"What the hell? I don't know anything about any statues." Smitty walked over to one of the councilmen.

"We need to get them into the lobby of City Hall. Johnny, give me your phone. We have to call some more people."

Johnny handed me his iPhone in the purple leopard-print holder. My gaze flicked to Mercutio to see if he approved of the color, but he'd gone up a tree and didn't seem to be paying attention.

I called Georgia and Kenny and told them it was an emergency. They didn't ask questions; they just drove straight over to help. And they didn't even complain about lugging the two-ton town leaders around the building, though Georgia talked nonstop and did ask me if there was any truth at all to the rumor about me running over Jenna Reitgarten and burying her in a shallow grave in the Macon Hill woods.

"Of course not."

"Hon, maybe you don't want to ask Tammy questions in front of the law here," Kenny whispered.

"Oh, it's just Smitty. Tammy Jo stood up in his wedding!"

I frowned. That hadn't stopped Smitty from arresting me plenty over the past couple of weeks.

We couldn't get the last one inside before the drizzle started so I'm sorry to say that Councilwoman Faber's designer suit lapels, plus her fingernails and kneecaps, kind of melted off.

We all sat down to catch our breath except Smitty, whose walkie-talkie crackled.

"Deputy Smith, what's your location?" Sheriff Hobbs asked.

"Moving those statues in out of the rain."

"The what?"

"Time for us to head out," I said, hopping up and hurrying to the door with Johnny, Georgia, and Kenny. We pretended not to hear Smitty when he told us to "Hold up a minute."

As soon as I walked out of the building though, I stopped dead. Boyd and Lucy were walking to the parking lot where about half a dozen other people, including Sue Carfax were gathered.

"Hey, Tammy Jo, the sheriff doesn't know anything about these here salt sculptures."

The group started toward us, their umbrellas bobbing angrily.

"Well me either, but someone had to get them out of the rain. You saw how they were going to melt out here. Merc, c'mon!"

The mob was between me and my car, but I thought we might've been able to make it to Johnny's BMW if we ran for it.

I was ready to dash when Smitty's beefy hand caught my arm. "Now just hold on there, girl. The sheriff needs to talk to you."

"You go get in the car, Georgia Sue," Kenny said, handing her the keys.

"Why? What are you gonna do?" she asked.

"What's going on here?" Sue asked.

Nobody answered.

"She was coming out of there," Sue said, hurrying past us along with her crew. They went into the City Hall lobby.

"C'mon, Smitty. I'll walk over to the station with you guys," Kenny said, clearly sensing trouble was about to erupt.

Sure enough, the lobby door swung open and Sue came out red-faced and shouting.

"Pillars of salt! She turned them into pillars of salt!"

From behind her a chorus of "The Lord is my shepherd" started up.

"All right now, y'all need to quiet down and tell me what you're talking about," Smitty said.

They didn't stop. They kept shouting as they rushed toward us. I suppose I could've pulled my gun, but they weren't armed, so that wouldn't look good in Smitty's report. Plus, it wasn't my gun, and I didn't have a permit to carry it concealed.

So I did the next best thing. I jerked my arm, pulling it from Smitty's grasp. In his defense, Smitty was probably distracted by the six people running toward us from City Hall and Boyd and Lucy coming from the station.

I took off toward the parking lot, figuring that getting past two people would be easier than getting past six. And I would've gotten to my car, if Mindy Glusky hadn't driven up in her truck, jumping the curb to block my way. Apparently, she wanted back in the group.

I looked over my shoulder. Kenny was body-blocking people in a way that was a real testimony to his days on the high school defensive line. Sue toppled over while Smitty got a hand on the shirt of a middle-aged man, but it only slowed them down. I darted down the path between the station and City Hall. I thought about doubling back to my car, but that seemed risky. Merc must've thought so too because he headed to a fence that led to a residential neighborhood.

I'd seen Zach practically fly over fences when we were growing up, so I did what I'd seen him do. I ran as fast as I could and when I was a few feet away I jumped as high as I could. I grabbed the fence links with my fingers and swung my legs up and over. Except I didn't quite clear the top, so the crossed metal ripped through the leg of my jeans and the leg *in* my jeans.

The other thing I didn't time right was letting go, so I almost dislocated my fingers when the momentum flung me toward the ground. I landed with a bone-jarring thud. At first I thought I must've popped both my lungs because I could not breathe.

Mercutio's face swam above me. I hadn't hit my head, but there were tears stinging my eyes, so he was blurry. I blinked them away and sucked in air.

"Zach . . . Zach makes that look easier than it is." I rolled onto my hands and knees. "Good thing I drink a lot of milk or every one of my bones would be broken to bits right now." My finger joints throbbed, but it was the burning along the side of my right leg that was really painful.

Mercutio nudged me toward the street as the drizzle started again.

"Keep your spots on, Merc. I need a minute." I rested my forehead against the fence links for a second before looking down at my shredded seam. I pulled the fabric wider to see the wound. It didn't look so bad . . . until I moved. The skin gaped open, and I could see inside a quarter inch to bright red flesh that I'm pretty sure is supposed to always stay covered.

"Yep," I said. "I need a minute." Then I crumpled to my knees, retching. Mercutio hopped back and forth on his paws like a prizefighter circling the ring, then he nipped my arm.

"Mercutio!" I snapped as sweat beaded at my temples.

Merc yowled and bumped my jaw. I looked up and saw cars rounding the corner at nonresidential speeds. There were also a couple of women running toward the fence, and they seemed to be pointing shotguns at us.

I jerked myself up, the pain in my leg one long burning scream. There was no way I could outrun the cars or make an effective escape. I yanked my gun out.

"It's times like these, Merc, when the Alamo really comes to mind."

Mercutio licked my leg, which stung like crazy. "Cut that out," I said, limping across the street. Just then a white Ferrari zoomed toward us from the other direction.

It screeched to a stop with the passenger door a few feet from me. I kept the gun firmly in my right hand and opened the door with my left.

Seeing the Winterhawk behind the wheel, I froze. I glanced at the cars bearing down on me. The devil you know? Or the devil you don't know too well, but are pretty afraid of anyway?

31

"DO YOU ENJOY bleeding in the rain?" she asked dryly.

I dropped into the passenger seat. Merc hissed.

"You don't have to come. You can run back to the house," I said, starting to pull the door closed. Merc leapt in, landing on my lap.

I shut the door, and Mrs. Thornton pulled away from the curb. Then she gunned it and drove through the neighborhood in a way that made my hair want to turn as white as hers.

I clamped my lips closed and held on. Oblivious to break-neck speed, Mercutio licked his damp fur. I could have killed him, if I'd had a free hand.

Once we reached the woods of the tor, she pulled over.

"Who taught you to drive? James Bond?" I asked.

She smiled and inclined her head at the acknowledgment of her skills. Unfortunately, her nod was the beginning and the end of the pleasantries. "You moved our salt bodies."

"You have to turn those people back into people."

"Have to?" she asked, then shook her head curtly.

"Well, you should. Isn't there some WAM law against turning innocent bystanders into spices and condiments? If not, there should be! Definitely."

"We're willing to negotiate. President Barrett said you stole something from him."

I opened my mouth to protest, but closed it again and glared at her. "If I took anything, it's because I wanted to return it to its rightful owners."

Her thin silver brows rose. "What rightful owner? What are you talking about?"

So she didn't know the truth about the brooch. What would she think of John Barrett if she did? Mrs. Thornton was a strong woman in her own right, and she'd been loyal to WAM long before John Barrett had taken over.

"What I'd like to know is how Mr. Barrett got the brooch of a murder victim anyway," I said, carefully watching her expression. She continued to look surprised.

"A murder victim," she echoed, weighing my words.

"Yes. A young woman was killed, and her brooch was never recovered. Until now."

"You're certain?"

"Absolutely certain. Someone else got blamed for the crime, but I have to wonder how the president of the World Association of Magic got it. Maybe it was just found and someone sold it to him. On the other hand, maybe he had something to do with her death. Maybe the brooch was his trophy of the murder he arranged."

"Who was this murdered woman? What was his supposed connection to her?"

"I haven't figured that out, but I bet you could, being an operative and all." If we could get the Winterhawk on our side that would be a huge advantage. She was probably pretty loyal to John Barrett, but she had come and picked me up to save me from the townspeople, so she didn't seem totally set against me. Plus, Lennox admired her and she'd said she wanted to help Bryn get out of trouble when she'd first arrived. Maybe we had a chance to win her over.

"Tell me how you identified the brooch as belonging to the murder victim."

I decided to go for broke. If she stayed on Barrett's side

and told him everything I knew, what difference would it make? Bryn and I were already Barrett's targets. I explained about seeing the visions and later seeing pictures of Cassandra Lyons.

"And someone mailed you the brooch? Who?"

"I don't know."

Her lips pursed, making her look a little like Meryl Streep in *The Devil Wears Prada*. "You don't know much, do you?"

"I know John Barrett had the brooch of a murdered woman, which is more than you knew."

She laughed softly and tapped a slender finger against the steering wheel. "Touché. We may claim you as one of us yet."

I was more pleased by her praise than I should've been. I guess I kind of admired her, even if she wasn't playing for the home team.

"Do you have the brooch with you?"

"Nope."

"If I do investigate this, you'll swear in court to the fact that you took the brooch from John Barrett's room?"

"So long as I don't get in trouble for stealing it."

She shook her head. "If he's a killer, you won't. Even if he isn't, if the brooch belonged to a witch, it should've gone to the family. The circumstances of how he got it must be uncovered, along with the truth, the entire truth, about the night of her murder." She ran her fingers over the wheel again. "You'll get the brooch for me, and I'll crack the spell that's holding her. Then we'll hear from her what happened. That testimony, no one will be able to dispute."

I shifted. "Those spells are hard to undo, aren't they? Will her soul be at risk?"

"No more at risk than she is now, trapped eternally by malevolent magic."

"Well, I won't just hand it over. I'll have to be with you when you try the spell."

"I have no objection to that." Mrs. Thornton started the car. "Are you staying at his mansion?"

"For the moment."

She drove the half dozen blocks to Bryn's street. "I know your grandmother."

I stared at Mrs. Thornton, leaning forward. I wanted to hear about my grandma. I was sure there was a good reason that Momma wasn't on speaking terms with her; at least I hoped there was, but whatever happened between them had happened a long time ago. Maybe if I tried, if I got them together, I could fix our family. "You know her?"

"Don't look surprised. I've been around forever. I know everyone."

"What's she like?"

"Josephine's talented. Like you. She's also exceptionally well educated. Unlike you. We'll have to see about remedying that." She stopped the car at the gates to Bryn's house. "Go inside and get the brooch."

"Um, yeah, I'll have to bring it to you later." After I cleared it with Bryn. "Mrs. Thornton, one more thing."

"Yes?"

"About my town? I'd like you to turn those people back to people and to leave the town alone."

"You and Bryn Lyons have yourselves to thank for the salt. You told the mayor and the city council to get in the way of our property acquisition."

"That's because you've got no right to scare people into selling their homes! This isn't your town!" I snapped.

"It is if we buy it. We'll be happy to return the mayor and his people to their rightful form once we're finished convincing your neighbors to leave."

I glared at her, opening the door. Merc hopped out and I followed him. I bent forward to look inside at her. "We're not going to let that happen."

She smiled. "Then pick a spice. Do you like curry? Or perhaps you'd do better as a pile of hot pepper flakes."

I gasped and slammed the door, then hurried over to the gate and buzzed Steve. "Let me in," I said, flicking off the gun's safety. She wasn't turning me into a pepper pile, and she wasn't following me onto Bryn's property either.

Mrs. Thornton didn't even wait for the gates to open. She just smiled, inclined her head, and drove off, cool as winter.

I WAS STILL shaking my head when Mercutio and I walked into Bryn's house. I called out, but didn't hear them. The security phone on the kitchen wall rang, and I picked it up.

"They're in the yard," Steve said. He'd obviously seen me on the security cameras, looking around and calling out. Turns out when I'm not nearly naked or sneaking into a room I'm not supposed to be in, the security cameras can actually come in handy.

"Okey dokey. Thanks," I said, waving Merc over to the back door. We walked outside, but I only got a few feet from the house before I stopped. Most of the time I can't see or feel magic, and except for chocolate sculptures and cake decorating, not too much stops me in my tracks with wonder, but Bryn and Andre's work did. There was an area of about a thousand square feet dotted with white lanterns and strung with cascades of tiny white and blue lights. Crystals hung from tree branches, sparkling like diamonds, and the smell of sandalwood and roses wafted through the silky air. A haunting melody played softly and male voices murmured in German and English, intermixed with low chuckles.

I glanced down to see what Merc thought of this modern wizard's garden party, but he'd left my side and was racing around the lit square, leaping and pawing the lights and basically doing some kind of kitty jig.

"Wow," I said, limping over to where Bryn and Andre were securing a huge chunk of rock crystal so that it hung from a tree limb in the center of things.

Andre smiled. "Nice, yes?"

I nodded.

He hooked my arm through his and took me on a tour of the stars and galaxies as they'd been laid out on the ground. Meanwhile Bryn had climbed a ladder and was flinging something on the swags of white netting that hung over the area.

"What's he doing?" I asked.

"Scattering dirt and herbs. This is to represent the Earth. We have reversed things. Earth above. Stars below. To use both kinds of magic. Celestial and elemental for each of you."

"Well, even if it doesn't work, it's sure pretty." I walked to the ladder and waited for Bryn to come down.

"What happened to your leg?" he asked when he was standing in front of me.

"Got into a tangle with a fence. I was trying to fly over it, but didn't quite make it."

"Gravity, she is a tough mistress," Andre said. "Nine-point-eight meters per seconds squared. It does not sound like much, but how it pulls." He rambled in German for a few seconds.

"We've got a problem. The Conclave's turned some people to salt. I think before we do anything else, we'd better turn them back to human."

"Organic matter into inorganic matter?" Andre said. I could tell by his tone he was skeptical.

"Turned them to salt?" Bryn echoed. "That can't be."

"I saw it."

"If they really have been altered in that way, undoing it will take the kind of power that is nearly immeasurable. To build that kind of power . . ." He blew out a breath. "Let's hope that the prophecy allows you to trust me because we will certainly need to be magically bonded to attempt a spell that changes one form of matter into another. The bond will need to be strong and permanent."

I took a step back, licking my lips. My stomach and muscles tightened. My body was saying yes, even though my mind was saying: hold on, not until we know what the prophecy says.

"Well," I said, clasping my hands together. "They did it somehow without a magical marriage. We should be able to do it, too. I shrunk Jenna to mini-Barbie size. My power should be enough right? You can draw it off like you do and cast a counterspell."

Andre clucked his tongue.

"What?" I asked.

"It wouldn't be so simple as you think. Ask him to swallow a lightning bolt. This would be easier than what you propose," Andre said.

"But they did it. If I get you the original spell so you could see how it was done, then could you undo it?" I asked.

Bryn shrugged. "Maybe, but how would you get the original spell?"

"I'll have to steal it for you."

Bryn stared at me. "You're not immortal, you know. You almost died last week, remember?"

"I know. My memory's not all photographic like yours, but those little things like nearly getting killed tend to stick in my mind."

Bryn's gaze swiveled to Mercutio and then back to me. "I can't figure out if you're getting more bold because you've survived the past couple of weeks. Or if there might be another reason. Like a growing attachment to your cat. As predators go, big cats are the top of the food chain. They don't really know fear. It could be influencing you. Or maybe it's the fact that some of your dormant genes were unleashed."

"I'm not fearless!" I said. "I'm just practical. These Duvall people are my people. I can't just let them get turned into Spice Girls . . . and guys. Whatever I have to do to get that undone, I'll do, whether it's scary or not."

Bryn nodded. "Whatever it takes?"

"Yes."

"Then let's find out what that prophecy says because if we enter into a spell to turn salt sculptures into people, there will be no going back for you and me. We'll be connected to each other for good."

I shivered. "So, time travel first. Then robbery. Then . . . whatever comes next."

32

WHEN BRYN TOLD me that I'd have to be naked except for a bolt of purple silk fashioned into a kind of toga, I decided we'd have to be alone in the yard, well except for Mercutio. Andre went to the library to do research on transfiguration spells.

Bryn turned off the security cameras for the grounds and changed into dark pajama bottoms and a black bathrobe. Swathed in purple silk, I followed him outside to the backyard star chart.

He positioned me between two lanterns, and I was happy to have the heat they gave off. It was so darn cold out, you could almost forget you were in Texas. The wind kicked up and drops of rain dripped from the dark sky.

"You're on Orion's belt," Bryn murmured as he took a position behind me. "What I want you to do is picture your aunt's house. If you can get your mind in that place while I cast, the spell should take you to the right moment."

"Do I need to do an incantation?"

"No, I'll do it. You're the energy. I'm the anchor. You'll travel with a metaphysical tether to me."

"Won't that hold me back?"

"We'll find out, but don't let go of my hands, Tamara. Whatever happens, hang on to me. If this spell doesn't work, we can try another, so long as you're not hurt in the process."

"Okay," I said, taking a deep breath.

He shrugged off the robe and tossed it out of the decorated area.

"Maybe the prophecy was that we'd die of exposure while trying to do a time-travel spell," I joked. "Wouldn't that be ironic?"

"Yes," he said, stepping close to me so that his chest pressed against my back. I felt his body heat and lean muscles through the thin layer of silk. He positioned my hands to my sides, slightly behind me, and laced our fingers together.

He brought his mouth close to me, his voice tickling my ear. "Look at the rock crystal and concentrate on your aunt's house. Picture what she described. Picture it all around you."

I stared at the hanging rock, seeing a reflection that wasn't actually there, myself and Bryn over my shoulder, black hair touching red. Lights flickered in the wind. Cut crystals swayed and sparkled. His words in soft Gaelic mixed with the music.

My vision blurred, and I smelled perfume, sharp and sexy. I strained my eyes, trying to get them to focus, but everything seemed fragmented, like long shards of broken glass. I turned toward a voice I recognized.

Edie!

"How could she prefer *The Covered Wagon* to Valentino in the *Four Horsemen*? Dumb Dora," she said. The voice softened, and I floated toward it. The images shifted so they weren't so much shattered as watery.

I pursued her voice. The carpet under her feet was deep red and edged with a gold border. Her dress was dark blue or maybe black with gold embroidery and crystal beads. The back had delicate swirls and circles around a central circle. Below the low waist, there were horizontal patterns of solid lines alternating with twisted swirls of beads. The bottom of the gown was asymmetrical, creating scallops of fabric that skimmed the floor. Her shoes were like old-fashioned clogs, but daintier, with a square pattern, like a witch's buckle, on the front.

She slowed, but I didn't, and, the next moment, a rush of air stole my breath and the colors vibrated around me as I saw them through her eyes. She gasped and stumbled. The world whirled as we fell backward. Toward the stairs!

The momentum took us, but her voice, sharp and scared, snapped, "Cradle catch."

A thrust of energy pushed us to the side, and her hand caught a rung of the banister, jerking us to a stop. She turned her head, and I saw down the stairs, at least twenty of them, to the marble checkerboard floor where we would've probably cracked our head or broken our neck.

"Out," she hissed, and a vacuum of air sucked me out of her body, leaving me cold and confused. "Grasping little bitch," she whispered, narrowing her clear green eyes as she twisted her legs around to get them under her. She kept her white-knuckled grip on the banister as she crawled up the stairs, looking carefully from side to side like she was trying to spot me. I was inexplicably drawn to her. The lights had been so bright and warm. I wanted back in.

"No spirit rides me. Try that again and I'll trap you in a hell you've never imagined."

Despite the warning, I floated nearer, which was scary, because I couldn't seem to control the way I moved. She glared and raised a hand. I edged closer, still not able to stop myself.

Help! Help me!

I felt a sharp pain, like a knife slicing me, but it pulled me backward, away from her.

Edie grimaced, touching her glossy finger-waved black hair. Her black-lined green eyes were almond shaped and beautiful, but deadly calculating. A Park Avenue Cleopatra.

She walked carefully but quickly to a door. I followed, very slowly. She entered the room and slammed the door. I passed through it, into a pretty-as-a-picture bedroom.

A porcelain-faced doll with auburn hair lay on the covers of a high four-poster bed. The cream-colored dressing table had panels painted with delicate branches and birds. The silver-handled hairbrush and cosmetics had been pushed to one side to make room for a journal. A woman sat in the table's matching chair, bending over the book, writing with a fountain pen. I could see her face in the gilded mirror. Edie's face, but softer. The waves in her long dark hair were natural, not coiffed, and she wore no makeup, which made her look young and fresh. Her teal green dress was high-waisted with a gold braided cord that laced the bodice together.

"Did I leave my cigarette case in here, Nor?" Edie asked.

Lenore didn't look up from her writing. "Yes, as you well know, since you did it on purpose."

Edie sighed as if very put out. "What if I did? If that little fiend found it in here, she wouldn't give it to Papa. She'd never get *you* in trouble. None of the servants would."

"You could try being nicer to them."

"Why should I? The wretched little snitches." She paused, calming. "Do you like this gown? It's from the French designer I told you about. Gabrielle Chanel."

Lenore looked up. "Very pretty, but I don't like the square neck. You know I don't go in for hard edges." Lenore looked past her, toward me. She tilted her head.

"What?" Edie said, whirling in my direction. "Do you see something? There was a strange ghost in the hallway. Rotten cow jumped right into me. Nearly broke my neck falling down the stairs."

Lenore smiled at me. "Poor dear," Lenore said, and I didn't know if she meant me or Edie. "It was an accident. She's not malicious."

"Well, who is she and what's she doing here?" Edie demanded suspiciously.

"I don't know, but I think she's just passing through. She's a tender heart. Nothing to worry about."

"Well, you can tell her to bloody well stay out of my body, or I'll stuff her into an ill-wish doll and stick her with pins like the Voudoun priestesses do."

"You know better than to dabble in black magic, Edes. You really must be careful."

Edie pursed her crimson lips defiantly.

Lenore sighed. "I'd think drinking bathtub gin would be enough lawbreaking for you." Lenore turned back to her journal.

"What are you writing in that infernal book?" Edie said, walking up behind her and peeking over Lenore's shoulder.

Their two pretty faces were framed together in the mirror. Identical bones and flawless skin, but one painted and clever and the other soulful and knowing.

"I have a new name for the list."

"You and your list."

"This one's the most dangerous yet," Lenore whispered. "He'll divide the family."

"The family could use some division. If I could get my inheritance early, I'd move in with the artists and young bohemians in Greenwich Village."

"And give up French silk evening gowns?" Lenore said with a soft laugh. "I doubt that."

Edie opened a drawer to retrieve an engraved cigarette case. She put a cigarette in a long black holder and lit it.

"Get Mama to talk Papa into giving me my money, and see where I go," Edie said without an ounce of self-doubt. She inhaled, then blew out a puff of smoke. "So what's the dastardly name then?"

"Lyons. I don't know the first name. Perhaps Brian . . ." Lenore trailed off, then added, "Something like it anyway."

No!

A crushing weight suffocated me.

"And what will he do to divide the family?" Edie asked.

Lenore's finger traced the edge of the journal, then along the swirls of dried ink where she'd written the name. "He oughtn't to be able to. They'll be forewarned, you know. They'll have my list. They'll know the name, but she won't get away quickly enough. She's drawn to that power, you see. He'll be so beautiful, that one. Spells so brilliant and hard to resist. When understanding dawns, it'll be too late." Lenore shook her head slowly. "The family's already splintered. Dangerous decisions. Terrible ones. But there's hope until . . . He'll take their child. Even when she begs him to give it back, he won't. He thinks he's better than us, and he'll want that darling girl more than anything. He lost something when he was young, you see. Something precious. So he'll never give up anything that he thinks belongs to him. No matter that the child is half McKenna blood; no matter how much it will hurt them to be separated. He knows how to be ruthless, and he will be." A round tear spilled over her lashes and rolled down her cheek. "The destiny they share will break the hearts of all those who live to see it."

Edie shuddered and exhaled a curl of smoke. "Well, it's their own fault if they know about the list and ignore it. Silly little fools."

"Yes . . . fortune finishes the fool."

A great dread pressed in on me, and I fumbled toward them, trying to speak, trying to promise that it wasn't too late yet.

But when I got close to Edie, she raised her hand sharply. "No you don't, tender heart. Be gone." She snapped her wrist, flicking me away.

Air rushed through me with a deafening roar. I was lost and spinning, my ears splitting. I tried to yank my hands free to cover my ears, but they were pinned behind me. I struggled and thrashed, needles pricking my skin, a sharp pain in my leg and side.

"Tamara!"

I gasped and opened my eyes on the blurred night. My body twisted to escape. "Let go, Bryn! I'm back now. Let me go!"

He did and I stumbled forward, my knees landing on the cold, wet ground. He bent near me, putting a warm hand on my neck. "Are you all right?"

I looked up into his dark blue eyes and wondered if I might already be pregnant. I'd been careless with Bryn because, in all the hundreds of times with Zach, we'd never made a baby. A specialist said there was nothing wrong with either of us, but it didn't happen. Maybe that was because I was part fae. Like Bryn. Maybe with him, making a baby would be easier. And maybe he'd love his little girl so much that, when we broke up, he'd decide I wasn't a good enough mom and he'd take her away. The fear was like a dagger poking at my heart over and over until all my blood and all my hope seemed to drain away.

"What, sweetheart?" he asked. "What?"

He'd lost his own mom. He didn't have much family. I could see why he wouldn't want to just let me have her if we broke up. What if I ended up with Zach? Would Bryn take the baby out of spite? Would he think his child would be better off learning magic from him? Living somewhere outside Duvall? And if he did, what chance did I have of stopping him? Bryn was a lawyer who specialized in family law, and he'd never lost a case. People joked that he'd made a deal with the devil to get juries to always see things his way. Maybe not. Maybe he just bespelled them. Or maybe he just persuaded them with a handsome face and beautiful, irresistible eyes.

I put my hand up to cover his eyes, so I could look away as the tears started to well up in mine. He jerked his face back so he could see me.

"What?" he demanded as I got to my feet. I heard the sharp note of unease in his voice. He could see the truth in my eyes.

"No," he said.

"We'll work together to save the town," I whispered.

"And then?" he demanded.

Then I'll get away from you, and, if I'm pregnant, I'll make sure you never find out. "Then we'll see."

He grabbed my arm and kept me from walking away. "Tell me! Tell me what you heard!" His teeth clenched, and dark power radiated from his body, all but swallowing me up in ice. I shuddered.

"Let go of me. I'm cold."

He pulled me toward him, but I jerked back. His vise grip on my arm tightened until it hurt. I was afraid, not so much of him, but that I'd crack, that I'd look at him and want to tell him everything. A part of me loved him, wanted him in spite of everything. That part fought to get to him; that part wanted to press against him and cry into his ear and

believe whatever he'd say to convince me to trust him. It
took every bit of my strength not to snake my arms around
his neck and turn my back on my family.

Tears dripped from my eyes.

Edie's words echoed in my head. *Their own fault. Silly
little fools.*

"Let go, Bryn." I tried to make my voice sound hard.

"Won't you tell me?" he asked, frustration laced with fury.
He could be ruthless. It was there in his voice and in the
things he'd done. The way he drove Edie away and blocked
her from reaching me. When he thought he was right about
something, he could be calculating and probably never
regretted it. Who would he think our baby would be better
off with? Him or me? Him. Of course, he would.

"Let's talk about it. Tell me what you heard," he said.

I stared at him, then turned my face away a fraction of
an inch. With my heart breaking, I said, "No."

Mercutio's yowl made Bryn loosen his hold on my arm,
and I pulled away. Mercutio rushed toward me, and I hurried
in his direction. I didn't hear or feel Bryn behind me. I
glanced over my shoulder to see that he'd turned his back
to me, shrugging the bathrobe back on while he stared out
at the water.

I walked without breaking my stride, anxious to put some
distance between us.

Merc was almost to me when he hissed and sprang toward
the tree I was passing. I slowed just as a hand shot out and
grabbed me. For a moment, I was face-to-face with Scarface
until he whirled me around, levering a forearm across my
throat and pressing a gun to my head.

33

SCARFACE KICKED VICIOUSLY at Merc, but only landed a glancing blow. He whipped the gun toward Mercutio and fired. Merc sprang forward, and the bullet missed him by a hair. Real bullets, not tranquilizer darts.

"Run, Merc!" I said. I'd tried to yell, but the arm across my throat made my voice a rasp.

Mercutio stood his ground, back raised, front legs slightly bent like he was ready to spring at us.

Scarface pressed the muzzle of the gun to my head. "Tell him to back off. I will shoot you."

"Go on, Merc. You get behind a tree," I said. Mercutio didn't listen. I'd known he wouldn't. Back down from a fight? Leave me on my own? Not a chance. It made me mad at him. It also made me want to hug him.

"Who are you and what are you doing?" Bryn's voice was soft. I almost didn't hear it over the blowing wind.

Scarface spun to face Bryn. "I'm here to collect some things." He rubbed the gun against my temple. "She took a brooch. Where is it?"

"I don't know what you're talking about," I stammered.

"She doesn't have it. It's locked up in my house," Bryn

said, making me scowl. I'd worked so darn hard to get that brooch. Also, lying to the bad guys seemed like the right thing to do on principle, and, I reasoned, the longer Scarface didn't have what he wanted, the longer he wouldn't be shooting me in the head.

I shivered.

"I'm unarmed. Let her go. You're better off with the gun on me," Bryn said.

"You go in and get the brooch. We'll wait here. And take the cat with you," Scarface said, drawing us back away from Merc and Bryn.

I stiffened as Merc yowled in warning when Bryn took a step closer to him.

"Don't bite him, Merc. You go on with Bryn. I'll be just fine out here," I said, trying to keep my voice steady. It was just sinking in that there was an actual bullet a couple inches from my brain. I gulped. Just a little pressure on the trigger, and I could be Tammy in a locket or a brooch. Or in one of the earrings I had on, which were mighty small. I wished I'd worn real gold instead of Wal-Mart junk.

Bryn grabbed Merc's collar and hauled him up. Merc twisted, and I winced as he scratched Bryn's forearm.

"Easy," Bryn said in a low voice to Mercutio. There was a lulling quality to the magic that dripped from his tongue. Bryn whispered something else. It sounded soothing, but I felt the back edge of the magic and knew that Bryn had said something dark, like: "You can kill him later."

Mercutio calmed, though he opened his jaw in a snarl to show off teeth that were made to tear things to pieces.

"If you bring anyone with you, they die and so does she. Better come back alone, Lyons."

When they were gone, I tried to relax my muscles. It didn't work all that well.

Raindrops turned to drizzle. Wet, cold, miserable, and scared. I'd had better days.

"What's your name?" I asked.

"Let's go," Scarface said, pulling me backward toward the woods.

"I thought you wanted the brooch!" I said, moving slowly, stalling our progress.

Uneven ground made his body jerk as he nearly stumbled.

"Hey, be careful! I don't want to get shot by accident!"

Just inside the woods, he shoved me face-first against a tree.

"Don't move," he said, pushing on my back so that my belly, which was only covered by the thin layer of draped silk, scraped against the bark. A moment later, he grabbed my left wrist, and I felt a metal cuff snap around it. The next second, he whirled me around and jerked my arms up. He brought the links of the shackles over the tree branch. I struggled against him trying to stretch me upward, but he lifted me by my right wrist and closed the cuff around it. He let me go and I dangled, my toes just touching the ground, my torso pulled so tight it was hard to breathe.

"If you cooperate, I won't shoot Lyons. If you don't do what I say, I will kill him where he stands."

My heart seized up at that. "You're not supposed to kill me, are you? You used tranquilizers when you came for me alone. But when you come to Bryn's property, you carry a gun with real bullets."

"You heard what I said."

I took a sip of air, feeling slightly dizzy. "Did you kill Gwen to get the brooch? Your boss, John Barrett, sure wants it back pretty bad. Want to know why?"

"Quiet," he snarled, pinching my chin viciously. It throbbed and I glared at him, trying to suck in a deep breath. My body swayed. Half dangling from the branch, it was hard to steady myself.

I brought my hands together, cupping the thick branch and trying to get some purchase. I had to do something. Bryn was going to be back soon, and I was pretty sure Scarface was lying about not killing Bryn if I behaved myself. He'd tried to shoot Bryn the last time he'd been on the property. I was willing to bet that when he got the brooch back for John Barrett, he was under orders to kill Bryn.

Lightning streaked the sky, and I jumped at the rumble of nearby thunder.

I cocked my wounded foot, trying to stretch the bottom enough to open the cut. Blood can ignite magical energy, and, whenever I bled on tree trunks or roots, it seemed to help the trees understand English better.

"I can't breathe like this," I complained, drawing in a ragged breath.

"Shame," he said coldly, making me dislike him even more.

"C'mon," I hissed. "Move me toward the trunk where the branch is a little lower."

Pain exploded in my jaw when he hit me with a closed fist.

Yep, I thought dazedly, *I hate this guy.*

"Make a sound, and they die," he said before disappearing behind me, leaving me to stare into the dark woods.

My left lower lip swelled like an inner tube, and bloody saliva filled my mouth. Yuck. The pain was like a miniheart beating in my face. I opened and closed my mouth slowly. No sharp pain. I didn't think my jaw was broken, but that was hardly the point. He'd clocked me with his fist while my hands were chained over my head. *Jerk!* If I didn't end up dead, I was going to get even for that.

My mouthful of bloody saliva had to be dealt with. My stomach roiled, protesting the idea that I'd swallow any of it.

I turned my head and spat. I felt something. Maybe just a rustling of leaves as the wind kicked up, but then again, maybe not.

Blood on the roots. I sucked some more blood from my cut lip and spit it on the ground.

"Hey, tree," I whispered. "Tree?"

My body dangled, and I tried to swing to get my toes onto something, a root, a higher mound of dirt. "I'm hanging here. Can't breathe too good." I sucked in some air. "Can you help me? C'mon, tree, swing me up."

The thwack across my calves was like a cracking whip,

and my body flew upward too fast for me to know what was happening. Afterward, I was lying on a branch. I clasped it with my elbows and knees to keep from losing my balance and falling off.

"Thanks, tree. Thanks," I mumbled and gave the bark a quick fat-lipped, slightly bloody kiss. I took a big breath and exhaled. "I've gotta get down."

I inched forward away from the trunk with the wind blowing under the silk toga onto my naked butt. I scowled, looking around. I supposed that doing magic naked, or nearly so, was a time-honored tradition, but I really felt that fighting evil—or anything else that I had to leave the house for—required underwear.

The branch curved up and my legs tangled in the leafy offshoots. Moving was awkward, to say the least, and slow going.

"Can you help me get down? Swing me off the end of your branch?"

I gasped as I felt the branch jerk. I was bucked from the bark, and a sharp yank on the back of the silk toga sent me flying through the air.

I only had a couple seconds to be terrified before I slammed into the ground.

It felt like a bomb had exploded from the inside of my body. Everything hurt, and warm blood dribbled down my leg from the formerly clotted fence wound.

My heart pounded painfully in my chest, reminding me with every beat that I had better breathe. I'd wanted to get back to the ground, but I have to say, when you ask a tree to help you, you've got to be careful what you ask for.

Andre's words came back to me. *Gravity, she's a tough mistress.*

"I have to get up," I told my innards. "Sorry about that. Try not . . ." I breathed deep to brace myself and gripped my aching torso to steady it. "Try not to be bleeding in there."

A brush of fur made me turn my head sharply. Merc's smooth head nudged me.

"Where'd you come from?" I whispered, getting to my

feet and wincing. That cut on the sole of my foot felt like someone was sticking a knife in it. I hissed in pain. Merc put steady pressure on my calf to get me moving.

"I'm going," I mumbled, staggering silently in the direction he was pushing me toward.

"Tamara?" Bryn called.

I didn't answer. I had my eyes peeled on the ground along the tree line where Scarface would be lying in wait. I spotted the bastard. He was on one knee, his body hidden from Bryn by a tree trunk. His gun was already aimed.

Bryn headed straight for me, probably drawn to my magic, but, to get to me, he would pass too close to Scarface. He was already too close, I realized with a start.

I ran, hardly feeling the ground under my feet.

Gotta get there!

"Trees, help!" I whispered fiercely.

A branch gave me a swoop and a fling. I sailed forward, like Tarzan without a vine. Some crazy primitive triumph gripped me. Yeah, I was going to land like twenty tons, but I was going to land on Scarface like twenty tons. And flying's all right, kind of exhilarating when you get used to it. It's only the landing that I could do without.

I tried to yell "Stop!" but I didn't really get it all out. My body nailed Scarface's, and the gun went off.

I'd knocked him facedown into the dirt. From his back, I jammed my hands over his head and jerked them so the handcuff chain caught him across the front of the throat. I dragged my arms back. Mercutio yowled.

"Bryn!" I rasped, looking up sharply. Had he been shot?

Scarface's gun was only inches from his hand. Fury and anxiety roared through my veins. I pulled the chain tight, cranking Scarface's head back.

Footsteps slapped the ground, then Bryn stood over us.

"Get the gun!"

Bryn kicked Scarface's gun away, and Bryn's hand emerged from his robe pocket with his own gun.

"Are you—" Bryn's gaze darted to my face for a second. "Are you going to kill him?"

"Nope," I said through clenched teeth. "But he's not getting the upper hand. Not again. Not if I can help it."

"He's turning purple, Tamara." Bryn's voice was so calm, like whether I committed murder or not was up to me. Bryn was just letting me know about the purple, in case I didn't realize.

I hadn't. I pitched forward, palms down on the ground, taking the pressure off Scarface's throat. I heard his raspy intake of breath.

Pulling my chain free, I dug my knee in his back as I climbed off him. I glanced at Mercutio, who was gnawing on the guy's calf. Served Scarface right, but . . .

"Merc, remember how you're an ocelot, not a tiger?" I caught my breath, the adrenaline wearing off slowly. "He's too big for you to eat. Except for maybe a foot or hand or something." I shrugged at Bryn's surprised expression, but I guessed it was kind of an odd thing for me to say.

I felt weird, shaky, and things began to ache. It was like I was becoming human again, but then what had I been before? I gazed up at the trees, whose curved branches looked like smiles to me. Their canopy kept most of the rain from drizzling on my head, and I knew something that I couldn't explain in words. It was like they were beckoning me, like they were telling me I could curl up in the crook of their branches and I'd feel okay. Part of me wanted to.

"Thanks, trees. Thanks for everything," I whispered.

"Tamara," Bryn said, drawing my gaze back down to the world of men. The cold, damp air seeped into my bones, making me shiver. He studied my face. "Your eyes are glowing gold."

"Yeah, I think—" My teeth chattered, and I looked down at Scarface. "I've got some of my dad's blood. It's in me for sure." I bent down to check Scarface's pockets for the handcuff keys. "I've really gotta be careful about it, or I'll end up living in the woods in a *Clan of the Cave Bear* outfit with dirty fingernails and twigs in my hair. Johnny and Rollie would be so furious."

Merc purred.

"Yeah," I said, looking at Merc's tawny eyes, which I knew were a lot like my own. "I know you'd stay with me, Mercutio. You're a wild thing, too." I plucked the key from Scarface's pocket and stood up. My body throbbed a protest, but I moved forward. Bryn pocketed his gun and took the key. He unlocked the cuffs, and I rubbed the scraped skin of my left wrist with my other hand.

Bryn bent down and cuffed Scarface's hands behind his back and whispered a spell. The magic curled around the shackles.

I gave him a questioning look.

"So that he can't use magic to get out of them."

"Oh, right. Good thinking. That's probably how he got loose the last time I handcuffed him." I picked up Scarface's gun. "Did you bring the brooch?"

"Of course," he said, taking it out to show me. "There is nothing that I have that I wouldn't have traded for your life."

"Will you trust me with her? I think maybe I can free her if you do."

"Tell me what you're thinking."

I couldn't be partners with him. I could barely concentrate while I looked at him. I kept thinking about the prophecy, believing it and not wanting to believe it. My heart ached for what I could never have with Bryn now that I knew the truth.

"You trusted me before to save your life. I know you didn't have a choice then, but you know me. I'll do everything I can to help her," I said.

He leaned forward and slipped the brooch between two folds of silk that were lying across my left shoulder and upper chest. He pinned it to the fabric, so it was hidden from sight.

"Thanks," I said and took a few slow steps out of the woods. Adrenaline gone, everything hurt.

"Tamara, wait," Bryn said. "It doesn't have to be this way. Whatever you heard—" He shook his head. "Won't you at least tell me what it was?"

The temptation was like a weight pressing down on me.

Tell him. He'll convince you it's not true. You know you want to let him convince you.

Except . . . you've heard it over and over. Lenore is never wrong.

I turned my head toward him, licking my puffed-out lip. Bryn studied me intensely with his glittering blue eyes. He was so handsome and so what my body craved that it was hard to look at him.

"Not everything we want is good for us," I whispered.

He clenched his jaw stubbornly. Exactly why he was dangerous. He refused to accept that I might know something important that proved what he didn't want to believe.

I touched my fingertips to my mouth and then extended them toward him in a makeshift long-distance kiss. "Try to let me go," I rasped.

I turned and shuffled into the whipping wind and falling rain, but still managed to hear his single spoken word.

"Never."

34

AS WE HURRIED back to the house, I poured my heart out to Mercutio. The heavens had opened up and sheets of rain were coming down so hard that I had to yell over the noise.

"I do care about him *so* much, but that's not the point, is it?" I shouted as we got to the screened porch. The door opened, making me jump back, but it was only Andre and Steve.

"Where is he?" they both asked at once.

"He's out there with the Conclave bad guy. You could help him bring the guy in, Steve."

Steve pushed past me.

"You might want to take an umbrella," I said.

He kept going without one. Andre yanked the star-chart quilt off the sofa and wrapped it around me.

"I'm okay. I just need a fast, hot shower and some dry clothes. And a raincoat or hooded rain parka," I said through chattering teeth. I shuffled into the house leaving muddy, bloody footprints.

Andre trailed along with me, mumbling in German and rubbing my arms to warm me up. Mercutio howled, and I looked up at the sound of pinging and popping on the roof.

"Hail," I said to Merc.

Then the alarm went off, and the phone rang. Mercutio yowled a complaint.

"I know it's loud. What do you want me to do?" I demanded.

The sound of crashing glass made me jerk my head toward the front. "That wasn't hail," I said, swinging around. I pushed Andre behind the kitchen counter and shoved his shoulder. "Get down."

He crouched down, and I shrugged off the quilt to get my arms free. He grabbed my hand.

"You down as well."

"No."

"Wait," Andre said, standing up when I started creeping toward the kitchen door.

"Get down," I hissed at him.

"No. I will help you."

I waved off his offer of help and opened the swinging door a crack. My eyes widened. One of the decorative windows that flanked the front door had been smashed, and Lucy Reitgarten was climbing through it.

"For the love of Hershey," I muttered as she opened the front door for her prayer-spouting posse. They were dressed in trench coats and cowboy hats and armed with shotguns.

I darted back into the kitchen.

"Change of plans," I whispered, grabbing Andre by the arm. "Backyard. Now." I glanced over my shoulder. "Mercutio, c'mon!" I shouted in a whisper.

Merc glanced at me and then back at the kitchen door.

"C'mon," I snapped. No matter how outnumbered we were, the concept of retreat was unappealing to Merc. Andre was more reasonable, and I pushed him out the back door.

"Merc!"

Mercutio darted across the kitchen and outside. I was backing out the storm door when the inside door swung open.

"Tammy Jo Trask!" Boyd said.

I grimaced and raised my gun with the rain pouring down

on my head. Boyd didn't have a gun pointed at me though. Boyd had a gun pressed against Johnny Nguyen's neck.

For pete's sake! It was just one hostage situation after another these days.

"You come on back in," Boyd said.

"I sorry, Tammy Jo," Johnny said.

I knew Merc was behind me. If he got into the kitchen, he'd attack, and Boyd would definitely try to shoot him.

I waved off Johnny's apology with my gun, stepping back inside. I pulled the door closed so Andre and Merc, who I didn't think Boyd had seen, were left outside.

"Hey there, Boyd."

"I want my wife."

"Yep, I can see how you would," I said, my voice sweet as peaches in syrup. "I'm sure she'll be back anytime. You know Johnny does Jenna's hair? You really think she'd approve of you shooting the only person in town who knows how to get her highlights right?"

Boyd scowled at me. "You put that gun down and get over here," he said.

Other people appeared behind him in the doorway. Things were getting more and more out of control. I needed to defuse the situation fast.

"I'll sure take you to Jenna on one condition. Y'all have to leave Johnny here. He's got nothing whatsoever to do with anything. You've got to understand that."

"Put your gun down and walk away from it," he said.

"And you'll let Johnny go?"

Boyd nodded.

"Your word?"

"Hand to God," he said.

I set my gun down on the counter and stepped away from it.

"Okay," Johnny said. "We talk this out, Mr. Boyd." Johnny tried to push down Boyd's forearm to lower his gun, but Boyd shoved him aside and waved me over.

I sighed and stepped forward. "Go on now, Johnny. You get behind the counter. I'm gonna be all right." I walked to them, and they grabbed my arms.

"This not a good idea, Mr. Boyd. We all sit down. Have coffee. Or better yet: no-caffeine tea. You like cinnamon?" Johnny asked.

They dragged me out of the kitchen.

"Or peppermint! That soothing!" Johnny shouted.

They ignored him and pulled me out the front door into the pouring rain. The last thing I heard was, "Don't worry, Tammy Jo. We come after you!"

THEY SHOVED ME onto the floor of an SUV and tied me up with rope, then Boyd's thick-necked, curly-headed cousin, Abe, and Lucy and Sue told me I'd better put a stop to all this evil or I'd be going to Hell sooner rather than later.

"Forget all that!" Boyd snapped. "Where's Jenna?"

"She's at the Duvall Motor Inn," I said, figuring that if John Barrett and the Winterhawk could turn people into salt lick sculptures, they'd be able to handle my latest band of kidnappers. Of course, I'd also be delivering myself into John Barrett's hands. Well, no plan is really perfect.

We passed the busted-in front gates that they must've rammed several times to get access to Bryn's property.

"Rain's really comin' down," Abe said.

"Yeah," Boyd agreed. "Streets are getting flooded."

"Uh-oh."

"What?" Sue asked. "What's wrong?"

I wrestled myself up into a sitting position to get a better look out the window. "Floods are kind of . . ." I trailed off as lightning streaked through the sky. A moment later, the ground rocked and thunder rumbled.

"What?" Sue demanded. "Floods are kind of what?"

"Biblical," I murmured, putting my nose against the slightly fogged glass. Another flash of lightning lit the night, and I saw water gushing out of gutters and lapping up the curbs. "This can't be good."

"Your fault!" Lucy accused. "You're an abomination that the heavens are planning to wash away."

Sue nodded. "We should drown her, don't you think?

Then all her cursed magic will die with her, and everything will go back to normal."

My heart kicked up a fuss in my chest. "Do that and you'll never find Jenna."

"So you admit it!" Lucy crowed. "You admit that you hexed her?"

"Boyd, the town's between two rivers," I said.

Boyd narrowed his eyes.

"Admit it! Admit what you did to my sister-in-law," Lucy said, giving my arm a hard pinch. "Jenna always knew there was something wrong with you and your family. I should've listened to her sooner!"

I glared at her, but then turned my head to look at Sue and Abe. "We need to wake people up. If the water makes the rivers overflow and the town floods, people will drown. People need to get out of town until the storm's over."

"This town doesn't flood," Sue sneered. "It's never flooded. Sure there's water in the streets, but even when we've gotten inches of rain, it runs off. Duvall never floods. It never has a drought. It's the perfect town. Or it was until you got a hold of it."

"Listen, we have to start calling people before the phone lines go out."

"First, we're getting Jenna," Boyd said. "I'm driving, and we're getting my wife back before we do anything else."

"C'mon now, y'all. We can drive and call. No reason we can't do both at the same time," I said in a cajoling tone I hoped would convince them.

"We could call. Or we could take a more direct approach to handling the problem," Sue said, looking me over.

"We're here," Boyd announced, pulling into the parking lot.

"She'll be in Room Seven," I said. "Or, if not there, in Room Five," I said, not giving them Mrs. Thornton's room. I didn't mind if Barrett got shot in the fight or if they discovered Gwen's body, but I didn't want them to take Mrs. Thornton by surprise when I was hoping for her help with the brooch and with clearing Bryn and me from the trouble with WAM.

Boyd and Abe got out of the truck with their guns and jogged through the rain to the motel room doors. Boyd kicked in the door to John Barrett's room. He and Abe went in and the room light blinked on, but a minute later, they came back out. Abe pounded on Room 6's door while Boyd kicked in the door of Room 5. He went inside and turned on the light. A few seconds later, he was back out, waving his arms and yelling. Abe bent his head forward, looking in the window of Room 6. Then they ran to the office. A few minutes later they returned to the truck.

"You lying bitch," Boyd yelled, rubbing water off his face. "The English people were staying in those rooms, but they checked out this morning. Guy on the desk says Jenna was never here."

Checked out? Then where were they staying? And what the heck had happened to Gwen's body?

"They said they all checked out? All three of them? Did they actually see the young woman?" I asked, sounding as bewildered as I felt. Had Barrett and the Winterhawk taken Gwen's body away? Like those CIA guys that they called cleaners who got rid of bodies and any evidence of a crime scene? On the one hand, that would've been kind of a relief. On the other, yikes! Really scary. Would they kill Bryn and me and make us disappear next?

"Abe, I'm going to drop you and Sue off. You need to get people organized," Boyd said.

"And what are *you* planning to do?" Abe asked.

"Nothing for you to worry about. Lucy and I will find out what she did with Jenna, then we'll take her to the police station. The sheriff'll lock her up for kidnapping. I'll see to that."

I wasn't exactly keen on getting locked up, but, compared to getting tortured or killed, it didn't seem so bad.

Boyd took Abe home and dropped Sue back at her place, telling her to get her neighbors up and out of town.

"What about Lindsey?" Sue asked, referring to Boyd and Jenna's daughter.

"My parents took her to Disney World," Boyd said.

"You sure you can handle the witch alone?" Sue asked.

I narrowed my eyes. "I have a name. It's Tammy. Or Tammy Jo. Or even, sometimes to some people, Tamara!"

Boyd's dark glance in my direction made me shiver. Something told me that I didn't want to be alone with him without witnesses.

"You should stay, Sue. I'm sure there's—" I started to say, but Boyd's sharp voice cut me off.

"Hurry and get out!" he said. "If Jenna's tied up somewhere on a ground floor, she could drown if it floods."

Sue got out, her feet slapping the water-soaked ground. "You both be careful. We don't know what else the witch is capable of." The door slammed shut, and Boyd pulled away.

"So, what's it going to be? My sister swears that you made Jenna disappear; that it wasn't some trick. I know—and we've seen—a lot of things the past couple of weeks that can't be explained. Me, I don't care which it is. Whether you tricked Lucy or whether you used some unholy power. All I care about is getting my wife back." His voice was angry, but there was also some fear, which made me feel bad. No matter how rotten Jenna and her people were, I wasn't trying to torture them with worry.

"Listen, Boyd, she's okay."

"*Where* is she?" he demanded.

Should I tell them about her being in Bryn's other house? That we'd left Bryn's butler Mr. Jenson in charge of taking care of her? What would happen if I took them there and they saw that Jenna was only a few inches tall? They already seemed to have a notion that killing me would undo my magic spells, which was true.

"She's safe, and if you let me go, I'll make sure you get her back right away. As soon as the storm's over."

"She's lying. She's stalling. She has no intention of bringing Jenna back. Not ever. If you want your wife back, we're going to have to get the witch to tell us where she is," Lucy said.

"Okay," Boyd said.

Uh-oh! "Hang on!" I said as Boyd turned left.

"Let's go to the cemetery. No one will be there this time of night in this weather."

"Wait! Okay, I'll tell you. The truth is she's in a whiskey decanter in a spare house outside town. She's okay, just a little short at the moment. She's not hurt."

They ignored me.

"It's the truth!" I said, struggling to loosen the ropes. Lucy grabbed my wrists to keep me from getting my hand out. "Leave me alone."

She slugged me. "Be still!"

I swung my arms and bopped her in the side of the head. Boyd slammed on the brakes, but the wheels didn't catch. We hydroplaned through the water, slammed into a curb, and rolled over and over. The last thing I felt was my head bouncing off the window.

I WOKE UP in a big metal tub of freezing water with huge stones on my belly and across my hip bones. The rocks were secured with ropes, so I couldn't knock them off. The tub sat just outside the Glenfiddle Whiskey factory that's shaped like a castle. It's where Lucy works, so I guessed that she'd used a key to get in, and they'd pulled the tub out.

It was three-quarters full, and the rain went on pouring down, but Corsic Creek was just on the other side of the factory, so if they were planning to drown me, there was sure a faster and easier way.

"She's up," Lucy said. I turned my head and had to crane my neck to see over the side of the tub. Lucy and Boyd were standing under the awning of the covered porch.

Boyd was drinking from a bottle. Liquor and good judgment, not usually the best of friends.

Boyd handed Lucy the bottle. "Get her to drink it. It'll help get the truth out of her."

"You don't have to get me drunk to get me to tell the truth. Really," I said as Lucy walked over. "I've got a crick in my neck. How about you let me up, and I'll take you to where Jenna's at? I promise I will."

"Drink," Lucy said, banging the bottle against my bruised lip.

"Ouch. Cut that out! You get more flies with honey than whiskey, and I'm just like flies in that regard. I don't want—"

She poured, and I choked and sputtered, most of the liquor splattering over my chest.

Lucy grabbed my hair and yanked my head back. She poured whiskey over my face, choking me some more until I was mad as hell.

"Come and help me, Boyd," Lucy said.

He did. He took my head and pinched my nose until I opened my mouth, then she poured whiskey into it. I choked it down, and I glared at her.

I couldn't resist trying a spell.

As bad as your sister, in every way.
Join her then, in a bottle–stay.

With a soft *pop*, she was gone and the bottle she'd been holding dropped to the ground with a splashing thump.

"What the hell? What the hell did you do?" Boyd said, backing away and looking around.

I gasped for breath, still shaking with fury. "You're next, bud, unless you get me out of this tub."

He pointed a finger at me. "You unholy bitch!"

"I'm not unholy or a bitch. You guys were pouring whiskey on my head when I'm half drowned already. I'm sure God is going to agree that I was provoked."

"Well, I was provoked, too." He reached in and grabbed my legs, pulling me so that my shoulders sank underwater, and my head was below the level of the tub's rim.

"Hey!"

Boyd walked away.

"Hey! Hang on."

He didn't turn back. I saw light when he opened his SUV.

"Boyd!" I called. The water was already to my chin. I needed to get out. "C'mon. I promise not to cast any more spells. Come back, and let's talk this over."

The door slammed shut and a moment later the engine roared to life.

"This is not good."

I heard Boyd drive off. I craned my neck, trying to get my head above the tub's lip. Not happening. What's more I could hear water sloshing against the outside walls. I wondered what would happen first, the rain filling the tub up and drowning me or Corsic Creek overflowing and drowning me. It was also possible that I'd freeze to death before I drowned because maybe the water was not quite as cold as the water that the *Titanic* sank in, but I swear it was close.

This abuse was the ultimate snub.
I need out; turn over this tub.

Nothing. I huffed a sigh and tried several more times without success.

"This is really not good." My heart pounded in my chest, and I closed my eyes, trying to stretch my mind out. "Edie!" I called. "Bryn!" I took a deep breath and exhaled, licking my swollen lip. "Mercutioooo!"

Unfortunately, I could tell it was no use. Even I could barely hear my cries over the sound of the wailing wind.

35

AT JUST THE right angle, I could keep my chin, my nose, and my lips above the waterline. I'd been trying to cast all sorts of spells to tip the tub over or to empty it or to be ejected out of it, but nothing worked. What's more, I kept getting water in my mouth when I tried.

I did have a strategy that was working. I held my breath, pulled my legs in and shook them back and forth to make the tub overflow as much as possible, then lifted my legs out, and I'd have a little more room to keep my mouth out of the water. I had no idea how long I'd been doing it for when I saw light through my closed eyelids.

"I'm here!" I said, barely hearing my own voice. I coughed on the nasty water that got in my mouth and spit it out.

My ears were underwater, plus there was the storm, so I couldn't hear much. If I hadn't been half frozen, the quiet would've been kind of peaceful.

I felt hands grabbing me, heard muffled shouts. Then the ropes were being cut and someone hauled the rocks off me.

I opened my eyes, but water blurred my vision as I was pulled from the tub.

Mercutio yowled louder than the wind, and I blinked several times. Bryn stood in knee-deep water next to the tub as Steve climbed back into a canoe. When Steve was sitting, Bryn, who was holding me, handed me to Steve, then climbed in himself.

Steve set me on a cushioned bench and wrapped a coat and blanket around me.

"Who put you in there?" Bryn demanded, glancing back at the tub.

"Jenna's people." My teeth chattered. "What's going on? Is the town evacuated? Where's Andre?"

"He wanted to come, but there wasn't room," Bryn said. "Lennox and Andre took another canoe to Macon Hill. I think Barrett must be casting from there. I'm not sure how he tapped into the tor's power. He doesn't have a connection to it. Lennox says the tor's core power can only be used by certain families. The first families who found it and, through a ritual, claimed it. Yours and mine and Tom Brick's."

"Huh." I shook, rubbing my numb legs.

Mercutio climbed on my lap, and I wrapped the blanket around us both. Bryn passed me an umbrella, but my hands were too cold and stiff to hold the handle. Instead, I put the blanket over my head and huddled inside it. Bryn recovered his paddle from the floor, and he and Steve started us going.

"How'd you find me?"

"Mercutio. He's able to track your magic with incredible sensitivity. And your power's mingled with mine, so it wasn't hard for me to feel it when we got close enough, even submerged in that water."

"The boat's filling up. We'll sink," I said, unable to stop shaking. My muscles and joints ached.

"We'll be all right."

"What happened to the bad guy? Scarface?"

"I didn't have time to question him. Andre handcuffed him to the banister at the top of the stairs."

"I can't feel my feet," I mumbled.

"I know you're freezing. We'll get out of the rain as soon

as we can," he said, shoving the paddle in and giving the water a hard stroke.

"Mr. Lyons," Steve shouted.

Bryn glanced over his shoulder.

"Current's pulling us south. I don't think we'll be able to reach Macon Hill."

"Just keep steering east," Bryn yelled. His magic flared as he whispered a spell. The boat surged forward, but the water lapped over the sides and tilted us to the right.

Branches and other debris banged into us, and the water continued to rise. The town was flooded. In some places, the water only filled the streets. In others, whole houses were partially submerged.

We passed through a neighborhood where people were being rescued from their rooftops. Our canoe rode low, half sunk from all the water we'd taken on. I cursed the rain and the wizard who'd brought it.

"We have to empty this water out," Bryn said.

The first couple rooftops Steve aimed for, we couldn't reach, but finally, we got to one.

The water ran down, but the shingles were ridged, and the texture helped me keep my balance as I climbed on it. Bryn and Steve flipped the canoe and lifted it upside down before flipping it back over.

Mercutio hissed, and I turned my head. His eyes shone in the moonlight, and I followed the line of his gaze to Steve.

The water streamed around Steve's ankles, but he seemed steady on his feet as he and Bryn lowered the canoe onto the water's surface.

"What?" I asked Merc as he darted forward.

I saw the swishing movement a moment too late. I screamed, "Snake!"

Mercutio's teeth clamped down on the middle of the water moccasin at the same time it struck, sinking fangs into Steve's forearm. Steve howled and jerked his arm. The snake recoiled and twisted toward Merc.

I lurched forward as it bit Merc's shoulder. I grabbed the

snake's slimy neck and squeezed. Merc's teeth tore the snake's middle open as he jerked his mouth sideways. The snake writhed and I yanked it back, pulling its fangs away from Mercutio.

I shook the heck out of its head until Mercutio let its body go and looked at me, giving a soft "We're done here" yowl.

It took me a minute to realize that there was no reason to hang on to a dead snake. I whipped it into the water, and the current dragged it away. I turned to see Steve holding his arm and talking to Bryn, who nodded.

When we returned to the boat, Bryn went to the back of the canoe, and Steve sat next to me in front. I helped Steve paddle as we maneuvered to a roof three houses away where a couple of deputies were putting people into a powerboat.

"He wants me to go. I can't help him like this," Steve explained, climbing out. His arm was already puffy from the venom.

I nodded.

Steve put his mouth to my ear. "You guys should come with me. You'll never make it all the way across town."

Smitty came over and ushered Steve to the bigger boat.

"The roads out of town are impassable, and there aren't enough boats with motors. Damn rain's still coming down," Smitty yelled, shaking his head. "I can fit two more. One of you will have to wait here, and we'll come back for you!"

Steve gave me a questioning look, and then Smitty gave him a little push to get him going.

"Go on," Smitty said.

Steve looked over his shoulder at us as he climbed in the boat.

"Your face is a mess, Tammy Jo. What happened to it?" Smitty asked with a frown.

"I fell."

"Right," he said, taking my arm. "Come on. I'll come back for Lyons."

"No, you go ahead. There are little old people over there," I said, pointing. "You have to get them first."

Smitty looked at Bryn, who was sitting in the boat. "You wait right here, Tammy Jo. I'll be back for you both."

As soon as the police zoomed away, I looked over my shoulder at Bryn.

"Can we make it?" I asked.

He nodded, so I picked up the front paddle and dipped it in the water.

Mercutio yowled.

"I know. I'm not sure about this either," I said.

I WAS HARDLY any help to Bryn when we dumped the water out of the canoe the second time. My arms shook from the effort, but I wasn't sorry that we'd decided to try to get to Macon Hill, because we'd found five-year-old Paige from my neighborhood and her teenage babysitter, Charlotte, along the way. I doubt the police would have checked the deserted area we found them in.

The teenager held Paige, who was fuzzy-headed from being half frozen. She kept squirming, trying to get her arms around Mercutio.

"Paige, honey, stop wiggling," I said. "Merc's not really the type to cuddle."

"Hang on to her," Bryn shouted at Charlotte several times. The last was just before a wave tipped us into the side of a tree.

Paige slipped like a greasy sausage from the girl's arms and disappeared into the water.

"No!" I shrieked, jumping up.

Bryn slapped my hands on to a tree limb. "Hold the boat here for me!" Then he dove in headfirst.

Charlotte wailed, and I shook my head, mumbling and biting my lip. The water was as black as tar and running fast. He'd never find such a little girl in all that. Tears welled in my eyes.

"Let him find her. Please, God, let him find her."

Merc stuck out his tongue to catch the rain, then gave a

soft yowl. A bluish light loomed under the surface, and I blinked. A moment later Bryn surfaced, dragging Paige. He swam to the boat with the current trying to sweep them away.

"Help him," I yelled at the girl. It took all I had just to keep my grip on the branch.

Charlotte pulled Paige into the boat, and Bryn hauled himself in, blue-lipped and breathless. He sat in several inches of water on the floor of the boat next to the bench where I sat.

"I have to let go," I said, my arms shaking from being so tired.

Bryn rose, teetering a bit. He grabbed the branch to help me keep us steady.

He had to yell above the noise of the storm. "We have to keep going. If we drift, we'll smash into trees, and the boat will break apart. Understand?"

I nodded.

"It's not much farther to Macon Hill."

"Okay!" I yelled. There was no choice. If we ended up in the water, we'd all drown except for maybe Bryn.

"I need power," he said. "I could invoke more black magic, but it would be risky—"

I tipped my face up and closed my eyes. Our mouths were so cold that our lips felt like rubber pressing against each other. The magic was sharp and spiky at first and then warmed up and surged between us.

He didn't hesitate. He sucked power off, then pushed a little of it deep into my chest. He took his place on the back bench.

"Hold on!" he told Charlotte and pressed her shoulder until she was sitting on the floor with Paige between her legs.

Mercutio sat next to me, but faced them, like he didn't trust Paige not to jump out of the boat again.

Facing forward, I rowed. I couldn't hear Bryn's voice above the storm, but I knew he was whispering spells because we bobbed over the water in the opposite direction of the current.

Finally, we ran into the slope of the mountain and saw a bunch of townspeople rushing toward us to help. I was so relieved, I could hardly speak. Then I remembered that our work was far from done.

Bryn gave the kids to the people, and we pulled the boat up onto the muddy bank to keep it from washing away. I saw bobbing light from men's flashlights. They were building a makeshift shelter about fifteen feet above the waterline.

As I straightened, I spotted a flash of red hair and froze. A woman dressed in an ivory-colored hat with plum trim and a matching rain slicker was with a group standing under a cluster of trees. Her white Wellington boots squelched in the mud as she turned.

It's her! She came home!

"Aunt Melanie!"

36

SHE HURRIED TO me, her boots slipping a couple of times in the slick mud. She didn't fall, but had to slow to keep her footing.

"Tammy," she said, hugging me tight. Then she flashed a small Maglite on my face and gasped. "What happened?" she demanded, her gaze darting to Bryn.

He scowled. "Of course not."

"A Conclave bad guy punched me in the lip, but I kicked his butt in the end. Well, the trees helped," I babbled with chattering teeth. I knew I looked like a refugee, bedraggled and bruised, while she was all shiny and pretty under the stylish straw cowboy hat that kept the rain off her face. How in the world did she do it? And why hadn't I inherited that ability? She was almost forty, but, come hell or flooding-the-town high water, she looked like a twenty-nine-year-old supermodel.

"What are you doing here? Edie said there was a curse," I stammered.

"There is. I was supposed to stay in the UK and earn its removal, but I didn't, so no powers for me for seven years. But I had to come, didn't I?" She clasped my cheeks gently in her hands. "You were in trouble. Of course, I had to come." She gave me another tight hug that squeezed all my aching body parts. I winced, but didn't complain. It was so nice to have that hug. She rubbed her hands over my arms. "Wow, that's a great partial protection spell. Very elegantly cast."

"Protection spell?"

She cocked her head. "It's subtle. Really nicely done."

I looked at Bryn. "Did you—"

"It's not his magic," Melanie said quickly, barely giving him a glance. "God, your skin's cold. Come under the trees," she said.

"Tamara."

We both turned our heads. Bryn looked tired, but resolute with his arms folded across his chest, his jaw set.

"What?" Aunt Mel demanded. "She's exhausted and freezing and injured. What can you possibly want?"

I almost smiled. Aunt Mel was a wild party girl and bohemian witch most of the time, but, when it came to me, she couldn't have been more responsible if she'd been my own momma. When I was growing up, they'd both taken care of me. I could hear the echo of a thousand things she'd said over the years. "Mar, what did our baby girl do this weekend? . . . What did our little girl learn in school today? . . . What did our little Tammy think of . . . ?" She'd loved me something fierce. And I still loved her, too, whether she'd lied to me or not.

"We're involved in something," Bryn told her. "It's a long story."

"Well, it's not as if I have something more pressing to do," she said, tugging me toward the trees.

"Hang on, Aunt Mel. There's something—well, we've got to climb this hill and stop a lunatic wizard from washing all the people away so he can take over the town."

"You can't get up there," Aunt Mel said. "The water's pouring down the side. It's a constant mudslide. Don't you think we've tried to get to higher ground? The trucks are all stuck in the mud. The road's unreachable. We'll have to wait out the storm. If it's powered by magic, it can't last much longer."

"I wouldn't count on that. Barrett seems to have a power store that's unprecedented," Bryn said.

"Well, you do whatever you want, but she's staying here." Aunt Mel nodded at me while tucking loose strands of hair behind my ears and pulling the blanket forward so the lip shielded my face better.

"I'd love to stay here. I really would, but I promised and I need to—" I began.

"No," she said, clasping my hands. "It's not your responsibility."

I bit my lip, which made my breath catch at the pain. "It is. I decided it is, but you don't have to worry. We'll be back before you know it." I gave her a hug and a quick kiss, which left a dirty smudge on her glistening cheek. I rubbed the mark.

"If you're going, so am I."

"But you don't have any magic!" I said.

"I have knowledge and experience, and, most importantly, *I* have your best interests at heart."

I didn't want to look at Bryn because I just knew he would look furious, but he cleared his throat, and I couldn't help but glance over.

He ran a hand through his hair and studied my face. "It's not a good idea for your aunt to come. The power I generated the other night is nearly gone. It'll be hard enough for me to protect the two of us without also having to keep her safe. And we can't afford her interfering with whatever we need to do to generate magic. Think about it," he said. "Take a minute while I assess things." He swiveled the flashlight and walked away.

"If you're going, I'm going," she said. "Now that he's gone, I can ask: What in the world are you doing with him? And what are you wearing under that blanket? It looks like shrink-wrap."

"Yeah, it's been kind of a rough . . . well . . . Aunt Mel, I sure love you. That's why you can't come with us, but I don't want you to worry. After Bryn and I take care of this,

I won't be seeing him anymore. In fact, I might be leaving town. Maybe you and I can take a trip somewhere. You always like to travel."

"What about your job and Zach?"

"No job, and no Zach, at least not in Duvall right now. So you and I could go anywhere, except not somewhere that cats aren't allowed. I have an ocelot. We're friends," I said pointing to Merc. "And we can't go until we're sure the town's safe."

Bryn came back with rope and a shovel. "Listen," he said. "There are plenty of dark places among the trees. We can get out of sight, generate magic, and I can draw power from you. Then I can go alone."

"No way. You've got a gun for me, right? You'll cast spells. I'll shoot. You know that's our best chance. It's just logical," I said, knowing he couldn't deny it.

"The side of the mountain is too wet and slippery, the incline too steep in places, for us to walk or climb without equipment. One of the guys has gardening tools in the back of his flatbed. We could use the small spades to climb with, but it would be a hell of a lot of work."

"We're both already so tired," I said.

Bryn nodded. "Going up the road would work better."

"But you can't get to the road," Melanie said impatiently.

Bryn didn't respond to her. "I have an idea about how to reach the road." His eyes were fixed on my face. "It'll be dangerous."

As usual. "Then let's get it over with before I get too nervous."

THE GROUND BETWEEN us and the road had sunk into a channel of gushing water. Beyond that, there were three fallen trees with branches sticking out everywhere that would prevent anyone from getting to the road by boat. This didn't look good.

"Bryn, what do you have in mind? Us growing some wings?" I asked.

Bryn stabbed the shovel into the ground until the whole metal piece was buried and part of the pole along with it. He tied an end of the rope to it.

Blood dripped off his arm. "Bryn, your wound."

"I know," he said, testing the knot's tightness.

"What do you think you'll—" Aunt Mel began.

"Melanie, can you hold this? To be sure the shovel doesn't come loose?" he asked.

She pursed her lips, but grasped the wooden handle. "What does he think he's going to do?"

He tied the rope around his belt. "I'm going to swim to the trees and secure the rope. I'll come back for you, Tamara, and we'll use the rope to keep the current from washing us away."

"You really think you can swim it?" Melanie demanded.

"I can. She can't," he said, then looked at me. "I don't think I could swim it with you holding on to me, but hand-over-hand with the rope for leverage, I can get you across to the trees. Then we'll climb through the limbs to the road. After that, getting up the hill should be straightforward."

I didn't need to tell him it was a crazy plan. He already knew.

"The water's so cold," I mumbled. "When this is all over, I'm going to soak in a hot bath for two weeks. Maybe a month."

He caught my face in his hands and kissed me. I didn't move, self-conscious at first from Aunt Mel's sputtered protest, but I felt Bryn twisting swirls of our magic together and coaxing it out of me. He needed a power boost, and that's the only reason I let him kiss me. Really.

When he let go, he turned away immediately, licking his lips before he dove into the icy water. He disappeared instantly into its darkness.

I clenched my fists nervously, straining my eyes, hoping to see him surface. I bit the corner of my lip where it wasn't hurt and chewed until that spot started to ache, too.

"There are other handsome wizards, you know. If you're really finally over Zach and want to meet some new guys, we'll find some for you. Ones who don't have the last name Lyons."

"Aunt Mel, can you be quiet, please?" My stomach knotted. Bryn was tired and bleeding. My fingers were so stiff that I could hardly move them, and I wasn't even in that frigid water. How could he make it?

I moved the light back and forth in a slow arc until it caught the gleam of his wet head. I exhaled, tears prickling my eyes. I might be planning on never seeing him again, but I still couldn't stand the thought of anything happening to him.

It took a long time for him to secure the rope. I shouted for him to stay there, but he followed the rope across the water.

He was breathless and shaking when he got to the make-shift bank. I put a hand out to help him from the water, but he shook his head.

"If I got out, I'd never get back in. Just come," he said.

"Okay. Merc, there's no way for us to carry you, so you stay here with Aunt Mel." I shrugged off the blanket and coat, knowing they'd be too heavy once they got completely soaked.

Merc gave a soft yowl, then hopped onto the rope and ran across it like some feline tightrope walker. Merc went all the way to the trees, where he hopped on the branches. He almost fell through them, but didn't. He was on the road in a few moments.

"Sometimes I hate that cat," Bryn mumbled.

I grabbed the rope and slid into the water. I couldn't help myself. I screamed. The water was like icicles, like needles. Like knives.

"I can't," I said about twenty times in a row.

Bryn grimaced, his dusky blue lips pursed tight. "Come on, sweetheart. Get close to me. You'll be warmer."

I moved to him, my legs numb. They dangled from my hips like dead weight. My fingers clamped around the rope and wouldn't move.

"I really can't," I sobbed.

"Give me your hand," Melanie yelled. "Come on, Tammy, come back."

"Put your arms around my neck," Bryn said, moving so that our chests were touching. He whispered a spell, and his body warmed. He moved his head next to mine, our cheeks touching. "Drop your arms around my neck, sweetheart."

My heart banged in my chest. "You won't be able to hold us both up. We'll fall in the water."

"For God's sake!" Melanie screamed. "Bring her back."

"We have to go. One way or the other, Tamara, we have to move," he said.

"I don't want to drag you down with me. Please. Back up."

"No." He moved his hands over mine, warming them. They stung like they were waking from being asleep. He pulled my fingers, and they lost their grip. I sank.

Bryn grabbed my waist with one arm and held the rope with the other.

"Get your arms up. I can't hold on like this," he shouted.

"Let me go."

He shook his head, and I knew he was about to let go of the rope. With a groan of pure pain, I forced my arms up and around his neck. I clasped my hands tight, dragging his neck forward. His face dipped in the water for a moment before he managed to lift his head and got his second arm back onto the rope.

He gasped for breath, his face a mask of concentration. His muscles corded tight as he walked us backward with his hands, straining against the force of the current. It probably only took about ten minutes, but it felt like ten hours, ten excruciating hours.

At the other end of the rope, we had to climb through branches. My muscles moved, but I didn't even feel like I was controlling them anymore. By the time Bryn dragged us out of the water onto the road, we were both covered in bloody scratches and oozing from our other wounds.

"I can't go back in that water. Not ever. I'd rather die," I said.

He was lying half on top of me, for warmth and from exhaustion. "I know. Part selkie, my ass," he said. "I think halfway across my feet turned into blocks of ice and fell off."

Mercutio hopped on top of us, across our shoulders like a warm, silky feline blanket. He licked our faces. It was nice to have his body protecting our heads from the rain.

"I really can't understand why you wouldn't want to ignore the prophecy and be with me forever," Bryn said. "I always show you such a good time."

I laughed and kissed the side of his face before I remembered I wasn't supposed to let myself do that anymore. "I'll miss you, but I won't ever miss all this craziness."

He pushed himself up and held out a hand to me.

"For the love of—" Aunt Mel snapped.

I turned my head sharply toward her voice. She was tangled in the branches, trying to climb through.

Bryn frowned, but, without a word of complaint, he went back in the water and helped her get to the road. Another reason a part of me would love him until I died.

Melanie shook, dragging her boots off and dumping the water out of them. "Awful. Really bloody awful."

I raised my brows.

"What?" she asked.

"You talked with an accent."

"Oh," she said, and then, in her normal American voice, she said, "I'm part English and I was just in England. Sometimes the accent comes back of its own accord."

I stared at her, flabbergasted. "Who are you?"

"Still the same Aunt Melanie who loves you, just with a few secrets to confess. I'll tell you everything," she said. Looking briefly at Bryn, she added, "Later. When we're alone."

Bryn rubbed his wounded arm. "Ready?" he asked me.

I nodded. "Aunt Mel, I guess you're coming with us, but you should stay back and out of sight. You can be our backup if we get caught or wounded or something."

She didn't answer. She's not much for taking orders from people her own age, let alone somebody she taught the ABC's to.

We walked up the road, our feet slapping in the water, rain blowing against us. There were no trees on the road to act as shelter, so by the time we got to the top, I felt ready to collapse.

"You know how in summer the concrete's so hot it can give you second-degree burns if you walk to the mailbox without flip-flops on?" I rubbed my arms, shivering. "I'm never going to complain about that again."

Bryn bent down and took a gun from an ankle holster. He handed it to me and pointed toward the chapel with a swirl of his finger that I took to mean we were going around.

I followed him, Mercutio sauntering along next to me and Aunt Melanie a few feet behind.

Bryn stopped abruptly and I bumped into him. "There are wards," he said.

I looked at him expectantly. He put a hand out as if to feel them. Melanie stepped forward, too. She put her hands up, then took a sharp step back. She drew her brows together, frowning.

"President John Barrett from the World Association of Magic is the one who's up here?" she asked.

Bryn nodded, still focused on the invisible wards. He shoved a hand out, and I felt a frizzle of Bryn's power arc through me. My breath caught, my stomach lurching. He grabbed my arm and pulled me forward.

We circled the chapel and stopped when we saw a tarp drawn across four posts. Sitting under it in a large deck chair was John Barrett. There was a fire in the center, and a cup of tea on a small table next to him. Outside the makeshift tent, there were six twelve-foot spikes whose pointed tips stabbed the sky. Lightning rods.

"You shouldn't have come. I suspected you would, but you really shouldn't have," he called.

"I had to come," I said.

"Not you, my dear. You're perfectly safe." He and Bryn locked eyes, and Barrett stood. "You should have been smart, Lyons, and got out when you could."

Aunt Melanie lurched forward and grabbed my arm, yanking me to face the chapel. "Say what I say," she snapped.

Earth alive within us free.
Enclose and protect just we three.

She squeezed my arm hard, and I spit out the words.

I didn't see or feel whatever hit us, but it crashed through the barrier I'd tried to create and knocked me and Bryn and Aunt Mel down.

"Enclose," Bryn shouted, putting his arms out.

Something hit his enclosure with a loud crash and a flash of white light.

The Winterhawk emerged from the building's doorway where she'd been out of sight. She wore a black slicker and hat, like a sinister version of *The Old Man and the Sea*. Sleek and calm under her large umbrella, she defied the blowing rain, seeming unaffected by its bite.

Aunt Melanie paled to the color of milk.

"I thought so," Aunt Mel whispered. Then, her voice a bit louder, she said, "Hello, Aunt Margaret."

What?

All the blood pooled in my feet, and I swayed.

What?

37

"HELLO, MELANIE. WHERE'S Marlee?" the Winter-hawk asked.

"Wait. What?" I asked. The superspy assassin/bodyguard witch was my relative?

Merc yowled that he wanted an explanation, too. Aunt Mel didn't respond.

"Your sister's not with you. That's a problem, isn't it? You're always so much stronger together. And recent intelligence reports that your powers have been drained. How did that happen?"

Melanie's posture was rigid, like she was made of white marble. Only the rippling of the wind through her hair made her look real.

The Winterhawk walked slowly in a semicircle until she stood in front of Bryn. "You have a single chance to live, my lad." Her voice was a terrible whisper that cut through the wind in the strangest, most ominous way. "No, don't harden yourself. Hear me out."

He stared at her.

"She," Mrs. Thornton said, pointing at me, "belongs to us, to our family. If you foreswear any claim to her, if you make a solemn vow to never approach any of us again, you may go unharmed."

He didn't move. Didn't speak.

"You can't hope to win a battle of magic. You're weakened, your magic depleted from the disastrous spell you cast last week. Even if you weren't drained, you couldn't defeat me."

She raised a hand and with a slight flick of her wrist, she whispered, "Slice."

He winced and blood appeared on his right cheek.

"Don't!" I said with a gasp and raised my gun reflexively.

Her cool green gaze skimmed me from head to toe, and I flushed. Apparently, she was kin to me and even if she hadn't been, I believed in respecting my elders. But I liked Bryn's face how it was. I wouldn't stand for anyone cutting it with razor-blade magic.

"Somewhat ironic, Maggie," John Barrett said with a low chuckle. "Little girl," he said to me. "Haven't you wondered why in the past few days, bullets intended for you never hit their target? You've been under a protective spell. One so smooth, I daresay, it's even sent bullets that were intended for others astray when you got in the way. Who do you think cast the spell on you?"

"Lower the gun," Mrs. Thornton said.

I looked at Bryn, then Aunt Melanie. Neither of them said anything.

"Will you promise not to hurt anyone?" I asked Mrs. Thornton.

"That is entirely up to your friend."

"It's not only up to Bryn. I can swear not to see him. In fact—"

"Would I believe you without something binding?" Mrs. Thornton scoffed. "You look at him as though he's a chocolate you'd like to swallow in one bite. Would I take your word you'd avoid him? Without a blood vow, I think not."

I blushed. "I don't—well, he's—What's a blood vow?"

"Tamara," Bryn said with a sharp shake of his head. "Nothing that's completely binding. Nothing irreversible. You need a way out, if you change your mind."

Mrs. Thornton flung her hand, and magic cut through the air, slashing his shirt and cutting the skin beneath. Blood welled.

"Stop it!" I said, putting my hand on the wound. It wasn't deep. *Yet.* His magic obviously couldn't keep hers from hitting us.

"Are you willing to give up the child?" Mrs. Thornton asked. "You know, by rights, she belongs to us, to the line that she was born to."

I cocked my head. She called me a child. And John Barrett had called me a little girl. Is that how they saw me? What had that prophecy said? Had Lenore meant me? What if I was the child Bryn wouldn't give up?

"Why does he have to let me go?" I asked.

"Because you're the key to mending a broken line," Mrs. Thornton said. "You're not to be used as a source of power for another family. If you are untrained, *we* will train you. It's our obligation and our privilege.

"You must understand, my dear. Some men are evil, but even the ones who are well-intentioned convince themselves that a woman is better off relinquishing her power to her lover. Anytime a witch gains the upper hand, it is because she fought for and won it."

I glanced at John Barrett. He leaned calmly against a post and shrugged.

"President Barrett hasn't tapped into the power of the tor. You're connected by blood to Momma and Aunt Mel and me. You're the one drawing power from the tor for this storm," I said.

"Yes." She walked slowly, dragging the tip of her umbrella in the mud to mark a circle around us. I glanced anxiously at Bryn, but he didn't seem worried that she'd trap us inside. "Young Lyons, will you take a spell to answer truthfully while in this circle?" she asked him. "So that the child can truly judge your motives for wanting her?" she asked.

He hesitated, and I stared at him, waiting.

"Can't you promise to tell me the truth?" I asked.

He walked to the groove she'd drawn and held the fingers

of his wounded arm over it, dripping blood. I felt a current of power close around us.

In this circle, I speak truth alone, as any may implore.
If not, then let my soul be lost and my heart stop
evermore.

I gasped. Not a vow that would kill him. "Wait!"

He held his arms out in a gesture of surrender, as if to say: "This is what you asked for."

"It's done," he said.

Mrs. Thornton didn't hesitate. "This child is so very untrained, and you're a Granville Prize winner." She narrowed her eyes. "You have magical synergy with her. You will subjugate her, making her a power source for you. You will be the one casting and controlling all the spells." The Winterhawk inclined her head. "Do you deny it?"

"Yes, I deny it," Bryn said. "I want her to develop her potential. I don't intend for her to be just a preternatural battery for me."

"She doesn't need your help developing her powers. I'm home now," Aunt Mel said. "Tammy, Aunt Margaret's harsh, but she's not wrong. You can't risk everything for a man, honey. No matter how good-looking he is. No matter how magnetic. Ask me why you shouldn't, and I'll tell you a dozen terrible stories—"

"Under what circumstances would she be the one leading the spell-casting with you supplying power for her?" Mrs. Thornton asked Bryn.

"If a situation were better suited to Earth magic and if she could write a better spell than I could to accomplish the desired ends, I'd give her my power to cast it."

"Would she be able to write a better spell than you?"

He hesitated.

"Come, let's have no false modesty. There are few in the world who could exceed your talent for spell-writing. Do you really believe that she could ever be superior in that regard?" she snapped.

My heart thumped hard, my body frozen, waiting for his response. He'd always had faith in me. All he had to do was confirm that.

He turned his head to stare at me. "I wouldn't exploit you, Tamara. I'm in love with you."

My eyes widened, and my heart sped.

"Love isn't enough of a guarantee," Aunt Mel protested. "It doesn't always last, and tapping into that kind of power, it corrupts. It always corrupts."

"I will have an answer to my question," Mrs. Thornton said.

Lightning bolts cracked the rods, shaking the ground. I jumped, putting up my hand.

"Stop," I said to her. "It's enough."

"What is your answer, young Lyons?"

He glanced back at her. "No, she'll never write a better spell than I could."

"Then if you love her, you must give her up, because in a synergistic relationship with you, she could never reach her potential. She could never have daughters with Earth magic. She could never inherit all that is her birthright. For her own sake and yours, let her go."

Bryn stared at me.

"Will you swear it?" Mrs. Thornton demanded.

His eyes never left my face. "No," Bryn said. "I won't promise to give her up." He shook his head slowly, his eyes smoky cobalt. "There's no place you can go, Tamara, where I won't follow. No matter how far. If you leave me, I will find you. So long as we're in love with each other, I'll be relentless."

My eyes swam in tears. The line between supernatural stalker and irresistibly romantic boyfriend can be kind of blurry at times. I stared at him with words caught in my throat.

"It's all right." His fingertips grazed my jaw. "Resist as long as you want. I'll seduce you in the end," he whispered. "I'll have to because I can't let you go."

I stepped close to him. "Answer me this," I said softly. "If there was a baby. Yours and mine. Would you swear never to take her away from me without my permission?"

He raised his brows. "Are you?"

"No—I don't know. Just answer."

"How could I take her away when I've just admitted I'm prepared to do anything to be near you?"

"Would you swear a blood vow, a permanent vow, never to take her? Even if you stopped being in love with me?"

"Tammy!" Aunt Melanie said with a gasp. "Was that Great-Grandma Lenore's prophecy? You can't risk it! For God's sake, you don't want to have to fight someone like him for custody. If you lose, you'll never get over it. He'll promise you anything right now, but long-term, you don't understand what magic and ambition can do to someone."

Bryn's glance at her was so cool that I took a step back. He caught my hand and held it.

"My will is stronger than that. Ambition doesn't rule me, and it never will. The way I've lived my life is proof of that." He pulled me closer and put his mouth near my ear. "I'll never take a child away from you, even if it's half mine. And yes, I'll swear to that in a blood vow."

Tears dripped from my eyes, mixing with the rain running down my face. Aunt Mel would think I was crazy and dumb to ignore her advice. The family I loved versus a guy I barely knew? It should've been easy to choose. Only it wasn't.

"Your children with him could have magic so distorted it may be unusable. Would you risk that?" Mrs. Thornton asked me.

I looked at her. "I'm not even sure my magic's ever going to work right, which is maybe why I decided a long time ago that magic's not the most important thing in life," I said.

She raised her eyebrows. "Yes, well, that is one philosophy." She glanced at John Barrett. "The lanterns have gone out."

He turned and exhaled, blowing blue-white flames toward the woods. Lanterns at the base of a pair of trees burned to life, revealing two men—chained and gagged, their sagging bodies bloody from a recent beating.

Oh God, no! Andre and Lennox. Bryn's best friend and his father. I cringed, ashamed to be related to her. How could she have done something so awful?

"Will you choose her over everyone? Over life itself?" she asked Bryn.

"Aunt Margaret, no!" Melanie said.

"I won't choose," Bryn said.

They all raised their hands at once. Bryn and Barrett and Aunt Margaret. The magic clashed in a thunderous roar. Her blast knocked us down. Aunt Mel tumbled onto the incline and screamed as she slid down the mountain. It was like she was on a waterslide, careening out of control into the darkness.

"Aunt Mel!" I yelled.

"I'm okay," she called back.

I swiveled and shot John Barrett in the leg. He crumpled, but my bullet aimed at Mrs. Thornton ricocheted off and hit a rock. She glared and jerked her hand toward Bryn. I threw myself in front of him. Ice sliced through my chest, and I felt my heartbeat hiccup and slow.

I couldn't move as Bryn dragged me behind a boulder. The pain in my chest suffocated me for several moments, then my heart's steady thump sped to normal.

"She meant to kill you," I said.

"I know." He extended his arms up and spoke in Gaelic. Light from the sky pierced his hands, bending and coursing through me, too. Black and stinging.

"Stop!" I wailed.

It was over in a moment, but the darkness around us was thick and oily.

"I'll create a diversion. You release Andre and Lennox and send them down the mountain," he said.

"We can't separate. She doesn't want me dead. You can use me as a shield."

"I can shield myself," he said, shoving me away. "Go, and be quick. This power won't last long against her."

38

WHEN BRYN STOOD, I ran. I fell and slid across the muddy ground until I careened into the trunk of an evergreen. I crawled from under it, covered in mud and pine needles. I got behind Andre and shot the chain between the shackles on his wrists and ankles. He fell to his hands and knees.

The sound of magic crashing against magic was as loud as the thunder rattling the earth. The flashes of light blinded me as I raced to Lennox. I shot the chains and he fell facedown, unconscious. I rolled him over and ungagged him. I checked and was relieved to feel him breathing. I shook his shoulder.

"Wake up, Lennox. We need your help."

A sharp tug on my toga made me jerk my head. Mercutio let go of the silk and yowled.

"What?" I asked, clamoring to my feet. I rushed back to the clearing. Bryn was on his knees, bleeding from his arm and neck, arms outstretched to ward off spells from both Barrett and Mrs. Thornton.

"Stop!" I screamed. "Stop it!"

Mercutio darted sideways, drawing my eyes.

Scarface! No!

With dead eyes and a black expression, Scarface pointed his gun at Bryn's back. My arm moved instantly, finger squeezing the trigger, and I unloaded the clip. Scarface's stunned expression fixed on me as he crumpled. I swiveled back to Bryn.

He lay facedown on the ground. I ran to him, sliding the last few feet.

"No!" I screamed, finding the bloody hole in his back. I turned him over and ripped open his shirt. No wound. The bullet was somewhere in his chest.

With labored breathing, he turned deathly pale, blue eyes wide with shock. "Can't breathe," he gasped.

"No," I sobbed, bending forward and holding his chest. I didn't know how to help him. "Please, please don't die. Take power from me." I kissed him, but his eyes rolled back.

I saw Mrs. Thornton's legs and I jerked up, shoving her back. "Don't touch him!" I snarled. "I'll kill you if you touch him."

"You won't because you can't. I'm the most powerful witch in the world," she said coolly. "Now move aside. He's dying. I'll end his pain."

I stood and stepped over Bryn's body, advancing on her. She flung a spell that knocked me to my knees. The pain was terrible, like all my bones were grinding against each other, crushing my insides.

I couldn't scream. I couldn't breathe.

She stepped around me. "I should have done this years ago," she said, leaning over Bryn.

When her spell released me, I fell forward. I rolled immediately and kicked her leg, knocking her down. She didn't strike the ground. Her body levitated, her magic stronger than gravity.

I crawled on top of Bryn, covering his body to protect him from her.

"Move!" she said.

"Maggie, let her say good-bye to him," John Barrett called. "Come help me with this leg. I'm bleeding badly!"

I twisted my arms around Bryn's neck and kissed him, trying to shove magic into him. It didn't work. He didn't inhale. He wasn't breathing.

Fear and panic swallowed me up, my heart breaking.

"Please," I mumbled, searching for the words that would keep him with me.

Blood of my blood. Bone of my bone.
Two bodies, one. Never alone.

I felt a white burning in my chest, like a balloon had been inflated too far, like my chest would explode. Mercutio yowled next to me.

"Ahhh! Bite him," I rasped. "Here. Make a hole," I said, shoving Merc's head down against Bryn's chest. "Something's in there. Let it out. Hurry—" I swayed, the world darkening. I was dying, too. I fell onto Bryn's chest.

The world lurched and faded through a haze of spots and stripes. Pain pierced my chest, like a spike stabbing me. A rush of hissing air escaped, and hot blood sprayed my face. My vision cleared. Bloody bubbles frothed out of Bryn's punctured chest, releasing the deadly pressure.

My eyes darted around. Mrs. Thornton had gone to John Barrett and was binding his leg where I'd shot him.

I drew my finger across my cut leg and mixed my blood with Bryn's, then rubbed it over my lips like gloss. "Blood of my blood, bone of my bone," I whispered as I kissed him. He breathed in, magic curling from my mouth to his. I pushed it into him, wanting him to have it all.

He mumbled against my lips.

"My God, no! My friend," Andre sobbed, kneeling over us. Andre lapsed into German as I stood.

"Watch over him, Andre," I said.

Mrs. Thornton finished tying a makeshift bandage around John Barrett's leg. I dug my toes in the mud, just as she turned her head and narrowed her eyes at me.

She stood. "What have you done?" she asked, stalking toward me.

"To kill one of us, you have to kill us both."

She sighed wearily. "And you think I want you alive more than I want him dead?"

"Don't you?" I asked, backing toward the woods.

"It's not too late for Melanie or Marlee to have another child. I have many things with which to bargain. One doesn't become the most powerful force in magic by letting sentiment rule."

The wind whipped rain across my face, making me blink. "I'm your own flesh and blood. Please don't do this."

"Undo the bond between you and Lyons. You can't save him, but you can save yourself," she said, edging toward me, a predator stalking prey.

I stood under an enormous oak, cringing. "Betray the people I love? I don't do that," I whispered, dragging my foot across the roots to make the cut gush blood. "Would rather die."

She sighed and raised her arm. "So be it."

Tears welled. I squeezed my eyes shut. "Protect me, tree. Stop her dead."

The branch cracked with a sound that drowned out the thunder. I heard her shriek, felt the ground quake.

I bit my lip, the pain almost as strong as the lump in my throat. I opened my eyes. Part of the branch had pierced her belly. She lay pinned and breathless, her lips bloodless white.

Tears overflowed as I knelt over her. "You made me," I whispered. "It didn't have to be this way."

She clenched her jaw and whispered a spell, lifting the heavy tree limb a couple of inches. She grabbed her skewered stomach with a cry of pain and let the limb fall. The rain ebbed and stopped, like heaven had turned off a faucet.

"I underestimated you," she said with a gurgling breath. "I, of all people."

"Hello, Margaret."

I looked up, and Bryn's mother's ghost stood a few feet away, all luminous light and glowing skin.

Mrs. Thornton didn't look at her.

I stared at the Winterhawk, horrified. "It was you? You killed Bryn's mom and trapped her soul?"

"She married a Lyons against our wishes. She was our student. We mentored her. She—she should have listened. She defied us. She wasted—wasted her talent. Wasted her life . . ." Mrs. Thornton clutched her stomach.

"Let's not forget my spells," Cassandra said.

"Yes," Margaret said fiercely. "I ruled—ruled the whole world with those spells." She coughed and moaned. "Ruled."

I felt Mrs. Thornton's soul leave her body, a rush of cold air passing me.

I looked up at Cassandra. Her light brightened.

"Hi," I stammered, tears spilling down my cheeks. "Your son's here. He'd give anything to see you."

She floated closer. "You freed me." Her phantom finger traced my cheek, down my neck, and came to rest over the spot where her brooch was under the silk, touching my skin. "Such a lovely, brave girl. Will you help me do one more thing before I go?"

I nodded, biting my lip.

A brush of silk and warmth, and then my body was crowded. I exhaled, squeezing smaller until the warmth closed around me. My hands and arms changed, like a glamour covering me. The hair hanging down darkened to deep chestnut.

We stood and walked to where Bryn lay. His breathing was even, but fast, his skin still pale, but not deathly so.

His eyes widened when he saw us. "Are you—Who are you?" he rasped.

"You know," we whispered, bending down. We brushed a kiss over his cheek. "My beautiful son. How much I've always loved you. More than life." Another kiss. "I'll see you again, but not soon." We smiled at him. "Not soon."

He clutched our arm, and we squeezed his hand.

"Where is he? Where is Lennox?" we asked, standing. We turned and returned to the trees.

Lennox sat propped against a trunk. He looked disheveled and dazed.

"Here you are," we said softly and knelt next to him.

With effort, he raised his battered face. He tipped his skull against the bark. "Am I dreaming or am I dead?" he asked, his voice hoarse.

"Have you written songs for me this week?" we asked.

He raised his brows. "I . . . don't write songs anymore. Not since you left me."

"My love," we whispered and kissed him.

He cupped the back of our head, the kiss deep and full of pain and passion. It got hard to breathe. We pulled back. He tried to hold on.

"Cassie, stay," he said fiercely.

"I loved you more than music. More than magic. More than life," we whispered. "Don't forget me."

"Never," he said with tears in his eyes. "Not for a day. Not for an hour."

As her soul tore free of my body, I fell back. I landed on the ground, staring up as she rose through the tree limbs into the star-studded sky.

The ground was so very cold, and I was so very tired.

39

I WOKE UP crying, but couldn't remember my dream. I felt Merc's fur against one arm and touched him, then rolled on my side. Bryn was next to me in the bed, an IV dripping in his arm. Dr. Suri was asleep in a nearby chair. Both of them had more than a day's worth of stubble.

I looked around the small downstairs guest room.

Bryn opened his eyes. They were bloodshot, but back to their usual bright blue.

"We're alive," I said.

"Apparently," he said in a raspy voice. "Against all odds."

I smiled. *Against all odds.* "You're probably not used to being the underdog. Lucky I was there to show you how it's done."

"Lucky you were there," he agreed.

I turned my head, hearing children's voices. "What's going on? Who's out there?"

"A lot of places flooded. This house didn't."

I sat up slowly, feeling a little woozy. "So?"

"People asked to stay here."

"And you said yes?" I didn't manage to keep the shock from my voice.

He nodded.

I smiled and kissed his cheek. "That is so sweet of you."

The corner of his mouth curled up as his lids drifted shut. "I knew you would think so."

My brows rose, but he didn't open his eyes again. I climbed out of bed, letting out a hiss of pain when my foot hit the floor. The problem with wounded feet is sooner or later you have to walk on them.

Someone had dressed me in white flannel pajamas. I didn't want to think about who, since I was sure Bryn would've been too weak to do it.

I shuffled out of the room. There were people scattered everywhere. On air mattresses and sleeping bags, sitting on couches and in chairs. The ladies from First Methodist were serving donuts and scones and coffee.

I heard agitated German and followed it to where Andre was arguing with Rollie the vampire, as Johnny tried to calm them down.

"What's happening?" I asked.

"Rollie bite Mr. Andre. Mr. Andre get mad."

Since Andre was standing and shaking a fist at Rollie, I took it that Andre was okay despite the pincushion treatment.

"Rollie!" I said.

"What? I would've bitten your boyfriend, but he didn't look like he could spare even a drop. What in the world did you do to him?" Rollie asked.

I shot him a harassed look. "Can't you get blood from a blood bank?" I demanded. "Put some of those packets in a foam cooler in your trunk for when you travel?"

"I only drink organic."

"This isn't a Whole Foods! This is a house. Behave yourself."

I marched back out into the hallway and smiled at all the people who were telling me good morning. I wandered into the kitchen.

Cookie and Mr. Jenson were at the countertop. Cookie

poured brownie mix into a pan. Mr. Jenson poured steaming water into a teapot.

Aunt Mel and Lennox Lyons were sitting together at the kitchen table, but stopped talking when they saw me.

"Morning," I said hesitantly.

"Hi, sweetheart," Aunt Mel said, getting up to give me a hug.

"You're not mad?" I asked.

"No. Whatever happens, we'll figure it out." She kissed me, and I smelled her black currant and flowers perfume, felt her hoop earring graze my jaw. *Home*. So great.

As she sat back down, I moved over to Mr. Jenson.

"Mr. Jenson, remember that *doll* you were keeping for me? What'd you do with her?" I whispered, thinking that the last thing I wanted was for anyone to discover the mini Jenna Reitgarten.

"I took her out of the glass case to let her clothes air out. She and her companion doll are in the locked library," he said in a low voice.

"Oh, good. I'll figure out how to get them back to their rightful owners after breakfast. Or if I'm too busy and Bryn's too tired, maybe after dinner . . . or, you know, tomorrow." I smiled. Just a little.

"Very good," Mr. Jenson murmured, totally unfazed as he got warm scones out of the oven. When I get old, I plan to be as unflappable as Mr. Jenson.

I started to the door, but caught Lennox's eye as I passed the table.

"Good morning," I said. "Are you—How are you?"

"Better than I've been," he said, his voice smooth. He poured coffee into a cup and nodded to the chair next to him. "You're welcome to join us."

The invitation shocked and warmed me.

"Um, maybe later? There are a lot of people around. I'm gonna get dressed." I reached over and took the cup, having a swallow of the dark roast and snagging a warm brownie drizzled with caramel. I took a couple fast bites and set the rest on the saucer next to my cup. "I'll be back in a few minutes." I got as far as the door before I turned back. "I'm glad you're better."

"Of course you are. You've taken it upon yourself to fix everything that's wrong with the world." His voice was dry, but the corner of his mouth edged up into a smile. Just like Bryn's. "What's on your agenda next week? Peace in the Middle East? Should take you what? Three or four days to clear that up?"

"Nah." I laughed softly. "At least a week."

He choked out a laugh.

I waved and left the kitchen, not able to wipe the smile from my face. I spotted Steve standing guard outside Bryn's library door.

I nodded. "How's the arm?" I asked.

"Still works," he said, glancing at Georgia Sue who was taking a group of ladies on a tour of the hallway paintings.

"Now this one's by that Pissarro. Isn't that so pretty? Just like a museum. Oh here's Tammy Jo," Georgia said, rushing over to give me a hug. "People are talking about you! You saved that little Paige and her babysitter after you'd already rescued a carload of little lost girls. Some people are even saying you saved the town. And Bryn Lyons told everyone you convinced him to open up his house so people would have a roof over their heads while the town dries out."

"People aren't mad at me?" I asked, glancing around. No one seemed to be giving me dirty looks. "No one's siding with the Reitgartens?"

"Haven't you heard? The sheriff's got proof that Mindy Glusky from Dyson is the one who arranged for those gunmen to come to the Fish-and-Fowl fund-raiser, and Mindy's claiming that Jenna put her up to it. Sheriff Hobbs wants those Reitgartens for questioning, and where are they? Some folks are saying they took off to avoid getting interrogated."

"Wow." I tucked my hair behind my ears. "So when Jenna turns up—"

"*If* she turns up."

"She'll be in trouble? She'll have a hard time convincing people to believe whatever wild explanations she has for her crazy behavior."

Georgia Sue nodded.

"Well, I hope it all dies down real quick, so the town can get back to normal," I said, extracting myself from them, feeling good that no one seemed to want to yell at me—or, you know, burn me at the stake. "I'll be back in a few minutes. I have to get dressed."

Craig Cuskin appeared in a doorway. I raised my eyebrows, surprised to see him.

"I snuck onto their computers and deleted the footage of you. I overwrote the disks with new stuff," he said.

"So it's gone?"

"Yeah, you forgive me?"

I nodded.

"Good, because you rock. We all think so. Maybe you'd let us do a calendar with pictures of you—regular pictures. Just swimsuits . . . to raise money for the Duvall rebuilding," he said. "You know, for charity, Tammy Jo."

"Aren't there enough girls in bikinis on the Internet for you?" I said, flabbergasted.

"It's not the same . . ." he said, but I didn't hear the rest of his argument.

I limped up the stairs on my sore foot and went to the green guest room.

I pulled the door open and walked in, surprised to find John Barrett lying on the bed in a nightshirt with his leg bandaged and his arm shackled to the bed frame.

"Oh. Hi there," I said. "Your leg okay?"

"Cracked tibia. Nice shot."

"Um. Thanks," I said hesitantly.

"I'm not angry about you shooting me. It was just business," he said.

I thought in his place I'd have taken it personally, but didn't say so. I perched on the chair next to the bed. "I guess you've lost your job now as president, huh?"

"You killed the president."

"You mean she was secretly in charge of everything? You just pretended to be?"

He nodded. "She never had the title, but she didn't need it."

"How come you went along with that?"

His eyes twinkled. "A great many reasons."

"Did you help her kill Bryn's mom? Cassandra?"

"No, but I helped her cover it up," he said with a sigh. "Lovely Cassie was the greatest spell-writer of her age, but she was going to expose Margaret for using her brilliant work. Spells that could wipe away any traces of dangerous or powerful magic. Spells that could wound from a distance. She'd written them as class assignments when she was in your grandmother Josephine's courses. Margaret saw their potential. She saved thousands of lives by eliminating threats to our world. She was a patriot. And later, she was a great leader. There was only one problem. Cassandra recognized the spells and confronted Maggie. A serious mistake. Cassie's death should've been the end of it, but then Cassie's son grew up and would not stay quietly in America, away from politics. And he got involved with you."

"What happened to Gwen?"

"She betrayed us. She was Maggie's apprentice. That girl could've been the first female president of the association. That's what Maggie was grooming her for. But Gwen found the brooch and recognized it, and her ridiculous obsession with Bryn Lyons made her take it. Gwen couldn't keep it on her person or in her things, not while she was traveling with us. Maggie would've been drawn to her own magic, the power coating the brooch. But Gwen didn't want to simply mail it to Bryn. She wanted to present it to him. She didn't realize Maggie hadn't bought the brooch, hadn't found it.

"She'd killed Cassie and trapped her soul inside it to keep Cassie from appearing to her family and telling them who had really murdered her. You see, Margaret lined up a scapegoat and planted clues that led to him. When she killed him, the family was grateful to her for exacting justice. We did such a good job of framing him, no one ever suspected he was innocent."

I clucked my tongue. "That's awful!"

He shrugged. "Maggie was a brilliant and talented operative."

"Did my grandma know what really happened?"

"No."

"Why did Gwen send me the brooch?"

"Gwen was investigating you. She saw that you didn't use wards, didn't seem to know how to safeguard your things. She mailed it to you, knowing she could easily retrieve it later. As she did."

"But Mrs. Thornton realized she took it?"

"Oh yes. Maggie had very powerful magic wrapped around that brooch, to prevent anyone, especially Cassie's family, from drawing her spirit out. But your family has such a strong affinity for ghosts, and your magic was too like Maggie's own. The brooch mistook you for her. The spell, you see, had an opening that Maggie had left so that she could speak to Cassie if she wanted to."

"Why?"

"Because Cassie was a stunning talent, and Maggie always hated to see a young woman's potential squandered. She had killed Cassie in an act of self-preservation, and that was a terrible and difficult thing for her to do. Maggie thought she could still immortalize Cassie in the world of magic, by keeping her spells alive. In fact, Maggie has a book of Cassie's spells. One that she intended to have published after we retired from politics. She wanted Cassie to have a great and enduring legacy."

"Wow, what a great humanitarian Mrs. Thornton was," I snapped. "Making Miss Cassandra famous and revered *after* she killed her. Not to mention planning to destroy Cassandra's best and most important legacy. Her son."

"Only the magic matters," Barrett said wistfully. "That's what she always said."

"How could you stand to be around her?" I demanded.

"Easily. She was remarkable. Years ago, the association

was crumbling. Witches were being burned and beheaded, being preyed upon by every other preternatural creature. Maggie Thornton changed everything."

I shook my head. That didn't justify anything, but I knew I wouldn't convince him of that. He'd been drinking the Conclave's crazy Kool-Aid.

"And you just go around killing whoever you want to cover things up? You killed Gwen?"

"Operative Lambert killed her. Under orders."

"Operative Lambert? Scarface?"

He nodded. "He was here to get you out of the way, so we could deal definitively with Lyons, but you proved harder to contain than expected."

"He painted Gwen's walls with antiwitch stuff?"

"Yes, we thought we'd frame the town's religious extremists. Get some of them jailed and out of the way, but Maggie said the investigation would be too time-consuming. So Operative Lambert went back and got rid of the body and the evidence."

"How did you expect to get away with it?"

"Do you see anyone arresting us for Gwen's murder? We did get away with it, my dear. That and so much more over the years."

I shook my head. Certifiable, the whole group of them. "What do you think will happen to you now?"

"I'll stand trial, and then I'll be executed."

I raised my brows. "You don't sound scared."

He shrugged. "Maggie and I were lovers and partners for many decades. I shouldn't think this world will be at all interesting for me without Margaret. Better to join her on the other side."

What could I say to that? I got up and went to the walk-in closet.

"What about you? What will you do?" he asked.

"Get dressed. Have breakfast."

"I meant with your life."

"I knew what you meant," I said, closing the closet door

with me inside. I put on jeans and a sweater, warm socks and turquoise cowboy boots.

"I hope that ring doesn't mean that you'll let him enslave you," he called. "A witch of your lineage has a responsibility to rise with the cream."

That ring? I looked at my hands, stared at them. One moment my fingers seemed bare, then a gold ring appeared on my right middle finger. My jaw dropped. *Magically hidden.*

The bright yellow gold was etched with a moon and stars and three blue-violet sapphires in a row. *Orion's belt.*

I pulled off the ring to study it. It was sure pretty. Had Bryn put it on me while I slept? The skin of my finger burned and ached. I looked inside the ring. In fancy old letters, it read, *Blood of my blood.*

My finger joints stiffened until I couldn't stand the cramp. I gasped in pain and shoved the ring back on. The pain faded instantly. What the Sam Houston?

I shoved the door open and rushed out of the room, hurrying down the stairs. I burst back into the downstairs guest room, startling Dr. Suri who nearly fell out of his chair.

"Good morning," he said, getting up. "Excuse me."

I didn't pay attention to him leaving. Instead, I grabbed Bryn's hands and stared at them until I saw it. A white gold band on his left middle finger. The pattern etched into the band was a leafy vine. I dragged the ring off, scraping his middle knuckle in the process. I peered inside. The same antique lettering. *Bone of my bone.*

Setting in my hand, his ring touched mine, and they both vibrated with power, a soft hum buzzing in my ears.

"Put it back on," he said, holding up his hand.

There was a fiery red mark on his finger where the ring had been.

"I finished the spell? On the tor when I said the words?"

He nodded, taking the band and pushing it back onto his finger.

"Where did you get the rings?"

"I had them made."

"When?"

"Last week."

"You couldn't have known that I'd agree back then! Why would you have had them made before we did the spell?"

He shrugged. "Most of the time, I follow my head. Once in a while, I follow my heart."

Speaking of hearts, mine thumped in my chest, adrenaline searing my veins. What had I done by finishing that spell?

"What if we don't end up getting along? What if you marry someone else? Or I do?" I said breathlessly. "This magical bond—it's forever?"

"For life or longer."

I took a deep breath and blew it out slowly. That sure was a long time. "You might live to regret it," I said.

He smiled. "No, I won't."

He interlaced our fingers, his left palm against my right, the rings touching. Magic and warmth rose up my arm and into my chest. It did feel so right, like everything always did with him.

Plus, I had to finish the spell or let him die. I shuddered at the thought of him being lost forever. He was too important to Duvall, to the world of magic, and to me.

I leaned forward, the curtain of my hair hiding my face and our hands. I kissed his knuckles and whispered, "I won't regret it either."

TURN THE PAGE FOR A PREVIEW OF
KIMBERLY FROST'S NEXT
SOUTHERN WITCH NOVEL

SLIGHTLY SPELLBOUND

COMING TO BERKLEY SENSATION
IN MAY 2014!

1

NO MATTER HOW many times people try to kill me, I never seem to get used to it. That goes for spying, too. I'm always startled to find a peeping Tom . . . or Craig . . . or fire warlock creeping around. The thing is they'd better not let me catch them at it. I'm a redhead. I'm armed. And I don't take kindly to interruptions when I'm trying out a new cake recipe.

I didn't always have a hair-trigger temper, or a hair-trigger weapon tucked in the top kitchen drawer behind the salad tongs, but a couple of months ago, my life changed.

My name is Tamara Josephine Trask—Tammy Jo to most of my friends—I'm twenty-three years old, and I'm a witch. Or I should say I come from a long line of witches. Until recently, I thought the family magic skipped over me. It turns out that I actually got a double helping of magic and that my two types of magic, like the creatures they come from—witch and faery—don't get along. It might have stayed that way, with the two magicks cancelling each other out, if I hadn't had a close encounter with a wizard named Bryn whose own magical heritage is also mixed. From the moment my magic met his, it was trouble for us and anyone within a twenty-mile radius.

Now it was late December, and the supernatural drama had died down. Country music Christmas carols played on the radio, and in my kitchen I was minding my own business as I sometimes do. I wore a white T-shirt, boot-cut Levis, and a black apron with a Julia Child quote in white letters that said, "If you're afraid of butter, just use cream."

I was in the middle of stirring cake batter that had both butter and cream in it when the trees started kicking up a fuss. I don't speak tree, but after an unfortunate incident involving pixie dust, I'm usually able to get the gist of what they're trying to tell me.

Woody limbs scratched the roof and scraped against the kitchen window, making me look up from the bowl. I slid open the window and said through the screen, "I'm not coming out to visit right now. I'm busy being a regular person."

The leaves crackled, and I rolled my eyes. A chilly breeze blew in. I shivered and closed the window. When I turned up the radio, Martina McBride drowned out the trees.

My ocelot, Mercutio, who'd just woken up, strode into the kitchen. It seemed like God couldn't make up His mind when He painted ocelot fur. There are stripes on their faces and necks like little tigers, but spots on their bodies like leopards. One thing's certain, they're the cutest cats of all, big or small, foreign or domestic. A person might say I'm biased and that person would be right, but that doesn't mean I'm wrong about ocelots being extremely cute. Just ask the Internet to show you some pictures.

"The racket woke you up?" I asked as I dripped a couple drops of cream on my finger and held it down to him.

He licked and swallowed. Another scrape against the roof made us look toward the yard.

"For foliage, that's pretty pushy," I said. "I'm not fixin' to go out there with bare feet. It's full-on winter and that ground's cold."

Mercutio tipped his head down, touching his nose to the top of my bare foot.

"I meant I wouldn't go *outside* barefoot. In the kitchen with the oven on is fine," I said. "In here it's seventy-five degrees. Out there, it's forty-eight, and rumor has it it's going down to thirty. By Texas standards, that's blizzard cold. Now I ask you, would anyone in her right mind go out in a blizzard without socks and boots?"

Mercutio cocked his head and opened his mouth to answer.

"I meant that to be rhetorical, Merc." I leaned over the bowl. I added finely chopped Texas pecans, a dash of chili powder, and another splash of cream to the cocoa cream cake batter. "Besides I'm real busy." I stirred and then dipped my finger into the bowl. As soon as the batter hit my tongue, I smiled. *Now we're talking.* I added pinches of nutmeg and pepper.

Mercutio jumped onto the counter, nearly knocking the mixer off, and darted to the window that's above the sink.

"Watch your step," I said, moving the mixer to the middle of the counter.

Mercutio's low purr raised the hair on the back of my neck. When it comes to announcing trouble, Mercutio's more accurate than a police scanner. I reached into the corner and turned down the radio, then I opened a bottom drawer and pulled out a flashlight. I turned it on and shined it out the window.

I jumped when I caught a glimpse of a figure in the tree. I instantly lowered the light and yanked open the top drawer. I reached behind spatulas and tongs and closed my fist on the handle of my gun.

I tucked it into the back of my jeans and moved away from the window. I yanked on the socks that were sitting next to my cooking clogs and slipped my feet into the shoes.

"What do you think, Merc? A neighbor boy trying to sneak a peek at me in my undies again? Or real trouble?"

Honestly, as good as most kids were with computers, it would've been a lot easier for the town's teen boys to look at naked people on the Internet rather than spying on live women with bad tempers and big boyfriends. According to my friend Georgia Sue, naked people are "all over *that web.*" I didn't ask how she knew that. When I looked up recipes and spells, I never got ambushed by naked pictures. Kenny,

Georgia Sue's husband, might want to spend less time playing pool with his buddies and more romantic time with her.

Mercutio crossed the counter in two strides and pounced down to the floor. I watched him approach the back door. He kept his body low, in full-on stealth and ready-to-rumble stance.

"All right then," I said and reached over to turn off the kitchen light. "Someone more sinister than a teen boy it is."

I crouched next to Merc. "Even with the lights off, he'll see the door open. So we'll have to move fast," I said and then rolled my eyes at myself. I didn't need to tell Mercutio about speed. He could give lightning a run for its money. He also didn't need lectures about how to stalk prey. I wasn't there the day he was born, but I'd met him when he was seven months old, and he'd already been tougher than overcooked steak.

I moved the flashlight into my left hand so it was ready to be flipped on and gripped the door handle with my right. I took a deep breath and opened it.

We burst into the yard. Claws out, Mercutio went up the trunk. I drew my gun with my right hand and shined the flashlight at the treetop.

One glimpse told me the figure was all wrong. For a split second, I froze, staring at the gaunt face. His skin was so thin I could see stark white bones beneath the surface as he gnashed his teeth at me. Was there even flesh on those bones? Or just a translucent phantom covering? Was he alive or dead? I wondered frantically as I squeezed off four ear-popping rounds. A bright flash of light blinded me as the man—or whatever he was—jumped. I dropped to my knees and rolled for cover. He didn't land on me—or the ground that I heard.

Tangled amongst the azalea bushes, I pointed the flashlight beam at the treetop. Mercutio howled a protest at the fact that the intruder had escaped before he'd gotten to him. I moved the light all around the yard, scanning every inch. I also checked the sky and the fence. No sign of the peeping skeleton.

Mercutio returned to the ground, strolled past, and padded into the house.

My heart thundered in my chest. "What the heck?" I

muttered, rolling onto the patio. "We're done, Merc?" I asked, following him inside. "Just like that?"

Mercutio meowed.

Apparently so. I locked the door, set my gun down, and brushed off my clothes.

"Well, what was that? I didn't hear it hit the ground. So was it a ghost then?" I frowned. "I haven't seen all that many ghosts, but the ones I have seen look like people. A little more transparent than a regular person sometimes, but not like a skeleton."

Merc sniffed.

"And maybe I'm old-fashioned but I think skeletons ought to either be covered with flesh and blood as God intended or buried in a coffin waiting to turn to dust. They don't need to be creeping around in a person's backyard, annoying the trees and giving me a heart attack when I'm trying out a new cream cake recipe."

Mercutio yawned and curled up on the floor a few feet from the door.

I waved an annoyed hand at him. "Sure, you go on back to sleep. No need for us to sort out what's happening. Or to prepare for trouble. Winging it has worked out so well for us in the past."

Oblivious to sarcasm, Mercutio put his head down and went back to sleep.

"For the love of Hershey," I said, grabbing the gun and putting it away. I turned off the oven and put the batter in the fridge. "I'm going to consult some witches' books. Not that I have many here to consult. But I'm not going to Bryn's house. I've made it twelve whole days without sleeping with him and no scary skeleton standing in a tree is going to send me to Seduction Central now that Bryn's big case is finally over."

Mercutio didn't move a whisker. When it comes to fighting for my life, Mercutio's the best friend I could have. When it comes to my messed up love life, I'm on my own.

And actually it's okay that Mercutio's not into that kind of drama. That's what the rest of the town is for.

2

THE ONLY LIVE-ACTION skeletons I found in Aunt Mel's magical reference book were zombies. In my experience, zombies were a lot squishier than the treetop creature. Not that I had vast experience with them or anything. The only zombie I'd ever met had been the re-animated wife of our town's retired psychiatrist and probably Mrs. Barnaby hadn't been dead long enough to be just bones.

Even so, I didn't think the skeletal creature in my tree was a zombie. If he had been, I'm sure I would've heard him hit the ground when he jumped down. Zombies weren't dainty. They also didn't climb trees or run off when you threatened them with a weapon. They tried to maul you until they succeeded or you stopped them.

The creature from the tree seemed smarter than a zombie. There was also the slight glow and transparency to it, which made me think it might be a ghost.

Frustrated that I couldn't decide what I thought it actually was, I returned to the kitchen. I'd get back to what was really important: cake. I whipped the batter and added a teaspoon of Kentucky bourbon. I was mid-taste when the doorbell rang.

Mercutio lifted his head and yowled.

"I'm not expecting company. You?"

Mercutio stretched and walked to the back door.

"Okay," I said. From Merc's laid-back attitude I decided the doorbell ringer was probably a person, and not one who had murder in mind.

I let Mercutio into the yard, and the person at the front door knocked. I swallowed another teaspoon of batter then did a rapid tiptoe to the foyer to confirm Merc's instincts that I didn't need my gun. I stared through the peephole, my pulse doing a two-step at the sight of the man on the other side of the door. As usual, Merc was right. A gun wasn't the kind of protection I needed. A chastity belt might've helped.

Bryn Lyons is ridiculously accomplished at many things, one of them being his ability to separate me from my clothes. He's blue-eyed, black-haired, and the kind of gorgeous that the devil might use to tempt a nun to sin. Not being especially nunlike, for me he's like a chocolate truffle. In large quantities, I might remember he's too rich for my blood, but intermittently he's too delicious to resist. I sighed and rested my head against the door.

My hand hovered over the knob. Why was he here? I often visited Bryn at his mansion in Shoreside Oaks, taking advantage of his giant library of magical reference books, chatting over tea and scones with his gentleman butler, and curling up with Bryn on the fancy cushioned furniture, but Bryn didn't come to my house. Because I never invited him.

I'd been raised with a family prophecy that made nine families, including Bryn's, off limits. Bryn's savvy though, and he might have shown up unannounced because he realized my keeping him out of the old Victorian house wasn't just about following family rules. It was also a way of keeping our relationship in a holding pattern.

I stepped back as the chemistry between us thrummed clear through the door. My fingers tap-danced on the knob as his knuckles rapped on the door. I folded like a falling soufflé and pulled the door open.

"Hey there," I said.

"Hello," he said, all sparkling blue eyes. Magic as enticing as the smell of cookies fresh from the oven surrounded me. "Would you like to help me celebrate?" he asked, holding up a bottle of champagne.

I grinned. He'd been doing battle with one of the biggest law firms in Dallas, and as the case had progressed, they'd kept adding lawyers to the team against him. Working until three in the morning, he'd likened it to David versus Goliath, with him holding the slingshot.

"It turned out okay?" I asked, pulling open the screen door. "When I didn't hear from you I was afraid to call, but I should've known!"

Under his dark topcoat, he wore jeans and a black V-neck sweater. He looked scrumptiously casual. High-priced suits had been his daily uniform for weeks. It was nice to see him dressed down.

"I was late returning to Duvall. The client insisted on taking me to dinner to celebrate."

"She has a crush on you," I said. "I would, too! You got rid of the cheating husband who browbeat her for fourteen years. You're a hero."

"I found a loophole in the prenuptial agreement. The judge awarded her ten million dollars."

I let out a low whistle and gave him a quick kiss. "Congratulations."

A few seconds passed, and I hadn't stepped back yet to let him inside. He gave me a considering look.

"Is this an okay time?" he asked.

"What? Oh sure, I guess," I said, finally moving aside. "I'm baking." *And seeing creepy skeleton guys.* I didn't tell Bryn that. I didn't want him to worry. I'd dragged him into more than enough magical messes. He deserved a night off.

"I have to get up early tomorrow," I said. "And you must be exhausted. We should celebrate a different night when we can do it up right."

He stepped inside and handed me the bottle. "You heard he's back in town."

"Who?" I asked, pretending I didn't know what he was talking about.

Bryn cocked an eyebrow, but didn't say more on the subject of Zach Sutton, my ex-husband.

Zach and I had been childhood sweethearts who'd gotten married too young. After the marriage went bust, we should've gone our separate ways, but the breakup was kind of a bust, too. We'd had an on-again off-again relationship for three years. Then I'd needed Bryn's help with magic and in a matter of weeks, I'd fallen in love with him, too. I can't recommend being in love with two men at the same time. Knowing I'd have to choose between them had my nerves as frayed as old wires; I got zapped whenever I considered it.

Bryn pulled a piece of rolled paper secured with a gold ribbon from his back pocket. He set it on the side table in the foyer.

"What's that?" I asked.

"Something for you. For the smoked salmon at midnight on Tuesday and the coffee and spice cake at two a.m. Thursday. I appreciated it."

"I was glad to do it. You were working so hard!" I said. "You didn't have to get me a present," I added, but snatched it up and pulled the ribbon strings to unravel it.

When I unrolled the paper, my heart about stopped. Sarah Nylan's secret recipe for amaretto caramel sauce is the stuff of culinary legend. The Hill Country candymaker's sauce elevates an apple crumble to a five-star gourmet treat. I'd been dying to get my hands on her recipe for forever.

"Holy moly! How did you—I wrote Sarah Nylan two letters with recipes to trade and sent her samples of my pastries. I promised never to serve the sauce without giving out her website, but she never responded. I would just order bottles from her, but she can't keep up with demand. It's a four-month wait to get one jar. What in the world did you do to get this?"

Bryn shrugged with a smile.

"You went to see her, didn't you? One visit from you and she would've handed over her firstborn. What's a little recipe for caramel sauce?"

"If you think I coerced her, you could tear it up."

"Probably I should. As a rule you should be using your

powers for bigger causes," I murmured. "But I really, really wanted this recipe," I said, staring at it like I'd found the Holy Grail.

"I know," he said.

I looked up when I heard the knob turn. He was leaving. A wave of guilt swamped me. He'd been working like a dog, and he'd still found time to do something really sweet for me. Of course, Zach being back in town might have been part of the reason Bryn had gone so far out of his way. Bryn could teach even Nick Saban, who'd won back-to-back college football championships, a thing or two about strategy.

"Hang on," I said.

"Yes?" he asked, turning back.

"Oh please," I said, rolling my eyes. "Don't look so innocent. You know I'm not going to let you leave without giving you something sweet for this."

"Something sweet," he echoed. "That sounds promising. What specifically?"

"I'm about to put a cake in the oven," I offered.

"That's a good place to start," he said, and I had no doubt where he wanted things to end. I knew I should push him back out the door, but his beautiful smile reminded me of all the reasons I'm crazy about him.

"We're not going to get carried away. If anything, you're in trouble with me."

"Am I?" he asked.

"I've warned you a bunch of times to stop doing things to make me fall more in love with you, but you just don't listen."

He smiled. "Yeah, me treating you well, it's a problem."

"It is," I said, waving a hand impatiently. "You know that I made a promise not to make a decision about my love life until . . ." I trailed off with another vague wave of my hand. "You could be a little more supportive."

"It's not in my best interest to encourage your indecisiveness. It's not in your best interest either. The past may seem comfortable and familiar, but that doesn't make your relationship with Sutton any less of a bad habit." He leaned close so that the magic sizzled. "Deep down, you know it," he said in a seductive whisper.

I bristled, pushing him away. "You only want me to make a decision because you assume you'll win. That's a bad habit of *yours*."

"Being confident?"

"Being overconfident and telling people what to do when they didn't ask for your advice. You're not my lawyer. Like I've told you, I need time. We can see each other, but you have to understand that I didn't mean to fall in love with you so fast, and I'm not happy about it."

He smiled and held out his arms in an "I surrender" gesture. "All right. Have a glass of champagne with me so I don't have to celebrate alone. Then feed me a slice of cake and send me packing."

"Really? You'll behave? You won't try to flirt your way into my bedroom?"

He shook his head. "Champagne, cake, home."

"Okay, then. See how when we negotiate, we're both happy?"

"Sure," he said with another innocent expression that I didn't trust. Bryn's a lot of things, but he's not guileless.

I narrowed my eyes at him. "As long as you agree that the only sugar I'll be serving up tonight is cocoa pecan cream cake, we'll get along fine."

"I'd never try to force you into anything, Tamara. You know that," he said sincerely. "Glasses?" he asked, taking the champagne bottle back from me.

The tension eased from my shoulders. I'd be safe for the night at least. Then I really did have to sort things out. It wasn't fair to any of us for me to keep the relationships in limbo. But it was going to be awful to choose, like trying to decide between hot apple pie a la mode and dark chocolate decadence. Each was perfect in its own way. Too bad men weren't really desserts. Then each one could have a turn.

I thunked myself in the head. *No matter how good they taste, men aren't desserts. Get over it, Lady Godiva Chocolates, before you turn into a tart yourself.*

*Welcome to Duvall, Texas, where new witch Tammy Jo Trask
has just unleashed an accidental Armageddon…*

FROM
KIMBERLY FROST

BARELY
BEWITCHED

A Southern Witch Novel

When Tammy Jo's misfiring magic attracts the attention of
the World Association of Magic, or WAM, a wand-wielding
wizard and a menacing fire warlock show up to train her for a
dangerous—and mandatory—challenge. But is there more to
their arrival than they claim?

   The town comes unglued when a curse leads to a toxic
spill of pixie dust and the doors between the human and faery
worlds begin to open. To rescue the town and to face the challenge, Tammy needs help from the incredibly handsome Bryn
Lyons, but WAM has declared him totally off-limits…

PRAISE FOR KIMBERLY FROST

"Frost can tell a tale like no other."
—*Fang-tastic Books*

"Filled with humor, sass, and sizzle!"
—*The Romance Readers Connection*

frostfiction.com
penguin.com

M1379T0913

*In the small town of Duvall, Texas, the only thing
that causes more trouble than gossip is magic.*

FROM
KIMBERLY FROST

WOULD-BE WITCH

A Southern Witch Novel

The family magic gene seems to have skipped over Tammy
Jo Trask. All she gets are a few untimely visits from the
long-dead, smart-mouthed family ghost, Edie. But when her
locket—an heirloom that happens to hold Edie's soul—is
stolen in the midst of a town-wide crime spree, it's time for
Tammy to find her inner witch.

Tammy turns to the only person who can help: the very
rich and highly magical Bryn Lyons. He might have all the
answers—and a double-oh-seven savoir faire to boot—but
the locket isn't the only heirloom passed down in Tammy's
family. She also inherited a warning: *Stay away from anyone named Lyons…*

"Delivers a delicious buffet of supernatural
creatures, served up Texas style—
hot, spicy, and with a bite!"

—Kerrelyn Sparks, *New York Times*
bestselling author

frostfiction.com
penguin.com

M1378T0913

Enter the tantalizing world
of
paranormal romance

Christine Feehan

Lora Leigh

Nalini Singh

Angela Knight

Yasmine Galenorn

MaryJanice Davidson

Berkley authors
take you to a whole new realm

penguin.com

M4G0610

Can't get enough paranormal romance?

Looking for a place to get the latest information and connect with fellow fans?

"Like" Project Paranormal on Facebook!

- Participate in author chats
- Enter book giveaways
- Learn about the latest releases
- Get book recommendations and more!

facebook.com/ProjectParanormalBooks

M883G1011